Eduard, a German ͟ ͟ ild of postwar
Berlin, has long been settled in California with his
American wife, Jenny, and their three children
when he discovers that he has inherited an apartment building in the former East Berlin. Lured by
the property and a promising new job offer, he
returns to his native city.

But post-Communist Berlin is a surreal and
baffling landscape to Eduard, who struggles to
orient himself in a city where he feels uncannily
at home and yet estranged. He finds his property
occupied by a hostile troupe of squatters. On top
of this, his marital relations have dipped toward
freezing as his wife resists Eduard's efforts at
repatriation. Convinced that Jenny's distaste for
Berlin is a rejection of Eduard himself, the neu-
rotic hero launches a series of quixotic stunts in
a mad scheme to win back his wife and at last
come to terms with his home.

A bewitching mixture of Kafkaesque absurdity
and domestic drama, Eduard's Homecoming
offers the most insightful, wittiest look yet at the
problems of reunification, personal and political,
in the new Berlin.

Also by Peter Schneider

The Wall Jumper
The German Comedy
Couplings

EDUARD'S HOME-COMING

Farrar, Straus and Giroux
New York

EDUARD'S HOME-COMING

PETER SCHNEIDER

Translated from the German by
John Brownjohn

Farrar, Straus and Giroux
19 Union Square West, New York 10003

Copyright © 1999 by Peter Schneider
Translation copyright © 2000 by John Brownjohn
All rights reserved
Distributed in Canada by Douglas & McIntyre Ltd.
Printed in the United States of America
Designed by Cassandra J. Pappas
Interior photographs by Orly Saddik
First published in 1999 by Rowohlt-Berlin Verlag GmbH,
Germany, as *Eduards Heimkehr*
First published in the United States by Farrar, Straus and Giroux
First edition, 2000

Library of Congress Cataloging-in-Publication Data
Schneider, Peter, 1940–
    [Eduards Heimkehr. English]
    Eduard's Homecoming / Peter Schneider ; translated by
John Brownjohn.—1st ed.
        p. cm.
    ISBN 0-374-14654-3 (alk. paper)
    I. Brownjohn, John.   II. Title.

PT2680.N37 E313 2000   00-028417

For Ruża, Lena, and Marek

1 IT TOOK HIM quite a while to figure out what he was doing in this bed. His forehead and hair felt cold, as if he'd only just come in from outside. The window was closed, but there was a refrigerator near the head of the bed, and someone had left the door open.

Someone, or himself? It seemed unlikely that anyone could have occupied the room before him. He thought he detected a smell of fresh paint. The space heater, an aluminum convector with flat vanes, the brilliant white paintwork on the door and window frames, the dimmer switch on the wall—everything was as new as if the workmen had only just moved out. The only curious feature was how old all this new stuff looked. In front of the window, which was filmed with greasy dust, hung a curtain of cream-colored linen so skimpy it failed to cover half the pane when drawn. At each end of the room the brown carpet ran up the wall for eighteen inches, as if allowing for future expansion or originally intended for different premises. The bed was a sofa bed whose surface hinged into two narrow strips. If Eduard didn't want to feel the intervening groove beneath his back, he had to opt for one overly narrow side or the other. It clearly hadn't occurred to the manufacturer that a sleeper might sometimes feel the urge to lie at full length. A person of Eduard's build had no choice but to rest his head on the arm or draw up his legs.

He jumped out of bed and went to the window. The front of the only surviving late-nineteenth-century town house across the street was pitted with bullet holes, presumably dating from the last war; thanks to fifty years of uninterrupted dilapidation, some of these had become enlarged, creating cracks in the stucco the height of a man. All the other buildings were relics of the pioneering age of prefabricated-slab construction and had long since started to disintegrate. Like huge concrete building blocks standing on end, they were probably identical, down to their door and window dimensions, to the building from which Eduard was presently observing them.

He had been delivered to the entrance of the high-rise the night before, after a fifteen-hour flight, by a cabbie who sent his Mercedes bouncing over foot-deep potholes without slowing down. An upward glance at the façade had made him wonder at first if he'd come to the wrong address. The building that contained the guest apartment assigned to him was a honeycomb structure some two hundred feet high, with squat, perfectly uniform windows. The entrance, the steps leading to the lobby, the bulletin board plastered with handwritten slips of paper, the porter's window through which a taciturn female custodian handed him the key—all radiated the authority of a highly organized disaster. Could it be that the Molecular Biology Institute housed its guests in a students' hostel? The "residential accommodations for teaching staff," so he was informed by the woman behind the window, of whom all he could see was a towering hairdo, were on the second floor. Having climbed a flight of stairs flanked by green walls, he opened a steel door beyond which everything had been suddenly, freshly whitewashed, and he now recalled the feeling that had overwhelmed him on going to the window. The newly painted and carpeted room might have been dangling from a gigantic crane above a cityscape destined for demolition.

He was feeling edgy and exhausted, as if he'd slept for only three hours. While looking down at the stream of curiously small, angular automobiles that seemed to be gliding past below on an invisible towrope, he recalled the dream that had woken him in the middle of the night. Or had he only dreamed that he'd woken up? The whole room, fitfully illuminated by lights roaming across the window, had suddenly been in motion. The outlines of the furniture changed shape from moment to moment, becoming merged and superimposed: closet-bed, chair-table, TV-fridge. The seat of the chair was suddenly a wine bottle's height above the desktop. And how had hundreds of people managed to fit into so small a room, all at the same time? It sounded as if a vast multitude had gathered around his sofa-table, book-couch, bed-shelf, and were producing the incessant, organlike continuo that had roused him: a somber, swelling and fading babble of voices punctuated by high-pitched, abruptly invasive cries of exultation. He put out a cautious right arm, but the room receded at his touch and conveyed nothing but sensations of cold and emptiness. All at once, not that he had taken a single step, he was standing at the window and had thrown it open. What he saw below struck him as absurd and menacing, for the cobbled pavement, too, was in constant motion. The cobblestones rose and fell, sprouted arms, legs, and bodies, and now he saw it quite clearly: hundreds and thousands of people with square, cobblestone heads, jam-packed without an inch between them, were milling around down there. Although their reason for assembling was obscure, what Eduard found most puzzling of all was their exuberance and lack of violence. They surged to and fro between the cars, which had simply been abandoned in wild confusion, wedged together with headlights blazing and doors open. Some were drumming on the hoods, others sitting on the roofs of their cars or cavorting around on them; many were holding bottles and passing them around, all were shouting or singing—celebrating, in fact. He now noticed that every window in the street but his own was illuminated. Perched on nearby windowsills in their parents' straining arms, little children were waving to the crowd below. Many local residents were spraying the revelers' heads with champagne. But the very absence of light in Eduard's window attracted their attention. He, the only one standing in the dark, was the real occasion and object of the huge gathering. "Go on, jump! Why don't you jump?" The injunction was uttered at first by one reedy voice, but it swiftly infected others. They started chanting:

"Why not jump, Ed? Don't be scared. We don't mind about your beard."

Beard? Why beard? He'd never worn a beard in his life—he detested beards.

Dozens, no, hundreds of hands were now waving to him, inviting him to take the plunge. People stationed themselves on the roofs of their cars as if to lessen the distance between them. With urgent gestures they signaled to him to leave everything behind and let himself fall just as he was, in shirt and underpants, into the bright, untrammeled depths. Why not obey their summons? The multitude calling for him below would surely catch him; they didn't have room enough to stand back and let him go splat on the asphalt. Yes, why not jump? He was ready. He stood poised on the windowsill, already savoring the glorious sensation of flight and about to push off with the ball of his left foot. He jumped—or would have done had he not, at the very last moment, recognized a figure that caused him to stop in mid-movement: a woman standing erect in the midst of the crowd. The only person not waving to him, she stood there in a black dress whose plunging neckline exposed her high, dazzlingly white breasts, looking incomprehensibly young although, if he added up the years they'd spent apart, she must have been his own age. It was impossible to tell at this distance whether she had seen and recognized him too. A childish, incorrigible feeling of joy pervaded him: her presence here gave promise of reconciliation. But the moment he caught her eye her features underwent a change: Laura became Jenny, but a Jenny equipped with Laura's breasts. He discerned a trace of sorrow—indeed, bitterness—in her face as it turned away. And, suddenly, everything seemed spurious and counterfeit. The images were ages old and worn out by thousandfold repetition. What he was seeing was a reprise of the German centennial celebrations, which he had missed. Some malicious producer had restaged them for him. Nothing was as it appeared: decades-old reproaches disguised as jubilant cries, destructive impulses concealed behind welcoming gestures, a desire for revenge and exposure camouflaged as offers of salvation. No, you don't deceive me, I have no intention of jumping (Will the transom hold?). My nosedive is all that really interests you, no one will catch me. You'd like to watch me fall, come crashing down, land with a thud! Then you'd bend over me, just to see how flat a person can become after taking the shortest route to the street.

Eduard discovered, even before breakfast, that he must guard against giving spontaneous replies. He sensed how the custodian, Frau Schmidtbauer, inwardly froze when he ventured a polite but truthful response to her express inquiry about his first night in the guest apartment.

"I hope you'll wake up in a better mood tomorrow," she said, as if his comments on the sofa bed's hinges were purely subjective. She added that the Institute's previous guests, including professors of sixty and seventy (endowed with heaven alone knew how many honorary doctorates and international prizes), had all, without exception, enjoyed an excellent night's sleep on the very same piece of furniture. Here was a pampered and, until yesterday, unemployed Western academic who had doubtless usurped the job of an East German colleague at least as competent as himself and had nothing to offer but pretensions. His complaints identified him as a representative of the German species that mistook its postwar good fortune, geographically speaking, for talent.

Eduard had the feeling that, even if his suggestions had cost nothing, they would have been not only denied consideration but rejected as presumptuous. His request that the toilet have its inlet valve replaced to prevent it from flushing continuously evoked nothing but the information that the existing valve was a new one. When he offered to trim the carpet to size, he was informed that it was Institute property and must not be damaged. The air of the other Germany in which he had taken a job was obviously mingled with a rarefied, highly explosive gas. The newcomer had only to obey his reflexes and, quite without noticing it, he gave off dangerous sparks.

Eduard had left the city, half in anger, eight years before. The unexpected offer from Berlin-Buch would not by itself have prompted him to embark on the long journey back. For a scientist who had since made a name for himself as an assistant professor at Stanford and published some of his work in *Science* and *PNAS,* there were more tempting challenges than that presented by a job in the gray capital of a gray ex-country.

The image of his native city entertained by those who trod the evergreen lawns of California was characterized by chilly curiosity. "An amazing place" or "Really interesting" were the comments most often heard there. In American social parlance, which forbade the giving of offense, such remarks conveyed a friendly warning. Besides, Germany was no longer one of the countries to which an ambitious scientist felt irresistibly drawn. In Germany, ran the murmur among Eduard's colleagues, there were a hundred regulations to every flash of inspiration. You had to fill out an application and get it approved if your laboratory needed so much as a box of pipettes. Project decisions that took an afternoon to clinch in the States could not be expected to jell at a German institute in under six months, and even when the project was finally approved you found the environmentalists and animal-rights activists breathing down your neck.

A single event had changed the city forever, it seemed. Late on the afternoon of November 10, 1989, Eduard was greeted in the corridors of Stanford's Medical Center with upraised thumbs and repeated cries of "Congratulations!" Acquaintances and strangers slapped him approvingly on the back as if he himself had ordained the breaching of the Wall. Automatically enlisted as an expert on this historic event, he was bombarded with questions. Didn't he feel an urge to go to Berlin? the chairman had asked, his rheumy old eyes agleam with pioneering spirit. Their East German colleagues' main claim to international renown had been the production of anabolic steroids for East German athletes. Didn't he itch to give them a bit of a leg-up? The quaint old man usually wore jeans and cowboy boots in the Center, which discreetly prided itself on the number of Nobel laureates it boasted per hundred square yards. His body language as he sat there regarding Eduard expectantly seemed to convey that, in Eduard's place, he himself would have left for Berlin long ago. "Thousands of books have been written on how to transform a capitalist society into a socialist society, but not one on how to reverse that process."

When the secretary handed Eduard a bouquet and a bottle of champagne on behalf of the department—"We're so happy for you!"—he was too overcome at first to speak. Then, feeling himself the cynosure of every eye in the library, he extemporized a brief speech on his "lucky day." He was dismayed to find that this little ritual aroused or reawakened emotions he thought he'd outgrown. By the end of his sardonically patriotic address there were—to his own bewilderment—tears of joy in his eyes. He spent the next few days trying to book a flight to Berlin. Finally, since all the affordable flights were sold out, he gave up. In any case, he'd felt uncomfortable about the idea of returning to his native city to marvel like a tourist at the breaching of the Wall.

Unwonted pictures of dancing, rejoicing Berliners flitted across American television screens for months on end, to be replaced before long by older images more deeply rooted in the American memory. Conjured back into being by neo-Nazi arsonists, the blond, blue-eyed, thin-lipped Hollywood German who clicks his heels and barks "Jawohl, Herr Obersturmbannführer!" was resurrected from the film archives.

The invitation from Berlin-Buch reached Eduard at a time when political disenchantment had already set in. The director of the newly founded Molecular Biology Institute evinced a keen interest in his work on the genetic mapping of human diseases, although the ancillary staff and research funds available were far more tempting than the salary on offer. What clinched it in the end was Eduard's spirit of adventure. It appealed to him to promote a new line of research in the familiar yet alien environment of East Berlin—"the German boondocks," as a German colleague in California warningly referred to it.

But Eduard had another reason for going to Berlin: he had to claim an inheritance. A letter had come one day from a Dr. Lorenzen, who introduced himself as Eduard's late father's tax consultant and announced that Eduard and his brother were the legal heirs to a building in Berlin-Friedrichshain containing fifty-six apartments. The very existence of this apartment house was news to Eduard. The letter, which had been mailed to his former Berlin address together with an application for a certificate of inheritance, had reached him only after making several detours. He was so surprised, he mistook it for an April Fools' Day hoax. It took a long transatlantic phone call to the tax consultant to convince him that, thanks to a mysterious clause in the German reunification accord, he had become one of millions of Germans entitled to reclaim property in the territory of the former German Democratic Republic. It took him several transpacific phone calls to discover the whereabouts of his brother in Christchurch, New Zealand. Lothar's initial reaction to the news was derisive. "Us, an apartment house in Berlin? In Friedrichshain? Are you pulling my leg? Or are you testing the strength of my principles by telling me I've only got to say the word to become a DM millionaire?"

"A DM millionaire twice over," said Eduard.

He could tell from Lothar's voice that his brother's conception of a Berlin apartment house in the Friedrichshain district was as nebulous as his own. But Lothar's tone changed with remarkable speed. Other considerations or instincts gained the upper hand. Should they sell the place or rent it? If they rented it, why not modernize it right away? What sort of rental income would such a building currently yield? Were there any charges on the property to be deducted?

Eduard was amazed at his younger brother's business acumen. Lothar, who had only a few years ago insisted that the acquisitive instinct was acquired, not genetically innate, was already debating the relative profitability of selling and renting! Did his ears deceive him, or had he detected an electronic beep? Could Lothar really be manipulating a pocket calculator?

"Selling would be a better deal in the long run, taking into account the intangible asset of not having to do battle with builders and tenants," said Lothar. At his request—"You're nearer our inheritance in California, you've got to admit"—Eduard declared himself willing to attend to the formalities and arrange the sale. He was fleetingly concerned, on hanging up, by the thought that avoiding trouble with tenants and bricklayers was the only intangible that had entered into their deliberations.

Having been sure he would never inherit anything in his life, he'd never given any thought to the potential benefits or disadvantages a bequest could bring in its wake. All that occurred to him when friends or colleagues found themselves in that position was that nothing, not even a chair, had come down to him from his parental home, and he'd actually felt rather proud of that nothing—not, of course, that it was any more to his credit than the abundance inherited by others. Suddenly, thanks to a ten-line letter, he belonged to a group of people whom he had hitherto regarded without envy, indeed, with a certain condescension—a sizable group, as he discovered on sounding out his circle of friends and acquaintances, for every other person he told of his unexpected bequest surprised him by proving to be a fellow legatee and expert on inheritance taxes. He suddenly felt he'd been admitted to a fraternity whose existence he'd never dreamed of. First, however, he had to pass a kind of entrance examination. He was abruptly subjected to searching stares by men who regularly entrusted him with unsolicited accounts of their extramarital escapades. Indeed, many of them asked him trick questions as if trying to determine whether they were dealing with an heir or an IRS investigator.

It became clear that most people possessed two private lives, of which their proprietorial life was the more private. Once confident of Eduard's new status, they promptly plied him with technical terms and tips on tax avoidance, subjects which they had hitherto shunned in conversation with him. "Devolution upon death," "lineal and collateral heirs," "statutory portion," "movables and immovables," "computation of taxable value"—he seemed to be learning the basic vocabulary of a secret language known to almost everyone but himself. Yacht owners, he was informed by a friend who had always turned up at their old Charlottenburg drinking den on a bicycle, wearing torn jeans, but now disclosed that he stood to inherit a Munich construction company—yacht owners were averse to discussing the tax deductibility of their yachts with the owners of rubber dinghies. It was he who first warned Eduard of the dangers of an inheritance. A bequest, especially a shared bequest, could prove a calamity, a source of unforeseeable and unwonted tribulations, a misfortune productive of ever more misfortunes. You could always turn down a bequest, of course, but unless you did so in time, or within two months of probate, it would dog you throughout your life like an unwanted child. Eduard must abandon his ironical attitude at once, said his friend. Any heir who took more interest in the psychological effects of property ownership than in property itself would inevitably lose the testamentary dispute that was bound to ensue. Like it or not, Eduard was doomed to dwell on his inheritance forevermore, even when he ought, for once, to think of something else.

2 | HE FOUND IT confusing that the new street map no longer distinguished between East and West Berlin. It had surprised him that the old East Berlin street maps showed nothing west of the Wall but an empty expanse. Now he wondered why the new map of Greater Berlin bore no reference to the Wall, as if the city had never been divided. It took him much page turning and folding to memorize the route to the apartment house on Rigaer Strasse, half of which was suddenly destined to be his.

The bulk of the S-Bahn station was encased in scaffolding and plastic sheeting. Eduard felt relieved to hear the sound of a train pulling in. It still emitted the familiar, mechanical but somehow human sigh he remembered from the days before his departure—a harsh, protracted exhalation.

There had been no transition this year between a hot summer and a tempestuous fall. The branches of the maples and beeches that glided past the window of his car jutted into the sky, black and dripping, with only a few leaves tremulously dangling from their withered stalks. But some trees, which appeared to belong to another, windproof species, had retained their foliage intact. Seen beneath a blue-black sky, their yellow and greenish-gold crowns looked unreal, as if painted. When a ray of sunlight fell on their leaves, they seemed to go up in flames and, with a final burst of refulgence, transform the backyards into banqueting halls. Nearly all the peeling, dark gray façades were covered with graffiti, but the paler, freshly stuccoed walls and even the doors and windows of the S-Bahn car were similarly adorned. When they first appeared, Eduard had regarded these aerosol inscriptions with curiosity and vague optimism as messages from an underground or future civilization. When they proliferated, he saw them merely as symptoms of disintegration and squalor, proclamations of a world without grammar. Like territorial animals urinating, the agents of this counterworld left their mark on any blank space big enough for a swipe with an aerosol can, and the only mystery these hieroglyphs presented was their sheer meaninglessness. They were indecipherable because they enciphered nothing. Their omnipresence implied a vast army of authors. Thousands of *guerrilleros* were engaged on mainly nocturnal operations intended to superimpose their chaotic messages on the works of diurnal civilization. And the world of daylight seemed gradually to be surrendering to the graffitists, indeed, doing their work for them. Eduard was infuriated to note that the green, black, and pink lines on the new plastic covers of the train seats were printed on them, not sprayed. The designers had simply adopted one of the graffiti warriors' basic patterns for the mass production of seat covers. "Not here, please," they were probably meant to convey. "Here you've already won the day!"

The car was crowded at this early hour. Eduard's eyes strayed to his immediate neighbor's face, which was bent over an open newspaper. The man suddenly looked up, only to refocus his attention on the newspaper because he clearly found Eduard's gaze irksome. The other passengers were also making strenuous efforts not to lock eyes with their fellow passengers. All stared studiously into the space they were obliged to share with the persons sitting beside and opposite them. Eduard's eye was caught by a headline on the front page of the newspaper which his neighbor was now holding protectively in front of his face. "EXPERTS FEAR GDR SEX TAKEOVER," it proclaimed in bold capitals.

Involuntarily, he lowered his head so as to decipher the lines in small print below. "At 37%," he read, "the female orgasm ratio in the former GDR is substantially greater than West Germany's 26%." What on earth could have induced the recently reunified Germans to pore over their compatriots' marriage beds and draw such comparisons? But what astonished Eduard even more than the headline that trumpeted the East–West orgasm ratio was the indication of how relatively few orgasms even "more fulfilled" women enjoyed.

The journey was proving an increasing strain on his stomach. The train kept braking sharply on open stretches, proceeded awhile at a walking pace, and then, with an unpleasant jerk, accelerated once more. Visible through the window were newly poured expanses of concrete with reinforcing bars protruding from them. Unlaid rails lay in heaps beside the track, as did towering stacks of precut wood and mounds of gravel or sand, all of them swathed in plastic sheeting. The workmen wore orange safety vests and hard hats of the same color. Their hands, which were bare, looked doubly unprotected in the midst of all that enshrouded building material, and Eduard was surprised that so few of the men wore gloves. But further away as well, on either side of the track, his eye met things that were packaged, crated, or corded. Every second or third building displayed a cocoon of scaffolding which itself was swathed in tarpaulins or lengths of safety mesh. It was as if half the city had been parceled up to await dispatch.

A remark of Jenny's popped into his head. A casual, wholly trivial remark of no significance. It had probably occurred to him only because she'd uttered it the night before he left. Or because she'd done so at a moment when other sounds are more to be expected than an articulate sentence. While he was soaring high above his ready-packed bags, borne along on the wings of sexual frenzy and under the impression that he had only to stretch out his hand to reach Jenny, who was flying beside or above him, she'd asked, in a voice completely devoid of breathlessness, "Did you remember to cancel your dentist's appointment?"

He had gotten up and traversed the darkened apartment, making for the faint sound of childish snores. Loris, lying relaxed on his back, had crept into Ilaria's bed and draped his arm across her face. Eduard hauled the boy toward him by the feet, marveling at how much heavier children are when asleep than awake. Having picked him up, he restored him to his allotted place on the lower story of the bunk bed.

The glasswork and iron girders of the station where he had to change were also swathed in plastic sheeting. Following some hand-drawn arrows, he made his way up and down through a number of boarded-up stairways until he found the right platform. The incoming train was covered with builder's dust. It wasn't until the doors had closed that Eduard noticed his mistake: the train left the station heading west, the direction he'd just come from. When he sought confirmation of this, the man beside him merely shrugged and said, "You've got eyes, haven't you?" A young woman stepped into the breach. She explained that the train was temporarily operating a single-track shuttle service. The next few stations were closed, so he wouldn't be able to get off before the zoo.

The serried buildings abruptly receded as they neared the former interface between the eastern and western halves of the city. Nothing could be seen for miles but raw or concrete-lined holes in the ground and expanses of sand interspersed with red and yellow site offices and isolated, mostly stationary construction plants. The ground had been ripped open to a depth of forty, fifty, sixty feet, the spoil bulldozed into huge mounds. The center of the city was a deserted wasteland, a vast cavity encircled by towering cranes. The Wall had vanished without a trace. It struck Eduard only on the return trip that the peculiar concrete figures with rounded tops that had been erected like sculptures on a site near the bend in the Spree were its remnants.

He got out at Lichtenberg station. The streets were paved with wet leaves that filled the gutters and potholes with viscous yellow mush. A restless light sporadically obscured by racing clouds played across the faces of the houses, which were slightly discolored by rain showers and sometimes glistened in a stray shaft of sunlight. Some of the buildings had clearly been renovated before the Wall came down. Their mosaic-adorned entrances and pink or pale green paintwork reminded Eduard of West Germany in the 1950s, when garish façades ornamented with interlocking rectangles and triangles were thought to betoken playful cosmopolitanism. Running repairs apart, however, most of the houses had been left in their postwar condition. There were whole streets where all but a few remnants of plaster had fallen off the walls, exposing the bare brickwork beneath. Many houses had gutters hanging askew from their eaves, many window frames seemed loose in their embrasures, iron balcony supports displayed huge rust holes and looked as if a vigorous tug would dislodge them from the masonry, and those who stood on or underneath such balconies appeared to be counting on someone other than themselves to meet with the inevitable accident. All this was somehow familiar to Eduard from the days before he emigrated. The sights he saw were not new to him, no, but instead of registering their decrepitude he seemed to have turned a blind eye to it. How could he have so stubbornly and persistently denied the monstrous dilapidation of the city's eastern half during his earlier visits? Even in default of any other indication, one impartial look at the state of these buildings should have sufficed to predict the collapse of socialism in action long before it occurred.

It wasn't easy to locate his inheritance. Some of the doors bore no numbers and the paintwork on others was so faded that a 3 and an 8 were hard to tell apart. Eduard vainly scanned the street for a property he would have *liked* to inherit. All the buildings were of that widespread type, unique to Berlin, which regularly aroused a kind of ethnological interest in visitors from abroad. Who on earth could have devised these residential barracks with two or three interconnecting courtyards that deprived both occupants and trees of light and were suitable at best as routes to the human habitation you never reached?

Having twice toured the entrances with numbers ending in 5 and 9, Eduard was in no further doubt: the unnumbered building with the barricaded windows on the first and second floors was the one bequeathed to Lothar and himself by their grandfather. He crossed the street to examine their inheritance at longer range. The building was indistinguishable from any other in the group of five: that it was still standing seemed miraculous. Its special feature became apparent only when he looked up at the tangle of wires on the façade. Whoever its remaining residents were, they couldn't be bona fide tenants. Running in and out of various windows were telephone wires, antennas, and electric cables, of which some led from the basement and others from the roof. Like climbing plants unable to gain a hold, they dangled down expanses of wall adorned with garish graffiti: FREEDOM FOR THE BASQUES, EAT THE RICH, THINK PINK, BUILDINGS BELONG TO THEIR OCCUPANTS. Eduard was struck by a novel consideration: he would have to discover, as soon as possible, what appliances all these wires were attached to and who was paying the gas and electricity, water, and sewage bills. To whom were all the invoices addressed? What bank account were they depleting?

The makeshift front door was a sheet of metal with several bullet holes in it. There were no doorbell buttons, and it seemed unlikely that the building still constituted an address to which the various suppliers could send their invoices. His own letter, addressed "To the Occupiers" and politely advising them of his arrival, had probably not been delivered either. The bottom two floors were barricaded and some of the windowpanes were missing on the floors above, but all the lights were on—in broad daylight. Any hopes that the uninhabitable building might really be unoccupied were dispelled by the rap music that blared from one of the gap-toothed windows. An upward glance at the roof disclosed the occupants' identity: fluttering from it was a black flag.

Pushing open the makeshift door, which was fractionally ajar, Eduard entered a hallway leading to a courtyard with two side entrances. He caught a momentary glimpse of a thin, childish face that gazed at him with a peculiarly earnest expression and promptly vanished. The sight of it kindled an emotion he was unprepared for. He felt he knew that face from another country, another life, as if its defiance were mingled with a kind of defenselessness—even of entreaty.

Barring his path was a multitude of bicycles, mopeds, and motorbikes, most of them unserviceable and unlicensed. The courtyard was piled high with crates, rusting refrigerators, burst and eviscerated mattresses, baby buggies and supermarket carts, all jumbled together as if they'd simply been hurled out of the windows overhead. Irresolutely, Eduard stood amid this junk and looked up at the windows for a while. Then he froze: a detonation was followed almost simultaneously by a hiss, and a projectile narrowly missed his left shoulder. Just as he heard the second report and ducked, he caught sight of two masked, black-clad figures crouching, like a brace of outsized ravens, on the apex of the roof beside the anarchist flag. They seemed to be welcoming him with outstretched arms. It took him a moment to make out the flare pistols in their hands. Too surprised to feel scared, he sprinted back through the junk to the shadowy hallway, from the cover of which he was able to watch more flares land in ever quicker succession. As soon as a projectile left the muzzle it described a fiery, swiftly fading arc between the roof and the rear entrance. Eduard could distinctly hear the empty cartridge cases clatter against the walls and fall to the ground. He felt a glancing blow on the neck and a slight burning sensation. When he touched the spot his fingers came away bloody. One of the cartridge cases must have bounced off the wall and struck him. To judge by the amount of blood, it had only inflicted a minor cut. The laughter from the roof seemed to indicate that the building's present occupants had been expecting their landlord after all, and that they considered this reception to be a heartwarming piece of fun.

Eduard didn't know how he got to the police station. When he breathlessly asked someone where it was, the man stared at him aghast and pointed him in the right direction, even running after him for a little way because he'd turned left instead of right.

At the entrance he asked for the precinct commander. The words made him feel a trifle uneasy as soon as he uttered them. What, he wondered, did he actually want to say to a man who bore that professional designation? He'd been almost automatically propelled here from Rigaer Strasse by sheer fury at the outrageous reception he'd endured on his own premises. Having been shot at with signal flares, he could hardly be expected to ascertain, by risking a second visit, if the occupants possessed any small-arms ammunition as well. Eduard was still holding his neck. The desk sergeant gave him a puzzled stare and directed him to the second floor.

The building seemed deserted. Red plastic footprints stuck to the floor, presumably intended to show the way, led only to doors without handles. More than once Eduard thought he detected echoing footsteps around a bend in a corridor, but they ceased as soon as he stopped to listen. If a new spirit had really taken up residence within these walls, there was no outward sign of it. The patterned linoleum was a travesty of oak parquet flooring.

The more flights of stairs he ascended and descended in search of room 215, the more futile his intention seemed. He felt as if he'd gone astray in time—as if he were trying to lay claim to an apartment house in Friedrichshain at a People's Police station ten years before the Wall's disappearance. The only minor indication that the end of the socialist era had not gone entirely unnoticed was a bulletin board: NO MORE ABUSE OF AUTHORITY! EQUAL TREATMENT FOR FOREIGNERS! RACIAL PREJUDICE IS OUT! It was hard to tell if the outstretched hand on the flier was black by design or because the photocopier had reproduced it that way.

A showcase beside the bulletin board displayed some gold and silver cups awarded to the police team for victories at table tennis and handball. They all dated from the years since reunification, Eduard noticed. You didn't become proficient in such sports overnight, so had the new masters locked away any trophies of earlier date because they couldn't tolerate the sight of the hammer and sickle engraved on them?

On the second floor Eduard at last heard voices and discovered a half-open door. The policeman who bade him enter was standing with his back to him and didn't turn around. Another, much older officer glanced up from the typewriter he was operating with the middle finger of his left hand and the forefinger of his right, but he was either unwilling or unauthorized to attend to Eduard, because he jerked his head at his younger colleague. The latter was standing in front of an open metal locker, buckling on a gun belt and clearly about to depart. Eduard watched him remove a service automatic from the locker, check the safety catch, and insert it in a holster on the wrong side, just above the hip. Evidently a left-hander. Eduard found the scene embarrassing, as if he'd burst in on a woman pulling up her panty hose, and stifled an apology. It surprised him that the policeman, who was obviously readying himself for action, should be wearing mufti. Who was in charge here, and what command structure prevailed?

Hanging on the wall above the head of the older man were photo portraits of Lenin, Dzerzhinsky, and Honecker. The last of the trio was still alive but had left Germany forever, now that his country had vanished.

The man with the gun belt swung around and looked at Eduard. He seemed to relish being observed while engaged in an activity that clearly discomfited his visitor.

Eduard described the Rigaer Strasse incident as succinctly as possible. Even as he spoke, however, his story began to seem limp and implausible. Perhaps it was the glances the two policemen exchanged. Did they hear such recitals every day? He searched their faces in vain for any reflection of the terror that had made him dive for cover in the courtyard. They seemed to greet an event he found incredible, almost incommunicable, with understanding—indeed, with barely disguised approbation. They evidently saw nothing unusual in the fact that a landlord had been fired on with flare pistols from the roof of his own premises.

Did he wish to press charges, asked the younger officer, whom Eduard for some reason tagged as a West Berliner. Eduard shook his head. For the first time, the policeman looked at him attentively, even with a certain curiosity. "Quite right," he said, "they're only kids. No need to send in a SWAT team just because they got fresh."

Eduard felt misunderstood. Who was he talking to, a policeman or a pistol-packing social worker?

"I can see you're a sensitive soul," the duty officer went on. "You get the picture. Tenants around here aren't used to being visited by landlords. I mean, put yourself in their place. A landlord from the West rolls up in his Mercedes—"

"On the S-Bahn," Eduard cut in.

"Whatever. The tenants have never heard of him and he knows nothing about them—as a rule, a registered letter is the first he's heard of the property in question. So he rolls up and tells them, 'This place you've been living in for twenty or thirty years belongs to me. We'll have to see how many of you can stay.' Well, no matter how nice and sympathetic he is, they're bound to see red."

"But I was shot at!" Eduard protested. "I want them evicted!"

He was surprised at his own decision. He hadn't entertained the possibility of eviction till now, but he felt boundlessly infuriated by the West German officer's perplexing adaptation to his new working environment and his readiness to empathize with his East German colleagues. In his fevered imagination, Eduard envisioned him sitting on the roof of the Rigaer Strasse building, drinking coffee with the masked figures.

"Try speaking with them first," said the younger policeman. "Once your tenants have come to trust you—"

"They aren't tenants, they're squatters! Besides, they're Westerners, every last one of them!"

This seemed to arouse the curiosity of the older man as well. The typewriter stopped stuttering for the very first time. However, Eduard got the feeling that the older man's sudden interest was centered less on the identity of the Rigaer Strasse perpetrators than on himself, the complainant.

"How do you know they were Westerners?" he asked.

"The slogans on the walls! Their sneakers!"

Both men, the duty officer and his colleague at the typewriter, seemed amused by this information.

"Their sneakers?" asked the younger one. "What make were they?"

"Nike, Adidas . . ."

"What century are you living in?" demanded the older man. "You expect them to go on wearing nationalized Red Star footwear forever?"

Disconcerted, Eduard glanced at the younger officer's black sneakers—Reebok?—and his close-fitting tapered shirt with the button-down collar. What made him so sure the man was a Westerner? And what about the older man, with his faint Saxonian accent? He wore the green uniform of the West German police, which had now become the police of all Germany. No, Germans had ceased to be distinguishable by their dress. Eduard decided to change the subject.

"Don't you think it's about time your communist saints came down off the wall?"

"They don't bother me," the younger policeman replied casually. "Besides, a lot of our colleagues are still attached to them."

Reunification had certainly succeeded here in this office, Eduard reflected angrily. Sympathy for the constraints of conformity under a German dictatorship was probably greater in police stations and army barracks than anywhere else. At the same time, he couldn't deny that he was finding the two policemen more and more likable. Didn't this duo represent the German version of that legendary pair of cops, one black and one white, whose squad car roared through the American streets on television every night at nine, blue light flashing? And didn't they, pigmentation apart, have to deal with very similar conflict situations? But the American TV cops didn't only hit it off together. They joked and swore at each other, they quarreled and made up, and—most important of all—they jumped into their patrol car and sped off if a citizen came under fire from the roof of his own home.

"So what do you suggest?" Eduard asked.

He learned that he had to fulfill certain legal requirements prior to an eviction. The building could be cleared only on the strength of a court order and only if it had been occupied before its restitution to the heirs. Even if the court decided in Eduard's favor, however, no eviction could be carried out unless he employed a gang of builder's laborers to brick up all accessible doors and windows thereafter—an operation which, in the case of a property as substantial as his, would cost in the region of sixty thousand marks. "When you've met all those requirements," said the older policeman, "only one thing'll stand between you and your property: your conscience."

"And until I get the building cleared who pays for trash collection, water, electricity, and so on?" Eduard inquired.

"You do," the two men said simultaneously. They looked at each other and chuckled.

3 JÜRGEN MATTENKLOTT'S OFFICE obviously hadn't been tidied for weeks. The lawyer's bulky figure was almost obscured by the stacks of files and reference books on his desk. He spent the whole of Eduard's discourse rolling back and forth on a peculiar form of seating, an inflatable rubber ball which, according to the latest school of thought, assured those with back problems of the sedentary posture most beneficial to them. Whenever Mattenklott leaned forward to fish a few jelly beans out of the jar on the desk, he seemed on the verge of losing his balance.

Eduard had known him since the days of the earliest sit-ins at Berlin's Free University, when the law students had caused a stir mainly by being the last to ridicule their lecturers' academic robes. As leader of these latecomers, Mattenklott had exploited his gift of

gab and flaming red hair to become a celebrity known only by his
nom de guerre: Klott. Eduard had later lost sight of him. For several
years Klott had vanished into a Marxist-Leninist splinter group
whose members lived in cultlike obscurity. They duplicated pam-
phlets far into the night and distributed them at factory gates at six
a.m., feeling rewarded if the objects of their revolutionary endeavors
at least bore them off to a wastebasket out of sight. Eduard recalled a
chance meeting with Klott shortly after Mao Tse-tung's death. This
news from the other side of the world had transformed Klott, like
thousands of other young Germans, into political orphans and
impaled them on the horns of a dilemma. Mao's death had divided
China into two factions, and it long remained uncertain which one
would triumph. For weeks no definite announcements or instructions emanated from Beijing. Eduard asked Klott which course was
the better. In genuine despair, Klott admitted he didn't know; he
knew only that the right one would prevail.

On reencountering Klott now, ten years later and shortly after
the Party's dissolution, Eduard found him unmistakably changed.
His girth had doubled, but he didn't seem the least bit hampered by
his new dimensions. He forestalled Eduard's discreet questions by
unashamedly volunteering information. Thanks to a small inheritance which he had managed to rescue from the clutches of the professional revolutionaries, he said, he had been able to fill the terrible
void created in his life by the Party's disappearance by gorging himself in French restaurants. What impressed Eduard even more than
Klott's readiness to confess himself a glutton was the way he carried
his new body around. He seemed to take pleasure in his corpulence
and bore it with a self-assurance that lent his movements a balletic
quality. Given the bulk he had to maneuver around, his footwork
made a nimble, almost graceful impression. His hands, too, seemed
suddenly dainty, and the eyes above his pendulous cheeks seemed
ever on the lookout for new, undiscovered delights. Eduard had seldom met anyone who had so happily put on weight and so willingly
bore the extra pounds. It was probable that Klott's revolutionary

experience with the Maoist party had proved to be a blessing in the long run, because the Party had exploited its members more or less in accordance with the principles prevailing in nationalized Chinese footwear or carpet factories. It had thus developed virtues in rebellious sons of the bourgeoisie which German parental homes no longer inculcated, and which were lacking in most of Klott's contemporaries: organizing skill, discipline, and a positively Asiatic love of hard work—qualities, said Klott, that now stood him in good stead as an attorney. In the Party he had learned to toil twelve or fourteen hours a day for a factory worker's handshake and an approving glance from the local chairman; now he worked with equal zest for his clients and his own pocket.

Eduard, who had called Klott several times since the notice of restitution arrived, informed him of his attempt to repossess the property.

"You must complain to a higher authority, of course," Mattenklott said when Eduard had finished. "Those officers had a duty to take the gunmen's particulars, even if they were only firing flares."

"And the running costs on the building?"

Klott pushed a small pile of opened letters across the desk. The Berlin Electricity Works had submitted an invoice in respect to the Rigaer Strasse building. It was addressed to Eduard and Lothar Hoffmann and covered the previous and present years. Eduard, who saw at a glance that five of the boxes in front of the decimal point were occupied, confined himself to reading the first two numerals, a one and a six. Beneath this invoice lay more documents of the same oblong format sent by other creditors: waterworks, gasworks, municipal trash collection, fire insurance, chimney sweep. Eduard stopped short. Why a chimney sweep? He'd seen no chimneys on the roof, only armed, black-clad street fighters. Not all the bills ran to five figures, but even the thousands added up to a sum in the region of thirty-five thousand marks, to be paid within fourteen days.

"You can't be serious!" said Eduard.

"Don't worry, we'll get it all back."

"*Back?* You mean I have to pay it first?"

Klott extracted a bulky tome from one of the piles of books, opened it at a certain page, and showed Eduard the relevant passage: "In accordance with Clause 16 of the Property Act, all rights and liabilities arising from any property on the site devolve upon its rightful owner."

The legal position, Klott explained, was clear-cut but complicated. Naturally, Eduard could not be expected to meet expenses incurred by people who were occupying his premises rent-free, not indefinitely. Any judge would find for him in the end. But until then, said Klott, some preliminary investment was essential. It was customary for the cost of water, trash collection, chimney sweeping, and the lighting of public spaces to be met by the landlord and passed on to his tenants—which was temporarily impossible in Eduard's case because the tenants or squatters were not registered with the authorities. He, Klott, had made inquiries. Eduard's apartment house had been condemned before the Wall came down. A housing association, which probably dated from GDR days, had taken over the running of it and concluded a tenancy agreement with the squatters' association. The latter no longer existed, so the Berlin electricity works and other suppliers were temporarily left with no one to invoice but Eduard. They took the view that it wasn't their problem if a landlord couldn't recover his expenses. All they wanted, after all, was payment for services rendered.

"Then they ought to stop rendering them! Either they cut off those people's gas, electricity, and water or we'll sue!"

Klott's face broke into the smile of an expert who has first to dispel his client's illusion that a civil suit can be fought with sound common sense. Water and electricity suppliers, he explained, were legally prohibited from taking such draconian measures; their hands were tied. The protection of the unborn took legal precedence over the claims of accountants.

"The unborn?" Eduard demanded. "What are you talking about?"

"To the best of my knowledge," said Klott, "there are pregnant women and mothers with young children on your premises. For as long as they choose to live there, the waterworks must continue to supply them at your expense."

"Not on your life! I'll have them evicted."

"Very well, but remember, the police won't evict them unless you bring a construction gang with you. Cost: around sixty thousand marks."

"I don't have thirty-five thousand, let alone sixty. I'll renounce the whole bequest."

Klott gave Eduard a look that would have been described, fifteen years earlier, as comradely. It was too late to back out now, he said. The deadline had expired long ago, as Eduard knew, but he could rest assured: he, Klott, had taken the precaution of contesting all the bills. Besides, no one ever got rich by mistake. A life of luxury entailed debts and determination. Eduard would soon forget all about these initial difficulties once the proceeds of the sale—which should easily amount to a million and a half!—had been credited to his account.

"A million and a half?" said Eduard, remembering the preliminary advertisements Klott had inserted in the *Frankfurter Allgemeine Zeitung* and *Die Zeit*. They had spoken of 3.2 million.

Klott cast his eyes up to heaven as if preparing Eduard to accept that it would be worth making the effort for a million or less. They were certainly justified in asking three million *then,* he said, but that was before Berlin's bid for the Olympics failed. Prices had rocketed, only to slump with equal rapidity thereafter.

"What do you cost an hour?" Eduard asked.

"Our office charges DM350," said Klott, "plus value-added tax. But we're patient, unlike the Internal Revenue Service."

Presumably to cheer Eduard up, he recounted some of his professional successes. Restoring big inner-city commercial properties and real estate to their original owners was the only way to make real money, he said, but that didn't prevent him from doing his duty by society at the same time. He'd won a reputation as attorney to the dispossessed. When former East German citizens had to be extricated from ruinous contracts into which they'd been bullied by West

German swindlers and loan sharks, his was the first name mentioned. Quacks, subscription hunters, and crooked insurance salesmen of every kind had roamed the new provinces in droves within weeks of the Wall's collapse, eager to sell their products to unwitting East Germans who could understand neither the big print nor the small. Western failures had pounced on the "natives" of the East. Only a few days ago he had rescued a group of East German smallholders, none of whom was under seventy, from an immoral contract. A West German real estate speculator, who'd had the effrontery to light his cigar with a hundred-mark bill during negotiations, had persuaded them to sell him a site near Berlin for one mark per square meter, payable when redevelopment work began in six years' time. How many of them would have lived to see that day? He had rescued another client from the clutches of two car dealerships. Being accustomed from GDR days to taking delivery of a car at least fifteen years after ordering it, the man had signed sales contracts committing him to buy two new cars, a Ford and a BMW. In the GDR this double order would have presented no risk. Anyone driving a new car away from the trading cooperative's lot could resell it at once for several times the retail price. The man was flabbergasted to be called by representatives of both firms barely two weeks later. His car was ready for collection, said the Ford salesman, so would he remember to bring DM36,000 with him? His jewel of a car had just been delivered, said the BMW dealer, so would he be sure to come armed with DM38,000 in cash? Checks, alas, could not be accepted.

Eduard wondered what it signified that, to Klott, handling his case clearly came under the heading of "social commitment."

Klott's office was only a few hundred yards from Eduard's former haunt, the Tent. The streets had changed so much during his years away, he was tempted to check the street signs to make sure he hadn't gone astray. Every last house was resplendent in a new coat of stucco. The little newsdealer's on the corner had been demolished and supplanted by a boutique selling Indian goods from Mexico. A computer store now occupied the site where a small grocery had made a meager living. In order to exploit every square inch of costly floor space the proprietor had inserted a mezzanine at the rear. Unless the people working there were children or Lilliputians they had to reach their desks in a stooping position and could straighten up only when seated in front of the outsized monitors. The launderette with the decrepit washing machines had closed and was now the preserve of a man in a turban who catered to lovers of Indian cuisine. All the features that had once differentiated West Berlin from West German dollhouses—crumbling façades pitted by shrapnel, windowless red brick walls bereft of plaster, incomprehensible wastelands in the midst of the inner city, buildings that were fissured, incomplete, and beyond repair—had been excised by skillful cosmetic surgeons.

But the burst of rejuvenation or renovation to which the entire district had been subjected seemed to point straight back to the past. Every sign of modernity had been replaced with brand-new replicas of what was modern in Grandma's day. It was as if the city had resolved to turn itself back into the form preserved in photograph albums from before the turn of the century. The fifties and sixties streetlights with their smooth, curved steel standards and neon tubes had given way to cast-iron, classicistic reproductions of Wilhelminian appearance: small, scrollwork-encrusted Corinthian columns that were obviously meant to look as if they'd been hand-crafted by the blacksmith on the corner. The frosted glass bowls emitted a subdued light produced not by gas but by four little neon bulbs in the shape of gas jets. Even the hooks for the lamplighter's pole, albeit wholly redundant in the age of automatic ignition, had been reproduced. The pharmacist's sign, the street signs, the clock faces—the new, old-fashioned characters and numerals seemed to have aged them all by decades.

The Tent looked like a foreign body in such surroundings. Peering in through the big picture window, Eduard thought the walls looked somewhat yellower and more fashionably ocher than they used to, but this impression might have stemmed from his peculiar powers of recall: his memory was better at retaining figures and symbols than images. He suddenly couldn't remember if the place had been yellow or pale green when he entered it last.

While he was inspecting the establishment from outside, someone gave him a two-handed wave from the bar. Pinka, ever pretty, ever slightly tanned, ever cheerful, opened the door and came to meet him with the smile she reserved for all her regulars. If anyone in Berlin did so, thought Eduard, it was Pinka who observed the obligatory American ritual that would have compelled you to respond in kind, even on the day of your self-appointed suicide: "How are you today?"—"Fine! How about you?"

"So empty today," said Eduard.

Pinka beamed at him. "That's because you've been away so long."

Seated around the freshly painted walls were a few unfamiliar customers who appeared to be conversing in whispers only. Every remark he exchanged with Pinka was doomed to be overheard. The place was filled with the inaudible frequencies of absence and expectation. Only half of the tables were occupied; the rest, like a defiant memory, bore black plastic triangles inscribed "RESERVED." To Eduard it was as if the magnetic field that had once linked a huge extended family—a jostling, elbowing, vociferous throng—had collapsed. The Wall had always been a politicians' obsession, remote from the customers' thoughts, and any mention of it was accounted a social blunder. Now that it had gone, however, the old regulars seemed to have lost the protective shield that had made them feel warm and snug.

Pinka registered Eduard's expression.

Of course, she said, trade had suffered a bit as a result of the new migration from West to East Berlin. A wonderful thing, really, except that there'd been no opposite trend. As it turned out, now that they were free to move around, the Ossis preferred to stay put. "And I wouldn't dream of switching over to Solyanka soups, just because my competitors in Prenzlauer Berg are serving overpriced *penne arrabbiate* to renegades from here. In two years' time, when ghastliness has lost its initial charm, all my old customers will be back again."

One person did wave to Eduard, who waved back as soon as he recognized L.M.'s gray hair and his celebrated omniscient smile. L.M. was wearing his usual outfit: a black jacket over a freshly pressed shirt, a violet necktie with a Windsor knot, and a pair of ancient, lovingly repaired shoes. His whole person radiated an aura of dispossessed nobility and marked him as one whose last remaining assets were good taste and good manners.

"About time too!" said L.M. as he gave Eduard a hug. "Not a sign of you, and you've been in town for days. But you've more important things to do, I know: that inheritance of yours!"

Eduard made no attempt to conceal his surprise. L.M. was famous for knowing everything—he could even speak of events that wouldn't occur until the following day. But how, asked Eduard, had he learned of the bequest? L.M. didn't answer, as usual; he smiled discreetly.

"May we drink to it? What'll you have?" he asked.

To the barflies of West Berlin, L.M. was a kind of celebrity. It was rumored that there were at least three L.M.s, not one, because it was impossible not to run into him wherever you went. L.M. came alone and departed alone. In the intervening hours one or two regular customers would entrust him with details of their private life they never confided even to their diaries.

No one could explain why L.M., of all people, should have become father confessor to a drinking population of several thousand souls. He was never pushy, never asked questions; he was simply there, and he inspired confidence. L.M. presided with care and discretion over the vast store of personal information he'd accumulated over the years. Admittedly, it had long been rumored that he worked for some intelligence service on the other side of the Wall, and many customers expected a file code-named "Macrochip" or "Long Memory" to turn up in the end. Unlike many of his detractors, however, L.M. had preserved an unblemished reputation; there was no known instance of his having abused his inside information. Any secret, however embarrassing, seemed safe with him because it was filed away in a mass of similar arcana.

L.M. had always displayed a melancholy streak, but Eduard now felt that this hitherto latent and rather charming quality had crystallized into a form of dementia. The years when he'd endeavored to escape his fate as a single were long gone, it seemed. He no longer told Eduard of his love affairs and breakups; instead, he showered him with political ill tidings: a Jewish cemetery in East Berlin had been daubed with swastikas a few weeks ago; trash cans in the eastern part of the city were crammed with works by authors for whom readers had been lining up in bookstores a year or two back; local youths attacked foreigners on the S-Bahn and threw them out of moving trains while fellow passengers looked on.

Although Eduard had heard of some of these incidents, it seemed to him that L.M. was blind to all but the frightful side effects of historical acceleration. Perhaps this was a feature common to all great upheavals: they spewed up such a diversity of material that it furnished a superabundance of grounds for any interpretation, whether euphoric or catastrophic. The jubilant and the Cassandras were equally right, and both refused to admit that all they perceived in the latest upheaval were developments that confirmed their opinions.

L.M. had heard in East Berlin that Poles in the frontier area were eager to be incorporated in the new Germany for economic reasons. When questioned by Eduard, he conceded that his only authority for this story was the East Berlin friend of a Polish friend who had heard it, in his turn, from some old man. For L.M., however, it was as cogent as a referendum.

"It won't be long before the Austrians rediscover their love for the Germans!" he declared. "And what about the Alsatians—had you heard? They want German as their first language. Now we're stuck with the consequences: nationalism, racism, intertribal slaughter— all the old horrors are making a comeback. You'll soon be yearning for the good old days under communism!"

"You mean they shouldn't have breached the Wall at all?" asked Eduard. "You think they should simply have left it standing?"

"For another three years at least."

Eduard didn't know what it was, the schnapps or L.M.'s apocalyptic mood, but the whole conversation annoyed and upset him. Absurd, he retorted angrily, you couldn't command an earthquake to happen by easy degrees. L.M. looked at him as if he were a fallen angel unaware of his cloven hoofs.

Not until later, when they were speaking of mutual friends and L.M., every inch the expert again, was linking every name to an anecdote dredged from the immeasurable depths of his long-term memory, did Eduard become aware that his excessive vehemence hadn't been directed at L.M. at all. He suddenly remembered that Jenny, too, had looked at TV shots of the Wall's demolition with eyes quite different from his own. While he was experiencing a surge of exultation at the sight of East Germans brandishing beer cans and making the V sign as they streamed westward through the Wall like a Levi's-clad army, Jenny had involuntarily drawn away from him. He knew that defensive flutter of the eyelids and thought he saw her hackles rise. Although she tried to share his exultation and didn't want to be a wet blanket, her reaction was anything but euphoric. He himself was so certain of his emotions that he took her detachment almost as a personal affront. Later, when she tried to explain her reservations, neither of them was satisfied with the form of words she used: "Forget it, I'm glad for you. What do you want to do, dictate how I feel?"

That was it: he had listened to L.M.'s dissertations with Jenny's ears and spent the whole time imagining how thoroughly vindicated she would have felt. One thing was certain: it wouldn't take any great powers of persuasion to convince her that she and the children were safer in San Francisco than in Greater Berlin.

4 I KNOW he's pleased, thought Eduard when he finally got through to Theo on the phone, so couldn't he at least try to sound like it?

He had called Theo regularly during the first few months after his move to San Francisco and had always been surprised, despite the echoing transatlantic tunnel that held their voices captive, at how quickly he readopted the intimate tone unique to their conversations together. But then, perhaps because he was always the one that called first, a hiatus ensued. The hiatus was followed by an exchange of letters, and since Eduard was usually the sender, seldom the recipient, that form of communication had also lapsed in the end. It was pointless to complain, Eduard knew. Where his nearest and dearest were concerned, Theo obeyed the rule common to children and cats: the people who count must be present in the flesh every day; the absent must expect to be forgotten—until they reappear.

Eduard had conducted long monologues with Theo since November 9. Above all else, he wanted his verdict on the latest developments. But Theo's phone had emitted nothing for days and weeks on end but the busy tone or a ringing that remained unanswered. Eduard could only speculate on the reasons for Theo's unavailability: love talk or rancorous farewells, foreign travel, yet another change of address. He'd been without news of Theo's whereabouts for all of a year after the Wall came down.

The lifting of this news blackout was attributable to pure chance. While attending a guest lecture on "German intellectuals and reunification" in the Pigott Hall at Stanford, Eduard heard the young female lecturer raving about a newly discovered writer from the former GDR, Theodor Warenberg. When he inquired which of his works had been translated into English, he was informed that Theo had abandoned the antediluvian medium of the printed word: he didn't write, he dictated. His fans disseminated his poems and short texts among German departments in the States by fax and E-mail.

Eduard was puzzled by Theo's electronic messages, of which he procured printouts in the next few days. "The victory of capitalism is sounding its death knell. Why? Because you cannot conquer what hurls itself into your arms." Or: "The future is the root of all evil" and "The Federal Republic has kept the Nazis' promise: everyone can zoom along the autobahn in a Volkswagen, the streets are swept by foreign serfs, the brothels are full of women from Asia and Africa." Or: "Communism exists in dream time and is independent of victory and defeat."

Eduard promptly recognized the sound of Theo's desire to hold up all the century's horrors at once and encapsulate them in a sentence that could be carved in stone. But he also detected a novel, alien sound that made him feel uneasy. He feared that, like all who had witnessed the flash of the huge explosion at close quarters and with the naked eye, Theo had undergone a change he didn't understand and never would. He was suddenly uncertain whether he and his friend would still be on the same wavelength. But then he convinced himself that Theo was now, after the collapse of communism, getting a special kick out of singing a dirge for the putative winner of the historical contest. He aspired to bury triumphant capitalism under poetic gravestones so monstrously heavy that his brilliant obituaries would be all that remained of it.

The lecturer who had discovered Theo for America and written a dissertation on him either couldn't or wouldn't give Eduard his current telephone or fax number. Eduard did, however, learn from her that the prickly and almost untranslatable writer had become a secret star of the German departments on the West Coast, "the last spokesman of the third world," as one of his honorific titles described him.

Sporadic fits of nostalgia had occasionally impelled Eduard to attend German department functions at Stanford. The focus of German studies in America had unmistakably and increasingly shifted. Back in the 1970s, postgraduate students and assistant professors had explored a hitherto neglected field of research: the literature of "the other Germany." This new discipline proved a boon to a faculty that was forever balancing on the knife-edge of its own superfluity: it was virgin research territory awaiting investment. Within a decade, ambitious pioneers had taken possession of the new territory and parlayed their projects into jobs for life. They demonstrated that the "other German literature" discovered by them was not only different from but infinitely better than the West German writing to which attention had hitherto been paid. American pioneers were particularly impressed by the female authors of the other Germany. Where, in West Germany, was their like? German departments developed cells of sworn supporters of East German literature who gradually came to include the political regime in their predilections and transmitted that infection to related departments. As late as the summer before the Wall came down, Eduard had listened to a lecture entitled "Why is the GDR so economically successful?" whose author based his assertions mainly on unpublished sources and on an interview with Markus Wolf, the East German secret service chief. Discounting the Saarland, Honecker's regime was nowhere more doggedly defended than at the Ivy League universities. Thus it was that the distant tremors of the earthquake that demolished the Berlin Wall reached the California West Coast and gently shook a few dozen careers there.

It seemed to Eduard now, as he spoke with Theo on the phone from a handful of miles away, that only an hour or two had elapsed since their last conversation. He knew he would find him, as in the old days, ensconced amid a jumble of papers, wine and mineral water bottles, cigarettes and cigar boxes, hemmed in by ceiling-high bookshelves whose contents lay higgledy-piggledy in some order known only to Theo himself. It slightly bemused him to realize that he and Theo had changed places. While he himself was standing in an East German high-rise, using a dial phone of GDR vintage, Theo, whom he had for years been able to visit in East Berlin only when armed with a visa that expired at midnight, was strolling around a spacious Charlottenburg apartment with a cordless in his hand.

Theirs had been a strange, improbable friendship from the outset. A literature-loving GDR physicist had taken Eduard along to a meeting in an East Berlin apartment at which writers from East and West Berlin took turns reading aloud from their works. Eduard and Theo had hardly been introduced before they became embroiled in an argument over Eduard's field of research. "Behavioral genes?" demanded Theo. "Didn't we have all that crap in Germany once before?" He'd heard of a rare species of apes, the bonobos, that differed from other anthropoid apes in eschewing war, rape, physical violence, and other forms of aggression. Experts were unanimous in believing that the reason for their peaceful behavior was a surplus of food in their natural habitat. This circumstance enabled the she-apes to accompany their mates on their wanderings and prevent them from forming male gangs.

All that surprised Eduard, who disputed this in a rather bored fashion, was the interest with which Theo listened to his opposing view, which he promptly condemned as "reactionary." Unfortunately, quipped Eduard, nature paid little heed to expert opinions, so no scientist should waste time wondering whether his findings would find favor with a left- or right-wing central committee and be consistent with the prevailing school of thought. Strangely enough, left-wingers found nothing particularly objectionable in the idea that, where falling in love was concerned, the brain was assailed by certain chemical substances known as endorphins, which induced feelings of bliss and rapture. If confronted by the logical assumption that similar chemical processes helped to stimulate aggression, on the other hand, the same left-wingers would brand any scientist who espoused it a latter-day Josef Mengele.

The two of them had often met thereafter, either in Theo's favorite East Berlin bar or at his apartment. They wasted no more time on the everlasting academic controversy over nature versus nurture. After emptying their first or second bottle of vodka, which was always consumed on a empty stomach, they turned their attention to other matters. To what extent had their own careers and views been influenced by those two political laboratories, the FRG and the GDR? In what way had those opposing "environments" helped to forge their respective destinies, their first childish impressions, their school days, their first love affairs, their first political leanings, their respective behavior during the brief, anarchic spring of 1968? How many of such differences were attributable to the "environment" factor and how many to the natural diversity existing between individuals? They often tried to imagine how entirely different—or entirely similar, perhaps—their lives would have been had each grown up in the other's country. Once, shortly before midnight, they had actually considered swapping clothes and identities.

"I'll go across with your ID and move in with Klara—for two weeks, say. You stay here, pay off my bar bills, and have a good time with Pauline."

"No border guard would mistake your nose for mine."

"So? I'll accuse him of anti-Semitism, that'll make him click his heels."

"Who's going to guarantee you come back?"

"Klara will, won't she? Maybe not. That's a risk you'll have to take. It'd be a genuine experiment at last: you improve your inadequate knowledge of socialism in action, and I'll tell you something about the power of genes."

One day Theo really did turn up at the door of Eduard's apartment. He refused to divulge how he'd made it to West Berlin, merely said that Eduard would have to be content with the information that he'd fallen head over heels for a female admirer who'd disappeared to West Berlin after an unforgettable night and had never been seen again.

"Well?" asked Eduard.

"Well nothing. I want to pay her a visit, that's all—tack a few whole nights onto the half we had together. I hate half-finished affairs."

Theo insisted it was just a weekend excursion. He'd told his wife Pauline he had to attend a reading on the Baltic coast. He didn't deny that his trip was highly unusual. All Eduard believed of Theo's avowed intention was that it would take him only a few days to make his escape a permanency.

But Eduard was wrong: Theo insisted on going home after three days. After the first night with his West German inamorata he'd spent the whole time bickering with her; now all he talked of was Pauline, whom he couldn't, he said, keep waiting any longer. He frankly admitted that he'd made no arrangements to return. Eduard realized why the kindly soul who had sneaked Theo into West Berlin was not available for the return trip. Whoever it was—a literature-loving diplomat, a professional smuggler—no one could have conceived that a man who had run such a risk would want to go home after only three days. Anyone who returned to the GDR of his own accord seemed suspect to the frontier authorities for that very reason. Prodigal sons returning to the GDR had to reckon with eight solid weeks of interrogation at a reception center.

Eduard eventually took it upon himself to return Theo to Pauline in the trunk of his Citroën. Although it was to be assumed that no one would search a car entering the GDR for concealed GDR citizens, the border guard spent an unconscionable length of time comparing Eduard's ear with its likeness on his passport photo. Only when he at last closed the document and handed it through the driver's window did Eduard allow himself to avoid the carcinogenic intensity of the man's X-ray eyes.

Ever since that long, tremulous wait at the checkpoint, during which Eduard kept expecting to hear a Gitanes cough from the trunk at any moment, Theo and he had been linked by something stronger than any argument over serotonin.

Theo had now landed in the West and Eduard in the East. They would be able to continue their argument under different auspices and from different points of view. Theo had certainly changed his ways in one respect, that much emerged from their phone conversation. He hadn't the least desire to go drinking, least of all at the Tent, nor did he want to "look in" at one of the newly opened bars in Prenzlauer Berg. "Had you forgotten how far it is from here to Schönhauser Allee? If you live in Manhattan you don't go boozing in Brooklyn, do you?" Theo declined to go out and asked Eduard to come to him instead. In his case, thought Eduard, that request would have been tantamount, before the Wall came down, to reporting sick.

Eduard found the door to Theo's apartment ajar when he reached the top of the stairs. Theo wasn't waiting there to welcome him, of course—he set no store by such gestures. Even if Eduard had just returned from an expedition to Theo's favorite apes, the bonobos, Theo would have greeted him in the same manner: seated at one of three tables in front of one of the eight unfinishable manuscripts on which he was resolutely engaged.

Eduard was shocked when Theo rose to welcome him. Always thin and frail-looking, he seemed in some alarming way to have become younger since they last met. His appearance had always elicited different reactions from men and women. Men were puzzled by his failure to put on weight and envied his slim, youthful figure; women thought he ought to consult a doctor. Theo had been living on death's doorstep for years, a slave to his dangerous habits, but had remained mysteriously hale and hearty—so much so that one was tempted to believe that the Grim Reaper, impressed by his death-defying courage, had granted him temporary immunity, renewable yearly, from all the diseases that had long been infiltrating his bodily organs.

"So one doesn't patronize the Tent anymore?" asked Eduard.

"'One' does," replied Theo, "I don't. 'One' calls the police when I turn up there."

He described a bet he had made with the woman sitting next to him in the Tent some four months after the Wall came down. He wagered that at least half the room would join in if someone at their table started singing the national anthem. The majority of the table bet against Theo, but no one was prepared to settle the matter by perpetrating the requisite outrage. To his friends, the singing of "Einigkeit und Recht und Freiheit," even in fun, amounted to desecrating the premises. Nobody joined in when Theo, his vocal cords ravaged by the combined effects of chain-smoking and vodka, croaked out the opening bars of the Haydn melody. After a note or two only, his rendition petered out in a fit of bronchial coughing and was followed by dead silence. Suddenly, to everyone's astonishment, the Turkish writer Ismail Özgür took up the melody in a surprisingly clear, true tenor at the point where Theo's coughing had extinguished it. No one was sure why Özgür, of all people, had set himself up as the precentor. Whether he simply wanted to take over where Theo had left off or was celebrating his recently granted German passport, two customers angrily hissed him from their bar stools. But there was no holding Özgür, who even seemed prepared to court physical violence. More and more customers were carried away by his glorious bel canto. The regulars heard the forbidden strains with disbelief, with every sign of horror. Then some of them joined in, at first only in fun, and the chorus gradually swelled. Other customers rose and began to sing with all their might. Finally, someone at the back jumped onto a table and took over the baton from Özgür. All who had bet against Theo left the place in a panic without settling their debts.

"And what did Pinka do?" asked Eduard.

"She isn't speaking to me anymore. She clearly finds it hard to tolerate the new customers who've made themselves at home in her establishment—gentlemen with briefcases who pore over architects' drawings and real estate plans. The thing is, they've only started coming since word of my experiment got around. Pinka's afflictions strike me as rather abstract, you understand, because the new customers spend far more than the old."

Eduard fetched himself a glass of wine, carefully avoiding the stacks of manuscript that littered the tables, chairs and floor. "This novel of yours," he said, "how many thousands of pages have you written?"

"I'm not writing, I'm reading. I'm reading a novel about myself written by someone else—by an authors' collective, so to speak."

Theo picked up some pages at random and handed them to Eduard. They were copies of official documents in typescript, the upper margins adorned with reference numbers. Eduard could make no sense of the passages he read, which referred to the everyday activities of a person named Poet. In describing their protagonist, the author or authors appeared to subscribe to the literary program of the *nouveau roman*. They recorded Poet's every discernible movement with incredible precision but never ventured any conclusions about what went on in his head. "Poet left his apartment at 21:14, waited some 30 seconds before crossing the street, glanced around twice, then opened the door of the phone booth on the other side. He dialed a seven-digit number ending in 451."

It went on like that for dozens of pages. Interpolated here and there were passages of direct or indirect speech attributed either to Poet or to one of his collocutors, but both he and the subsidiary characters were invariably described as if they were hollow inside—made up of nothing more than their visible and audible manifestations. The most important rule underlying this literary program, which was scrupulously adhered to, seemed to be that any distinction between the important and the trivial was prohibited. Not until he reread certain passages did Eduard become aware that the interminable text was enlivened by something akin to a secret interest: every remark, however unexceptional, seemed to confirm the suspicion that even Poet's non-activities and non-utterances were considered worthy of note and recorded by the authors. "It is noticeable that Poet never consorts with his fellow tenants and keeps himself to himself. In an occupant of the building in question, this is considered abnormal." What at first sight seemed random attention to detail was clearly an adherence to the principle that all the hero's recurrent or fortuitous activities, especially those of an unexceptional nature, furnished hidden allusions in need of decipherment.

"It's three years of my life according to the State Security Service," said Theo, "recorded in thirty-two files each of four hundred pages. Reading them would take me just about three more years of my life—unrecorded years, presumably—to read. You know Borges's paradox: The perfect map would be one with a scale of one to one."

It was only now, he went on, that he grasped why the State Security Service had come unstuck.

Several hundred thousand East German citizens had been assigned, under oath, to investigate the lives of six million fellow citizens, or roughly every other adult inhabitant of the country. It was an unprecedented undertaking, the most gigantic field study in human history, and its sole purpose had been to detect any stirrings of emotion, however slight, that presented a danger to the state. Thanks to its instigators' paranoid basic premise, any manifestation of life was suspect on principle. The result was a corpus of material as vast and imponderable as life itself. So many man-hours were required for the collecting of evidence that little staff remained to evaluate it. In the end, even definitely incriminating evidence could no longer be distinguished from the boundless mass of largely trivial data, so the principal difference between suspects and snoopers was that the former got on with their lives while the latter devoted their lives to watching the former. The futility of this immense expenditure of effort did not become apparent until the system collapsed. The huge network of informants, recruited and trained to detect danger signs even in popular inertia, had proved incapable of predicting the demise of its own employer—the state—and its own liquidation.

"Why read this crap at all?" Eduard asked.

"Because most of the information about me was typed on my brother's machine. He reported on me at least twice a week for fourteen years, or roughly as often as he visited me. What you see there is a diary written by my best enemy."

Eduard had a vague recollection of meeting Theo's younger brother on one occasion, and of being startled by their resemblance. An even faster talker than Theo and even better, if anything, at witty repartee, all he lacked was Theo's self-assurance, but he'd promptly become the center of attention. One of their friends, not Theo, had told Eduard that, at a time when Theo was distinguishing himself as the saxophonist of a long-forgotten rock band, some highly regarded poems by his younger brother had appeared in the magazine *Form and Meaning*.

"Have you had it out with him?"

"I'm getting worried. He hasn't been seen for three months."

"What was his motive? Money worries?"

Theo's expression conveyed that Eduard must already know the answer.

"I think it's a bit more complicated than that," he said at length. "A brother versus brother affair: he occupied the space I left. He couldn't compete with me as an enemy of the state; the only role open to him was that of custodian and defender of all the beliefs I was infringing. His reports on me described the path he might have trodden himself if I hadn't got there first, so he naturally made an ideal informer."

"And you don't blame him at all?"

"I'm more curious than resentful," Theo replied. "He's showing me a way of life I was spared only by chance, by the order in which we were born. I recognize a variant of my own characteristics in all his preoccupations and obsessions. When I read him I imagine what I might have developed into if I'd had an elder brother like me."

"You mean he didn't have any choice?"

"You always have a choice between being a bastard and a reasonably decent person," said Theo. "But what makes one person opt for one thing and another for another?"

Eduard didn't reply. The old controversy. They'd hardly taken each other's measure yet, knew nothing about their latest love affairs, their wives, their work, the CDs they listened to, and already they were involved in the same old argument. Freedom of decision didn't exist: human beings were products of their environment and all behaved similarly if subjected to enough pressure. Eduard's opposing theory that they did have a choice—a chance to decide, be it ever so slim—even in situations characterized by extreme lawlessness or oppression, was thought by Theo to be a pious fiction. "Singing in the forest," he called it.

Once upon a time they'd speculated on how life in each other's country might have rewritten their biographies. His brother's treachery was now compelling Theo to submit his theory to a test that could no longer be passed with the aid of flippancy and intellectual curiosity.

5 SEEING JENNY come through the automatic glass doors into the airport arrivals hall, Eduard felt as if months had elapsed since he took off from San Francisco. He recognized the smooth, dark hair whose very appearance triggered a preperception of its scent, the nose with the tremulous nostrils so fine they verged on transparency, the eyes that seemed shrouded in the cloud belt of an unknown planet. Although he could have cited every detail of her face and walk as evidence of why he found Jenny beautiful, her beauty came to full flower only at a distance. A kind of electric current seemed to emanate from her whenever she stood or moved around in a sizable space. Yes, the space had to be large and almost deserted, like this arrivals hall, to generate the attraction that caused him—and, he believed, any man who set eyes on her—to feel this peculiar tug in the gut. Either Jenny was unaware of the effect she produced, or she was protected by her invisible bodyguards. The first time he sighted her from afar—in a shopping mall—he seemed to see two big, bright birds perched on her shoulders. They spread their fluttering wings to keep their balance as she strode briskly along. By the time she paused and looked at him blankly, they had vanished. She had absolutely no recollection of meeting him at a recent party.

Now, as he watched her coming toward him, he discerned something unfamiliar in her face, an expression—a furrow—that couldn't possibly have developed in the short time since his departure. It was as if some secret passion or sense of deprivation had worked its way through the epidermis and taken up residence in the lines around her eyes and the corners of her mouth. How could he have overlooked this change for so long? He had obviously been observing her in the same way as he studied his own reflection every morning. The image in the mirror didn't age; the eye corrected the daily, imperceptibly deepening wrinkles by substituting a remembered image for the one perceived. In the end, the constant retouching of these tiny drawings canceled out the broad brush strokes of perception, so that a fifty-year-old looking in a mirror seemed to see the young man he used to be twenty years earlier.

Jenny greeted him in the rather irritable, alcoholic state of wakefulness that sets in after a fifteen-hour flight. She hadn't the least desire to sleep in any bed, let alone a sofa bed in a prefabricated shoebox. She insisted on going right away to one of the Prenzlauer Berg restaurants she'd heard about in San Francisco. These days, she said, East Berlin was where the action was.

Eduard didn't recognize the area around Käthe Kollwitz Platz, where he'd first been some ten years ago. The whole district had transformed itself into a rendezvous for strollers and idlers who had never before been seen in this half of the city. The sidewalks were lined with powerful new automobiles, and the visitors who alighted from them didn't seem to notice that the only people they encountered in these unfamiliar surroundings were their own kind.

In one of the many restaurants they found a table beside the windows, which were open wide. The decor followed a pattern that had become popular in West Berlin ten years earlier: stripped pine doors and window frames, white tablecloths bearing black "Reserved" signs, an unplastered red brick wall, and paintwork that wavered between orange and ocher, forming the background for an enormous oil painting in the postfigurative style of the young Turks of the Berlin art scene.

Jenny looked up in disbelief as the waitress approached their table with shining eyes that pounced, as it were, on her customers. She enumerated the specialties of the house in singsong voice: *"Le carré d'agneau sur un lit de choucroute," "Le loup de mer et sa purée d'épinards," "Le filet mignon aux beignets de poireaux."* Reading the menu, Eduard and Jenny tried in vain to get their bearings. The legendary words and combinations of words to be found on any green Mitropa menu—"Soup of the Day," "Ham and Two Fried Eggs," "Hamburger and French Fries"—had vanished, and with them the dishes in question. Jenny decided at random on a *"Chariot de salade"* and stared intently at the waitress as she repeated the order in a kind of coloratura; obviously, the girl had just completed a short course in customer care. But Jenny seemed less upset by the waitress's comportment than by Eduard's amusement at it. She said she missed the lazy, haughty waiters who used to lounge around in deserted GDR restaurants before the fall of the Wall, never condescending to take an order until a customer had summoned them several times. What was more, she said, she was disgusted by the quasi-ethnological interest West Germans were suddenly taking in their compatriots from the East.

Outside the restaurant a dense stream of pedestrians flowed past in the slanting fall sunlight, eagerly making the most of what might well be the last summery day. The promenaders were almost indistinguishable in outward appearance from a New York crowd. In the midst of all these pleasure-seekers an elderly woman was steering a little girl through the crush by means of a leather harness and reins. The scene resembled a clip from a black-and-white documentary of the postwar period. Many of the restaurant's customers had noticed the unwonted sight and most were pointing out the pair in amusement. Eduard saw Jenny turn pale and laid a hand on her arm, afraid she might jump up and liberate the child.

Any young dog that leapt at Jenny, barking joyously, only to be brought up short and half throttled by the chain that fettered it to its kennel, could wring her heart and unleash impulses she blindly obeyed. Like all other four-footed, two-footed, or winged creatures trammeled by chains and cages, the dog had to be released at once. Jenny gave no thought to the consequences of her emancipatory acts until she had carried them out. No matter what town or country Eduard and Jenny were living in, their home was regularly populated by animal asylum seekers which discovered, once aboard Jenny's Ark, that they were biological foes, and that the partitions she erected between them were too flimsy. The dog bit off the rabbit's head, the cat caught the bird in the cage and the fish in the aquarium and scratched the dog's eye out, the dog severed the cat's hamstring with its teeth. Eduard was always having to ring the vet's doorbell in the middle of the night, dig shoebox-sized graves, deliver funeral orations, and watch his children shed tears they would never have shed for him.

He was relieved when Jenny averted her gaze from the child in the harness, but he feared the scene had already imprinted itself on her mind's eye as an epitome of the life that awaited her if she decided to move here.

And he suddenly recalled the vehemence with which she had— days after the event—explained her uneasiness at the sight of the television pictures of the Wall coming down. She regarded the happy release of all these long-oppressed people as an irruption, a flood, a seizure of the West by the East that would destroy the precarious, insular cosmopolitanism of West Berlin. What would come to pass, doubtless applauded by the unsuspecting West Berliners, was nothing more nor less than the Germanization of their city. She couldn't understand their feelings of triumph. On what did they base their belief that the West had won? Wasn't it far more likely that the morsel of the West on display in West Berlin would now be sucked into the vortex of the East? Far more docile and compliant than the Poles, Hungarians, and Czechs, the East Germans had submitted to forty years of indoctrination by an "antifascist" dictatorship and were singularly proud of their "better" Germany. Had they genuinely become democrats overnight? Wasn't it inevitable that the old habits, ideas, and emotions lived on under the Levi's that had become their new uniform? What about the hatred of capitalism drummed into them since childhood, their obedience to superiors, their unavowed anti-Semitism, their inherited, never eradicated mistrust of foreigners, their defiant feeling of superiority, their unsublimated urge to redeem others? What did the sheltered West Germans, who'd never had to fight for anything, have to pit against those energy-charged orphans of socialism? Why the certainty that communism had abdicated? Its official departure from the stage of history might simply be a brilliant survivor's ploy, the ultimate way of taking over the West.

Jenny's fears had evaporated in the weeks that followed. If only because it irked her to play Cassandra in the midst of enthusiastic Americans, she sought proof that her fears were unfounded. She realized that the fall of the Wall was a universal occurrence transcending Berlin and Germany. The world was not rejoicing for the Germans in particular, but for the captive inhabitants of half a continent who were at last, after twenty-seven years, permitted to emerge from behind their Wall. Anyone who failed to join in was a spoilsport!

At the same time, Eduard sensed that these and other counterarguments only scratched the surface of her skepticism. It was as if Jenny were trying to quell her emotions by belatedly denying their validity. Barely three months later, when the Monday demonstrators chanted "We're one people!" and marched through Leipzig with GDR flags from which the hammer and sickle had been excised, Jenny's forebodings regained the upper hand. No, she had nothing against

German reunification, still less against the breaching of the Wall; that was all irrelevant. So what *was* her problem? Either Jenny didn't know, exactly, or she didn't want to say exactly what she knew. Their arguments on the subject were about as productive as an argument about a Hollywood movie that causes one person to shudder with disgust and moves another to tears. Where, Eduard wondered incredulously, was the connection between his married life and an event that definitely merited a bold heading in the history books? Until now, he would have dismissed the very idea of such a possibility as political kitsch.

In Eduard's opinion, Jenny spoke better and more melodious German than most of his compatriots, but she herself wasn't German. The daughter of an Italian father and a German Jewish mother, she had grown up in a small, sleepy town near Rome. The family had emigrated to California at the beginning of the 1960s. Although it had hurt her parents and provoked an interminable correspondence when their defiant young daughter went to university in the land of war criminals, the guilt of the Nazi generation had never, even during their most heated arguments, led to an open rift between Eduard and Jenny themselves. They both felt that it was the first and most important right of two lovers to thumb their noses at collective history.

Sometimes, when he shouted or bellowed certain words in an emergency, he saw Jenny wince. Those he learned to avoid. He forbade himself to shout *"Halt!"* even when one of the children was about to cross an intersection when the pedestrian lights were red. Other forms of imperative such as *"Stehenbleiben!"* and *"Achtung!"* and *"Schnell, schnell!"* he deleted entirely from his vocabulary and substituted "Stop!," "Hey!," and "C'mon!" If other people used those baneful words he walked on fast or crossed the street; he heard them with Jenny's ears, even if she herself was nowhere near. On the rare occasions when he inadvertently blurted out one of the banned injunctions and glimpsed the sheer dismay in Jenny's eyes, he wondered how it could possibly have retained its murderous resonance for decades.

Not until after the birth of their first child did Jenny confess that she had sensed the whole burden of her family history in her belly throughout her pregnancy. Most of her relations on her mother's side had been carted off and murdered by the Nazis. Not long before giving birth Jenny had been revisited by the scene she had once described to Eduard at the beginning of their affair but never mentioned again: how the Gestapo had herded her mother and the other Jewish occupants of an apartment house together in the inner courtyard. The youthful SS officer had promptly shot one of them who was "trying to escape" and hustled the others into a truck with the aid of German shepherd dogs and shouts of *"Schnell, schnell, schnell!"* Her mother had managed to slip away from the assembly point by flirting with one of the guards.

Jenny knew that her mother had long wanted a grandchild. When the baby began to stir inside her she wondered desperately how to avoid telling her that it had a father as well—a German, no less. In those days she sometimes envied the Virgin Mary her inspired recourse to the Immaculate Conception.

After Ilaria's birth, however, she soon succeeded in convincing her mother of the new earthling's innocence. What might have contributed to this happy development, she said jokingly, was the fact that the child bore little resemblance to its father. Her two succeeding pregnancies were unaccompanied by any inner voices of warning and protest; Ilaria's cries would probably have drowned them in any case. Whatever altercations Eduard and Jenny had during their years of unremitting sleep deprivation, he couldn't recall one that might have been accounted for by the conflict model "perpetrator versus child victim"—or the other way around. Remarks of that kind would have done little to resolve the question of who should get up when one of the sirens in the nursery started wailing.

And was this rule no longer to apply, just because Mayor Schabowski of East Berlin had mumbled a halfhearted and widely misinterpreted announcement at the television cameras—the one that had brought the Wall tumbling down?

Eduard breathed a sigh of relief when the old woman and the child had gone by.

Strangely enough, it was only now that Jenny really lost her temper.

"What do they think they're doing!"

A few tables away, two people had stood up and were obstructing each other in their attempts to snap a shot of the woman and child.

"For years," Jenny said angrily, "these Mercedes drivers opened their trunks at the checkpoints unasked if they so much as saw an East German policeman in the distance. Now they whip out their cameras to take a snapshot of child-rearing under a dictatorship! A harness like that may not be so unpractical after all. A pity we never thought of it. Come on, I'm tired, let's go!"

Although she refrained from commenting on his temporary abode, Eduard regretted not having taken a hotel suite, at least for their first night together, when he saw her eyes roam over the bleak gray façade. She fell asleep at once on the uncomfortable sofa bed. In the middle of the night she nestled against him and touched him, seemingly wide awake after only a few hours' sleep. Eduard was too drowsy to respond. All he felt was a vague sense of relief that the distance between them, a product less of their days apart than of their reunion in Berlin, seemed to be wordlessly dissolving.

6 IT WASN'T until the next morning that Eduard remembered the note in a sloping handwriting he'd found lying on the carpet just inside the door of the apartment. He apologized to Frau Schmidtbauer and said he'd mislaid it.

"A parcel for you," she told him. "There weren't enough stamps on it."

"How much do I owe you?"

"Twelve marks eighty," she replied in a reproachful tone that neither a tip nor expressions of gratitude could have appeased.

Eduard expected it to be one of the sixteen parcels of books he'd mailed in San Francisco. But the octangular monster which Frau Schmidtbauer hauled out of a cubbyhole and dragged across the lobby's linoleum floor was of a different shape. It didn't come from overseas, either; judging by the stamps, it had been mailed in Germany. Only the Molecular Biology Institute knew his temporary address in Berlin, so he assumed that it came from there.

When he picked up the parcel with an effort, some heavy, bulky object inside it seemed to slither toward him and slam him in the chest. Simultaneously, a cloying smell of decay filled the air. Frau Schmidtbauer must have noticed it too, because her nostrils, which doubtless had much experience in identifying smells, began to twitch. This particular, swiftly spreading aroma was not, however, listed in her olfactory archive. Eduard thought he read a single question in her eyes: Why in the world should this Westerner get perishable foodstuffs sent to him? Didn't he trust good local produce?

Jenny, who had at last subsided into her Californian midnight sleep, didn't budge when Eduard tiptoed into the apartment and deposited the parcel on the desk. In the cutlery drawer of the kitchenette he found a carving knife.

His hand was as steady with apprehension as a surgeon's when he finally proceeded to slit open the cardboard container with the carving knife. Through the slit he made out some gift wrapping, two or three superimposed sprigs of fir, and a few blackened, discolored lettuce leaves. When he continued to wield the knife the repulsive smell, which had seemed so remote in the lobby downstairs, burst upon the room with the force of an explosion. Swiftly tearing open the paper, he espied something fleshy beneath the lettuce leaves. Incredulously at first, then with panic-stricken certainty, he identified the greenish-violet proboscis with the big nostrils as the snout of some animal—more specifically, when he tore off the wrapping completely, of a pig.

He flung open the window with a smothered cry. Only the image of that severed head in Christmas wrapping paper prevented him from using the name of the animal that now lay there *in carne et osse* as a swearword and hurling it at the walls.

You didn't have to be an expert on the history of political symbols to surmise that the pig's head had been parceled up on Rigaer Strasse. The pig had been misused for centuries as an emblem of hatred, generally by people intellectually far inferior to that animal. In recent times the pig's head had been used as a political weapon mainly by left-wingers and self-appointed antifascist groups which either didn't know or didn't care that the Nazis had employed the same means to denigrate the Jews. Thanks to the bequest that had descended on him from the heaven of reunification, the squatters had clearly labeled Eduard a representative of the "pig system," and their parcel was intended to advertise this relationship. All that puzzled him was how they had obtained his address. He'd only disclosed it once, as far as he could recall, and that was at Friedrichshain police station.

Without a moment's hesitation he picked up the half-open parcel and dashed out of the apartment with his head averted. He didn't care what Frau Schmidtbauer thought as he hurried past her window. The stench and the pinkish drops he left behind on the lobby floor would now have justified any of her suspicions, however dire.

Halfway to the trash cans it occurred to him that it might be better to go to the police station instead. The parcel was material evidence, after all. When he was shot at, the only description he could give the duty officer was of two shadowy figures on the roof; now he could dump a severed head on his desk.

The bulky parcel wouldn't fit into the trunk of the car he'd rented for Jenny's arrival, so he maneuvered it onto the back seat and drove to the police station with all the windows down.

There, without waiting for an invitation, he deposited it on the counter. The desk sergeant, a different one this time, sniffed suspiciously but seemed uncertain whether the smell emanated from the parcel or from Eduard himself. What was Eduard doing here, he demanded, this wasn't a post office. Eduard opened the flaps and saw the man blanch. It suddenly struck him that, being a member of a profession regularly greeted while on duty by cries of "Pig!," the desk sergeant might misunderstand the situation. No, no, he said quickly, he himself, Eduard Hoffmann, was the target of this hate mail, he'd only brought the parcel along as an aid to detection. The desk sergeant glared at him.

"What is it?"

"A pig's head."

"Get it out of here at once!"

"But there are bound to be fingerprints! I've a right to have the sender traced and prosecuted!"

"What right? It isn't an offense to send a pig's head through the mail. This is a democracy. People can mail whatever they like."

Eduard's head seethed with drafts of complaints to higher authority. He would be back with his attorney, he said, and demanded to know the desk sergeant's name. The latter was already turning away, clearly lulled by the sense of security that had remained undisturbed for decades by citizens' complaints. Still, Eduard couldn't exclude the possibility that the desk sergeant's knowledge of postal law was better than his own. For the moment, he had no choice but to leave the police station with the parcel clamped beneath his chin.

Two streets further on he parked the car in front of a bakery whose stripped pine fascia bore the legend OVEN FRESH in sweeping letters. The open sandwiches, croissants, and pastries in the window were laid out like pieces of jewelry; only the little velvet cushions were missing. The whole building was resplendent in fresh, Italianate ocher stucco, though this was embellished at eye level with even fresher graffiti and slogans: WESSIS GO HOME! FUCK THE LANDLORDS—ASSHOLES OF THE UNIVERSE!

The building next door, its gloomy walls deeply eroded and ulcerated by long years of dilapidation, was clearly considered politically blameless and had thus remained unscathed. Eduard crept along a passage leading to an inner courtyard with the parcel clutched to his chest, puzzled as he went by some curious figures on the walls to the right and left of him. Using a broad brush, the painter had conjured a whole animal orchestra into being on the moldering plaster: a donkey blowing a trumpet, a goose saxophonist, a pig playing a double bass. Eduard emerged into the courtyard, which was enclosed by bare brick walls. There amid rusty bathtubs and dismantled doors stood some mysterious sculptures resembling skeletons, and hanging above a lean-to was a large photograph of

Brezhnev gazing with statesmanlike appreciation at a recumbent Marilyn Monroe. It took Eduard some time to find the trash cans, which were arranged according to contents, like books in a library, under a wooden roof of recent construction: WHITE GLASS, GREEN GLASS, PAPER/CARDBOARD, PERISHABLES, PACKAGING, and, on the left, the anonymous dark green receptacle for the residue. Resolutely, he made for the one marked PACKAGING, lifted the lid, and crammed his parcel into it without making the due distinction between packaging and perishables. The lid wouldn't shut. However much pressure he exerted, the frightful pig's snout seemed to force it up again.

The phone booth outside the bakery was too new to have been adorned with graffiti. To Eduard it seemed like a radiant spacecraft that had landed in another world for a day or two. How wonderfully silently, almost politely, the glass door slid open to admit him; how agreeably, unaccountably light the plastic handset felt! He inserted his phone card in the slot, approvingly noted the credit on the display, and keyed in the number for directory inquiries. After a brief conversation, a mellifluous, supraregional, computerized voice informed him of the number of the Hilton Hotel in Gendarmenmarkt.

7 JENNY WAS SITTING on the desk, swinging her black-sheathed legs, when he got back to the guest apartment. She eyed him with a faint smile, as if expecting him to say something. The window was half open, but all he could detect in the room was the smell of fresh paint, which he now found agreeable. He'd never noticed before that the morning sun shone through the window. The light caught a strand of Jenny's hair, which had escaped from her chignon and lay across her cheek like a gleaming ribbon. Her complexion, a trifle darker than he'd known it in German latitudes, looked even darker and more exotic on the shadowy side of her face, which was toward him, and seemed eloquent of the sunlight and breezes of another continent. When she stretched out her arm to him the black satin shirt rode up, as if by chance, and he saw that she was naked beneath it except for her garter belt and stockings. His fears had been absurd. Jenny wasn't thinking of any pig's snout; she had other images and odors in mind. He'd quite forgotten that, in the days before their sex life succumbed to the dictatorship of the diaper, she'd often staged such unexpected performances.

Right at the start of their affair, on the way home from seeing a movie at the Zoopalast, Jenny had suddenly paused before some display windows. On the left an antique dealer's, on the right a store specializing in espresso machines. Jenny's attention was focused on the window in the middle, which exhibited high-heeled, thigh-length leather boots, garter belts in silk, rubber, and leather, and panties with button-up crotches. "If you buy me those boots," she said, "I'll model them for you. They'd suit me, don't you think? Or are you into latex lingerie?" Another time she told him of her erotic voyages of discovery with a Greek art dealer. Citing the quasi-ecological legitimacy of his ancestors' passions—they were all, allegedly, shepherds and goatherds—he had introduced her to the world of anal delights. "How many of my fingernails should I cut, one or two?" Jenny had asked, showing Eduard the nails on her right hand. He'd stared in disbelief at those dangerously long, bright red weapons, then into the girlish face with the eyes of a Madonna. Jenny's audacity, her determination to be the object of all his desires, had impressed him in those days. If a formula existed for the chemistry of his infatuation, it was the crazy mélange of Jenny's characteristics: innocence plus intelligence plus perversion.

He went toward her, then stopped dead: he couldn't possibly touch her with the hands that had just been holding the parcel. He not only felt like a butcher but was pretty sure he smelled like one too. He saw Jenny's nostrils flare. Fortunately, she failed to identify the odor that so clearly puzzled her.

He'd resolved not to trouble her with the events of the morning, at least for the present. The child in the harness, the high-rise apartment, the pig's head in the parcel—it was all too much too soon. As if overcome by another, more imperious urge he took a step backward, bathroomward. But Jenny wouldn't let him go. Our old problem, he thought. In their erotic arrangements they remained as dependent on sign language as new lovers who have yet to evolve a sign for explanations and delays. Jenny gripped his hand, drew him close, wrapped her legs around his hips, and signaled to him with her heels that she wanted to be carried over to the sofa bed. He complied—and marveled at all that happened thereafter. Normally a fairy-tale princess capable of detecting a piece of Lego under a dozen feather mattresses, Jenny wasn't worried by the groove beneath her back. Her nostrils, which quivered like the wings of a butterfly about to take off, were agitated not by extraneous smells but by the sirocco of her desire. As for Eduard himself, he forgot where he was and with whom. The sofa bed rose, soared miraculously through the half-open window, hovered for an incomprehensible length of time in the leaden air between the high-rise buildings, banked sharply in the direction of the Brandenburg Gate, and, with a jolt, touched down again in the guest apartment.

Eduard heard Jenny say, in a voice that conveyed no hint of acrophilia or acrophobia, "By the way, did you see that note inside the door? I think there's a parcel for you." He cupped her face in his hands. "Jenny," he said. But her eyes betrayed not the smallest inclination to respond or explain, just a glint of sarcasm. "Don't say you're going to ask me the worst question any man can ask!"

By the time he emerged from the bathroom with a towel around him, Jenny was ready to go out. Standing there in her black pantsuit, lipstick and mascara applied with intimidating precision, she looked all set for an embassy reception. But she had other plans: Eduard was to show her—yes, now, right away—his dilapidated apartment house, the future family mansion in which their children and children's children would take up residence. "And on the roof we'll install one of those swimming pools you see in New York!" No, she refused to change into something more "suitable." "It's wrong to conform, especially when you're going to see some squatters." Eduard would kindly put on his best suit and a silk necktie. Total surprise was the only way to achieve results.

The sun was setting by the time Eduard chauffeured Jenny to Friedrichshain. He noticed only on the way there that his visits to Theo in the old days were no help at all in finding his way around East Berlin. This time he was coming from a quarter he'd never started out from before—making for the city center from the east. Before the Wall came down the so-called capital had consisted for him mainly of the three or four big thoroughfares that took him via the crossing points in Heinrich Heine Strasse, Invaliden Strasse, and Bornholmer Strasse to the same two or three addresses he regularly visited. He'd driven along those streets as if they were tunnels, looking neither right nor left, eyes more often on the rearview mirror than the road ahead and ever on the lookout for the police Wartburgs that were only waiting to catch and stop a Westerner for any traffic violation, however minor. His gaze kept straying to the rearview mirror even now, although the People's Police had long been driving Volkswagens and working for their erstwhile archenemies. Instincts and emotions changed more slowly than cities and social systems.

He got his bearings by the television tower, which now and then jutted above the roofs like a gigantic pointer. The city's chunky outlines stood out crisply in the cold, dry air; only in the far distance, at the limit of one's vision, did they soften. The haze on the horizon seemed to transform buildings into slowly drifting icebergs. Sometimes there emerged from between them the huge, fiery orb of the sun, which appeared to be resting on the roadway, right at the foot of the television tower. At such moments the light burst through the windshield like water through a breached dam, dazzling Eduard so much that the city ahead of him dissolved into seething clouds of luminosity and blinded him for seconds at a time.

Jenny was surprised at how close Friedrichshain was to the new city center. Long before they got to Rigaer Strasse she was mentally drawing lines across the roofs of Frankfurter Allee from the television tower to the Plaza Hotel and fitting Eduard's property into a sketch map of the surrounding area. Several big department stores had recently opened on Frankfurter Allee, and the sidewalks were crowded. As they turned into Rigaer Strasse they sighted a vast new supermarket. Some investor—probably another West German heir—had faced the front of his apartment house with marble up to the third-floor windowsills. Eduard's inheritance, declared Jenny, even before she'd seen it, was obviously situated at the focal point of urban renewal; it was surrounded by new developments, not decay. "You must look at the street and its surroundings, not at the building alone. The first thing a buyer wants to know is whether people are moving into the neighborhood or out of it, and what kind of people they are. Hey, why didn't you tell me you owned a bar?"

Leaving Eduard to park across the street, Jenny surveyed the property. Having said she was prepared for anything, she bravely hid her consternation. Eduard, on the other hand, found the building a little less forbidding than on his first visit. One of the roll-up shutters on the ground floor had been raised, the door beyond was open, and the wrought-iron lettering above it really did seem to indicate the presence of a bar. Standing on the sidewalk, lean and lanky as a basketball player, was a young man in black leathers with an open beer bottle in his hand. He sported a buzz cut and a ring in his ear with a tiny brilliant in it. To Eduard, the look he gave this couple in their glad rags seemed less hostile than inquisitive. Jenny slipped her arm through Eduard's and steered him straight toward the young man, who eyed them like two errant representatives of another civilization.

"Hey," said Jenny, abruptly adopting an unmmistakable American accent, "this is the bar we heard about in San Francisco. Can we get a beer here?"

The leather-clad youth looked first at her, then at Eduard, as if she'd asked an extremely complicated question. Eduard got the feeling he'd already been classified as an enemy. The glossy woman in the pantsuit, by contrast, did not fit into any category and might merit a different reply.

"Wait a minute," said the tall youth in English, in answer to a call from inside the bar. An arm reached through the doorway and handed him a cell phone. Eduard heard him use it to order a long list of the most multifarious items dictated by the voice from the bar: lengths of timber, crates of beer, forks, CD-ROMs, candles, china adhesive. The last item obviously puzzled him. "China adhesive, Jeff? What the hell d'you need that for?" But "Jeff" hadn't completed his list of urgent requirements: two crates of noncarbonated mineral water, a dozen organically reared chickens, a pack of diapers. While the lanky youth was repeating these orders their originator emerged from the building. He looked at first glance like a younger brother of the man with the cell phone. Also dressed in black but not in leather, he was wearing a Champion track suit and Nike sneakers. He had the same haircut and earring but was shorter than the youth in leathers. The two of them spoke a sort of patois, but mutual communication was rendered difficult by the fact that Jeff spoke English with a Southern German accent and the lanky youth German with a British accent. Eduard was struck by an unpleasant thought: although it had been impossible for him, the target, to identify the masked figures on the roof, the gunmen, if these two were indeed they, might very well recognize him as the visitor they'd greeted with a fusillade. Unlike them, he'd been standing there completely exposed and brilliantly illuminated by the light from their flares. Had one of them been holding a pair of binoculars? If anything protected him from recognition, it was his Italian silk suit and the scent of eau de toilette that wafted from Jenny's décolletage. Where their clothing was concerned, Berlin landlords were probably not too easy to distinguish from Berlin squatters. Berliners were proud of not attaching much importance to chic and fashion.

"San Francisco?" said the lanky youth, handing the cell phone back to Jeff. "Are you sure? You probably saw our home page on the Internet."

"Oh, do you have one?" Jenny replied. "No, no, a colleague of mine on the *San Francisco Chronicle* was here. He had some great things to say about this building and its occupants."

"Hear that, Jeff? These tourists are from San Francisco!"

"Journalists," Jenny amended.

"The light in San Francisco is great," said the lanky youth, eyeing Jenny. "Here we have to make do with the Berlin Electricity Board." He introduced himself as Sam. "I'm from Manchester," he said in answer to Jenny's question, and "Pleased to meet you," when Jenny told him her first name.

How had they ended up on Rigaer Strasse? "We came by sea," Sam explained. They'd crossed the English Channel in their houseboat, chugged along the waterways to Berlin, and tied up at Moabit. The Rigaer Strasse address was popular not only in Manchester but in Dublin, Warsaw, Moscow, Lisbon, and Riga itself—"As a last resort," Jeff put in.

Did the squatters include any East Germans? Jenny asked.

The two youths looked at each other, apparently thinking hard.

"My girlfriend's from Leipzig," said Sam. "She's the only one of the old bunch left."

The people from Prenzlauer Berg had gradually moved out, Sam and Jeff explained. Living rough without water and electricity, clashes with the police, hand-to-hand fights with neo-Nazis—their East German comrades in arms weren't used to that sort of thing. In the end they'd been squeezed out by tough urban guerrillas from the West.

"What an amazing story! Really intriguing!" Jenny exclaimed delightedly. She flashed a professional journalist's encouraging smile. "Would it be right to say that here in this building, at squatter level, the Ossis were more or less expelled by the Wessis?"

"You've got it wrong," Sam retorted, slightly riled but still polite. "They didn't like the rough stuff, that's all."

The pair raised no objection when Jenny asked to see the bar. It took a while for their eyes to get used to the violet lighting. The bar was a converted living room. A few young people were standing around with bottles of beer in their hands. Another, wielding a broomstick with a piece of board attached to the end, was sweeping up last night's harvest of bottles, broken glass, cigarette butts, and cardboard cups. One of the walls, each of which was a different color, bore a screen on which a video was being projected. The video showed dozens of masked figures on a roof. They were defending themselves with slingshots and other weapons as a detachment of heavily armed policemen tried to storm their redoubt with ladders, riot shields, and nightsticks. Triumphant yells went up whenever a missile struck a policeman. Although every shot of a policeman getting hit and falling was repeated in slow motion, the video showed none of the defenders' casualties. But the occupants of the bar appeared to be ignoring the video. Excessive repetition—and, perhaps, its poor technical quality—had clearly made them tire of this epic devoted to their heroic deeds. Eduard was suddenly unsure whether the cheers and guffaws that greeted each direct hit were issuing from the throats of those present or the loudspeakers.

The counter and the shelves for bottles had been knocked together out of orange crates stacked on top of each other. Behind the counter stood a slightly built woman of about thirty with short hair and a thin, very pale face. Eduard couldn't catch what Sam said to her, but his manner conveyed that she was the decision maker around here. Initially reserved, her expression seemed to brighten at the words *San Francisco Chronicle*. She nodded to Eduard and Jenny and slid two glasses across the counter.

"Our bar list is rather special," she said with a smile that betrayed no curiosity as to how they would react. "We never have more than two or three different drinks on it at any one time, but the selection changes every week. Our choice is inspired by the novels we read. Yesterday it was *Green House*. That suggested Chartreuse. Today we're on *One Hundred Years of Solitude*."

Jenny gave an infectious laugh. "You must read a lot."

"We do," the woman replied, "but I have to admit we repeat ourselves occasionally."

Eduard could tell she'd taken to Jenny. He eyed her long fingers and blue nail polish as she dipped a glass in a saucerful of salt and filled it to the brim with tequila. He wondered if hers were the hands that had garnished the pig's head with sprigs of fir and lettuce leaves. When she stepped back from the counter, replaced the bottle on the shelf, and turned around again, he saw she was pregnant.

"How long have you been running this fascinating establishment?" Jenny asked.

"Ever since the electricity works cut us off and we all met up in here by candlelight. That was when we developed our craze for reading, incidentally. We found that books and electricity aren't an essential combination."

The electricity works had obviously knuckled under since then, Eduard reflected. At least three space heaters were generating room temperatures fit for García Marquez's Macondo. In his mind's eye he saw the dial of the electric meter counting off kilowatt-hours at a dizzy speed, ready to yield printouts that would unfailingly be sent to him, the landlord. The water meter, too, must be whirring away at a similar rate, because he could see a finger-thick jet of water gushing from the rusty faucet above the sink behind the bar. The very sound maddened him, not to mention the thought of the expense. He only just suppressed an urge to lean across the counter and turn off the pointlessly running faucet himself.

Jenny and the woman behind the counter were clinking glasses. He hurriedly picked up his own drink, marveling at Jenny's audacious fabrications. According to her they were *San Francisco Chronicle* reporters sent there to enlighten the American public on how the new German capital was treating its minorities. Whether or not the world could stomach a reunified Germany would depend on how the reunified Germans dealt with foreigners and minorities.

Sam had suddenly appeared beside them and was listening.

"Wouldn't it be better to chuck 'em out after all?" he asked the woman quietly. The question was seriously intended, but his British accent made it sound quite polite. The woman seemed to take it as a suggestion that needn't be acted on right away. It appealed to her, but Jenny appealed to her more. She was obviously intrigued by these journalists from the States. This, thought Eduard, was a generation of anarchists to whom the sixty-eighters' ingrained suspicion of the media was entirely foreign. Like Big Macs and Nike sneakers, the media formed part of the basic equipment of the world as it stood.

When they asked if they might look around a little, the woman gave Sam a nod.

He conducted them along the passage to the courtyard in which Eduard had been shot at. Although the trash and junk were untouched, the character of the courtyard had changed in some strange way. The cramped space seemed enlivened by an artistic aura that had even transformed the dismantled TV sets and refrigerators into sculptures. Embedded in the middle of the courtyard was a wooden mast of immense length, a thin, straight pole at least a hundred feet long. This gigantic spear divided the space between the walls at an oblique angle and jutted high into the sky. Almost the same diameter from shaft to tip, it prompted the beholder to wonder what era and form of vegetation could have produced it, and how it had ended up in a courtyard off Rigaer Strasse. It was as if a mighty javelin had been hurled across the roofs by some giant hand, to implant itself in the ground at this particular spot.

Sam showed no inclination to solve this enigma.

Eduard quickly counted the windows of his inheritance insofar as they were visible from the courtyard. Although he couldn't ascertain the number of apartments in this way, he could clearly see that many were unprotected from the elements by windowpanes and temporarily uninhabitable. The building was separated from the property next door by an eight-foot wall topped with broken glass and barbed wire. In the event of an eviction, Eduard reflected, this wall would be too long for the squatters to defend and might help the police to gain access when they stormed the building. They could always use scaling ladders, after all.

He suddenly caught sight of the small boy he'd noticed on his first visit. All alone in a deserted, brightly lit room, he was perched on the edge of a billiard table with a broken cue in his hand. The window was smashed, and Eduard wondered how the bare-armed youngster could endure being exposed to the cold night air. The object ball was invisible to Eduard and obviously hard to reach, because the boy was leaning as far across the green baize as he could with his head inclined and a lock of luxuriant fair hair flopping over his eyes. He spent a long time aiming and eventually cued, only—it seemed—to miss. He tried once more, again without success. There was something immensely single-minded and, at the same time, clumsy and futile about his efforts. Watching the boy as he sat there under the harsh white light, Eduard was gripped by a sudden, inexplicable feeling of compassion.

He was on the point of asking about the boy when another squatter emerged from a side entrance and, ignoring him and Jenny, walked up to Sam. He spoke so softly that Sam had to bend an ear to hear him. All of a sudden the newcomer extended his right arm in Eduard's direction, leveled a forefinger at him, and laughed. After whispering together for some time, the pair disappeared through a side door. Eduard, feeling more and more uneasy, was sure he'd been recognized. He now thought it incredibly reckless of himself and Jenny to have wangled their way into the building. Of their own free will, they'd placed their defenseless persons at the mercy of people who regarded them as mortal enemies. In theory, these squatters could do as they pleased with them: lock them up and interrogate them, hold them for ransom. He'd read somewhere that a decomposed body had been found in the attic of a squat, and the crime had never been solved.

Jenny didn't appear to sense his uneasiness. He saw her standing, pale and vulnerable, in the darkened courtyard. A shaft of reflected light was slanting down on her. In the midst of all that trash and decay she looked like a black-swathed statue stolen from a museum— no, he thought, like a hostage, a beautiful hostage whom he might at any moment have to defend against overwhelming numbers of abductors.

"Hey, like to see my pad?" called someone.

It was a while before Eduard managed to connect Sam's voice with Sam. He was standing in the rear passage with his head sticking out of yet another broken window.

Jenny didn't seem averse.

"Sorry," Eduard called back, "we have to go. We've got tickets for the opera."

"The opera? Are you sure? It's lousy, the opera in this burg."

"Too bad," said Eduard. He took Jenny's arm and propelled her vigorously across the courtyard toward the passage leading to the street. She insisted on saying goodbye to the woman in the bar.

"We're most impressed," she told her, and apologized for their abrupt departure.

"You must come to one of our parties."

"Like when?"

"Like every night, but the biggest one'll be in three or four weeks' time. To celebrate our tenancy agreements."

"You mean you've got tenancy agreements?"

"We're getting them," said the woman behind the counter. She laid a sisterly hand on Jenny's arm.

Eduard was dumbfounded; Jenny looked exultant.

"Good for you! Who from?"

"The woman that owns the building, who else?"

"Really? You'll find life pretty unexciting after that. Are you absolutely sure?"

"We're in luck," said Sam's girlfriend. "Our landlady's a wonderful old woman. She had to leave Germany in the 1930s. I think she likes us, too."

Back in the car again, Jenny flew into a rage. With his rapidly deteriorating eyesight, she said, which vanity deterred him from correcting with the reading glasses he'd needed for ages, Eduard was quite capable of having misread the name or the address. She wanted to see that restitution notice right away!

Eduard had difficulty convincing her that he really did possess such a document from Lichtenberg District Court and had studied every word of it. The squatters' assertion was a shrewd piece of lying propaganda concocted especially for two famous journalists from the *San Francisco Chronicle*. He did, however, concede that he knew almost nothing about the history of the building. Like millions of other equally astonished heirs, he'd benefited from a kind of historical lottery whose winners were often unaware they'd entered it.

"And you really have no idea how your grandfather came to own that dump?"

"None at all."

"You mean it's the old story of the long-lost uncle from the Bahamas?" she said sarcastically.

"If you like to put it that way," he replied. He wasn't the only one to be bowled over by his good fortune. Thanks to reunification, he said, many if not most of the new heirs had suddenly become nephews of uncles from the Bahamas and were now inheriting private houses and office buildings, factories, forests, and real estate they'd long abandoned hope of owning or didn't know existed.

"But surely you must know whether or not your grandfather was a Nazi?" she exclaimed.

Eduard vaguely remembered his father and grandmother talking about "Herr Egon Hoffmann," the bon vivant and lady-killer whom they always referred to in that dismissive fashion. The family's oral archives related that every Sunday morning, while his wife was in church with the children, Grandfather would disport himself in the marital bed with one or another of his mistresses. One Sunday, when Grandma and the children returned from their devotions earlier than usual, she found him jacketed but trouserless and his playmate clumsily camouflaged by rumpled bedclothes. Grandma shooed the children away from the scene of the crime and, in her Bach-choir-trained soprano, launched into a tirade that Eduard's father had never forgotten. The same day, she and the children moved in with one of her sisters. From then on Egon Hoffmann's name was mentioned only in an undertone: emigrated to America, married a hotel heiress, gambled away a fortune, ended his days in the gutter with tinhorns and prostitutes. "He certainly wasn't in the Resistance," said Eduard. Grandma, on the evidence of photographs and his father's allusions to her, had idolized the Führer. Even had his only claim to fame been a refusal to perform the Hitler salute, an anti-Nazi Egon Hoffmann would undoubtedly have been rediscovered and rehabilitated by his family in 1945. If only because of its usefulness during the postwar years, the existence of such a forebear would definitely have been bruited about.

Jenny was incensed at the vagueness of Eduard's information. How could a grownup man recall his grandfather's given name, albeit with difficulty, but have nothing save conjectures to offer about his age, his career, and the year of his death? What would he say to their children when they questioned him about their fore-bear? Didn't he have any anecdotes to tell, for instance, about the carving on the stock of Great-Grandfather's hunting rifle, or the smoke rings he used to blow, or his lace-up boots, or his fads and for-getfulness—some personal and inimitable characteristic a child could hang onto?

Eduard shook his head. No adult or adolescent representatives of his generation of Germans were keen to delve into their parents' or grandparents' antecedents because they risked coming across unpleasant details that were far from suitable as bedtime stories. They preferred to devote any such meticulous research to the past lives of unrelated persons.

"So who *did* you settle accounts with?" Jenny snapped. "With an age group? With some aliens who'd landed in Germany by acci-dent? How did you yourselves turn up in Germany? Like angels who tumbled out of hairless angelic pussies and little pink clouds onto that particular patch of ground? You Germans can't even tell your children who bequeathed them their red hair or talent for music or predisposition to diabetes!"

What was the matter with Jenny? Why was she getting so worked up? The whole subject had been thrashed out between them umpteen times. He had long ago conceded that the Germans' "structural settling of accounts" with their parents' generation had been anything but inadvertent. They favored the plural and eschewed the singular; referred to "the generation responsible for Nazi fascism" but seldom to their own fathers or grandfathers; focused on "the social and psychological preconditions" for the megacrime; devoted no attention to their relations' little cowardices, the gratuitous denunciations and despicable acts that had combined to facilitate the Holocaust. They had no patience, either, with minor acts of decency on the part of some aunt or grandmother which, if only they'd been more frequent, might have prevented the genocide. One of the advantages of structural analysis was that it absolved the accusers from researching their own family history.

But everything was different now, thanks to a magic formula termed "restitution." This complicated and unexpected law was bringing the history of the last sixty years home to the present generation in the form of family history. Fictitious or not, the female squatter's reference to "the woman that owns the building" would compel Eduard to explore the history of Egon Hoffmann's bequest in every detail. He would have to prove that his grandfather had acquired the property "honestly"—whatever that meant—and not, at all events, as the proceeds of "a forced sale arising from persecution." History was being rewritten as the history of family property. And, because this new branch of research related more to the individual pocket than the collective conscience, millions of amateur sleuths would engage in it.

All the streets around the Gendarmenmarkt had been transformed into cul-de-sacs. Eduard had to circumnavigate the square several times before he found the entrance to the Berlin Hilton amid a labyrinth of arrows pointing left and right. Ignoring Jenny's questions, he handed a bellhop the rented car's ignition key and ushered her into the lobby. The desk clerk confirmed his reservation in Saxonian-accented English. Where was Eduard taking her, Jenny asked as he steered her toward the elevator, room key in hand, back to America? She was astonished to note that the lobby, with its fountain, white stucco columns, glass-canopied atrium, and twin flights of stairs leading nowhere, was an exact replica of the lobby in a hotel she'd overnighted at in Arizona.

Once inside the room Eduard restrained her from switching the light on. He went over to the French windows and opened the curtains. The room was illuminated only by the yellow lights in the square and the red beacons on the towers and cupolas. Just above them they saw a wall of cloud, equally bright all over but with sharply defined edges, like a backlit white stone building suspended in the sky; at eye level in front of them were the blackish stone figures on the cathedral's frontal and lateral pediments, and, high above, the golden angel at the summit of the dome, which seemed to be flying along beneath the imperceptibly moving wall of cloud. The domed towers with their numerous columns and the seemingly free-standing figures on the pediments conjured a hint of Mediterranean, baroque cityscape into the Prussian sky. Only the view from the east-facing window reminded them of where they were. Visible against a wall surmounting some excavated foundations, a crane's long arm was pivoting through the darkness. Heavy machinery could be heard tamping and scraping away in the depths of the abyss.

Eduard saw Jenny's face silhouetted against the French window, all but her nose and the curve of her lips veiled in shadow. He drew her toward him. A speck of light danced across her bare arm as she let her jacket slide to the floor. The darkness and the unfamiliar room made strangers of them. As if for the first time, his hands traced the outlines of her body, first those he could see, then those he could only touch. He whispered endearments he'd never uttered before.

And then, as if time were suddenly being measured by another clock, they tore off their clothes. They were too impatient to undress completely—only the bare essentials were discarded, and Jenny's satin blouse and Eduard's socks weren't among them. Somehow, instead of finding themselves under the canopy of the bridal four-poster, they ended up on the carpet in front of it. But in the midst of their lovemaking Eduard seemed to hear a warning note that made him hesitate. It had nothing to do with him or his libido, but with the invisible piece of grit that brought Jenny's pleasure machine to a premature halt. Jenny didn't seem at all concerned that he should restrain himself and was adept at inflaming him to the point where a man forgets all his good resolutions. Eduard's restraint and hesitation and Jenny's urgings developed into a strange duel. Did he only imagine that she was averting her face from his kisses? That she froze, alert as a wild beast, when he fondled her, and clasped him roughly to her as if trying to prevent him from pursuing his futile activities? Could it be that his own wife, the mother of his three children, found his caresses distasteful?

This suspicion altered the rules of the sexual game. Surrendering to one's libido meant swallowing one's pride and losing the contest.

Let it happen, he said or felt like saying; let yourself go, I love you, what more must I do for you to grant my wish? Slay a dragon, serenade you on bended knee, climb the balcony railings and threaten to jump? Are you saving yourself for something or someone?

There came a time when he genuinely felt that her breathing matched the rhythm of his own, that he could hear a gentle sigh and a moan of pleasure issuing from the ultimate depths. He surrendered and promptly regretted it, for when he gently stroked Jenny's body, sated and soothed, he found that her skin was completely dry—as dry as it would have been after a siesta on the beach beneath a sun umbrella.

In the middle of the night he woke up and sought to make sure in the dark. There were no two ways about it: lying beside him was a full-grown, flawless woman, a swan-necked princess with the face of a wayward, enchanting child. She was his wife, she had borne him three children. But she didn't belong to him—had never belonged to him, perhaps—and he would lose her unless he contrived to guess her riddle.

8 DISCOUNTING A BRIEF INTRODUCTORY visit to the head of the department, Eduard had yet to show his face at the Molecular Biology Institute. He still had to discover a route to Berlin-Buch that promised to get him there at a reasonably predictable hour. The bumpy suburban roads he had to traverse were interspersed with construction sites every few hundred yards and correspondingly choked with traffic. His attempts to bypass them ended either in blind alleys or in open countryside. He clearly had no choice but to cover the final stretch to the Institute at a walking pace, and there was no sign that this state of affairs would improve in the foreseeable future. Most of the construction sites he passed were quite unconnected with road improvements; the technicians and workmen were primarily engaged on all the other services to be installed beside or beneath the streets. Gas, water, and sewage pipes, telephone and power cables had to be laid or relaid. The whole of Berlin was topsy-turvy: the city center was a temporary desert and looked like the outskirts; the outskirts were as crowded as city centers elsewhere.

The immediate vicinity of the Institute was reminiscent of municipal vegetable plots that had, with slender resources and great perseverance, been transformed into a permanent housing development. The gabled single-family dwellings, most of them two-storied and each enclosed by a small, neatly fenced garden, reminded Eduard of impoverished suburbs in the States. These houses were built of stone, not timber, and could not be mounted on wheels and hauled away. But the development's simple, uniform design, its almost deliberate sterility, and the rectangularity of the roads and building lots—all these features struck him as familiar. There were other strange resemblances, too. The numbering of the streets, the minutes-long wait for the lights to turn green, the compulsion to turn right off a main road when you wanted to turn left—had the town planners of the GDR copied these things from the imperialist foe across the ocean? Did the same apply to the central allocation of restaurant tables by the headwaiter, the modest menus, the obligatory garnishing of your plate with lettuce leaves? Could those who shaped the other Germany have been inspired by an unavowed love for the world power across the Atlantic? Such an attraction would certainly have possessed an inner logic, Eduard reflected, because American immigrants and the founders of the GDR had both been animated by the idea of starting from scratch. The revolutionaries held that traditional culture must bow to rational principles, and that history really began with themselves. It was quite inevitable, Eduard realized suddenly, that the young socialist state should in many respects have been a copy of poor America, a mini-USA. To him, the tragic error inherent in this imitation seemed to be that the German tyros had overlooked the shameless inconsistency of their American exemplar. The ideal of equality had not been mitigated in the GDR by an acknowledgment of human selfishness and its products. That was why you never glimpsed, rising above these conformist rabbit hutches, the glittering backdrop of the downtowns where the rich and powerful indulged their frenzied urges; never the shimmering façades, the Romanesque or Gothic, baroque or arabesque roofs and towers of the soaring residential castles to which even the poorest of the American poor could lift up their eyes from their shadowy abodes beneath expressway overpasses or in U-Bahn entrances.

Around the Institute, in the innermost circle of the development, a small colony of brand-new, partly occupied dwellings had grown up. Eduard surmised that they had been built by some of the Western colleagues who had managed to obtain permanent posts at the Institute. Many of these houses, which had overhanging eaves and wide balconies, looked like mountain hotels, others were reminiscent of vacation homes in Ibiza or Mykonos, still others boasted little oriels and turrets and struck a postmodern pose. Seen among the single-family houses of the GDR era, these new buildings resembled exotic blooms transplanted into an overly cold climate. The sole principle observed by the architects and planners of victorious Western civilization seemed to be that of the botanical garden which aspires to display the widest possible range of varieties. On discovering a Swiss chalet cheek by jowl with an adobe Mexican villa, however, Eduard wished houses were equipped, like plants, with sensors that forbade them to thrive in an unsuitable climate, causing them to wither and decay.

The barrier in front of the Institute's gatehouse did not rise until the gatekeeper had carefully compared Eduard's face with the photograph on his official pass. The driveway ran through well-kept grounds filled with tall trees—beeches, birches, oaks, yews, lindens—each of which seemed to represent a particularly rare species. The buildings among the shrubs and trees assumed the usual unmistakable boxlike shape and were faced with the usual brownish, pimply stucco. In the shade of a silver fir Eduard sighted the bronze figure whose likeness he'd been puzzled to see on the cover of the Institute's in-house magazine. Entitled *L'homme,* this work of art had been bequeathed to the Institute on permanent loan by a sister establishment in West Germany. It seemed clear that the East Germans' Western colleagues were worried about their aesthetic as well as their professional development. The naked male figure in bronze had both arms outstretched as if eager to embrace the world, but he looked so unsteady on his pins that anyone surveying him for long developed sympathetic muscle cramps.

Eduard parked in front of the "White House," which presumably owed its name to the recently completed labors of a gang of painters but was still unfinished inside. There you bumped into ladders, buckets, crates of building materials, and workmen who steadfastly waited for you to say sorry first. Eduard lost his way several times before he found Professor Rürup's study. The professor nodded as if to a close acquaintance he'd like to see more often, though Eduard had barely exchanged a personal word with him until now, merely settled a few administrative matters. He wasn't sure how he would get on with the slim, ascetic-looking man, whose body language he had yet to learn. The professor had addressed him by his first name right away, American fashion, but Eduard didn't know whether to return the familiarity—it might be just a superior's prerogative here. It also puzzled him that the professor spoke so softly. Did he purposely dispense with all authority rituals, or was he simply too shy to insist on them? Eduard was uncertain even of Rürup's age. Only the myriad tiny wrinkles on his neck and his long, thickened earlobes confirmed the date of birth Eduard had come across in a bibliographical footnote; his skin, his youthful, darting eyes, and his movements seemed to belong to another person.

Eduard was surprised by the spaciousness of the premises and the laboratory work stations. At Stanford they'd had to make do with much smaller desks, often in windowless rooms shared by two or three members of the staff. He was equally impressed by the laboratory's cleanliness. However, the expressions of many of the colleagues and lab technicians to whom Rürup had briefly introduced him on their tour—his official welcome was scheduled for a few days later—betrayed a rather studied affability. In any case, Eduard thought he detected the beginnings of laughter in the wrinkles around the professor's eyes. Rürup seemed only to be waiting for this technologically pampered newcomer from the celebrated Medical Center to pour scorn on the Institute's equipment. In fact, Eduard was favorably surprised by the standard of the laboratory. If genetic research in Germany really was limping along five to ten years behind that of the States, it certainly wasn't for want of the relevant gadgets. Perhaps there were too few people who knew how to use them. Besides, he didn't feel the slightest inclination to utter some expert opinion that would instantly brand him as a guru where machines and computers were concerned. Even in a computer heaven like California, 30 to 40 percent of the working day was devoted to rectifying breakdowns in communication between computers and their human operators. In Eduard's new, postcommunist working environment that figure would have to be pitched considerably higher.

Rürup, who seemed constantly at pains to build bridges between Eduard's old and new work environments, had ended their tour by inviting him to a coffee break in the canteen. The echoing room was almost deserted; only at one or two tables near the window could Eduard make out a few people sitting in front of beige-colored trays with dirty cups and plates on them. Was it his imagination, or had they lowered their voices when he came along the passage with Rürup? The professor steered him to a table at the back—"equidistant from the daylight and the kitchen clatter," as he caustically remarked.

He asked in passing whether Eduard had ever gone into Riggs Bank in Washington, D.C. Clearly proud of his "first visit to the West for exactly thirty-one years," he was undeterred by Eduard's negative shake of the head. In every branch of Riggs Bank, he went on, the manager and possibly his deputy were both white men. Any customer privileged to be greeted by one of the two would never forget that encounter. In his case they had been so effusively courteous that he wondered if they'd mistaken him for a Hollywood star. It wasn't until he joined the line in front of the counter that he realized he'd crossed the threshold of another world, the customers' carpeted hell.

The cashiers were all black and predominantly female, among them beautiful beings dressed like African princesses who manipulated their computer keyboards with chunky, glittering rings on their fingers. Even when they beckoned you over they were still engrossed in amusing telephone conversations, possibly of an amorous nature. When you finally caught their eye they inquired what you wanted so brusquely—indeed, with such undisguised contempt— that you were half inclined to apologize for being there at all. What Rürup had found most remarkable of all, however, was the patient, almost subservient demeanor of the customers, or at least of the whites among them. They behaved as if they deserved such mistreatment, nor had he ever heard anyone complain. American colleagues whom he'd questioned on the subject had either disputed his observations or found them politically suspect. As "slaveholders' descendants" they'd been almost amenable to the fact that "slaves' descendants" should punish them in this fashion. "You must think of this place a bit like Riggs Bank," Rürup concluded his account. "The faces behind the counters are white, admittedly, but there are other distinguishing characteristics."

Until 1991 the Academy of Sciences had employed around twenty thousand scientists. At the end of that year it was closed down and split up into small units. All scientific personnel had received dismissal notices; only a few hundred of those who reapplied and found favor with the Scientific Council had been reemployed, mostly on short-term contracts.

The outcome of this reconstruction was unsurprising, said Rürup. Most of the senior posts had gone to West German applicants, quite often people who had never obtained a professorship on the other side of the Wall. Personnel from the former GDR, on the other hand, were reunited in the middle echelon, in administration, security, catering, et cetera. Although Rürup refrained from pronouncing on the wisdom and justice of this arrangement, he questioned whether it had been a good idea, in the bankrupt GDR of all places, to provide highly desirable colleagues from the West with jobs for life. "What are the shipwrecked to think of lifeboatmen who occupy every last place in the boat that's supposed to be rescuing them? You mustn't be surprised if you see a lot of discontented faces in this place."

Middle management personnel were particularly ill disposed and ill paid, said Rürup. "They're all going to night school and learning English," he added with a fleeting malicious smile.

Eduard couldn't fathom the man. Wasn't he himself a living refutation of the statement that all the senior posts were occupied by West Germans? But Rürup seemed temporarily uninterested in resolving this contradiction.

Eduard was distracted by some loud, echoing footsteps behind him. It wasn't just any old sound that caused him and most of those present, Rürup apart, to turn their heads; it was the provocative, almost painful clatter of a pair of platform soles. The woman seemed unabashed by everyone's attention. Looking neither right nor left, she strode past the windows on her way to the counter. She was wearing a costume of some light, flowing material that translated her every movement into shimmering billows. A lock of her black hair, which had a reddish glint, rose and fell at every step. The sun had drilled a big hole in the gray autumnal sky and was streaming through the long row of windows. The bare canteen was suddenly filled with thousands of dust particles that went whirling into the air as though the light had turned to liquid. The room seemed pervaded by a tumultuous presentiment of spring. Eduard saw the sunlight reflected on the woman's face and felt as if his bleak surroundings were momentarily warmed by its glow—as if all present including himself were relaxing a little in their chairs. Did he dream it, or had she noticed him? With unaffected curiosity, she looked into his eyes in passing, perhaps because he was alone in not averting them at once. Rürup noticed his reaction but forbore to remark on it. Resuming his monologue, he answered the question Eduard hadn't ventured to ask.

"Where my own job's concerned," he said, "I owe it to a kind of writer's cramp." In the latter years of the Wall's existence he'd been gradually frozen out of the Academy's research projects because of some minor misdeameanor. In 1982, three days before his scheduled departure for a biology conference in Amsterdam, for which he had, to his surprise, been granted an exit visa, the cadre leader had walked into his office, deposited a printed form on his desk, and requested him to sign it. From now on and without further prompting, Rürup was to report on his every unofficial and unauthorized contact with persons from the West, irrespective of whether he met them in a professional or private capacity. A mere formality, the cadre leader assured him with a comradely wink, and one that every scientist visiting the West had to comply with. In practice, he added, it was about as effective as the nationwide ban on watching West German TV programs.

Rürup thought it important to stress that he was no hero. He had already picked up his ballpoint in readiness to scribble the signature that would not only guarantee him this and any future trips abroad but shape the subsequent course of his career. But some form of obstinacy, some mental block, some sudden stiffness or paralysis of the wrist had prevented him from applying the poised ballpoint to the dotted line with the cross against it. While he and the cadre leader were staring in bewilderment at the blank space that simply refused to be filled, it dawned on him that momentous decisions of this kind are made without long deliberation. He realized that far more important people than himself—internationally celebrated colleagues whom he much admired—had yielded to this moment of weakness. Who did he think he was, refusing to do what they'd all done? If he'd at least had an illegitimate child or an Italian mistress in the West, he'd have understood himself and his recalcitrance.

The consequences of his refusal surpassed all his fears. That he couldn't travel and wouldn't become a departmental chief he'd considered an acceptable price to pay. What he had not been prepared for was that, in addition, all his seminars and lectures had been canceled and his permission to use the laboratory and its equipment withdrawn. He was even denied admission to the Academy. Although his salary continued to be paid, he was expected to remain at home. He'd spent the last few years before the Wall came down playing chess against his own computer, and had been depressed to find that, although he was a novice at the game, he'd consistently defeated his antiquated machine.

"So you see," he went on with a wry smile, "I can't ascribe my sudden jump up the ladder to any major scientific discoveries or publications." He felt rather like those Germans whom the Red Army had appointed to be mayors, judges, factory managers, and school heads half a century ago. Generally speaking, their sole proof of competence was the fact that they'd refrained from collaborating with the Nazis or had even opposed them. But weren't they far too few, and had they been up to the job? Rürup regretted that he still knew enough about his specialty to realize that the talented colleagues who had compromised with the regime and retained access to international congresses and exchanges of information were definitely his superiors today. It was right, in a way, that they and not he had been appointed to permanent posts at American and Japanese universities.

"A fascinating problem," said the professor, curiously eyeing the pale brown freckles of senescence on the hand that held his coffee cup. "Sometimes I even wonder if resentment of toadyism and opportunism isn't symptomatic of a lack of talent. Would Mozart, Einstein, or Marx have opted for rebellion if compelled to pay for it with silence? Wouldn't they have preferred to make any compromise that enabled them to exercise their genius rather than do nothing and lapse into mediocrity? If the price of moral integrity is isolation, inactivity, and, ultimately, bemedaled stupidity, what is there to be said for it?"

He had uttered the last few words in an even lower voice and was nodding at someone behind Eduard's back. A young man with sparse fair hair paused briefly beside them and then, without waiting for the professor's invitation, sat down at their table. Rürup introduced him as Dr. Santner, *the* rising star in medical genetics and one of the few members of the old Academy of Sciences to pass muster with the Scientific Council.

Dr. Santner scrutinized Eduard intently. He had a swift, slurred way of speaking that caused Eduard to lean forward a little, quite involuntarily, while listening. Eduard promptly asked himself—and guessed the answer—how Santner would have reacted to the cadre leader's request before his first trip to the West. He was all the more surprised at the veiled disrespect with which the younger man behaved toward the head of the Institute. It was all Santner could do not to interrupt the professor every two minutes. Why did Rürup, who in Eduard's eyes merited admiration or even reverence, treat him so indulgently?

It transpired that Dr. Santner had made a close study of Eduard's papers on "behavioral genes, so called." He also knew that Eduard had recently attended a conference in Maryland on "The Biological Bases of Violence." Eduard found his interest obtrusive and unpleasant. Even the theme of the conference had aroused fierce reactions in the States and prompted the German press to draw comparisons with Nazi racial theory. In fact, he thought he detected a readiness to pounce in Santner's questions, as if the other man had aimed to expose the flaws in his scientific ethos before the first half hour was up.

But Santner had something else in mind. He surprised Eduard by telling him that GDR scientists had been secretly pursuing aggression research for many years—with peptid and steroid hormones, to be precise. The target group for their research had been athletes whose sports called for concentrated bursts of aggression, for instance high jumpers, fencers, and boxers. Although he couldn't say how many world records had been set with the aid of such hormonal preparations, it was noteworthy that the Scientific Council, which was dominated by West Germans, had attached particular importance to research in this field. When the Wall came down a colleague of his had decamped to Austria with all their data, which suddenly belonged to no one, and had made millions there in license fees.

The GDR researchers had encountered an interesting philosophical dilemma, Santner went on. Official doctrine stated that there could be absolutely no genetic basis for human aggression; acts of violence were held to be symptoms of a misanthropic capitalist environment for which the preconditions no longer existed in the GDR. However, since crimes of all kinds were committed in the GDR but could on no account be attributed to environmental factors, the guardians of pure theory were confronted by a painful choice. They had either to define acts of violence as relics of capitalist culture or to take a radically biological view and derive them from human nature. To all appearances, aggression researchers had finally surrendered to the latter hypothesis.

Professor Rürup looked at Eduard suspensefully, as if to convey that he owed him a rejoinder to Santner's outline of the problem, but Eduard hadn't the least desire to accommodate him. Santner had attempted to disenchant him, the colleague from California, in short order. He had intimated that his Californian colleague's research into behavior-altering genes was old hat here. At the same time, he had skillfully placed Eduard's project in a line of descent from Stasi research.

But that wasn't his present concern. What puzzled him was a sense of having already lived through this day—many such days, in fact. His presence seemed as unreal as a daydream that sets in at a moment of inward abstraction. He couldn't have said why he'd come here, felt he'd banished himself to this place without any discernible need and was at risk of losing something that still defied definition. Remarkably, the image of the unknown woman recurred to him, walking past in slow motion. He was grateful for her ocular greeting. For some reason, he perceived it as the welcome he'd been awaiting since his arrival.

9 OVER DINNER at the Hilton that night he asked Jenny the question that had been gnawing at him ever since he left the States. Jenny took a sip of her red wine, gave him a ravishing smile, and said in the tone of a rather bored talk-show star accustomed to indiscreet questions, "Yes and no. It was lovely, really it was, but the thing you're referring to didn't happen, of course. It very seldom does, with me. Please don't be silly. Don't act like we've never talked about it."

"Seldom, or never?"

"You want to know how often? How often in all these years? Whose happiness are you worried about, mine or yours?"

Her sarcasm infuriated him. She behaved as if he were casting her in the role of a bookkeeper compelled to search her memory for how often she'd fulfilled her quota of conjugal bliss. Any minute now, and she'd be counting on her fingers. To the best of her recollection, said Jenny, she'd reached the stage around which all his thoughts were suddenly revolving only a few times in the years between and after having children. And although he hadn't the slightest reason to develop a complex about it—"You're the best lover I've had, just so you know!"—she would probably be able to grant him and herself such an experience only on rare occasions in the future as well. To tell the truth, she'd only enjoyed "it" utterly and completely— Eduard promptly asked what that meant and earned himself a pitying smile—once in her life, and that was in an extremely dangerous, wholly unreal situation which she wouldn't attempt to describe because it was, quite simply, unique and unrepeatable.

The interior of Eduard's head felt peculiarly light and clear, but a yawning gulf had opened in the neat terra-cotta tiles beneath his feet. "I won't presume to ask the name of this expert," he said, "but would you, for the sake of a twelve-year marriage, be kind enough to explain why his performance was so unrepeatable?"

He saw Jenny's eyes light up. She might have been laughing at some successful childish prank.

"I don't know, it was crazy and dangerous, that's all—very romantic, too. Picture a couple on the north face of the Eiger, and the man tells his female companion, whom he's never even touched before, that he must either take her on the edge of the precipice, here and now, or jump to his death right away."

"*Was* it on the north face of the Eiger?"

Jenny hooted with laughter but promptly bit her lip, as if reluctant to push him too far. "You can't expect me to give you a formula," she said. "After all, I'm talking to someone who appreciates metaphors. Women are princesses—you know that, or you should. They may adore you, but they still want you to risk your life to conquer them."

Hadn't he made all the declarations of love she could wish for? asked Eduard. Jenny seemed to be thinking hard. "Rather a long time ago, I guess," she said eventually.

"So what do you suggest?"

"Nothing," she said. "In this area, good intentions are the worst possible thing. I'm nuts, probably. I entertain absurd demands and expectations that would drive even Sir Lancelot to despair."

"Can't you be a bit more explicit?"

"Just forget it."

He saw a drop of red wine sparkling on one of her incisors just before she captured it with the tip of her tongue. She smiled at him as if that would enable him to construct a more conciliatory version of her reply.

Jenny's revelation left Eduard too bemused to think straight. Swiftly changing the subject, they had run through the three children's accomplishments and bad habits in order of age—a subject capable of occupying an entire evening. Despite their like-minded approach to parenting, this had its customary effect on them: it totally dispelled any erotic tension. Now and again Eduard stopped listening and took the liberty of leafing through his album of earlier sexual successes, but his inward groans of rage and self-pity—"Why should this happen to me, of all people?"—had brought him no closer to evolving a strategy.

He woke up beside Jenny during the night. A look at the clock told him that he'd already had three hours of trauma-induced sleep and was unlikely to doze off again before dawn. That gave him plenty of time for reflection. Recalling the individual phases of his married life, he made a surprising discovery: the main obstacle to unbounded marital happiness, he found, was parenthood. It was only two or three years before his departure from California that they'd reached that intermediate plateau signaled on the parental calendar by the exclamation: "The baby slept through!" Loris, who had hitherto been woken by one of his fragile nightmares every few hours, had finally slept through with one small hand beneath his cheek—"like a cherub," to use an expression doubtless coined about children by the childless. Counting three years of nocturnal screams for each of their two daughters and only two for Loris, the prodigy, they'd suffered a total of eight years' sleep deprivation. True, Eduard had survived the bulk of that period by digging Jenny in the back— "Can't you hear? Katharina's woken up—no, I think it's Loris!"— but the balance was restored in a mysterious way. Eduard, whose nightly exertions were largely confined to prodding Jenny with his forefinger, couldn't get back to sleep after that exhausting activity, whereas Jenny, having made her way to the nursery with the unerring tread of a somnambulist, usually without switching a light on, and silenced the din by means of pacifier, bottle, or sweet reason, was asleep again within seconds. After lying awake for hours, Eduard came to the conclusion that interrupting one's sleep was less arduous than hours of sleeplessness. Agreements on sharing responsibilities according to the day of the week seldom lasted long and brought little relief. Even when Eduard had earned the right to eight hours' sleep by keeping vigil the night before, a privilege he exercised in a distant cubbyhole beside the kitchen, he woke up unsummoned after only four hours and did not drift off until six a.m., shortly before the alarm clock sounded.

Sleep deprivation was accompanied by another deficiency which Eduard came to regard as a natural phenomenon. Even his protests against it were silenced by Jenny's premature descents into the arms of Morpheus. Their love life became increasingly limited to lying, exhausted, side by side. Eduard had been quite unprepared for this consequence of parenthood. Neither in the late-night talk shows in which a sex expert, seated beside some oafish urban guerrilla, prompted well-rehearsed guests to divulge every detail of their aberrant sex lives, nor in the countless TV sex comedies, nor in popular international fiction, were parents of small children granted a hearing. The openly discussed sex life of the West was carried on by childless people of all ages. Although Eduard had sometimes heard of parents who, with their four- or five-year-old offspring looking on, strapped each other to brass bedsteads, transfixed their erogenous zones with fishhooks, or diverted themselves with whips and rubber accessories, his own inquiries yielded another picture altogether. To the extent that their erotic needs weren't met by nursing babies and changing their diapers, young parents suffered from a sexual apathy such as had hitherto been discovered and researched only in the drug dependent. Clearly, there was a never-mentioned precondition for sexual interest of any variety: a good night's sleep. "Sooner or later," said Jenny, indulging her malicious streak, "children teach their parents to be Catholics. After their birth, if not before, their procreators grasp that the purpose of sex may, after all, have been procreation. They're simply too exhausted to disprove the teachings of the Church and consoled by the belief that they're doing God's will."

Nonsense, thought Eduard, that's just an excuse. He suddenly realized what had disconcerted him most about Jenny's revelation: that it was no news to him. He had noticed certain shortcomings from the outset but attached no importance to them. Later on, in the continuous stress of the prenatal months and postnatal years, he'd repeatedly put off resolving the problem, aided by a man's habitual sexual megalomania. He thought it simply inconceivable that a woman who found him attractive, and who enjoyed the privilege of being loved by him, might not be happy with him. He did know that there was no area in which a man could err more tragically than in that of his sexual triumphs and abilities. He was acquainted with plenty of relevant examples, intelligent and otherwise rational individuals who blithely perjured themselves when it came to presenting their sexual performance in a good light. The impotent bragged about the dimensions of their erect members, the premature ejaculators brazenly described their hours-long foreplay, and the able-bodied, instead of quietly rejoicing in their endowments, differed only in lying still more blatantly than the rest. If locker-room stories were to be believed, the sexual contest produced Olympic victors only, no silver or bronze medalists. Jenny had hinted a couple of times that she'd attained the climax he considered so important—hadn't he noticed?—and Eduard had been only too ready to believe her.

There was probably no better candidate for persistent sexual deception and self-deception than a cocksure man in love. To suspect

that the caresses which aroused him might in Jenny provoke bore-
dom, if not displeasure or even revulsion, seemed at odds with the
logic of lust. Vigilance of this kind was all the harder to develop if
the only person at whom it was directed was forever urging its opposite. Jenny sternly scotched Eduard's questions. A woman's orgasm
began in the head, she told him, not below the waist. His anxious,
semimedical inquiries would only generate disastrous stress, and as
for technical virtuosity, that would get him nowhere with her—less
than nowhere, in fact. He would do better to concentrate on himself
and his own libido. Eduard had followed this advice so faithfully
that he knew almost nothing of Jenny's wishes and desires.

All he had heard, even now, were vague intimations. What had
been so crazy, dangerous, and, above all, unrepeatable about the
gratifying situation she'd declined to describe? Jenny's reluctance
and his own fear of falling into an imitator's role had dissuaded him
from insisting on a detailed account. In his imagination, the places in
which she'd found self-oblivion with her anonymous lover assumed
increasingly fantastic forms. Sometimes he pictured her going at it
with an unknown virtuoso on a precipitous rocky ledge at a dizzy
altitude; sometimes he discovered the pair beneath the altar cloth in
a quiet church at night; sometimes he envisioned their figures on the
moonlit terrace of the Mayan temple of which Jenny had once told
him, he now seemed to recall, with a strangely faraway smile on her
face. Or was her essential prelude to sex a successful bank raid, or an
endless climb up the steps to a Mexican bell tower? But it wasn't
mere jealousy that brought such images to his mind. If he was to
redeem Jenny and himself he would have to follow up every lead
like a detective. And the first lead he resolved to follow up was
Jenny's allusion to the extremely perilous circumstances attending
her blissful experience. He knew, of course, that there was another
possibility, namely that he was the wrong man for her, but he
decided to shelve that line of inquiry because it would dispel all
Jenny's mysteries and lead straight to the end of their relationship.

A story of Theo's occurred to him—a fairy tale, actually, but presented in a version heavily edited and modified by Theo himself.

Eduard couldn't recall exactly when Theo had told it to him, before fleeing to his girlfriend in West Berlin or after fleeing eastward again. It began like all traditional German fairy tales. Armed with a slender purse, a young man named Johannes goes out into the wide world to seek his fortune. As chance would have it, he sees two men dumping a corpse in order to sell the coffin, the dead man having allegedly owed them some money. Virtuous Johannes promptly assures the deceased of eternal rest by handing his purse to the evil creditors. He never guesses, of course, what any connoisseur of German fairy tales knows: that his good deed will be rewarded. From now on, kindly Johannes can count on the assistance of an invisible friend or traveling companion such as everyone wants and no one possesses. He soon has greater need of this benevolent spirit than anyone on earth, because he takes it into his head to win the hand of a capricious and extremely prickly princess. She's still available—not surprisingly, having had all her previous suitors beheaded for not being smart enough to solve her tricky riddles. She was quite fair, though: she warned the luckless men in advance—indeed, she took them on a tour of her open-air sculpture collection, where they could gaze at their predecessors' heads skillfully mounted on marble plinths and read the cause of death inscribed below in letters of gold: "He got it wrong."

But Johannes is undeterred. When the bewitched princess dons her wings at dusk and flies off to join her troll in a distant cave, his enviable, invisible friend follows her through the air, lashes her bare back with hazel twigs, and overhears the riddles she devises with her quizmaster.

One can well imagine the princess's fury when Johannes, far from the smartest and handsomest of her suitors, solves three riddles in succession and wins the right to enter her hitherto virginal bed-chamber. Is she, the pampered darling whose palace grounds are filled with the finest heads in the land, to give herself to this son of a peasant?

His only reason for telling this story at all, said Theo, was its remarkable ending. Thanks to the whispers of his invisible friend, good Johannes learns that his real test is still to come: now that his wife belongs to him, he must win her heart. Johannes's traveling companion gives him three swans' feathers and a flask containing three drops of liquid. He also instructs him to place a capacious barrel of water at the foot of the marriage bed and induce his bride to get into it first, the devising of a plausible reason being—for once—left to him. As soon as the princess condescends to dip one of her adorable toes in the water, he is to give her a vigorous shove, grab her by the neck, and, heedless of her screams and splutters, immerse her completely. He is then to haul her out, let her get her breath back, and promptly dunk her again. Only when he has completed this procedure thrice, each time adding one of the feathers and one drop from the flask to the water, will his bride truly belong to him.

And so it turns out. The first time Johannes thrusts his princess into the barrel she swears like a fishwife and struggles so hard he can barely keep hold of her. When he hauls her out he finds himself clutching a big black swan with sparkling eyes. After the second dunking the swan has turned white all over except for a black ring around its neck. It is only on the third occasion, when Johannes thrusts the struggling bird to the bottom of the barrel and holds it there until the scrabbling and the wingbeats grow fainter, that the miracle occurs: out comes a flawless white swan that turns back into the princess under his very gaze. With tears in her glorious eyes she thanks him for releasing her from the spell. As for Johannes, he gives thanks to God.

Eduard had a wry recollection of Theo's concluding comment. Unfortunately, he said, the fairy tale made no mention of how long the princess put up with her rescuer after this happy release, because it went without saying that good old Johannes, for all his heroic deeds, had not become any smarter or more inventive.

10 AFTER VAINLY TRYING to get Klott on the phone for two whole days, Eduard stormed into his office. Had he checked the restitution notice with sufficient care? Eduard demanded with an unmistakable note of reproach in his voice. Had he known but concealed the fact that there were other claimants to his inheritance? Lothar and he would never set foot in a building they might have inherited because the rightful Jewish owners had been driven out.

"With all due respect to your conscience," Klott replied curtly, "you aren't the only person in the world who's got one. Why so worked up?"

The testator, he pontificated after listening to Eduard's account of his second visit to the property, had acquired the building on

Rigaer Strasse in November 1933 and was listed in the real estate register as the successor of a certain Frau Edita Schlandt. The supervisory authority responsible for sales of property prior to September 15, 1935, did not assume any "loss of assets arising from persecution and/or forced sales" insofar as a current market price had been asked and demonstrably paid. It would, however, be extremely useful to submit the relevant acknowledgment of receipt.

"How?" Eduard demanded indignantly. "Where am I to find it?"

"In your late father's papers or those of his tax consultant."

"Nothing doing. The family severed relations with my grandfather long before 1933."

"Then we'll have to find this Edita Schlandt," said Klott. As if the woman in question lived just around the corner, he dictated a request to trace her, complete with particulars from the entry in the real estate register, into his tape recorder.

Perhaps in order to render one testamentary absurdity more palatable by recounting another, Klott told a personal anecdote. Some two years ago his elder brother Fred had called him from Duisburg. The very day after the reunification accord was signed, he had suddenly been visited by childhood memories of a villa on the Baltic coast. The redrawing of the German frontier after World War II had located this house in present-day Poland. Klott knew it only from a black-and-white photo, but he also, after interrogation-like questioning by his brother, managed to recall a deceased aunt in whose senile, rambling reminiscences two phrases had recurred with great frequency: "green dot" and "family treasure." Although it was odd that their parents had never mentioned this hoard during their lifetime, Klott's brother was sure that he and their aunt had buried it in the plot beside the Baltic shortly before the family fled westward from the advancing Russians. Having jointly lodged a claim to the house and land, the brothers set off armed with a certificate from the Office for Unrecovered Property and two brand-new spades.

Since one was starting out from Duisberg and the other from Berlin, they drove to the tumbledown bungalow on the Polish frontier by separate routes, each in his own Mercedes. People were still unused, in the early months of reunification, to the sight of two fifty-something gentlemen alighting almost simultaneously from gleaming sedans, each with a spade in his hand. A local inhabitant stood frozen in the doorway of his dacha, gazing at them much as the native Aztecs must have marveled at Cortez and his men-at-arms when they disembarked on the shores of the Yucatán.

The place hadn't changed much in forty years, as far as Klott could tell, though everything was infinitely smaller and shabbier than he'd pictured. The plot of land, which he remembered as a vast expanse that would have accommodated three seaside hotels, shrank when paced out to a mere hundred feet. Nor did the house itself have two floors, as he seemed to recall, but turned out to be a one-story bungalow. His brother Fred could not come to terms with this brutal clash between recollection and reality. He expressed doubts as to whether they were in the right place at all. He looked in vain for the branch from which the swing had hung, for the veranda from which he had fallen almost half a century before. The house and garden had been bigger, the trees smaller, the plot enclosed by a wooden fence, not a cinder-block wall. Fred couldn't understand how the little beech tree he remembered had become the skyscraper whose topmost branches presented themselves to his incredulous gaze. Klott had been too young at the time to be disconcerted now; château or toolshed—either one could have been sold to him as his former parental home.

Wasting no time on a further examination of the house, the brothers set to work. The sandy soil was ideal for digging. Within an hour they were standing in a deep pit with a sizable mound of sand alongside. It turned out, however, that Fred's childhood memories were as fickle as the ground they were excavating was soft. Before they turned the first spadeful he had definitely identified the site of the buried treasure: "It's here, where the green dot is: beside the right-hand corner of the house!" There was, in fact, no green dot to be seen in the relevant place. Although Klott initially accepted his brother's explanation—a green dot would hardly have survived forty years of sun, rain, and wind—the longer he shoveled sand in the midday sun and the bigger the mountain of spoil became, the more his doubts intensified. When they reached the water table Fred smote his brow and suddenly remembered that the hoard had been buried beside the left-hand corner of the house. As a child he'd confused the two directions because of the disastrous German mnemonic that ran: "Left means when your thumb is on the right."

But the new location, too, yielded nothing but groundwater. When the pits were wide and deep enough to have served as a family grave, Klott inquired how big the treasure chest had actually been. Under his searching questions the distance between Fred's hands, which was meant to indicate its length, steadily dwindled. The chest became a coffer, the coffer a casket, the casket a cigar box. The ground being soft and their enthusiasm unabated, the brothers continued to dig. By late that afternoon they had excavated a trench around the bungalow so deep and close to the walls that the whole building suddenly keeled over. In their eagerness to leave no cubic foot of ground unturned they had undermined the front of the house. While Klott braced his massive bulk against it, his thinner brother collected some ludicrously small stones with which to fill the yawning abyss. While engaged in these emergency measures they were bombarded with missiles. Unable to dodge them with the house propped against his back, Klott stared in disbelief as a lump of coal struck his chest and bounced off into the trench. On the far side of the garden wall, five or six senior citizens were hurling briquettes at them and uttering cries of rage: "That's right, strip the place! Goddamned Westerners!"

Toward evening the brothers finally came across something that resisted their spades, not right beside the house but near the big beech tree. It was a suitcase of medium size, and so light that it could have been taken as hand baggage on a transatlantic flight. Having broken the locks, they found that it did not contain their grandfather's coin collection, nor the family jewels of a noble ancestor on their mother's side, nor the twenty-four-piece Meissen dinner service whose loss their aunt had mourned so bitterly, nor the legendary eighteenth-century violin on which Paganini had once played. What they did find was their father's neatly folded major's uniform complete with helmet and World War I medals, a few rounds of ammunition loose in the pockets, and a complete set of silver tableware whose owner could be identified by the green dot with which every piece was marked.

By the time he was back in his car, Eduard realized that his return to Berlin had presented him with two problems at once. He had come into an inheritance that threatened to ruin him financially, even though it might not legally be his, and he was leading a married life which, though blessed with three children, lacked nature's ultimate seal of approval. Only Jenny knew what this deprivation meant to her. Where he himself was concerned, he had no illusions. Every unfulfilled night Jenny spent with him would erode his male self-esteem a little more until nothing remained of it but an uncertain smile.

The matter of the inheritance could be temporarily delegated to Klott. As for his conjugal happiness, there was probably only one person capable of salvaging it: himself. And a "traveling companion" named Theo.

11 WHEN EDUARD SAW Theo plodding around in the debris of his notes and drafts, he felt as if his friend had lost yet another battle in his war with death. Legends about his invulnerability served only to console those who recounted them. But then it struck him that Theo threaded his way among all these stacks of paper with almost balletic assurance, without ever bumping into them. Perhaps they were arranged in some order known only to himself—perhaps they marked the phases of a quest that ran in a circle. Wasn't this man embarking on a process of remembrance and clearance, doggedly going it alone and following the thread of his own history, while others in the city outside were hurriedly erecting palaces of glass and marble on the ruins of the past?

Mightn't it simply be that Theo was seizing an opportunity more dauntlessly and with greater presence of mind than the rest?

"If you're interested in hearing how the story of my brother continues . . ." said Theo. Unerringly, he reached for a folder lying on the floor and leafed through it. He read the odd page, shook his head, browsed some more, read a few more sentences, commented on them, shut the folder and opened it again. One sensed that the affair had captured his imagination, that it fascinated as much as hurt him.

It transpired from the records that Theo's brother, whom the authorities had deported to West Germany two years after Theo for his "negatively hostile" attitude, had remained in the Stasi's employ even then. He had been "released" from the GDR only on condition that he would spy on his elder brother. But why, once in West Germany and thus beyond the Stasi's immediate reach, had he performed his task with such horrifying exactitude? What source of energy had fueled his urge to pump Theo and report on him for so long? For fourteen long years he had fulfilled his mission with a single-minded attention to detail that put Anaïs Nin's lifework in the shade. Even his Stasi case officer had clearly marveled at the productivity of his source. It would be wrong, his superior wrote in an assessment, to attribute "Informant Eckehardt's" motivation solely to envy of "Poet's" talent. The said informant was cooperating for more exalted and idealistic reasons.

> Quite correctly, Eckehardt considers Poet an ideologically unsound element, a class traitor. But he himself, it emerges from other informants' reports on him, is plagued by similar doubts about the legitimacy and success of the socialist system, except that he refuses to admit them to himself. He keeps his own doubts at bay by detecting them in the brother he hates, ascribing them to his defeatism and corrupt character, and informing us of them.

Theo picked up another sheet of typescript.

Public meeting at the Academy of Arts. Poet ill-prepared and half drunk as usual. Obligatory collarless shirt and black jacket, palpably suffers from the Brecht syndrome. Had quite obviously failed to read the book by the author he was to introduce. Speaks in an undertone the whole time—another trick borrowed from Bert Brecht and Bob Dylan: a low voice or silence is reputed to make an audience listen harder. This lends Poet a kind of ring of conviction when he haltingly parades his dissident opinions. He almost trembles at his own audacity in violating taboos. He read out a poem by Ernesto Cardenal (mediocre Nicaraguan poet, currently minister of culture) which referred to the beauty of the empty shelves in his country's stores. The empty shelves of Nicaragua, Poet repeated softly enough for all to understand and take in, are hopes. (His implication: the full shelves of the GDR are disappointments.) The white-haired author sat there like a frozen-faced statue. The audience obviously liked this feeble agitprop poem, all except a loudmouth who asked about the writers detained in Nicaraguan prisons. Poet demanded in a low but nonetheless audible voice that the heckler be thrown out.

"Did you really have someone thrown out because of that interjection?" Eduard asked.

Theo stared at him intently. "See how effective it is, Stasi poison? Not even one's friends are immune to it. Here's something better still." He picked up another sheet and read:

We began by discussing his new stage play, a few scenes of which he read aloud to me (see appendix herewith). Poet is grossly overrated and will probably never become a truly great writer. His ambivalence is too German, his indecision he considers a poetic asset. The ideological mishmash he has concocted out of his contempt for our worker-and-peasant state and his hatred of capitalism is worthy of note. In my estimation, he's still a communist at heart and thinks practical socialism has watered things down. He spoke of the beauty of gradualism and expounded the following theory:

the socialist alternative's only hope consists precisely in *not* trying to rival capitalism. It was mistaken from the first to attempt to defeat a system geared to rapidity, to consumption and swift obsolescence, at its own game. (Like most of his confrères, Poet knows nothing about economics and isn't even interested in the subject.) No idea is too absurd for him to explore it in hesitant tones. He has lately been advancing some wild theories about the USA. That, he believes, is where communism will be reborn.

Eduard was feeling more and more uncomfortable. It dismayed him, the curiosity, indeed, the insatiability with which Theo seized on his brother's reports.

"Why take it lying down? Why not have it out with him—why not give him the hiding he deserves?"

"His reports are telling me something I've always known about us both, but never with such cold precision. A writer who doesn't suspect himself of the worst and isn't interested in the worst possible version of his personality is in the wrong job. Writing takes precedence over condemnation. Of all our cognitive processes, condemnation is the least productive."

"Even if he was the finest ghostwriter your innermost self could have had," Eduard burst out, "his object was to denounce you!"

"I'm not so sure he did me any harm," Theo replied curtly.

Eduard said no more. Issuing from the loudspeakers was one of Piazzola's coruscating right-handed runs on the bandonion, and it suddenly reminded him of other sounds and tonal colors he'd heard in the city in the old days: the Doors, Eric Clapton, Leonard Cohen . . . They were always in the nature of swan songs, captivating legati enclosed by bare, high walls. Theirs was the enchantment of a melancholy decline, the promise of an endless descent. The sense of freedom the city had once conveyed was largely that of a free fall, nothing more, and he once more became aware, without having to put his finger on any specific events, of what had prompted him to leave there in the 1980s. Berlin had lain under a kind of spell, a fine web of discontent and mistrust that paralyzed all spontaneity and left you with only enough energy to crack cynical jokes. To praise anything or anyone was an automatic act of self-betrayal; to spot the hidden flaw, the latent and suppressed, was a mark of shrewdness and superiority. Life in the city had been governed by a beguiling, infectious apathy, a defiant absence of courage whose maintenance almost required courage in itself—a self-prescribed, arrogant cowardice. A large, well-educated minority lived in the shadow of a vaguely sensed defeat, like a basketball team whose morale is low. Was it still like that? Eduard had been surprised to hear that Berlin intellectuals vied with each other in pronouncing themselves capable of all manner of misdeeds (which they had never committed and would never, one hoped, commit even in a pinch) so as to be able to impute presumption to those who condemned the misdeeds of the communist dictatorship. A society that had never truly settled accounts with Nazi crimes, so the argument ran, had no right to sit in judgment. Crazy logic. Did (alleged) complete moral failure in the first instance entail further such failures forevermore? Was Theo's refusal to feel hurt and indignant a mark of strength or weakness? Those who put nothing past themselves and others couldn't be disappointed; ergo, it was a strength. But those who shunned the risk of disappointment by denying themselves any hopes (or illusions) would never stick their necks out for anything or anyone; ergo, it was a weakness.

Theo was still picking his way between the stacks of paper like a surefooted charger traversing a battlefield without touching a single one of the dead and wounded that litter it.

"It's good now and then to see things through the eyes of your worst enemy. Here's a piece about me . . . and you," he said suddenly, and read it aloud: " 'Yesterday I met him with R., his fifty-third and latest ladylove. From the way Poet treats women, one wonders if he ever knew anything about them. It's amazing how much intelligent, good-looking females will put up with from a man they consider a genius . . .' "

Theo handed the sheet to Eduard.

"He can neither believe nor accept that somebody loves him and inevitably punishes anyone that does," Eduard read. "Not even the love of the entire world would satisfy him. He scents calculation, perfidy, and deception where all that exists is a desperate desire to be loved in return."

Theo looked at Eduard as if searching his eyes for some sign of recognition, perhaps of alarm as well.

Eduard impatiently laid the sheet aside. He felt he'd been lumped together too quickly in a "we." His own plight seemed less considerable and more clear-cut than that of Theo, with his insatiable need for love. He'd come because he felt better able to confide in Theo than in anyone else, but he couldn't find the right words at first. He fought in vain against the feeling of embarrassment or absurdity that promptly blue-penciled every phrase and handed it back to him for correction. "Jenny and I . . . something's wrong between us" would invite the question: "Really, like what?" Better to come straight out with "Jenny isn't coming"—or would that be misunderstood? "Why," Theo might ask, "were you expecting her?"

But Theo caught on at once and didn't try to conceal his surprise. "I always thought Jenny was a human volcano," he said.

"If she is," Eduard replied, "she's a dormant one."

Instantly, he regretted his candor. He seemed to detect a trace of pity, even of amusement, in Theo's expression. Or was it merely a projection of his own wounded self-esteem? His conversation with Theo differed from the usual man-to-man exchanges on the subject of women. Men recounted their affairs and amatory successes; if they spoke of their amatory disasters at all, they were the heroes of those disasters, not their authors. However innocent of the misfortune Eduard might be, a suspicion of doltishness clung to him. The embarrassing thing about his problem was that it didn't invite identification. All he could count on, more or less, was the sympathy aroused by someone who puts a cup of coffee to his lips and finds that he's sweetened it with the saltshaker. Mountains of literature on sex education had done nothing to alter the fact that, in the minds of men and women, certain responsibilities were set in stone: the latter were to blame for not conceiving, the former for failing to give the latter orgasms.

"What's so bad about it?" asked Theo. "Which of you raised the subject first? As you see it, which of you suffers more from the problem, Jenny or you?"

Eduard found the question disconcerting. It was possible that Jenny didn't really know what she was missing, but if she didn't, where did his problem lie?

"What are you after, joyful recognition of your virility—a medal for outstanding sexual achievement, maybe—or Jenny's happiness?"

"I never had to contend with this problem in the old days," snapped Eduard, "so I've no reason to suffer from any complexes." Even as he uttered it, that statement seemed to transmute itself into a white lie. It obeyed the tortuous logic according to which every denial inevitably reinforces the rumor that contradicts it.

Theo smiled indulgently. "We're all world champions in bed, that's common knowledge, and we're correspondingly easy to deceive. Never swear on a woman's orgasm or you'll find yourself convicted of perjury."

"Come on, you don't believe that yourself. Any reasonably experienced and observant man knows perfectly well when it happens. He can't be fooled that easily."

"Fooled, you call it? We're talking about a noble art developed over the millennia. Pardon me for drawing attention to the findings of some of your colleagues, the sociobiologists. To the best of my knowledge they're unanimous that the female orgasm has never played a major role in the history of evolution. It isn't essential to the reproduction of the species. Scientifically speaking, it's just a pleasurable irrelevance, mere icing on the evolutionary cake. Men can do their duty only when they scale the ultimate pinnacle of lust— and simultaneously impose a program on women. Unlike them, women can fulfill their natural function without such peak performances. Theirs is a freedom we're denied. I don't say it's any less important to them, but I suspect that the compulsion to demand this so-called proof of love is largely a product of male fear. He-apes and lion kings don't give a damn about their mates' happiness when they copulate."

Eduard resented Theo's attempt to lecture him on his own specialty and to go scientific on him, now of all times.

"As I'm sure you're aware," he said professorially, "observations drawn from animal life aren't automatically applicable to human mating behavior. Can your sociobiologists explain why nature should have evolved such a pleasurable irrelevance, so called?"

Theo cocked a finger like a schoolboy who knows the answer to a difficult question. The subject was beginning to amuse him.

"There are some interesting theories," he said. "But let's stick with apes for the moment. As everyone knows, male chimpanzees are preoccupied with disseminating their own genes as often and as widely as possible. At the same time, their main fear is of similar promiscuous tendencies on the part of the females—of dilution, in other words. Jealousy is primarily a defense mechanism against alien genes. The female orgasm—or its simulation—is biological proof of fidelity, a pledge that no other male is intruding into the biological chain. Its absence, on the other hand, warns the man that he has no guarantee of being the father of his offspring."

Eduard has grown more and more impatient of Theo's dissertation. "What are you implying? That I should stop worrying about this so-called irrelevance?"

"Far from it. I'm simply pointing out that the problem lies mainly with you, not with Jenny's alleged or genuine deprivation. You won't admit to yourself how much it bothers you. You're wrong, you know. You're chock-full of complexes—an absolute wreck, in fact. You doubt your ability to make a woman happy, now or even in the past. Maybe you forgot how to do so a long time ago, poor guy. You're afraid your children don't respect you anymore because they've noticed your wife has written you off as a man. I'm sure you never take the initiative in bed because you feel unwanted and don't want to force the pace at any price. You're convinced that all your creative energies are being frozen by the cold wind of deprivation.

Above all, though, you're afraid Jenny's secretly on the lookout for a savior. Don't waste another day, your life's at stake."

"Thanks for the advice!"

"How much do you know about Jenny?" Theo asked. "Have you ever asked her what her wildest, most secret desire is? Personally, I can't go to bed with a woman until I've kindled her imagination, and I never shrink from letting her know my own predilections. The truth's irrelevant, mendacity is a better source of ideas. Besides, no one ever tells the truth in this area. Love is a stage production that starts in the head, and if the performance goes wrong at least it's been entertaining. There's an inexhaustible fund of sexual whims, desires, and specialties, but most people go to the grave without ever discovering what their own ones are."

Eduard spoke of Jenny's allusions to her unique experience and the mental images they'd unleashed in him. Using "crazy" and "dangerous" as his building blocks, Theo promptly constructed a whole series of scenarios and overrode all objections. Eduard was suddenly overcome with fatigue. He said a monosyllabic, almost surly goodbye. On the stairs he struggled with the feeling that his friend had long ago found the key to the riddle he himself was still trying to solve.

12 HE WAS AWAKENED by a roaring sound overhead, but when he opened his eyes the mechanical din grew so loud that he tried to dive back into his dream. He'd seen Jenny sitting on the sofa bed with her head averted. She seemed to be watching the movements of her right hand on his crotch, but he could tell from the side that her eyes were tightly shut. While she was speaking to him he saw the blood drain from her face and her lips grow as pale as if frost were forming on them. To reach orgasm, she whispered, she needed things that surpassed his wildest imaginings. Things like what? he demanded when she fell silent, clearly overcome with embarrassment. Honey, she whispered, genuine honey plus plenty of fresh thyme and sage, and something else as well. So tell me! he shouted, because the roar of engines was growing steadily louder. A helicopter, she said in a suddenly clear and intelligible voice—yes, a helicopter, but a helicopter would cost too much, of course. Even as she spoke, however, he saw her soar past the window upside down with her foot in a trapeze. She waved to him, laughing exuberantly with her legs wide apart as if to show him how good she felt, and disappeared from view.

Eduard sat up with a start, went over to the French doors and shut them with a crash. The noise of the rotor blades was so loud, he stuck his fingers in his ears and stared anxiously at the ceiling. For a moment it seemed the machine was hovering directly overhead, about to land or pancake on the roof of the hotel, but however much he craned his neck the source of the noise itself remained invisible. He didn't even see a shadow when, to judge by the sound, the aerial monster rose once more and flew off toward the television tower.

He froze when he looked at the alarm clock. It was just before eleven. Not until he was half dressed did he remember that, for once, he had nothing to do and no matters to attend to. His sole commitment this Saturday morning was a reception at "Europe's biggest construction site," as the invitation rather vaingloriously phrased it. Jenny, who had an appointment with the personnel director, had left earlier on. In addition to the invitation card lying on the table, she'd left what he considered to be a superfluous sketch of the route. Potsdamer Platz wasn't one of the places he needed to look up on the street map.

He parked on the wasteland outside the fence, which enclosed an area of vast size but displayed no entrance anywhere. In the distance he saw some dump trucks driving through an opening in the galvanized mesh. On going closer he sighted a ramp leading straight down into a pit so immensely deep and wide it looked big enough to accommodate a subterranean city. All that could be seen of the building project itself were the aids to its construction: stacks of pipes, steel girders, winches, reinforcing bars, tracked vehicles, portable site offices. Situated in and beside the pit were dozens of cranes, the tallest he'd ever seen. It was only when one watched their huge jibs swinging around that some idea of the true scale of the project became apparent. Berlin, it seemed, was marking the end of the millennium by emulating the pharaohs.

Eduard marveled at the small number of workmen engaged on this gargantuan task, the desertlike silence and lack of movement behind the fence. Inside the cab of the tallest crane, which was pivoting almost noiselessly on its steel turntable, he made out the head of the operator seated some 250 feet above ground level. Unless his eyes deceived him, the man was, for some unaccountable reason, wearing a hard hat.

On the far side of the disemboweled wasteland Eduard made out an old building. Seen against the invisible outlines of the latter-day pyramids, whose contours were sketched on the sky by the cranes' jibs, the modest turn-of-the-century edifice with the temporary roof and the absurd little observation towers on the front resembled a foundling from another age. Looking from a distance as if it had been secured against an impending barbarian invasion, it seemed to be standing in a lake on piles and was girded on every side with a double framework of scaffolding poles that came up to the second-floor windows. Eduard knew from Jenny that the piles were very expensive ones, for what he saw was only the upper extremity of a steel structure driven sixty feet into the ground. Its purpose was to protect the building from encroaching groundwater while excavation work was in progress and prevent it from sinking or floating away. This safety measure had cost as much as a medium-sized skyscraper. An insane but somehow touching endeavor, thought Eduard, and only to be accounted for by the unique nature of the whole scheme. Seldom if ever had a metropolis been confronted with the task of erecting a new city in its midst. Although no Acropolis, the Weinhaus Huth was the only building far and wide to have survived the war, so the city fathers had declared it a historical monument and insisted that the developers preserve it at all costs—financially speaking, eighty million marks.

The prospect of having to circle the fence in search of an entrance was enough to make one turn tail. Eduard followed a party of festively attired fellow guests who were trying to communicate with the construction workers and truckers behind the fence with shouts and gestures. The workmen pointed to the putative location of the ears beneath their helmets but didn't remove the latter. Just ahead of Eduard, a woman wearing a broad-brimmed straw hat came to a halt. With one arm through that of her smartly dressed escort, she lifted the hem of her coat and looked at her left leg. Visible on her bare calf, like a pair of birthmarks, were two splashes of black mud. When she raised her head after wiping them off with her finger, her eyes met Eduard's and her indignant expression dissolved into a smile. He nodded for no reason—approvingly, as it were—and continued to follow the party with his eyes riveted to the woman's shapely calf, which promptly got besmirched again. Somewhere, someone discovered a hole in the fence. A man in an Armani suit held up the wire for the rest to pass through, Eduard last of all. With their glossy oxfords and high heels sinking into the tracks made by dump trucks and bulldozers, the party made its way to the building contractor's shindig at the Weinhaus Huth.

He found Jenny conversing with a dark-haired young man who seemed unaware that her overly frequent nods betokened total lack of interest and inattention. She caught sight of Eduard and intimated to her companion that she must leave him. Her bare, California-tanned shoulders and arms glowed against the little black dress she was wearing. Watching her as she threaded her way through the other guests, Eduard seemed to detect a ubiquitous surge of male desire. It was as if Jenny's body strove, quite unashamedly, to show off its full splendor and stem the advancing years with every pore. Hers was the body of a woman who looked all the more seductive because she sensed the signs of aging but had yet to betray them. Women submit themselves to far stricter scrutiny than men. They implacably note the barely discernible signs on their skin that herald their gradual exclusion from the market of yearning glances, and not even the most extravagant compliments can invalidate their findings.

As soon as Jenny had fought her way over to Eduard she took his arm and propelled them both toward a tall, mustachioed man in a white linen suit whom she introduced as the personnel director. Beside him, shorter by a head, stood the star of the occasion: the Italian architect of the new city district. Eduard was surprised by his insignificant appearance. Why in the world had he pictured the author of such a gigantic project as tall, corpulent, and white-haired? The creator of the latter-day pyramids was a man of his own age dressed with studied negligence in a houndstooth jacket, checked shirt, and brown corduroy slacks, as if to demonstrate that genius is shown to best advantage by a modest appearance. He eyed Eduard with discreet curiosity when Jenny introduced him.

The personnel director invited Eduard and Jenny to accompany him by elevator to the roof of the building. It was apparent from Jenny's surreptitious but cheerful glances that her interview with him had gone well. Rather offhandedly, she had answered an advertisement in the *Frankfurter Allgemeine Zeitung* from San Francisco. The Debis Corporation of Potsdamer Platz was looking for a press officer. Jenny was not particularly well qualified for such a job by her previous experience. Although she worked in the San Francisco office of an urban-development and environmental-planning agency, she had never handled the public presentation of the projects developed there. To her surprise she had nonetheless been invited to present herself in Berlin, perhaps because she spoke Italian and French as well as German and English, or perhaps because her job application had read more brashly and flippantly than the others.

Many of the guests had preceded them onto the asphalted roof, which was enclosed only by a temporary rope barrier. Most had glasses of champagne in their hands and some were trying to dance to the strains of a New Orleans combo that had installed itself and its instruments between the two chimneys. Eduard spotted the woman with the memorable calves and missed the spots of mud. Already rather tipsy, it seemed, she was dancing perilously close to the edge of the roof. Holding onto her hat with one hand, she was using the other to fend off her escort's necktie, which kept wafting into her face. Eduard noticed only now that the roof was being buffeted by a surprisingly warm, gusty breeze. Although the building had only six stories, there was nothing as high, near or far, to serve as a wind-break. The woman waved, whether to him or to someone behind him Eduard couldn't tell. Just as she was about to replace her hand on her hat the wind whipped it off and sent it pirouetting through the air in a wide arc. For a moment it seemed about to perform a balletic downward spiral and land on the other side of the roof. Some of the guests ran over there, whooping with delight, and one even scaled the chimney to lessen the distance between himself and the airborne object. Just before he could capture it, however, it gained height once more and then, to the oohs and aahs of all present, went sailing into the depths. Abruptly reduced to silence, everyone followed the hat's descent. The New Orleans combo, puzzled by the universal commotion, had stopped playing. The owner of the fugitive hat leaned so far over the safety rope that her escort grabbed her roughly by the waist. But Eduard, too, had to contend with the ver-tigo that momentarily assails you when one of your belongings falls from a great height and demonstrates, by proxy, how your body might have plummeted to the ground.

Having playfully circled several landing places, the hat at last touched down on the flooded pit at the foot of the Weinhaus Huth. For a while the broad-brimmed yellow confection floated motionless on the stagnant water. Not far away a floating crane was in the process of lowering a steel girder. All at once, something extraordi-nary happened down below—something which only a few of the guests noticed at first and tried to describe to their immediate neigh-bors: as if propelled by an unseen hand, the hat drifted leisurely but unerringly toward the floating crane. When it reached the hull a black arm emerged from the water, visible now with the naked eye, and lifted it clear of the surface. The arm was followed by the shoul-ders and torso of the diver, who was ascending an unseen ladder rung by rung. Finally, when he was standing fully exposed on deck, he raised the hat in a salute to the partygoers on the roof, who rewarded him with some gracious applause.

The personnel director explained this miracle in a faint French accent. The diver, he said, was one of an underwater team engaged in laying the foundations of a three-hundred-foot office building on the bed of the temporary lake. He had probably been surfacing for a breather just as the hat came sailing down, though it was also possible that the crane operator had instructed him to salvage it by radio.

As if eager to plunge into the role of a future press officer, Jenny asked why the foundations had to be laid by divers. She was quite right, the personnel director replied; a press officer would have to answer such questions from journalists and visitors. The Potsdamer Platz development was an undertaking of Herculean proportions, and it was the details that mattered. Its vast dimensions presented the architects with entirely novel problems. The construction site was so large and so deep that they'd had to forgo the usual practice of pumping out groundwater. If groundwater kept flowing into the excavation, the trees in the Tiergarten might die of drought. And if even half a dozen trees perished, the Frenchman added with a smile which obviously delighted Jenny but Eduard found flashy, Germany would be threatened with a Green revolution—hence the decision to build underwater. The divers could see for a distance of only two feet on the muddy bottom, and so, in order to locate the girders and the flow of concrete accurately, they had to communicate with their colleagues on the surface by radio. The mixture of languages that reigned on the construction site was a special problem. Since a diver operating at a depth of fifty feet weighed even less than a child, he lost his footing every time a girder swung. In order to insert the end of the girder correctly in the bottom of the excavation he had to be held in place by one or more colleagues who, weighed down by lead boots, had in their turn to steady themselves by holding on to each other. Only when the concrete basin was completed and firmly anchored could a start be made on pumping out the water. Then would come the moment of truth: if the basin had a crack in it somewhere, groundwater would inexorably pour in, and then . . . The personnel director drew an elegant forefinger across his Adam's apple.

Eduard couldn't understand the rest. Ignoring his presence, the Frenchman suddenly lapsed into his native tongue, and Jenny seemed uninterested in keeping Eduard au courant by interpreting, especially as the New Orleans combo had struck up again. Eduard left them to it and devoted himself to the view from the roof.

Until now he had always seen Potsdamer Platz from a pedestrian's viewpoint or from an airplane, never from such an intermediate height. The Wall had still been standing in those days, and all he really remembered was the wooden observation tower on the west side that enabled tourists to gaze out across the wasteland through their binoculars, themselves under surveillance by border guards in the watchtowers on the east side. He had preserved a mental image of the two groups' binoculars exchanging stares.

All the frontier installations had now been demolished, apart from a short section at the very foot of the Weinhaus Huth. It occurred to Eduard that the vanished Wall and its appurtenances had been erected on the debris of an earlier wasteland. He recalled postwar photos showing the skeletons of the big buildings that had once occupied it—relics of a square in which Europe's first traffic lights had been installed to control the overwhelming growth of traffic. The Wall had been erected on the bulldozed dust of those ruins, only to become a skeleton, a fragment, a relic, in its turn.

But even in the built-up environs of this enormous void he spotted only sporadic indications that urban life had existed here for centuries. From rooftop level the city looked as if most of its buildings had been dropped by helicopter. He looked across some anonymous flat roofs at the Trade Center. Visible in the haze beyond it, like quotations from another city altogether, were the twin domes of the Gendarmenmarkt and the fortresslike Berlin Cathedral botched by Kaiser Wilhelm II, then nothing for a long way except the television tower and the massive outlines of the Charité Hospital, and finally the grim Reichstag. It wasn't the ugliness that dismayed him so much as the absence of a regular cityscape. By far the strongest impression he gained from this height was of the huge gaps separating isolated buildings of varying quality. It suddenly struck him as the height of presumption, this five-year scheme to overpaint the center of a canvas from which so many historic inscriptions had been expunged.

In the distance he saw the personnel director guiding and adjusting Jenny by the arm as he indicated the wasteland with sweeping, expansive gestures. With the precision of a batonless conductor, his hands seemed to be conjuring up individual groups of buildings in the still-invisible urban landscape. Jenny's eyes were alight with a kind of infatuation when the Frenchman took his leave. All he spared for Eduard was the approbative nod of someone complimenting the escort of such a woman.

They climbed back through the skylight with the last of the guests. Jenny insisted on using the stairs, not the elevator. The marble staircase with its mosaic friezes and tall, elaborately ornamented bronze doors still conveyed a hint of bygone splendor, but the stone inlays around the doors—as Jenny demonstrated to Eduard by running his fingers over them—were only painted on. She'd been told by the personnel director that Huth, a wealthy wine merchant, had run out of money when he got to the fourth floor. But that wasn't all Jenny knew. There was talk, she whispered to Eduard, holding him back by the hand, of a pleasure house or pleasure tower somewhere. When the last of the guests had disappeared around a bend in the stairs below them she pushed a door open with her foot and drew him into the room beyond.

They were just beneath the roof on which they'd been promenading only a minute or two ago. The top floor, which got its light from a number of slatted windows, was not subdivided and had probably been used as a studio by the last tenant or owner. Eduard felt uneasy, all alone with Jenny in this ridiculous building beside a lake of groundwater—a building whose roof had so recently been the scene of a public function. The gates were probably being locked behind the last of the guests at this moment, but Jenny seemed quite unperturbed by such considerations. She made an exploratory tour of the windows and suddenly threw her weight against a door. It gave, and she vanished. Eduard's panic-stricken forebodings were dispelled by the sound of her voice calling him. He made his way through the door and up three steps into a turret constructed of pale stone. Inside, on a weatherworn bench stripped bare by the fall and winter winds, sat Jenny.

This, she said jubilantly, was just the kind of turret she'd always dreamed of sitting in. If such an exposed and vulnerable place had survived the attentions of Allied bombers and demolition-obsessed German architects unscathed, it had to be lucky. Propping her elbows on the stone parapet, she gazed out across the city center in the direction of the Brandenburg Gate.

The oriel tower was surrounded by the steel framework of towering cranes from whose jibs, controlled by invisible operators, steel cables of unimaginable length were gliding up and down. Eduard and Jenny had no business here among all these centrally directed, electronically supervised workmen and technicians toiling for the new German capital. They were as redundant as the birds that darted restlessly to and fro between the steel monsters or sometimes folded their wings and dropped like stones from the summit of a crane.

Jenny had stood up. As he watched her leaning against the parapet in her flimsy dress, Eduard seemed to hear the imperative of the place from afar. For a moment she looked startled when he lifted her skirt, but he sensed that she was enjoying his caresses, and that her body—despite or because of the warm breeze that was issuing from the turret's five arrow slits—welcomed his inventive tongue. With a resolute movement, she hoisted her bare buttocks into the cross-hatched limestone parapet, stretched out on it, and made the V sign with her legs. Who could see her, after all, apart from the moldering green charioteer on the Brandenburg Gate? Indeed, wasn't the faint possibility of witnesses a part of the performance? The coping stones were wider than Eduard had thought, but not wide enough. Lying on her back, Jenny vigorously shuffled further out on her elbows until her head and neck were in space, then pulled Eduard toward her. What she could see with her upturned gaze directed at the sky and the cranes, Eduard, who was looking down at the groundwater lake and the vicious steel spikes below, could only guess. But the precarious nature of their situation was taking effect. He sensed that Jenny was on the point of forgetting herself under the eyes of crane operators seated in the sky, of darting black birds, of the resurrected spirits of the buildings around them, and of the freshly refurbished bronze Valkyrie piloting her quadriga toward them from the Brandenburg Gate, ready to take them with her. All at once, though, a sort of shudder ran through Jenny's body. Eduard clutched at her in a panic-stricken but futile way—futile because all he could have done was plunge over the edge with her, not prevent her from falling. Brusquely, she pushed him off her, sat up, and hoisted her panties.

"Don't you hear it?"

"You mean that high-pitched whine down below?"

"That isn't just a high-pitched whine, it's core drilling, can't you tell? It's the only noise on the site that sets even lifelong construction workers' teeth on edge. It's the diamond-tipped drill that does it."

They had to climb over a fence to reach the street.

"So what went wrong that time?" he asked when they were in the car.

"Wrong? What do you mean?" said Jenny. "It was lovely. If they hadn't started that core drilling . . ."

Eduard told her about his helicopter dream. She asked if she should be prepared for more such experiments in the future.

"There are other possibilities," he replied coldly. "For instance, I've been wondering whether to ask the operator of one of these enormous cranes for his key. The cabs look tiny from down here, but they're supposed to be huge inside, regular three-room apartments."

She laughed. "Seems to me you've got a pretty mechanical idea of the female orgasm. You think it's all a question of pulling the right lever."

"You're the one who's obsessed with heights. Don't tell me nothing happened up there just now."

"There was something missing," she said.

"Like what?"

"The thyme, maybe."

BOOK **2**

1 TAKING LEAVE OF Jenny at Tegel Airport turned out to be a strangely casual business.

Like nearly all the city's major buildings, the departures hall of the airport was barely twenty years old but undergoing reconstruction: the floor ripped up, the walkways attenuated by temporary partitions, the passengers herded from one gate to another by loudspeaker announcements. Throngs of nervous passengers jostled Eduard and Jenny or thrust them aside and bruised their heels with baggage carts. The limbo between checking in and last call was filled, almost as a matter of course, with the little omissions no one ever remembers until half an hour before takeoff. Signing a power of attorney, promising to send the children's school reports, renewing an application to the John F. Kennedy School—to Jenny it seemed that a family's administrative problems were little less demanding than those of a large-scale development scheme. Eduard had spent the previous day buying presents for their offspring: for Loris a Lego set not to be opened until he'd read the children's book that accompanied it, for Katharina some platinum earrings and a turquoise velvet dress, for their eldest a videocassette of a German screen comedy and a tennis racket signed by Boris Becker. Jenny had expertly nosed around in the merchandise, extolled German toy manufacturers' unrivaled skill in producing teddy bears, and poked fun at the obsessive way in which they provided dollhouses not only with furniture but with kitchen utensils in "ecologically harmless" materials.

"Look," she said, holding up a toy gas stove, "wood! Will Siemens be mass-producing this model before long?" She had made several attempts to curb Eduard's enthusiasm for shopping. "Don't bother, one can get all these things back home, and for half the price."

"But not with German on them," he retorted.

"Afraid they'll forget their mother tongue?"

"Their father's tongue," he amended. Then, noticing Jenny's surprised and rather compassionate expression, he added, "Besides, they won't realize the presents are from me if I simply give you the cash to buy them with."

"But we'll be seeing you again soon," said Jenny, "won't we?"

Of course we will, he'd felt like saying, but where, here or there? Jenny's question had touched a nerve, kindled a fear he now admitted to himself. A scenario he'd never considered took shape in his mind's eye. They'd agreed that Jenny should return to San Francisco immediately after her interview and remain there at least until the end of the school year. If she got the new job at Potsdamer Platz she wouldn't be able to start until the summer. But what if they turned her down? Wouldn't she have renewed misgivings about what she was doing in Berlin at all? Why be dependent on a man she missed only in his capacity as the father of her children? Why not remain with them in San Francisco, where—to quote her own words—they all felt more at home than anywhere else on earth? Or was it just a delusion provoked by hurt male pride, the idea that a woman he failed to make happy couldn't really love him?

He had often been annoyed by Jenny's remarks during the days before her departure. Her opinion of Berlin changed hourly. Sometimes she liked the city's unfinished condition, its "construction-site Gothic," the cabbies' sardonic local patriotism. "In the eyes of God," one of them had told her, "everyone's a Berliner." At other times she seemed to be amassing arguments, perception by perception, against her return. Why did his friends have this awful predilection for wearing black? Wherever you went—a concert, a show, a party, a bar—you felt like a guest at a wake and kept looking, quite instinctively, for the coffin in the corner. She had also been struck by the fact that most of the German TV movies she channel-hopped were set in interiors, in stiffly furnished, brightly illuminated rooms that held no mysteries. The actors' faces, too, were bereft of all magic by merciless electricians. Every scene was dominated by harsh, somehow pornographic lighting.

"How do you mean, pornographic?" Eduard had asked.

"Pornography's a question of lighting," she replied firmly. "A woman's bare backside isn't pornographic; what's pornographic is the harsh lighting that shows up every pustule on it. Why this fear of the obscure, the latent, the allusive and suggestive?"

The soundtracks annoyed her too. Actors finished off every sentence neatly, as if they were onstage, and hardly ever overlapped each other. Every noise, from the rustle of a table napkin to the shooting of a cuff or the patter of footsteps, sounded razor-sharp and was dubbed in with excessive clarity and precision, as if the human ear did not possess the wonderful knack of filtering sounds according to their acceptability and importance. It seemed to Eduard that Jenny was testing an entire country for its ability to make her happy.

And he? What would he do if she remained in San Francisco and confronted him with a choice: Berlin, or me and the children? Lead a bachelor existence in the renovated attic of that godforsaken apartment house on Rigaer Strasse?

Shortly before her flight was called Jenny asked him to wait a moment. On the way to the bathroom she caught her heel in a crack in the unfinished floor, twisting her ankle and losing her balance. A young man whom she'd just overtaken saved her from falling by grabbing her elbow. He retained his grip a trifle too long for Eduard's taste, staring in utter perplexity at this unknown woman who straightened up and unfolded before his eyes, rearranging her limbs like a ballerina jack-in-the box. They held each other's gaze for a long moment. Then Jenny thanked her unknown cavalier with a smile and the young man stood motionless awhile, staring after her as if he'd just encountered the woman of a lifetime.

When the flight was called Eduard drew Jenny close and gave her a long hug. Jenny parted her lips and sought his tongue as if eager to display, now of all times, an alacrity she'd denied him in the bedroom. He cursed himself for being so subservient. And suddenly, amid the jostling passengers and the squawking of the public-address system, he thought he recognized the reactive mechanism he'd obeyed like a dumb animal. Wasn't the fact of the matter that Jenny kept him in a state of eternal preparedness and perpetual courtship, like an attentive suitor forever ready to prove himself and fulfill his function twenty-four hours a day? Wasn't her inaccessibility just a brilliant ruse designed to keep him in suspense? If assuaged, his interest in her might have waned a long time ago.

He pushed her gently away. She joined the line in front of the barrier and gave him a brief backward glance when the immigration officer returned her passport and boarding card. All he saw thereafter was her silhouette through the tinted glass wall, bending over to show security the contents of her purse. He also thought he saw her shadowy arm give a wave and waved back just in case. It distressed him to think that she could likewise perceive him only as a shadow—banished, so to speak, to the realm of possibility.

He got the cab to drop him at a sidewalk café on Savigny Platz and sat down without removing his overcoat. A few white plastic tables were standing on the terrace as if left there by mistake. Occupying them were people such as he'd seen in Munich or Frankfurt during the years before reunification, but never in Berlin: somberly attired men and women sitting by themselves in front of bottles of Perrier and low-calorie snacks, each holding a newspaper or a computer printout—harbingers of an alien way of life that had infiltrated the city and begun to familiarize the natives with the culture of deadline stress, no smoking, and nonalcoholic working lunches.

The ridges and gables of the surrounding roofs, which were tiled in bright red or aubergine, stood out with crisp, unnatural distinctness against a blue sky so pale it was barely distinguishable from the wan clouds overhead. The air had the warmth and clarity of a glorious day in early spring, but the only effect of the feel of it on Eduard's hands and face was a melancholy shiver. His skin seemed to know that the warmth would not endure and was inexorably declining. One nearby building was enveloped from eaves to entrance in a cascade of luminous red and yellow creeper, but most of the sidewalk trees had already donned their armor of sable bark, and their bare branches, which jutted into the sky like antennas, would receive only messages of cold from now on. Eduard found it nonsensical that plants should prepare for the cold season of the year by stripping themselves naked; he suddenly seemed to feel how differently the senses and emotions developed under an ever-dependable sun that shone down from the zenith. In a fit of nostalgia he recalled the strong, sure blue of the California sky, the robust greenery, the broad horizons and brilliant light. Vegetation here was doomed to lose its foliage from spring onward. By the time its shoots ventured forth into the light and put out leaves, they had three or four months of life left. The leaves celebrated their brief existence in a colorful fireworks display, then curled up and became road sweeper's refuse.

2 THE ALEXANDERPLATZ S-BAHN STATION was also draped in plastic sheeting and barricaded with scaffolding. The "Way Out" arrows that led up and down dusty flights of stairs and along plywood-encased walkways changed direction so often that Eduard finally emerged into the open feeling like a child taking its first sighted steps after a game of blindman's buff. He vainly tried to get his bearings by the television tower. He didn't know whether the tower lay east or west of the station, but, even if he had known, he could well have believed that someone had shifted it in the interim.

Many of the front doors in the streets he traversed were still fitted with antiquated bolts that denied access to anyone, whether friend or foe, after eight o'clock at night. The names next to most of the doorbell buttons were handwritten and many of them had been crossed out. There was scarcely an intercom to be seen. The sidewalks were lined with cars that might have been conceived by one and the same designer and looked, despite their varied paintwork, like products of a single, internationally dominant manufacturer: Fordvwbmwmercoyota. How had all those new automobiles materialized so quickly outside the old front doors? What had become of the indigenous vehicles, the millions of Trabants and Wartburgs? Had they all been rejected by their owners and consigned to junkyards overnight? If all the motor vehicles owned by a nation of seventeen million were bulldozed together in the same spot, how high a mound of scrap would they produce?

Eduard was reminded of an American colleague who, immediately after the breaching of the Wall, had come to Berlin on a Humboldt Scholarship and taken it into his head to go everywhere in a Trabi. Having spent six months driving through Berlin in that antiquated jalopy with the unmistakable brand of perfume, he'd become a field researcher. The diminutive car with the plastic upholstery proved to be a lightning conductor that unfailingly attracted all the city's emotional tensions and tempests. In the eastern part of the city he'd had to get used to being greeted by overtaking motorists with the communist salute, in the West with an upraised middle finger. On one occasion a mother had wrenched open the driver's door, hauled him out, and compelled him to apply his nose to the tailpipe in demonstration of the exhaust fumes to which he was subjecting her child in its baby carriage. His American English made no difference. The Trabi marked him out as an Ossi fundamentalist and rendered any linguistic peculiarities irrelevant. It took him only a few weeks to acquire a complete overview of the fund of swearwords, curses, and threats on which the city's inhabitants could draw.

His pleasure in the experiment eventually palled. When he caught himself wondering whether to list these spontaneous utterances in alphabetical order and compile a dictionary of Berlin motorists' "benedictions," he decided to treat himself to a change of scene and Trabanted off to Paris. On the Champs Élysées he had an experience that compensated for all the injustices he'd suffered in recent months. He had just parked his Trabi when a young couple in evening dress paused beside it. The man looked first at him, then at the Trabi. Finally, throwing up his arms in a rhapsodic gesture, as if calling on the streetlights to bear witness, he exclaimed, *"Quel chic!"*

As he made his way along Rosa Luxemburg Strasse, Eduard saw the Volksbühne looming at the far end like a mighty fortress. The street seemed to run straight up to the semicircular entrance, with its six massive columns, and preclude one from going anywhere but into the theater itself. Eduard would have expected to find such an urban vista in Rome or Paris rather than Berlin. Narrow streets bounded a surprisingly spacious and elegant triangular square, one whole side of which was taken up by the theater. With its imposing colonnaded entrance surmounted by a circular superstructure reminiscent of a gasworks and another of boxlike shape, the theater looked as if its architect had striven to reconcile the design for a refuse-incineration plant with that of a Germanic temple. On the flat roof, glowing like a beacon for errant angels and airplanes, was the word OST in outsize neon capitals. Below it, inscribed in black letters on a huge red banner, was the announcement THEO WARENBERG'S "THAT'S HOW IT WAS!" To the left and right of this, kept in vigorous motion by the wind or a fan, two anarchist flags fluttered above the lateral wings of the portico. Eduard briefly wondered if he wasn't standing outside the headquarters of that numerous group which had chosen to pitch camp in his inherited apartment house.

He was also reminded of Rigaer Strasse by the theatergoers he saw streaming through the doors into the foyer. They were all young people dressed in black, many of martial appearance, with spiky, carefully lacquered hairstyles resembling beds of nails. Quite a few of them wore steel or wire jewelry in their ears or nostrils—which, Eduard had to admit, suited some of the girls extremely well and led one to suspect that they wore similar embellishments in their navels or labia. He quickly averted his head when he thought he spotted the barmaid from Rigaer Strasse in the crush.

Theo he couldn't see anywhere. He'd had the utmost difficulty in persuading him to attend the premiere of his new play. Theo disliked showing up at premieres, especially his own, and it was only for the sake of "the tourist from Stanford" that he'd requested two complimentary tickets. Eduard finally discovered him in the lee of a mobile TV transmission truck parked in the courtyard. An emaciated figure with a cigarette in his mouth, he seemed to be carrying the whole of the theater's ten thousand tons on his shoulders.

They entered via the stage door. Eduard was surprised no one recognized the author when they made their way to their seats. It might have been because Theo had conformed to the basic color prevailing in the auditorium: he was wearing a black jacket over a black T-shirt. Besides, Eduard knew that the only publicity photo he ever circulated was ten years old. But perhaps there was another reason: perhaps they all recognized him and paid homage to him by treating him as one of their own.

The curtain rose to reveal an almost empty stage. In the background, a table with a black-shaded light on it and three or four chairs; right foreground, a mound of scrap metal; center stage, a rectangular trapdoor of the kind occasionally found in the sidewalk outside a store for the use of delivery men unloading crates into the cellar. The cast, who gained the stage by way of the auditorium's lateral aisles, seemed unaware of this hole and astounded the audience by skillfully—accidentally, as it were—avoiding it. There were never more than two or three people onstage at any one time. The play took the form of snapshots loosely strung together, scenes from the upheaval that had followed the downfall of the GDR. An elderly man armed with a video camera prowled around a square drawn on the ground in chalk. Inside the square, watering a withered houseplant, sat another senior citizen. Three wooden rails and a barbecue indicated that the square was a backyard. The two old men didn't notice each other at first; one watched, filmed, and measured the square, the other raked and watered it. Some laconic dialogue ensued. The first old man proclaimed himself the owner of the square in which the second was sitting and demanded its return. The one with the watering can retorted that the square had been vacant when he moved in, that he hadn't left it for forty years and had made everything—the fence, the garden, the little shack—with his own hands. He could take them all with him when he went, said the owner of the square, but go he must, because he himself, the original owner, was a refugee. Nobody could call himself a refugee after forty years, rejoined the other. There followed a scuffle in the course of which the two old men tore off each other's clothes and buried their dentures in each other's flesh.

Meanwhile, on the other side of the stage, another scene was unfolding: an East German ex-general was cutting up a tank with a pair of scissors, bit by bit, and delivering a soliloquy. He recounted his own and his huge toy's career in the vanished People's Army, picturing the fate that was about to overtake the tank's beloved caterpillar tracks, its gun, its turret, and the degrading forms in which he would rediscover them later on: as knives and forks, as tools, as reinforcing bars. Tanks were environmentally friendly products, he insisted; they were almost 100 percent recyclable. And, still soliloquizing, he proceeded to dismember himself as well.

Next, two women met in the middle of the stage. Their fragmentary conversation and body language disclosed that they were mother and daughter but had never seen each other before. The mother had been caught escaping from the GDR and given a prison sentence, the daughter taken away by the state and adopted by a Party-lining couple. The mother had finally traced her child and engineered this longed-for reunion, but it turned out that they had nothing in common. The daughter regarded her mother, who had betrayed the "better" Germany, with suspicion and revulsion. The mother, for her part, could not tolerate her daughter's reproaches and pious Party platitudes.

It only gradually dawned on the audience that all the scenes were played by the same four or five actors, who swapped roles in the process. Those who had just played Westerners had to slip into the

skin of their counterparts and vice versa. The scenes and the con-
flicts that provided their momentum were never resolved. No sooner
had the audience taken someone's part than the scene was reenacted
in a slightly different form. The elderly East German in the chalk
square reappeared onstage as a young Stasi officer and confessed
that he had cheated his neighbor out of the plot by denouncing him.
The next variation showed his victim, the man from the West, being
made to explain how his father had acquired the plot during the
Nazi era . . .

Theo seemed less interested in developments onstage than in
what was going on in the auditorium. He often turned and scrutinized the faces behind him when applause or laughter could be
heard. Eduard's attention, too, was increasingly distracted by the
interaction of cast and audience.

The recently divided Germans' mutual hatred, to which Theo's
text lent visual expression, was more and more uninhibitedly por-
trayed as the evening wore on. The cast seized on any opportunity to
bare their backsides, pass excrement or urine, smear each other with
blood or mucus, and practice other forms of humiliation. A man
masturbated into some potato soup, a sixty-year-old defecated on
a cloth imprinted with the German eagle, a Nazi bridegroom suspended his bride by her panty hose and compelled her to listen to
his declaration of love in that position, women in dirndls lay down
on the floor, spread their legs, and, with joyful cries, were bestrid-
den by swastika-wearing men with their underpants around their
knees. Enemies were symbolically beheaded or mutilated, embryos
ripped from wombs and hurled across the stage while roars of German barroom laughter issued from loudspeakers. The audience sat
there stunned and bewildered at first. Once the moment for protest
had passed, however, they seemed to watch the ranting and puking
onstage with growing fascination. Possibly ashamed of their horror
or disgust, some of them started to clap during a torture scene and
others laughed hysterically when a woman set to work on a man's
penis with a chain saw. After a while Eduard became convinced that

the performance was precisely what it purported to attack: an exercise in barbarity, a celebration of German repulsiveness. At the same time he was overcome by a kind of pity for the spectators and marveled at their lack of pride or self-esteem. Any other theatergoers in the world would simply have stood up and walked out, whereas these were only just beginning to enjoy themselves. It was as if they didn't feel really good unless they were reviled, deluged with spit and shit, and generally besmirched by the cast—as if life outside suffered from an excess of beauty.

Theo was lying back in his seat like a sleeping child. He'd retracted his head in such a way that Eduard could only see one ear and the jutting outlines of his nose. It was impossible to tell whether he was horrified or amused by the performance, or whether he was following it at all. Suddenly he sat up, nudged Eduard in the ribs, and intimated that he wanted to go.

But Theo's motives for leaving differed from Eduard's; he simply felt it was time for a drink. What might have detracted from his interest in the premiere was the knowledge that his play was to be presented at four other theaters in the next few days. He listened with only half an ear to Eduard's impressions of the performance, as if he himself had noticed none of its abominations. All that whetted his curiosity was Eduard's contention that they'd been witnessing genuine ritual violence disguised as a simulacrum of the same.

"Even if you're right, would that be so bad?" he demanded. "Forget Schiller's 'moral institution.' The theater may have become the last place in which to work off, in a relatively unconstrained and ultimately innocuous way, all the Teutonic blood-and-soil and omnipotence fantasies that no longer have any place in real life."

Theo pursued his theme quietly, as if testing the words while uttering them, but with great conviction. Art was traditionally rooted in frenzy and euphoria, and the sole effect of society's attempt to suppress this aspect of it was that suppressed energies erupted from some vent or other. Here in this part of the country in particular, people had been kept in a state of colonial submission for decades. Artistic frenzy and all forms of creative and emancipatory energy had been forced underground, there to become warped and distorted; that was why they could regain the surface only by venting themselves. Redemption from dictatorship would not be an entirely nonviolent process. All that he and, even more so, the producer had done was to lift the lid a little.

Eduard disputed this. What made artists—he stressed the word with a hint of sarcasm—so sure that the enacting of scenes of barbaric violence helped to contain or dissipate the said energies? The so-called safety-valve theory had long been refuted by aggression research. "I can cite you umpteen studies proving that the 'exorcism' of violence—your euphemistic expression—has precisely the opposite effect and reinforces the violence potential. A well-enacted rape is more likely to provoke imitation than condemnation. Any series of images that successfully depicts an unprecedented act of brutality, whether documented or fictitious, enlarges the range of possibilities and ends by functioning as an advertising campaign. This is because there's clearly no genetically built-in authority that condemns and prohibits such emotions. The word 'brutalization' is misleading. It implies that the capacity for brutality has been instilled by adverse circumstances, whereas it probably isn't secondary but as much a part of human nature as the capacity for love."

Theo seemed quite unfazed, let alone provoked. "Can't you conceive of a society that has civilized itself so swiftly and spuriously that it has forgotten what it is and was capable of? Can't you empathize with a writer's compulsion to remind himself and all the good people around him—all those nonviolent mothers and fathers and their badly behaved children—that they are, among other things, brute beasts?"

When they emerged from the bar at dawn it was like a scene from the old days: a dim, deserted street and two men on the lookout for two taxis to take them in two different directions. Except that this time Eduard went Theo's erstwhile way and Theo went Eduard's.

3 | IT HAD GROWN COLD. Under the southern skies of California Eduard had almost forgotten what a Berlin winter was like. The cement-gray, unbroken overcast intensified the gray of the housefronts. The bare branches and tree trunks seemed to be coated in a colorless varnish that robbed them of all luminosity. The leaves on the sidewalks and in the gutters lost their resilience and disintegrated into colored ashes when fleetingly brushed by your foot. Eduard reacquired the forgotten instinct that made him probe a mound of yellow leaves with the toe of his shoe before treading on it to make sure it was really all it seemed. Every brown or yellow leaf was under suspicion of serving as camouflage or wrapping for the turds daily deposited on the city's sidewalks by its hundred thousand dogs. You saw them standing there every morning, those members of a numerous Berlin minority: men and women of all ages who observed the extrusions of their canine pets and expertly appraised the coloration and consistency of what they brought forth.

The dankness rising almost visibly from the ground crept up pedestrians' sleeves and trouser legs and into their very souls. To Eduard the faces that surmounted their muffled torsos looked unpleasantly pallid and exposed, like genitals on a nude beach. It was a malign quirk of evolution that had stranded paleskins in colder climes; the few dark-skinned people he encountered looked far better suited to the cold; their faces radiated an optimism and beauty easily overlooked in the summer. From one day to the next Eduard had arrived at that season of the year when Berlin's evenings began in the mornings and its inhabitants, after one glance out the window, sought some pretext for pulling the bedclothes over their heads again.

Eduard spent the weekend viewing apartments in the three city districts Jenny favored ("if only because of the schools") and regarded as comparatively secure bastions against the flood tide from the east. She wanted four bedrooms and a southern exposure. "Why not a penthouse apartment with a roof garden for a change? Berlin looks quite different from above."

Finding such apartments was easier than coming to terms with their owners. Eduard often suspected that he was dealing with cult leaders, not landlords at all. Even before he crossed the threshold they compelled him to remove his shoes and put on a pair of the slippers that lay in wait for visitors. Then they glided with him across Italian terra-cotta or marble floors, showed him bathrooms the size of living rooms with oval or circular bathtubs, demonstrated how to set the codes for the electronic burglar alarm, the lights, and the electrically operated picture window, conducted him out onto the one or more terraces with the automatically watered palms and oleanders, nodded when asked whether full allowance had been made in the rent for the areas under the mansard roof that only an infant or a midget could have stood up in, and finally named a figure little less than Eduard's net salary. The dust from the Wall's demolition seemed to have acted on landlords and real estate brokers like cocaine. They were putting up apartments and offices for fantasy customers—Arab sheiks, West German and American millionaires, Russian nouveaux riches, Italian counts, British investment bankers—and never appeared to wonder why such people should suddenly descend on Berlin in droves.

Among the properties on offer was a penthouse apartment in the poorer part of Charlottenburg, on the other side of Kant Strasse, whose rent bore an acceptable relationship to its condition. The rooms with the sloping walls were far too small and cramped, but the terrace proved to be disproportionately spacious. Eduard was so taken with this unroofed section of the apartment, which ran around the sides of the building to the rear, that he promptly proceeded, while returning to the car, to remodel the interior in his mind's eye. Moments after starting to make a right at an intersection he was jolted out of his cogitations by a yell from behind. Startled, he braked hard, then satisfied himself that the lights were green. His incipient turn to the right having been halted, the car was now blocking the intersection at an oblique angle. A set of knuckles rapped on the passenger's window. When he lowered it, the aperture was filled with the face of a helmeted cyclist whose mouth transformed itself into a gaping maw—Eduard could see between the teeth as far as the base of the tongue and the uvula. "You blind or something? Check your wing mirror before you make a right, asshole!" Before he could reply, a circular object flew through the air, expended its momentum on his nose, and flopped onto his lap. He stared at the missile in disbelief: a salami roll with a bite out of it. Now wide awake with rage and disgust, he wrenched open the driver's door, but all he could see were the black, Lycra-encased back and taut bare calves of the cyclist-zombie pumping up and down like pistons. A composite of muscles, sinews, and lightweight alloy, the fighting machine was receding at automobile speed.

Just as Eduard took off in pursuit his eye was caught by a dark red blob on his shirtfront that seemed to replenish itself in some mysterious way. No sooner had the material absorbed it than another round blob took shape in almost the same place. It wasn't until he put his hand to his face that he discovered the origin of this miraculous phenomenon: a nosebleed. Cursing, he drove to a nearby playground he remembered from the old days and lay down on a bench. He'd often sat there with other parents when the children were young, but never so early in the morning, still less at this time of year. The surrounding silence, the cold and damp—everything about the place repelled him. He could imagine what a sight he presented and hoped that no one had seen him, let alone recognized him. While raindrops left over from the most recent downpour beaded the chains of the children's swings, the metal slides, and the wire-mesh fence, Eduard lay supine on the parents' bench in his bloodstained shirt and gazed, sniffing, at the sky.

The city had obviously gone mad. The newspapers carried almost daily reports of acts of violence committed for trifling reasons. A father strapping his child into its car seat was too tardy in the estimation of the motorist waiting to take over his parking slot, who hurried him up by punching him in the face. Another road user took umbrage at the number of times the driver behind him changed lanes. At the next light he got out, ax in hand, and demolished the roof of the offender's car. Yet another felt that the driver ahead of him was being too considerate to someone on a pedestrian crossing and lent expression to that view by spraying Mace into the man's eyes while overtaking him.

Although Berlin had always been famed for such hostilities, it seemed to Eduard that their incidence had definitely increased. After their first romantic encounter at the Brandenburg Gate, the city's inhabitants had maintained their East–West contacts not as pedestrians but mainly as motorists ensconced in the coachwork that constituted their working attire, as it were. There followed a thousandfold process of mutual education administered with sign language and clenched fists.

Cyclists represented a new and insufficiently heeded group of participants in these daily bouts of close combat. They were specially to be feared because they deemed themselves the best road users of all, being ecologically legitimized. Armed with helmets and clear consciences and mounted on steel chassis little cheaper than compacts, they raced at near-Olympic speeds along the new cycle tracks, scattering dogs, children, and old people and bellowing instructions on the highway code as they sped past.

Eduard used to consider it a privilege to disarm the city's traffic barbarians by remaining studiously good-natured. He had rewarded them with approving waves, sometimes two-handed, and censured them at most by clapping or cheering ironically. Now he sensed that he wouldn't be able to withstand the pull of brutalization for much longer. In the future he would repay one yell with another and counter salami rolls with a jack.

A light breeze stirred the tips of the bare branches and blotted out the threadbare patch of blue sky overhead with huge, dark billows of cloud. The silence conjured up sounds from another time, almost from another life. He suddenly heard the creaking and squealing of pulley wheels on the steel rope that had slanted across the playground like a miniature cableway. Loris used to climb the wooden tower again and again, call to him to make sure he was watching, grasp the stirrup with both hands, and push off with his feet. It saddened Eduard to recall the boy's little featherweight body and his lack of fear. A few weeks' unthinking patronage of McDonald's drive-throughs had sufficed to change the boy completely. He'd become sluggish, moody, and unsure of himself. Shortly before Eduard left Loris had asked him what he, Loris, was really good at. His only response when Eduard enumerated his talents was to shake his head and say that everyone else in his class was better than him at all the subjects mentioned. Eduard resolved to call Jenny and the kids at one a.m. Central European time and rhapsodize about the apartment, and he knew what idea he must implant in Loris's mind to gain his support against Jenny's misgivings about Berlin: "The terrace is so big, you could install a regular swimming pool on it." Any exaggeration was justified, he felt, it if helped to reunite a family.

4 A FEW WEEKS' INUREMENT to living in Charlottenburg forced Eduard to concede that Dr. Santner had been
right. There was only one way of avoiding the traffic jams on
the Berlin ring road or in the city center, and that was to purchase
two bicycles. With the first he rode to Charlottenburg station, with
the second from Buch station to the Institute and back.

His route to the Institute took him through a small urban district
in which relics of the first generation of prefabricated concrete high-
rises were crumbling away in company with the remains of a baroque
mansion. The latter had been blown up in 1963 by the masters of the
Workers' and Peasants' State, who had left only the politically unob-
jectionable barns and stables standing. Some of these two-centuries-
old buildings were now being renovated at great expense, creating a

suddenly glamorous neighborhood in which the GDR buildings stood out like the barracks of an invading army. Not far from the Science Center a large, châteaulike pile had withstood the onset of the socialist innovators—an eighteenth-century government building which now housed a section of Buch Hospital. On his cycle tours Eduard had dismounted there and spent a long time standing outside the vestibule as though meditating deeply. He needed time to take in what he was seeing. The GDR architects had grafted a species of entrance hall onto the baroque edifice, a small boxlike structure with a roof whose edges abruptly tilted upward in a series of inexplicable duck's-ass scallops as if the designers had suddenly sought some relief from their eternal rectangles. The walls consisted of grimy glass panes set in blue metal frames. This annex looked far more decrepit than the main building. Eduard surmised that the members of the licensing committee must first have looked askance at the unspeakable design, suspicious of its scalloped roof, before approving it in the certainty that it at least betrayed no hint of bourgeois cultural decadence. Instead of residing in baroque country houses or the mansion of their princely predecessors, the new masters had preferred to withdraw to some unadorned residential shoeboxes in nearby Wandlitz.

Rürup had told Eduard how the television cameras first explored the socialist big shots' private quarters in the months succeeding the fall of the Wall. Utterly nonplussed, the televiewing public had followed the cameras from house to house, room to room, bathroom to kitchen, gas stove to refrigerator. Probably the worse feature of these tours was the realization that the mystery-enshrouded, closely guarded temples of the Nomenclatura harbored no secrets at all. The GDR's big shots had been content with amenities such as any West German butcher would have treated himself to. The most the cameras discovered in the way of luxury was an occasional underfloor heating system, a heated swimming pool, or a collection of blue movies. There was, of course, the obligatory public outcry over bathroom fittings, gold-plated door handles, and multifarious bottles of whiskey, but it was probable that what really aroused popular indignation and horror was disappointment at the measly nature of these luxuries, at the socialist priesthood's lack of imagination, refinement, and taste.

One of the late GDR's insufficiently well-known crimes, said Rürup, had been its rape of the aesthetic sense. The Politburo had even proclaimed itself responsible for automobile design and compelled millions of drivers to sit hunched over their steering wheels like astigmatics. The greatest frivolity the planners had sanctioned was one day introduced under the slogan "Berlin Diagonal." At the Politburo's behest, every means of transportation in the capital of the GDR—buses, trolley cars, river and lake craft—had been adorned with three diagonal lines. The acme of creative freedom had consisted of allowing construction workers, when withdrawing materials from stock, to pick out the prefabricated concrete slabs they liked best. They could choose between the following finishes: "Hand," "Snail," "Maze," or "Plain."

Sometimes Eduard got out a station early and took the longer route through the development area. It astonished him each time to see how quickly the district was taking shape. New streets and squares came into being day by day and week by week, at a rate made to seem still faster by a kind of selective mechanism affecting his perception of them. He noticed new buildings only when they were completed; excavation and foundation laying, framework erection and topping-out ceremonies were intermediate phases he excluded from his range of vision.

The whole breathless venture seemed to be progressing quite automatically. The development's speed and organization implied the existence of a power center of immense capacity, but the stager and coordinator of it all was nowhere to be seen. The cranes, rollers, and graders formed parts of a complicated machine that seemed to be powered by clockwork, and someone had thrown away the key. Eduard felt as if some alien, unaccountable being were, for some mysterious reason, erecting these colonies for a future population that had yet to land on earth.

Among the locals, rapid changes in their surroundings seemed to evoke a kind of visual block. As if in a dream—as if following the invisible signposts of memory—they made their way along the pass-able stretches between the fenced-off construction sites in thick, zippered-up jackets, women arm in arm with men, mothers holding their children by the hand. The numerous windows of the light, airy, colorful new buildings, which didn't lend themselves to cur-tains, must have seemed to them like beacons of another civilization that felt no need to shield itself from the gaze of neighbors and passersby.

The White House changed its entrance every few weeks, so Eduard was never sure which direction to approach it from. Outside he would tramp through churned-up mud to a new plank walkway spanning some old or new trench in front of the building. Inside he would make for the laboratory by circuitous routes that took him over exposed pipework and up temporary flights of stairs, to end by wondering vainly how he had gotten there *this* time.

So far he had killed time at the Institute by doing the minor jobs that Rürup or Santner, casually apologetic, had given him while he was looking for an apartment and settling in. An animal-protection league requested a ruling on whether a female biologist at Tübingen University was violating scientific ethics by experimenting with fruit flies; she had even received death threats for "torturing" them. Another group was hard at work on an animal-rights charter and wanted a decision on whether this should apply only to mammals or to vertebrates in general. Eduard amused himself by espousing the theory that, in principle, bacteria and viruses, AIDS viruses included, had a right to be included in the community of species deserving of protection. It was morally untenable, he said, to eradi-cate such viruses merely because, without malice aforethought, they were killing thousands of members of a species they couldn't care less about, to wit, *Homo sapiens*. His last job was an expert opinion requested by some "alternative foresters" from the vicinity of the Science Center. They asked for information on whether and to what extent foreign varieties of trees and shrubs such as cypresses, pines,

and oleanders could endanger the indigenous vegetation. Dr. Santner didn't hesitate to twit Eduard on his role as an oracle for dis-
traught citizens; in any case, he said, problems with his complicated
inheritance must be leaving him little time to spare for his behavioral
genes project, at least for the present.

When Eduard had finally installed his computer and stored the
data from the Stanford laboratory on his hard disk, further work was
precluded by a straightforward burglary. At some time between
three-thirty and six-thirty a.m., so the police established, a small
truck had pulled up outside the White House. After gaining access
to the premises, obviously with a night key, a team of burglars, number unknown, had expertly dismantled sixteen of the new computers, Eduard's included, and borne them off to an unknown
destination. The general verdict was that it might have happened
anywhere. What Eduard found unique to this part of the world,
however, was the sequel. Inquiries into how the thieves' vehicle had
managed to pass the checkpoint without hindrance disclosed a hiatus in the security guards' duty roster. Decades ago the labor-union
management had won the right to suspend guard duty in the early
hours of the morning. At the time, this change had been advocated
by a sense of realism. Nothing but foxes, hedgehogs, and rats had
passed the Institute's barrier for thousands of sleepless nights. But
what if circumstances changed? What if, when the Wall came down,
electronically savvy burglars from the environs of Berlin seized the
opportunity to storm this suddenly undefended treasure island?

Eduard had forgotten that German duty rosters, once agreed on,
are proof against any historic upheaval. All at once, the scientists'
meetings were dominated by battle-hardened labor-union representatives who threatened strike action if the progressive regulation
dating from 1973 were rescinded. The result of their negotiations
was that the stolen computers had to be replaced out of the Institute's research funds. The security guards' duty roster remained
intact.

Santner, whose laboratory had not been affected by the burglary,
eventually thought up a way of utilizing Eduard's "criminally

underemployed expertise" until the new computers arrived. Since the study of behavioral genes was still in its infancy in Germany, he said, a public hearing on the subject should be held. Eduard's research into serotonin-amine, which allegedly helped to determine aggressive behavior, would make a particularly good subject for debate. One possible title would be "Genes and Crime"—or, less provocatively and couched as a question, "Does violence have any biological roots?" Who was better placed than Eduard to organize such a colloquium, both thematically and in terms of personnel? After all, he alone commanded an overview of the current state of the debate in America and possessed the requisite contacts. A conference of this kind, well prepared and designed to appeal to a wide public, would be a novelty in Germany and gain the Institute more publicity than a hundred learned articles in the house journal.

This stung Eduard. He sensed that Santner's proposal was an attempt to make him the instigator of a controversy that would activate largely ideological reflexes in Germany, among scientists as well as the general public.

He was grateful to Dr. Santner for having so much faith in him, he rejoined. If his esteemed colleague wanted to become embroiled in a public debate about the genetic roots of aggressive behavior, all that he, Eduard, could say was, "After you, Dr. Santner!" The suggested title for the conference would itself unleash a storm of indignation. Discounting any other misapprehensions it might arouse, in the end a meeting of that kind would be construed in Germany as a scientific conspiracy against foreigners and exploited as such in certain quarters. He suggested starting at the opposite end of the scale. How about a conference entitled "Love and Genes" or "The Chemical Prerequisites of Love?" Eduard's listeners felt he was pulling their leg and interpreted his objections as symptoms of a certain transatlantic arrogance. Human genetics was far more advanced, he was told, than American institutions were prepared to accept. Someone came up with a cunning semantic compromise on Santner's suggested theme: "Crime and the Myth of Genetic Factors."

Eduard forgot his annoyance when he found all three children's voices on the answering machine in his office. Ilaria, who had a math problem, regretted that her father couldn't give her some coaching and guarantee her an A as he used to. Katharina had clearly been bullied into sending him a recorded message. She merely wished him good night—"Good morning, I mean. What time is it over there, anyway? Never mind." When he heard Loris he deplored the fact that the two elder children had grown out of the magic age so quickly. Adult common sense had already descended on them like the hand of some almighty disciplinarian who insisted on a strict distinction between fantasy and reality, whereas Loris still commuted freely between those two worlds. His voice sounded as if he were half asleep. It conveyed infinite trust and intimacy, and also a sadness Eduard couldn't define. He felt a pang at the thought that he was leaving the little boy alone with his uncertainty and self-doubt.

5 EDUARD HAD NEVER IMAGINED that calculations involving interest rates and repayment installments would ever take up more than five minutes of his time. A five-digit figure—37,500—had now begun to monopolize his thoughts and his emotions in turn. To be added to that sum were the running costs of the Rigaer Strasse house: water, electricity, trash collection, fire insurance, chimneysweep, realty-transfer tax. The sum had even appeared in one of Eduard's dreams, on the check for a dinner with an unknown woman who watched him imperturbably as he looked for the requisite cash in his wallet. She vaguely resembled the woman in the Institute cafeteria, whom he had since encountered— but never exchanged a word with—on two or three occasions. In his dream he had readily paid the absurd sum by check, his sole complaint being that the value-added tax hadn't been specified.

This time Klott greeted him with the news that he had made some headway with his inquiries into the previous owner of the Riga Street property. Until October 1933 she had lived at the address listed in the real estate register, a house in the Grunewald suburb of Berlin owned by a family named Marwitz. If Frau Schlandt was still alive, he would trace her. Eduard needn't worry, though; he was the possessor of a legally valid restitution notice, and that was beyond dispute.

Klott's attempts to persuade the water and electricity works to cut off supplies had only led to some bureaucratic pirouettes. It was inadvisable to cut off supplies, declared the waterworks, because the pipes would be bacteriologically contaminated and might become furred, and cleaning them out would be more expensive than the present running costs. In addition, the building housed a pregnant woman whose right to running water was legally paramount. Furthermore, the payment of water bills was always a landlord's responsibility. This did not, of course, preclude him from pursuing his claims in the courts.

Klott cracked his knuckles while explaining the legal position. He'd had it with the waterworks. His final plea to them had been to address every future invoice to the police commissioner on the ground that he'd so far ignored all requests to clear the building and was responsible for the squatters' quasi-legal theft of water. The waterworks solemnly wrote back that they regretted their inability to charge the police commissioner for the water consumed because he hadn't personally consumed it.

Klott explained the reasons for the mayor's unwontedly indulgent attitude toward squatters. His Social Democratic predecessor had deemed it good policy to display exceptional rigor—three weeks before his reelection—by clearing a dozen squatters' houses in the immediate vicinity of Rigaer Strasse. The result had been house-to-house fighting on a scale hitherto known only in Northern Ireland.

The police were compelled to work their way upward, foot by foot and floor by floor, until they gained the attics and roofs. The brutality of this police operation had caused the Greens to resign from the ruling coalition. The Social Democratic mayor was compelled to resign and his conservative rival took over. "He really owes the squatters his job," said Klott. "That's why he's temporarily courting his involuntary allies. The last thing he wants is to suffer his predecessor's fate."

Only in the case of the electricity bills had Klott achieved a provisional settlement. One morning he had gone on his own initiative to Rigaer Strasse, thrust his pudgy fingers through the mailbox slit, and fished some letters out of the rusty cage. He had then forwarded the addressees' names to the Berlin Electricity Works. Subject to acceptance of liability by the squatters, the company had declared itself ready to send all future invoices to the consumers. Klott shrugged his massive shoulders when Eduard asked what would happen when the invoices were—predictably—returned marked "Not known at this address."

In addition to running costs of DM37,500, Klott remarked in passing, another five-digit figure awaited Eduard's attention, namely, DM71,238. This was a mortgage originally granted by the GDR State Bank and refinanced after its sudden demise. Klott took his time explaining this item too. Rents in the GDR had been kept so low by the state that they were not even enough to cover maintenance costs. The cost of repairing roofs, fractured water pipes, collapsing balconies and stairs, et cetera, could only be met by borrowing from the State Bank. These profitable debts had passed after reunification to West German banks and devolved upon the original owners. "But it's always like that," said Klott. "People who inherit property always find themselves up to their ears in debt to begin with."

It was clear that Eduard had no choice but to take out the necessary loan himself.

Incidentally, Klott went on, he had some good news to report. A former client from Berlin-Spandau was interested in the building—

"not the type of person one would normally consort with, but very well-heeled. A designer-kitchen supplier. That's one of the by-products of your new status as a property owner: it'll bring you into contact with all kinds—people you never even dreamed you shared God's good earth with."

Eduard was spared any more mental arithmetic, when he emerged onto the street, by a meteorological phenomenon. He noticed at once that something unforeseen had occurred, but he didn't know what. All movement on the street—activities he never noticed as a rule because of their sameness—seemed suddenly slower, contrived, and stagy. Pedestrians on the sidewalks, cyclists and motorists on the road—all were going along as if pondering or rehearsing every movement. The sight was so puzzling that Eduard didn't grasp the reason for this transformation until he stepped out onto the sidewalk and promptly fell over. Propelled on all fours by the momentum of his fall, he slowly and inexorably slithered toward an elderly couple who were approaching with tiny, cautious footsteps. Still taking tiny footsteps, they swerved to the right for fear of becoming entangled with him. "It doesn't do to take big strides," the man said with an amiable smile, as if apologizing for the belatedness of his advice.

A thin, almost imperceptible drizzle had coated the entire city with an invisible film of ice. This ice inspired an outgoingness and readiness to laugh that was absent in normal times. Everyone, children and adults alike, waited for something funny to happen. At an intersection Eduard saw a poodle turn the corner too sharply and skid willy-nilly, with all four paws braced, across the sidewalk and onto the road. The poodle was called a stupid mutt by the young man whose whistle it had obeyed, who then burst out laughing, grabbed the streetlamp beside him, slid down the slippery shaft, gazed briefly into his pooch's eyes on a level with them, and, almost as soon as he'd scrambled to his feet, came crashing down again. A woman leaning on a walking stick waved to Eduard with her free hand as if inviting applause for her ability to stand upright. Eduard was struck in general by how many old people were venturing out.

The sidewalks and stores were populated by cheerful senior citizens who appeared to relish the fact that the frozen rain had suddenly imposed a universal speed limit they themselves had had to observe for years.

Jenny's latest fax had complained that Loris was pestering her almost daily about the swimming pool on the terrace of the penthouse apartment; she said nothing about the possibility of moving in earlier than planned, nor had Eduard suggested anything of the kind. The movements of parents with adolescent children were permanently circumscribed by the beginning and end of the school year. Their agenda did not include secondary factors such as an inheritance, a new job, or efforts on behalf of marital happiness. Where the latter was concerned, the distance between himself and Jenny might even be an advantage. Living in close proximity hadn't brought them any closer; perhaps the ocean that now lay between them was a pointer to the distance they should preserve. Their happiness depended on their landing on a tiny, uncharted promontory whose discovery might entail as many odysseys as an expedition to the island of Atlantis.

Immediately after Jenny's departure Eduard had E-mailed her a suggestion: "Since we're going to be prevented from having any more 'amatory accidents' for a while, what could be more natural than to agree on their causes by letter? I read somewhere that one of the reasons for the successful evolution of the human race is its ability to lend verbal expression to its desires, and also to its feelings of distaste. It's a myth that lovers the world over communicate such emotions by looks and gestures alone. Since my/your bright idea (up in the tower) ended by arousing your misgivings rather than your enthusiasm, how would it be if we let our hair down at a safe distance?"

Jenny's reply included some passages that had angered him at first and then, because anger failed to silence them, signaled a red alert. "I'm not too sanguine," she wrote, "about your giving advance notice of your erotic fantasies in writing. Still, I was touched that you should have tried, up there in the tower, to create an almost exact replica of the scenario that once succeeded quite by chance— by accident, so to speak. It may have been a 'typically masculine' idea, but that doesn't bother me; what I liked about it, perhaps, was its very directness. So you're welcome to carry on and surprise me again in the future. To spare us future disappointments, though, bear one thing in mind. The famous 'O' around which everything suddenly seems to revolve—What do you call successful lovemaking without an O? A minus-O?—anyway, in my case and that of most women, the famous O originates in the head, not the pussy, and this cerebral O is certainly not induced by sexual fantasies, nor by bonuses such as an unusual location, helpful though these can sometimes be. The sensation of height and danger up there in the turret overlooking Potsdamer Platz can be experienced equally well on a single bed at ground level, provided your imagination is stimulated the right way. Preparation is far more important than location. If you want to seduce a woman at night you must start pampering and wooing her in the morning. Please don't get me wrong. I'm only telling you all this because you're obviously obsessed with the idea that my engine's stalled in some way, and that you only have to go about it with sufficient sensitivity to find the right starter button." (An odd question flashed through Eduard's mind as he read this: What was the significance of his wish to induce a sensation that other cultures forcibly eliminated by means of ritual female circumcision?) "But there isn't a starter button, or none that you could put your finger on. Perhaps I'm just a hopeless case in that respect. In answer to your question about my sexual fantasies: I don't have any at present, to be honest, nor do I miss them."

There spoke the Jenny he knew and loved, dauntless and forever ready to lock horns with anyone, not only with the superior forces of the sexual gurus and therapists whose talk shows daily revived the dictatorship of the "satisfying sex life" but with Eduard himself. Any woman who confessed that she harbored no sexual fantasies at all and didn't miss them cut the ground from under their collective feet. He admired Jenny's courage; of the role allotted him by that courage he was less enamored. Her letter embodied two contradictory messages. The first: Don't blame everything on me, there's still a chance, but only if you mend your ways. The second: It's futile, rooting around and asking questions; the real way to show your love is to take me as I am. Did Jenny mean to imply that by indulging in his risky act of love in the pleasure tower of the Weinhaus Huth he was yielding to his own peculiar cravings rather than complying with her wishes?

Eduard had always imagined he could form a kind of alliance with Jenny. The idea of such a pact had occurred to him long before he met her, as a young man's defensive strategy against the fate suffered by various couples of his acquaintance. He was convinced that marriages failed because of insufficient mutual curiosity—because of cowardice, in fact. Hardly had the brief firework of infatuation petered out when the disillusioned pair came to terms with its smoldering ashes and, for the rest of their long years together, sentenced each other to exotic and expensive forms of torture: macrobiotic food, physiotherapy, and orthopedic shoes; initiation by Indian gurus and Native American shamans who either hailed from California or aspired to go there; yoga, tai chi, NIA exercises. But it was now apparent that Jenny wanted nothing to do with such a pact. She was diverting his thoughts to love, to the art of courtship, to gallantry and romance. The role model she allotted him was that of the medieval troubadour who roams the world on horseback, lays the wicked low, gives the good a helping hand, ever devises new ballads dedicated to the unattainable love of his life, and, when he has finally presented her with his effusions after triumphing in the lists and been rewarded with an unforgettable look from her softly shimmering eyes, blithely rides on.

He studied the old vacation snapshot she'd E-mailed him: Jenny leaning against a ship's rail with her rebellious hair tied back but fluttering in the wind; frozen in the background, blue-black waves that flattened out toward the horizon and imperceptibly merged with the paler blue of the sky; knees and calves as slender and almost fragile-looking as a schoolgirl's; sturdy thighs that seemed to belong to another woman; upper body slender again, like the ankles; the face above the long, bare neck displaying noble shadows such as every fashion photographer's camera seeks; the smile of an adventuress, a little too triumphant, perhaps, but certainly carefree, conveying "Nobody puts one over on me!" To Eduard, that had taken on a different meaning. Jenny was intrepid, almost reckless, the first to bar a stubborn motorist's path or complain of rudeness in a supermarket, a born leader among women whose radical suggestions sometimes astonished people. She was forever disconcerting Eduard's friends with her outbursts against the opposition consensus, which either aroused their unyielding, unspoken hostility or caused them to compliment him after the event. They sounded as if they were congratulating him on sharing his bed with a Brunhilde; they forbore to add that they'd never considered him a Siegfried.

6 DR. SANTNER HAD DROPPED IN to remind Eduard of a weekend invitation he'd sent him. It was a mystery to him why Santner should set so much store by his attendance, but his curiosity had somehow been whetted by a piece of verbal bait: "You'll meet some very bright but highly incompatible people." Santner's invitation conveyed a certain magnanimity Eduard found surprising. Not only magnanimity but—why not?—pugnacity.

The first-floor apartment in Pankow formed part of a housing development dating from the 1920s. It was there, Santner remarked with a belligerent smile, that "the GDR's intellectual elite" had settled.

Several tables had been set up in the spacious, interconnecting reception rooms, giving the apartment the look of a small restaurant. The guests stood or sat around in groups with glasses of sparkling wine in their hands. Some had taken over the kitchen, others were braving the cold on the terrace. A few were colleagues from Eduard's department, but most of them he'd never met before. Would Rürup be coming? he asked when Santner led him over to one of the tables and introduced him. Santner shook his head as if Rürup's presence would distress him immeasurably. Scarcely had Santner introduced Eduard as "our German star from San Francisco" than he was engaged in conversation by a young man with lively eyes and a plump, boyish face. "Then we're almost companions in misfortune," he said. "My name's Füllgraf. Like you, I'm a relative newcomer from abroad—from Frankfurt, actually. Heavens, Berlin really is a hothouse with a microclimate of its own. It's hard to tell if you're one of the plants that can survive here. Come with me."

Eduard found something instantly engaging about the friendly way Füllgraf took his arm and offered his services as a guide.

"This scene you're looking at is deceptive. See all these people casually sitting or standing around in groups? See how outwardly homogeneous they are, how casually they stroll from room to room? Look a bit closer and you'll note that all movement takes place inside a group. If one member goes off to refill his glass, another goes too— they stick together. These little, chattering nuclei only communicate internally, never externally. But beware of classifying them too quickly. The lines of demarcation have long ceased to follow a straightforward East–West pattern."

Half obtrusively, half unobtrusively, he indicated two tables in the same room, slightly staggered but only a few feet from each other.

"A fascinating sight," he whispered to Eduard. "There you see, standing or sitting in echelon behind each other, two strong teams of GDR intellectuals. Both pride themselves on not having collaborated with the communist regime, and both, incidentally, still profess to be socialists. Each of the teams is now receiving attention from West German trainers, doctors, and fans, but that doesn't matter. What's important is that every player at one table knows every player at the other—from dozens of home games in the former GDR. They're on first-name terms, and that goes for their wives and lovers as well. But they don't talk to each other and won't do so for several years to come. Wessis versus Ossis—that's boring. The true line of demarcation runs between those Ossis who remained here and were showered with Party prizes for their noncollaboration, and the others, who were jailed or exiled for noncollaboration and showered with West German prizes for the same thing."

"And whose side do you take?" Eduard asked.

"My views are very clear-cut, but I can't afford to hold them, to be frank. My newspaper's owned by a West German corporation, and I have to help sell it here—to those who stayed behind. Anyway, does either of us know exactly which table we'd be sitting at today if we'd grown up in the east wing of the German edifice?"

Füllgraf took Eduard's arm and towed him over to one of the tables, at which an elderly man with long, sparse white hair was holding forth. Eduard failed at first to make sense of what he was saying. It sounded like a graveside tribute to a much loved, universally celebrated woman who had died an untimely death. She must have been an exceptional personality, a difficult but highly gifted woman—an artist?—whose occasional fits of cruelty and caprice even her admirers found hurtful but couldn't change. It appeared that the late lamented had one terrible failing: an almost intolerably dogmatic and incorrigibly arrogant attitude toward life and living. She was so convinced of the infallibility of her ideas that she cast all warning to the winds. She was clearly unable to conceive that she'd been surrounded from birth by enemies who had nothing better to do than finish her off. Those enemies had ultimately gained the upper hand and were now, in an unprecedented orgy of despoliation, purloining all that she had left behind: the physical and spiritual assets of that wonderful, difficult, enigmatic creature named the German Democratic Republic.

A young woman at the same table disagreed. Although she didn't deny the despoliation of the late GDR, she said, it had nonetheless conferred one or two benefits on the bereaved. Phone booths and phone connections, gas and electricity mains, roads . . . Air quality had improved, too. The stench of burning lignite in the winter was sometimes imperceptible.

"The development of the infrastructure is an undertaking like the colonization of India by the British," the old man thundered at her. "Investment in the new 'provinces'—the conquistadors used the same term for their colonies in America—has benefited West German industry alone! In the old days wars were fought for access to new markets. West Germany came armed with a single weapon: a trusteeship organization designed to break up our great nationalized industries and destroy them piecemeal!"

"When entrepreneurs decide to disfigure our countryside with supermarkets, factories, and power stations," said someone else ("A third-rate university lecturer from Frankfurt," Füllgraf whispered in Eduard's ear), who obviously felt called upon to lend the old man's complaint some scientific backing, "they naturally demand the requisite infrastructure. Expressways, phone networks, and railroads must work. But all such investments serve the capitalist exploiters' needs, not the so-called reconstruction of the East. The West German foodstuffs and luxury-goods industries reported a 20 percent growth in turnover during the first year after the currency union, whereas their East German counterparts lost over half their business. West German breweries introduced night shifts; Meisterbräu Halle had to tip its beer into the Saale."

The old man with the snow-white hair had been nodding grimly throughout this speech. At the same time, he seemed to find it irksome that his visions should be seconded by someone not authorized, either rhetorically or careerwise, to endorse them. He cleared his throat mightily.

"It'll end in tears," he cut in. "The unemployed won't be fobbed off with social security forevermore. Yugoslavia isn't as far away as those gentlemen imagine. There'll be civil war, chaos, fascist demonstrations. Marx was right: the worldwide victory of capitalism we're now witnessing is the prelude to its demise."

"But what comes after that?" asked the young woman in an audibly shaken voice. The old sage brushed this aside. Her question would be answered in two or three generations' time, he said, by unprejudiced young people whose brains had not been addled by talk of the failure of socialism.

"But shouldn't we warn them?" the questioner persisted. "I mean, socialism—as we experienced it, at least—really has failed, hasn't it?"

But the old man might have been addressing an unseen congregation.

"Terror is the first concomitant of the New. Childhood diseases like scarlet fever, measles, and chicken pox have to break out before the organism becomes immune to them. It took centuries for the bourgeois revolution to liberate itself from the relics of the old society, from religious wars, slavery, and colonialism. It will take just as long for socialism to reach maturity."

"Wonderful, isn't it?" Füllgraf whispered to Eduard as he drew him away. "They're obviously quite unperturbed by the prospect of a new series of experiments in socialism, if only because it won't reenter the historical arena for two or three generations. That means they're temporarily restricted to the pleasanter enormities of capitalism. There won't be any lack of volunteers from the West, either. After all, they only saw the blessings of socialism from the train window, as glimpses of a landscape flashing past. What I don't understand is that no one questions the economic basis of this new, 'mature' socialism. A lot of intelligent people staked their reason and their careers on a utopia whose primary difference from other utopias was an economic theory. Only the abolition of private ownership of the means of production would create an equitable society—so they believed. But now they don't want to know what really sank their utopia. They know nothing about economics. Not only have they never taken an interest in such matters, but they're proud of the fact. They've firmly diagnosed the cause of death without examining the cadaver, even at a distance. The experiment didn't fail of itself, they claim; it was sabotaged and wrecked by hostile elements. Let's not delude ourselves: these righteous souls aren't concerned with the good of humanity, only with justifying their own curricula vitae. They'd sooner lead humanity into another disastrous experiment than admit they were wrong."

Eduard had been listening with only half an ear. Terror is the first concomitant of the New . . . Wasn't that one of Theo's maxims? "You know Theo Warenberg?" said Füllgraf, surprised at Eduard's question. "You won't find him here. He doesn't go to parties like these, he restricts himself to being present in spirit! Now here," he went on as they entered the kitchen, "we're among Wessis—our own kind, or *their* kind, if you prefer."

The occupants of the kitchen were discussing the prize question of how to convey to grownup individuals, without offending them, that nearly everything they'd learned and done in life to date was worthless. After all, big firms trained their executives to perform such ticklish tasks. Not so Greater Germany, Inc., which had unleashed its representatives on the East Germans entirely unforewarned, complete with the know-it-all arrogance people found so insufferable at home. "Trust doesn't come into it," someone said angrily. "It's all to do with ownership. Reunification has degenerated into a means of self-enrichment. The property clock has been turned back sixty-five years—a unique historical development!"

Santner materialized at Eduard's elbow. "Aren't you yourself an expert on that subject?" he said. "What's it like when the good fairy of reunification lands you with a building you didn't know existed? When your claim is disputed and you have to turn the whole of your family history inside out to discover how Grandpa acquired the place?"

Eduard had no time to wonder how Santner had obtained his information. As succinctly and graphically as he could, he recounted the story of someone who, having emigrated in all but name, unexpectedly receives a letter from his late father's tax advisor informing him that his unknown grandfather has left him an apartment house in Friedrichshain, finds it a ruin, and is fired on by the squatters who are occupying it.

Füllgraf was entranced. Incidents like that, he declared, were a historical godsend. What was happening at the present time was the reacquisition of history by the individual. Because of the quasi-natural miscarriage of socialism, a whole generation was suddenly being compelled to abandon its self-indulgently aloof attitude, its pseudocritical equidistance from the competing systems, and run its colors up the mast. "What remains," said Füllgraf, "is a surprisingly simple truth. The system that has proved its superiority is the one that acknowledges the principle of error and the fact that human planning stands in constant need of correction. A society in which the truth cannot be uttered or published will never prevail over it." When leaving he asked if Eduard would make himself available for an interview in the next few days.

7 ONCE INSTALLED in his Charlottenburg penthouse, Eduard had to admit to himself that something was missing. He hadn't felt half as ill-at-ease in the Institute's ridiculous guest apartment as he'd told everyone. In the utterly unfamiliar, plowed-up environment of East Berlin he'd seen himself as a kind of pioneer. In Charlottenburg, where he knew his way around, he felt spuriously and deceptively at home.

He sometimes paused outside the lighted windows of former drinking haunts but could find no valid reason for entering them. The old neighborhoods and their landmarks had lost their power, the old cliques had disintegrated or quarreled and gone their separate ways. Involuntarily, he peered through the windows in search of a familiar face but averted his head as soon as he saw one. He didn't exactly know what he was trying to avoid, just felt a definite need to remain incognito. So his evening tours ended up in bars he'd never formerly noticed, even though he passed them every day— street-corner hostelries whose lighting and decor hadn't changed for decades. The counters were still illuminated by lights with cloth-covered shades, the ceilings shrouded in fishermen's nets, the pinball machines against the wall overlooked by hand-painted pictures of gypsy girls with plunging necklines, the rooms at the rear equipped with billiard tables. The amazing pertinacity of such establishments suddenly appealed to him. Amid a storm of redevelopment, thousands of street-corner bars in both halves of the city were steadfastly resisting any hint of change. Where their decor and clientele were concerned, they obeyed the natural law of endless repetition. Like their wallpaper, glasses, and selection of beverages, their customers didn't seem to have changed for twenty or thirty years. If a bar stool remained vacant for any length of time, it was taken over and occupied for decades by a younger regular. These hostelries preserved an eternally postwar atmosphere—with one strange difference, for women were lacking now instead of men. Men were always in the majority, and every male eye was focused on the one woman present, who was serving behind the counter. The same tipsy or thoroughly befuddled men had probably sat in front of the same barmaid for years, shaking dice in the same leather cups and laughing at the same old jokes. They all developed wrinkles, paunches, and bald patches, brought all kinds of bugs and diseases with them, but they never wearied of the hairstyle, blouse, and voice of the barmaid who simultaneously united the homeless army and kept it at arm's length, unerringly jotting down the number of drinks her customers consumed on their beer mats. Although Eduard remained a stranger among them, the rounds he bought were not refused.

He found to his surprise that, in other respects, his bachelor existence in the empty apartment hardly bothered him. True, a certain alertness returned from near oblivion and reasserted itself. The eyes of approaching women suddenly sent out signals again, their ankles and the curves beneath their coats regained their voices and spoke to him, a half turn of the head and the bobbing of a hem against a nylon-sheathed calf awakened old desires. That was a nuisance, but he could handle it—he wasn't twenty anymore, after all, and anyway, a grass widower's life was easier to endure in the winter. What he did miss sometimes, when cycling through the grounds of the Institute at dusk, was one of the glass torture chambers erected to combat such impulses on every campus in the States. At Stanford his route from the laboratory to the parking lot had taken him past the gym. Behind its glass walls he would see scores of half-naked individuals of both sexes staring intently at the digital displays on their consoles, utterly undisturbed by the language of the bodies around them. They walked on the spot, sprinted up steep hills on stationary bicycles, overcame absurd mechanical opponents with sweat-streaked arms and legs, steeled their knee joints. Solitary, self-absorbed islands in a sea of humanity, they all seemed to be trying to shake the Siegfriedian oak leaf off their backs and plug the treacherous hiatus in their physical armor. Now, Eduard sometimes wished he were torturing himself like them.

His dreams were making him restive, becoming populated with unheralded encounters. Women whom he knew only vaguely or not at all bewildered him by brushing up against him or making passes. In one dream the boy with the billiard cue conducted him trustingly through the occupied apartment house. Seeing it from the inside, Eduard felt he'd been tricked and wondered if it was the right address. He suddenly grasped why the squatters had blocked every previous attempt to inspect it: the shabby façade was merely camouflage, the interior differed entirely from what the exterior implied. The rooms had been papered and provided with new parquet flooring, the pipes plastered over, the ceilings lovingly painted pink, green, and blue. He glimpsed marble bathrooms and Siemens kitchens. Behind a half-open door he caught sight of the woman from the bar. Attired in a bathrobe, she was standing with her back to him in front of an elaborate baroque mirror. Without turning around, she made a bored gesture of invitation to come closer. Hesitantly, he obeyed her summons. Just as he crossed the threshold she half turned, and one of her bare breasts popped out of the bathrobe. She stared at him coldly as if waiting for the sight to take effect and elicit an appropriate reaction.

Strange that Jenny wasn't among his nocturnal visitors. The producer of his dream plays had evidently barred her access to the stage, but why? The law of marital erotic attrition didn't apply to Eduard. It was odd that his desire for Jenny had never waned, perhaps because it had never been entirely assuaged. In his case an altogether different mechanism must be at work. But it's unsuitable for our performances, replied the imaginary producer of his nightly playlets, it's just too complicated. Our audiences are after entertainment, simple plots, instant gratification. We don't go in for Herculean tasks, they only alienate our season ticket holders.

But the populist's reply was no consolation. Didn't Jenny's tacit banishment from his dreams imply that he was secretly, behind his own back, beating a retreat? This was denied, quietly at first, then more and more audibly, but by whose voice, his own or Jenny's? You're always resentful, he seemed to hear her say, always imagining I've hurt you on purpose. You blame me for something that's happening to me quite as much as to you. You look for disposable causes and reasons—and all, of course, in the interests of my happiness. Why can't you get it into your head that *you're* missing something, not me? People who love each other don't make demands, they live and let live. If it's yourself and your deeply impugned virility you're worried about, give me a break. Prove yourself some other way . . .

He was jolted out of such soothing reflections by an E-mail from San Francisco.

"Hey Daddy, sorry I didn't write you for ages, but my darling kid brother keeps hogging the computer. War Games, hate it! It's real fun here, but today Mom grounded me for 2 days 'cos I came home at 6 o'clock. She thought that was late for some reason. Anyway, we

had German dictation in school today, but I don't think I messed it
up. Pretty easy. Right now Mom's at a PTA meeting and I'm lissen-
ing to the old Boyz 2 men cd real loud. I love their cd, that's why I
bought it. Well, guess I'll stop now. Can't wait to see ya. I hope
Mom'll become more normal sometime, she's always cursing and act-
ing nervous, we've all noticed it, not just me. We figure she misses
you, that's all. Bye for now, love Katharina."

Did he detect, amid his younger daughter's talk of German dictation and CDs, a distress call? After all, the little contretemps he was
trying to sort out between himself and Jenny couldn't be confined to
a double bed's forty-odd square feet. It was bound to have minor and
major repercussions in the wider vicinity. Wasn't it only logical that
Jenny should work off her disappointment in the bedroom beyond
its walls? All her assurances notwithstanding, didn't she nurse an
unacknowledged grudge against him?

As if it had happened only a few hours ago, he was revisited by a
mental picture of a scene he thought he'd long since forgiven and
forgotten—a public put-down and humiliation. At a dinner party
one night Jenny had launched a blitzkrieg, so to speak, initially on
some other men and then on him. She'd later blamed her loss of self-
control on overtiredness and two glasses of red wine on an empty
stomach. In fact, the immediate cause of her ferocious onslaught was
so trivial that only its consequences had lodged it in his memory:
one of the predominantly male gathering had addressed her as "Frau
Hoffmann." At that, Jenny had blown her top.

"Don't call me Hoffmann," she snapped. "My husband neglected
to introduce me properly yet again. My name is Jenny Valenti. All I
have in common with Herr Hoffmann is the fact that he's the father
of my children—their begetter and provider, to be more precise.
Ultimately, whether married or divorced, we're all single mothers."

Just wait, Eduard didn't say but thought with great intensity, go
on talking criminal nonsense and you'll discover what it really feels
like to be a single mother! Until now, only their immediate neighbors
at table had been enjoying this exchange. Whether or not Jenny was

momentarily puzzled by the silence that had fallen, she pursued her embarrassing theme undeterred. Indeed, the other guests' increasing interest redoubled her flow of words.

"I've always thought of you and Eduard as the ideal couple," said someone, and promptly bit his lip.

"Ideal if you think it's bliss to spend most of your nights with earplugs in your ears. The Almighty may have intended men and women to have fun together. He simply neglected to say how many times a year!"

Almost at once, the company's outward show of surprise yielded to barely disguised curiosity. What could be more titillating than the sight of a beautiful woman beside herself with rage! Eduard ordered two taxis, one for himself and one for Jenny. She got in beside him.

Eduard clutched the taxi's grab handle to quell the itch in his palm. Of course, he hissed, her fascinating revelations had been the whole point of the party. The guests had only turned up to hear her confession. That and that alone had been what they badly wanted her to confide—so badly that the whole gathering would now spend the rest of the evening debating what her outburst really signified and what Eduard, so memorably introduced as the begetter of their children, would be saying to his wife in private.

That same night he advised her to catch the next flight to Italy and go to stay with one of her four Valenti sisters or five Valenti uncles. Jenny concurred. She accepted banishment, but she couldn't grasp what had happened. "Forget all that nonsense about begetters and providers! Easier said than done, I know . . ." Her anger and aggression hadn't been directed at him, not for one moment. She'd wanted to light a squib under that tableful of conceited males and make them look ridiculous, but she'd been like a child that tries to tell a joke, completely forgets the essential lead-in before the punch line, and stares in consternation at the grownups' faces when they fail to laugh. "But still, it happened. I shouldn't drink red wine, that's all." She got out the phone book and looked up Alitalia's number.

Her contrition dissipated his anger. Under his gaze, the remorseful man-killer caught in flagrante turned back into an orphan child, a wild and dainty forest creature perched on a branch like some way-ward little monkey. Deserted by her father, neglected by her mother—so much for child-loving Italy! Eduard's chivalrous instincts were aroused. He decided, in the name of a knowledge he alone possessed, to endure his public humiliation and forgive her.

Now, after his daughter's distress call, he felt like an idiot—twice over, in fact. He should have let Jenny catch that plane. Hadn't she herself told him she hated men who sacrificed their pride for her sake? "If a man knuckles under, if he doesn't stand up for himself, it sets off an awful process inside me. I have to make him feel smaller and smaller until he becomes invisible!" He'd never related that confession to himself, perhaps because Jenny had assured him in the same breath that, discounting his other merits, she'd chosen him to be the father of her children on account of her inability ever to subject him to such treatment. Since then, however, he couldn't help wondering if he'd unwittingly shrunk a couple of sizes and was wearing things far too big for him. The conscious aversion Jenny expected him to tolerate was not only wearing him down but affecting his children. It sounded like a sad joke: if only as a responsible father, he had a duty to bring her relief.

Jenny didn't express herself in words. To her, perhaps because she obeyed the millennial dictates of her Italian ancestors, the spoken word was primarily a means of disguise, of playful provocation and deception. "For God's sake, why does everyone here always take what I say so literally?" When they were living in Germany she often seemed, to Eduard's horror, to want to set other people's alarm bells ringing. Her remarks were seldom prefaced by the introductory turns of phrase that warded off false applause. Eduard had vainly tried to make it clear that one couldn't utter certain words, which she used in all innocence, without putting them in quotes, for instance emotive nouns such as "heroism" or "pride" or phrases like "risking one's life for a cause." Jenny had never learned to insert these quotation marks or adopt the useful expedient of the two pairs of upraised fingers. Polite silences greeted her announcement that she refused to let her children grow up in a cowardly cultural environment imprinted with supine remorse and images of death. Jenny was against five-year-olds being indoctrinated by their toys with environmental protectionism and ten-year-olds confronted by photographs of Auschwitz. She held that children—and adults too, for that matter—had a right to good examples, to "heroes."

Eduard recognized Jenny better by her mute interventions than by her verbal thrusts and sallies. Once, shortly before he left America, the children had found a bird's nest in the backyard containing four chicks and their injured mother and brought it into the apartment. When the mother succumbed to her injuries Jenny took over. Eduard saw her sitting in the kitchen every morning, trickling specially prepared gruel into the gaping beaks of the four orphaned chicks, which were almost too young to cheep. He and the children were unwanted during this emergency feeding procedure. For a while it seemed that the chicks had accepted Jenny as their surrogate mother. Eduard and the children, too, were suddenly struck by her resemblance to a bird. Didn't she turn her long neck to and fro like a mother bird, and didn't she, too, utter avian noises while ministering to the little beaks? Her devotion to the orphaned chicks was eloquent of an identification impossible to choose for oneself.

In a book dealing with "sexual desire disorders" Eduard came across the following passage, which might have been addressed to him: "Being raped means that I cannot now relax enough to let go. I have to be in control at all times and will make every effort to divorce myself from a situation where I don't feel I have some control . . . I'm a control freak in my relationship." Didn't Jenny behave exactly like the patient who was speaking? Like a victim of rape?

The image of Jenny the adventuress wasn't the whole story. Sure, she was courageous, sometimes recklessly so. She would have risked her life for her children—and, probably, for a creed as well. Fifteen years earlier she might have been a candidate for a terrorist group provided it was led by a woman, not a man like Baader. But did her heroic armor conceal a wound whose existence she admitted to no one, not even herself, because she thought it irremediable? Where the potential causes of her sexual disinclination were concerned, dauntless Jenny became as sensitive as a dewdrop in sunlight. When he thought of all the reasons she advanced to portray it as a passing, temporary indisposition! A headache, too tired, pains in the gut, the children will be home from school any minute, I didn't think you wanted to . . . The problem remains, dearest Jenny, that all such respectable grounds for nonparticipation are common to couples everywhere. If they had the effect you ascribe to them, the world would be populated exclusively by unhappy women.

The more situations his memory adduced in evidence, the more certain he became: Jenny's behavior was consistent in every respect with the profile of a rape victim, a "survivor," as the textbook repulsively termed it. But where was the relevant trauma? Was there some secret she kept from him and herself? Did his Jenny, like the princess in Theo's fairy tale, live under the spell of some inimical spirit, a troll who had broken her will at some stage, perhaps in childhood, and whom she still unconsciously obeyed even when lying in his, Eduard's, arms? And did she fly back to the troll's cave at night, while he was asleep, if need be through closed windows, to join her guru and arm herself against her husband with new decapitatory riddles?

He wrote Jenny a letter in which he asked her, "if only for the children's sake," to abandon her game of hide-and-seek, break the evil spell with his help, and find a way out of the troll's cave. "Where I'm concerned," he wrote, "please don't imagine that my love for you will ever persuade me to become inured to the present state of affairs. I tell you this: even at eighty I'd sooner jump out of my wheelchair than spend the rest of my days with a woman who always evades me."

He photocopied the most important pages from the piece on "sexual desire disorders" and enclosed them. What he omitted was the following passage: "The survivor may confuse the partner with the perpetrator. In fact, survivors may often find themselves with partners who share similar characteristics with the perpetrator, especially when the latter was a parental figure."

8 IN THE MAIN BUILDING, the oldest part of the Institute, Eduard had discovered a subterranean snack bar he patronized whenever he wasn't feeling hungry at all. Ducking low to avoid ancient electric cables and gas and water pipes, you made your way through a maze of neon-lit passages, past superannuated desks and chairs, floor lamps and computers, and were surprised every time when the whitewashed entrance came into view. You ordered at the counter right outside the kitchen in which omelettes, grilled sausages, soups, and German hamburgers were prepared on an open range, or you helped yourself to one of the prepackaged egg-and-salami or roast beef sandwiches from the chilled cabinet with various salads in the refrigerator beside it. Then you lined up at the cash register, paid a paltry sum, and sat down in one of the rectangular, uncomfortable wooden booths in the side rooms. The daylight slanting down through the barred semibasement windows was outshone by the neon tubes.

It wasn't the low prices, still less the range of food on the menu, that attracted Eduard to the place. Prevailing down here were a language and a rhythm that differed from those of the world above. These people weren't compelled, for the sake of some higher purpose, to restrict their whims and desires to the weekend. They didn't shun physical contact, they sought it. "Embarrassing" wasn't in their vocabulary. They communicated by means of jokes, aphorisms, personal remarks. Speech didn't serve to communicate; words functioned as signals, as the distinguishing marks of some affiliation or other. Conversations subsisted on secondary sounds, on the laughter or abuse provoked by a gibe intelligible to insiders alone, on shoving and jostling and feigned apologies, on welcome or unwelcome advances.

The basement snack bar was the Institute's power station, the realm of in-house engineers, electricians, and plumbers, of secretaries, cleaning women, and security guards. Of the predominantly male doctors and professors ensconced in their whitewashed offices upstairs, most hailed from the West. Down here natives predominated, and they performed the duties necessary to keep the place in operation heedless of whether the people overhead were running a research institute, a secret-service headquarters, or a lunatic asylum. The Institute had its own motor pool, its own teams of bricklayers and electricians, its own fire department and its own experts on hardware and software problems. The building's electrical circuits had to be maintained, the daily leaks and fractures in the gas and water pipes repaired, the expensive electronic gadgets checked. As for the expensive scientists, it was possible that they were merely a pretext for the real purpose of everyone's activities: to ensure the establishment's survival.

Late one afternoon Eduard had been sitting in the library on his own, preparing for a lecture the same evening, when two men in Institute uniform marched in and started to arrange the chairs for his evening performance. They didn't think to lower their voices, nor did it occur to them that their conversation might disturb a solitary reader. If anyone in the library was being disruptive it was Eduard. There were some hundred and fifty unoccupied chairs in the room, but his was the first that had to be lined up. He sat down on other chairs, only to be politely but relentlessly obliged, again and again, to get up and sit somewhere else. That was when he first suspected that he and the other scientists here were only playing bit parts; the stars were the people who arranged the chairs.

Eduard was not the only scientist who found his way down to the basement snack bar. More and more often he encountered colleagues from the upper floors who divested themselves of their jackets and their studiously remote expressions and looked as if they were noticing each other for the first time.

Although he knew the way, or ought to have known it after so many visits, he often got lost in the subterranean labyrinth. He would come to a halt, peer along the tunnel ahead and behind, and wait for someone to direct him. One Friday afternoon he had to wait so long he grew uneasy. Had the snack bar already closed? He was hurriedly retracing his steps when he heard the crisp, curiously precise clickety-clack of footsteps. The sound was hard to locate, but he roamed the passageways in pursuit of its echo and suddenly found himself following a woman who couldn't have failed, in her turn, to hear him pursuing her. Her high heels brought her head perilously close to the roof of the tunnel. Although she didn't turn around, he thought he recognized her upright carriage and long strides. Two or three times in the upper regions he'd come across the unknown woman whose glance had so affected him that first day in the cafeteria, but there had been no repetition of their mutual scrutiny. The clickety-clack of her footsteps in the narrow passage, the accumulated heat, the gurgling of the pipes above his head—all these seemed to efface the time between then and now. He froze when the unknown woman abruptly halted, distressed by the thought that she'd sensed a pursuer behind her and meant to let him pass or give him an earful. But she hadn't stopped because of him. More amused than annoyed, she looked at the pipes above her, ran a hand over her hair and shook it as if a whole flock of birds had defecated on her head. Lodged in her dark curls were one or two threads and fragments of metal that shone like little silver stars. She must have brushed against one of the fuzzy excrescences that hung like stalactites from the burst insulation on an overhead pipe. Eduard had stopped just behind her, but she showed no sign of recognition. When she raised her head again and threw her hair back, a strand of it grazed his cheek. Simultaneously, her eyes met his.

"My hair okay?" she asked.

"Yes."

"Why say yes when you mean no?"

"Like me to defuzz you?"

She laughed, ran her hands over her padded shoulders, and turned. Eduard now saw all of her at disturbingly close range: the sturdy, black-stockinged legs, the short skirt drawn taut over a distinctly pneumatic posterior, the long back beneath the flowing jacket. She lifted her hair and presented her neck and collar for inspection. He discovered a few pale fibers on the collar of the jacket and quickly tweaked them off, reluctant to touch her for such a fortuitous reason.

"Thanks," she said, "but why apologize?"

"I did nothing of the kind," he said.

She had turned around again and was now looking at him judicially. Despite himself his gaze strayed to her breasts, which seemed to be regarding him from beneath her jacket like two hidden eyes. He was sure she'd noticed. Her violet lips were slightly parted as if about to add something or waiting for him to do so. Close above his head he could hear the rush of water, hear and smell the gas that was seeping along the narrower of the pipes, sense the perturbations in the numerous cables, the flux of all the subterranean forces that sped from one point to another whenever a faucet was turned on or a valve opened somewhere. The whole of the building's bulky frame seemed to breathe and vibrate. "Just a few fibers," he said. "Apart from that, you look charming. If we weren't so far below ground, I'd call you a gift from the gods." She didn't smile; in fact her expression was curiously grave. She seemed surprised but not alarmed. "That's not all you wanted to say, was it?" As if she could hear someone coming, she turned her head a little to give him another few seconds to respond. Her composure amazed him. She wasn't giving him the brush-off or evading him, just waiting to hear some more before she made up her mind.

"You attract me," said Eduard. "You've attracted me from the start, and I know we'd hit it off together."

"Quick, aren't you?" she said after a pause. "Sure you've dialed the right number?"

But there was no sarcasm in her expression. She seemed to be compiling an instant profile of this candidate from all the available data: voice, body language, dress, hands, eyes. Somehow, Eduard envied women their prognostic faculty. A man's intuition sufficed at best to picture the first night in bed together, whereas a woman, far quicker than any computer, could mentally spend whole years with an aspirant. If he failed the long-term test he didn't even rate a one-night stand.

"We might meet for dinner sometime," she said eventually.

Eduard was disappointed to note that the route he'd taken led out of the underground maze. Before leaving the office he switched on his computer again. His electronic mailbox held a vigorously worded communication from Jenny.

"I'm sorry," she'd written, "but I can't confirm your theory by producing a rape or some other childhood trauma from my sleeve, just to provide a handy explanation for us to work on. You act in general as if you're suffering from some unique and unbearable affliction. Make an effort—discuss the subject with a member of your own sex. You'll be amazed how many men will own up to the same problem—if they're honest. From what my women friends say, the figure must be around 50 percent. Men like to keep quiet about these things and imagine they're doing so for their partners' sake. In my opinion they're only thinking of themselves. A man who fails to satisfy his wife is regarded by other men as an ineffective member of the breed. That's why every man tends to hold a fig leaf over this blot on his married life and justify his secrecy by pleading the discretion he owes his wife. The truth is, he's scared of looking a failure in front of his friends.

"While we're on the subject, I'd like you to consider the mirror image of our problem. Just for fun, picture our situation with the roles reversed. In the United States alone, so I've read, the number of men who can't produce a satisfactory erection, or can't manage one at all, has been put at twenty million. How do women cope with their partners' 'erectile dysfunction'? There must be roughly the same number. Given that they're deprived of children as well as pleasure, don't they have far more valid grounds for complaint than you? Think of all the worldwide dramas, evasions, and lies, all the touching, desperate, tragicomic 'final attempts' of which one strangely hears nothing. Compared to the millions of women afflicted with impotent partners, you can think yourself lucky. As for that 'traveling companion' of yours, I suspect he knows nothing about women. The only thing he's grasped is that they want the men who aspire to conquer them to take risks—lethal ones if necessary. That apart, he's a frightful German boor. He may impress poor Johannes with his uncouth recipes for rescuing the princess from her fate, but there isn't a woman in the world who'd go for them. He seriously believes that Johannes can coerce his princess into happiness by grabbing her around the neck and dunking her. The bloodless spirit's oafish advice is just a means of retaining his power over Johannes, hadn't that ever occurred to you?

"Perhaps the princess genuinely does love Johannes after their wedding night, but the idiot simply won't believe it, so she obliges him by feigning an orgasm. After undergoing all the torments ordained by his traveling companion, she wants some peace at last. If you're looking for a guru, why not try a female traveling companion? In case of doubt, she'd know more about the problem."

9 EDUARD SHUNNED the snack bar for some days after his encounter in the basement passage and forbade himself to make inquries about the unknown woman. Then, quite suddenly, she materialized in his office. He always left the door open, American fashion, and must have failed to hear her knock. She evidently enjoyed surprising herself and others by making radical changes in her appearance. This time she seemed to be aiming at a low profile. She was wearing dark slacks, flat shoes, and a round-necked, coarse-meshed woolen sweater. Not a trace of lipstick or makeup; all that betrayed a skillful hand was the well-nigh imperceptible enhancement of her curving eyebrows. Undisguisable and untamable was her dark, curly hair, which looked phosphorescent.

"Doing anything tonight?" she asked.

"No so far. Any suggestions?"

"I'm eager to try an Italian restaurant that has just opened in Neu-Karow. Don't ask me how good the food is, the whole neighborhood's only three months old."

"So why eat there?"

"I like out-of-the-way places," she said. "I thought you might too."

Eduard refrained from telling her that he'd arranged to meet a hard-pressed American colleague who had insisted on taking a quick look at the remains of the Wall—"Sure, why not by night?"— on the eve of his departure for the States. He invented an excuse and left it in writing at the man's hotel. He'd only just heard that the city fathers, in their infinite wisdom, had had the last interesting section of the Wall demolished. Rumor had it that a true-to-scale replica was to be erected in Las Vegas, where he'd be glad to act as a guide when the opportunity arose.

Being used to the rush-hour traffic, he turned up half an hour early. Whatever lay behind the unknown woman's suggestion, the Palmetto was the strangest imaginable venue for a first assignation. Eduard stared incredulously at the blue neon sign, the two *T*s of which had been clumsily distorted into greenish-yellow palm trees. It was the one speck of light in a row of brand-new buildings, many of which were clearly still unoccupied. The muted strains of a Neapolitan melody were issuing from the restaurant. Seen beneath an infinity of clear, starry sky, the district looked like an experimental space station. Most of the windows were in darkness and had probably never been opened.

Eduard didn't feel like waiting inside. He looked around him, ejecting spurts of white breath into the gloom. If he didn't want to freeze he would have to move. One end of the street terminated in open countryside, the other in an American-style shopping mall. The sidewalk slabs still had to be cemented in position, and visible through the gaps between them were the remains of the field that was the only thing to be seen here a year ago. The trees had clearly been delivered by truck and planted not long before. They were staked to prevent them from falling over and encased in jackets designed to protect them from collisions with cars and bulldozers, and perhaps from the cold as well.

It wasn't an ugly complex. The architects seemed to have tried to display as much variety as a mass-produced, prefabricated urban district had to offer. True, one could tell even at second glance that the colors, window shapes, and angular or rounded ends of the buildings were varied in accordance with a pattern relentlessly laid down in the minutest detail. The front doors were pale brown, the façades egg-yolk yellow, the second-floor apartments in every building provided with a balcony, the third-floor with an oriel. Every other second-floor window was round-arched, the windows on either side were rectangular, the central sections projected, the lateral sections were set back. Compared to the suburbs of the 1950s and 1960s these variations looked positively frivolous. But the impression of greater vivacity and individuality was merely the product of an advanced technology that made it possible to mass-produce an illusion of anarchy.

He heard voices nearby. Three youngsters were standing around a brand-new, marble-faced municipal toilet, reading out the instructions in thick Berlin accents. It cost one mark to enter the facility, and a notice in four languages detailed the actions to be read, understood, and performed before one was privileged to lift the seat.

"Go on, get in there."

"But I don't need to."

"Never mind that, get in there."

"Not me."

"What's the matter, scared?"

"Some guy got stuck inside one of these things, spent half the night in there."

"Sure, he was having so much fun, that's why. The seat's heated, honest. Even your ass gets wiped automatically—showered to start with, then blow-dried."

"Okay, lend me a mark?"

Eduard couldn't make out the face behind the tinted windows of the speeding Alfa Romeo, but he waved just in case. She skidded to a halt, reversed just as fast, and opened the passenger door.

"You look frozen," she said.

"This is the most ridiculous rendezvous I've ever kept. We might as well have met at the North Pole."

"Good idea for the next time. Anyway, what's so bad about it? A place without a past or a present, only a future—could be just the ticket for you and me. Besides, I'm bored by stylish restaurants where the maître d' and the decor set the tone. Here I'll be entirely dependent on you."

"Do all your new acquaintances have to pass an endurance test? What's your name, by the way?"

"Marina."

Up to door height Marina's choice resembled a fishermen's restaurant in Rimini, above it a ski lodge in the Carpathians. The mustachioed waiter looked disconcerted when Eduard asked him for a table in Italian. Eduard couldn't associate the broken German in which the man replied with any country he knew of. He obviously couldn't expect to get any *spaghetti al dente* here.

Marina made no attempt to enlighten him on the singular establishment, but she, at least, was charmed by it. She suffered the waiter to take her coat and shepherd her across the almost deserted restaurant to the table by the window. Clotheswise, she had changed the program yet again. She was on display. Her black stockings were surmounted by a startlingly short velvet skirt, a skintight top, and an open jacket in some iridescent mixture of man-made fibers. Marina, the glittering apparition . . . The woman Eduard followed to the table was one who knew—and didn't mind the fact—that any man walking behind her was momentarily robbed of his reason by the interplay between flowing fabric and swaying hips. He was determined not to ruin the powerful attraction she'd exerted on him from the first by making any half-baked advances. Her choice of a rendezvous half an hour's drive from the nearest available bed was probably deliberate.

"Was that a Russian accent?" he asked while she was studying the menue.

"No idea," she said. "Why do you ask?"

"I thought you might have learned Russian."

"What gave you that idea? Your Russian is probably better than mine."

Although this had really exhausted the unproductive subject, something seemed to be bothering her, so she reverted to it.

"You take me for someone who grew up and went to school here?"

"Would that be an insult?"

"Not at all, but what made you think so?"

"*Did* you grow up here?"

The look on her face intimated that the answer was self-evident, or that she preferred to leave the question open. "Does it matter? Perhaps it does. Do you associate something specific with an East German woman, something a West German woman doesn't have?"

"Like what?"

"That she's somehow more feminine, more straightforward, less tricky, easier to handle. All the things a Westerner associates with the East. That camels walk slower, smoke rises differently, alarm clocks go off later or not at all, children are better behaved, women wear higher heels . . ."

"You like wearing high heels, that's all I know."

"At least you know something about me."

Although he'd formed no definite opinion up to now, her questions proved to him that he really had thought she came from the East. He couldn't have said why, or rather, he could have said it and probably made a fool of himself. Above all, he didn't know which was the bigger gaffe: mistaking a West German woman for an East German woman or vice versa. On his guard now, he deemed it wiser not breathe a word about the inadequately chilled rosé. He took big, hurried gulps of it, unable to tell if he found it delicious purely because he'd forbidden himself to be revolted by it.

"You remind me of a woman I missed by a split second," he said. "And it was forever."

"Does that often happen to you?"

"It wasn't my fault. A friend of mine was quicker off the mark."

"You don't strike me as slow. Tell me about it."

It had happened at a biologists' symposium in Canada. They'd spent almost a whole week cloistered at a hotel in the depths of a forest. During that time Eduard had made friends with a Peruvian colleague whose brilliant but tormented personality had attracted his attention. Manuel's mood changed almost hourly: sometimes he felt confident of a Nobel Prize, sometimes of a final descent into insanity, and he held those moods in balance with an infectious sense of humor.

The final session took place in Montreal, whither they were transported by bus. On boarding the vehicle they were simultaneously transfixed by a vision: a young woman the sight of whom was almost unendurable after their days of seclusion in the forest. Neither of them could imagine what had stranded such a glorious creature in such a remote place. Eduard, who had instantly noticed that the place beside her was unoccupied, was about to take it when Manuel's bag sailed past his shoulder and landed beside the lady, to be followed a moment later by its seemingly exhausted owner, who flopped down on the stolen seat as if it had been reserved for him weeks ago. Eduard had no choice but to make do with a seat on the other side of the aisle. The bus had only just moved off when Manuel, so vague as a rule, resolutely made the most of his location. It took him only a few minutes to dispel the unknown girl's forbidding air and make her laugh. Hesitant at first, then more and more unrestrained, the longer her laughter went on the more it aroused an irresistible urge to know what was causing it.

Actually, said Eduard, laughter wasn't the word for it. What Manuel unleashed in his still-unknown companion was a tempest, a cataclysm, an eruption of mirth that began by convulsing her face, gradually encompassed her whole body, and set off one paroxysm after another. At first she laughed with her shoulders and breasts alone, then with her pelvis. She braced the tips of her toes against the floor in an attempt to steady herself and used a succession of handkerchiefs to staunch the tears of laughter that ran down her cheeks in rivulets, black with mascara. In the end, everything was out of kilter: her pinned-up hair straggled over her eyes, her teeth were smeared with lipstick, her face and hands looked as if she'd just emerged from a coal mine. When they reached their destination barely an hour later, the austere beauty was utterly transformed. Still crimson-cheeked and fighting for breath, she said goodbye to Manuel, embraced him passionately, and thrust a slip of paper into his hand.

The bus journey had wrought a transformation in Manuel as well. He informed Eduard, in all seriousness, that he had just made the acquaintance and decision of a lifetime: he was going to move into the unknown girl's apartment that very day and spend the rest of his life there. He wouldn't become Peru's president or leading terrorist. Instead of returning home he was going to send a heartless telegram to his wife and children, who were supposed to meet him at the airport the next day. There were moments that determined the whole course of one's existence. Most people let such moments slip, not because they never encountered them, but because they weren't decisive enough.

Marina's expression conveyed that Eduard had omitted a crucial part of the story.

"Well, what became of the courageous couple?"

"I never heard from them again. Do you think such things really happen: you meet someone, gaze into their eyes, and your whole life changes?"

"I'd much rather know how your friend managed to make the girl laugh so much," said Marina, regarding him expectantly. Her violet lips parted a little in readiness to laugh. Eduard suddenly felt that the rest of the evening depended on whether he could conjure it up, that irresistibly hilarious story. He thought hard, dredged his memory, but no, he was caught in a trap of his own making.

"I'm sorry," he said at length, "I'll have to pass. Besides, the element of surprise would be missing. I'd only disappoint you."

"Better not try, then," she said simply.

Strange, though: the ensuing pause wasn't awkward in the least. Marina continued to look at him with the beginnings of laughter in her eyes, but she didn't seem disappointed that he wasn't giving her the smallest ground for amusement. On the contrary, this sudden, disastrous anticlimax had made her more curious than anything else.

"Know something?" she said. "If your friend really did meet up with this woman of a lifetime, he'd have looked just as sheepish as you're looking now."

"What makes you think so?"

"Well, let's theorize and take the story a little further. Let's assume that Manuel met his laughing lady that night. In a bar."

"At her apartment," Eduard cut in.

"Unlikely, but still. First of all, how did the pair of them look? What was their state of mind when they met up again? She'd calmed down, showered, changed, repaired her makeup. What about him?"

"He'd still be carrying that stupid Peruvian shoulder bag of his. He'd also have sunk five tequilas by that time."

"That she wouldn't mind, but what else? He couldn't gladden her heart with another funny story; the surprise factor would be missing, as you say. So what next? Would he tell her about the telegram to his wife and three kids, if he'd sent one?"

"Why three? Did I say three?"

"Five, then. If you wanted to win over a woman, would you tell her about your wife and five children?"

"Hardly!"

"In that case, what?"

"He'd tell her he was close to curing humanity of impotence, multiple sclerosis, and AIDS."

"That wouldn't interest her particularly."

"So what would?"

"She'd be itching to know how this man with the shoulder bag, the one who'd made her laugh so beautifully, would set about seducing her."

Having donned their overcoats and left the Palmetto, they lingered for a long time in the glare of a brand-new streetlight. The pastel façades glimmered against the inky sky like huge monitors, switched on but blank. He showed her how their breath rose into the air like pillars, unraveled in the white light, became entwined, and finally dissolved. He saw something glitter in her curls as if a few particles of insulation from the basement passage were still lodged there, and, with a reflex gesture weeks in arrears, ran his hand over her hair. She quickly averted her head when he tried to kiss her, but she didn't reject his embrace and gently thrust her crotch against his. When they walked on she suddenly turned and kissed him on the mouth, bit his lower lip.

That night they each got into their cars and drove home separately. But their affair was already under way. Perhaps when he'd failed to account for the unknown girl's laughter in the bus, or possibly earlier still, in the rain of dust from the pipe on the basement ceiling, they had developed an almost violent mutual curiosity that no "See you around sometime!" could have assuaged.

Marina avoided meeting him at the Institute in the weeks that followed. They usually arranged to meet in haste, with little advance notice, and always at a different secluded rendezvous. Marina seemed not to want them to be recognized, even by strangers.

She was moody, capricious, hard to please. Once aroused, however, her passions were unbridled. They were enchanted with each other, with the easy, innocent way they communicated and coordinated their desires. Wordlessly, almost without a sign, they divined each other's favorite evolutions like a couple treading the dance floor together for the first time and instantly performing the most complicated tango steps. He was disconcerted, even slightly shocked, when Marina embarked on her first solo performance. Once she'd attained a certain voltage she ceased to heed him anymore. Borne away on the wings of her preliminary orgasm, she left him trailing and soared off into the blue. Somewhere out there in her own orbit she moaned and bellowed her exultation at the cosmos so loudly that Eduard, who knew that the cosmos had walls, debated whether their vigilant neighbors, depending on their conception of what was happening, would call a patrol car or an ambulance. The first time he heard Marina's mighty cry of pleasure he almost fell out of bed. After that initial shock he'd been smitten with positive nostalgia for the quieter delights of Jenny's bed, muted by consideration for childish ears. And although he promptly allowed himself to be carried away once more by Marina's typhoons of lust, he'd been briefly disturbed by a thoroughly inappropriate thought. Could it be that, quite coincidentally, the well-meaning angel who had put Marina in his path had histrionic tendencies? Erotically speaking, the woman he'd been sent pursued a course diametrically opposed to his own. He once told Marina that he felt like a ground station whose only function was to launch a rocket which, once it achieved liftoff, blithely ignored all signals from earth and made for its own destination in space. Marina had merely laughed, tickled by the analogy. She was like that.

But such irritations were soon forgotten. Their place was taken by gratitude. What bliss it was not to feel indebted to a woman. Not to feel too heavy, too clumsy, too hasty, too late. Not to have to entertain the most ludicrous of all male self-doubts, questions which the incorrigible cerebrum kept raising even though it had long been proved how harmful they were. Nothing chafed, nothing pinched. Limbs and bones found their junction points with ease and clicked gently into place. He sensed the smooth descent and touchdown of the body-ship after its intoxicating flight, the postcoital prickle in the veins, and relished the long-lasting moment thereafter.

What he had lacked most in previous years, perhaps, was this feeling of serenity. Whether or not he imagined it, Jenny's body had always seemed to be transmitting a demand he failed to meet. It was this physical state of alert that Marina consigned to oblivion. Suddenly everything was light and buoyant, body and conscience alike.

He sensed at the same time that Marina was seeking a suggestion, a form of words that would define the transitional nature of their meetings. "An affair without a past, without a future. The present is all there is . . ." He had told her about Jenny and the three children right at the outset, and her quarrel was more with herself than with him. "I promised myself I'd never get involved with a married man, let alone one with children." She declared that they must part, but first she tried to devise a temporary formula that would guard against false hopes.

"You're my in-between man. I'm using you just the way you're using me. I'll make a platonic friend of you sooner than you think. It'll be me that gives you your marching orders, not the other way around. I'll tell you when the time comes. By the way, if you know someone who's free and would fit into my life better than you, please introduce us."

10 NIESSLING? It wasn't until the unfamiliar voice on the phone mentioned Klott that Eduard recalled the latter's forewarning. Niessling was the prospective purchaser, the man who'd made a fortune out of designer kitchens in East Berlin after the Wall came down. He had to hold the receiver a hand's-breadth from his ear. The voice at the other end of the line was several decibels too loud, like the voice-over for a TV commercial. Furthermore, Niessling seemed obsessively reluctant to let Eduard get a word in, possibly motivated by a salesman's fear of those silences in which the customer makes a final attempt to weigh things up before coming to a momentous decision. Even the question of where and when to meet spawned so many suggestions that Eduard had no chance to ponder them or reply. "If it's okay with you, I'll send my chauffeur to pick you up right away," Niessling offered. And, when Eduard hesitated, "Or would you prefer me to fetch you in my private chopper? Provided there's a landing pad on your roof, of course!"

Eduard laughed. "A helicopter would be just the thing for a preliminary inspection. I'm sure Herr Mattenklott told you how difficult it is to get into the building."

"Don't worry, I can get into any building. You have to strike the right note, that's all."

"Meaning what?"

"I've got a genuine East German admiral working for me. When the GDR was still a going concern he had eighteen thousand men under him. They've all disbanded, but the admiral's still in command—of my customers. He's my top salesman. A man with natural authority. Even you would click your heels if he marched into your kitchen and said 'Here's what we're going to do!' Old ladies or squatters—they're all easy meat to him."

"Your admiral won't get anywhere with *my* squatters," Eduard replied. "I suspect a large proportion of them are draft dodgers."

"No problem, I've got an ex-squatter on my team as well. He isn't as good a salesman as the admiral, but he knows the ropes. He's handy with his fists, too. I'd better bring them both, the admiral and the squatter. Let's go there right away. Surprise is the grandmother of success, that's my motto. Be with you in ten minutes."

Eduard was getting hot under the collar. "Ten minutes? Impossible, I'm afraid."

"Why impossible? The realty market never closes."

"Precisely. I've got an appointment with another interested party."

"Are you sure? Who is it?"

"I can't tell you that."

"It wouldn't by any chance be a Dortmund conglomerate by the name of ZIAG?"

"How did you know?"

"I don't want to jump the gun, but I'd strongly advise you not to do business with them. They're tax evaders, been convicted more than once. They'll sign a binder and then renege on it."

"And you?"

"I always come armed with cash. Want to see it? I can drop in right away."

Eduard fixed an appointment for the weekend. As soon as he hung up he reproached himself for indulging in the luxury of this delay. He urgently needed some money to remedy the debit balance on his bank statement. His only reason for withstanding the temptation was Niessling's voice. He simply couldn't have borne to hear it in his apartment ten minutes later.

For form's sake he sent the squatters a registered letter informing them of the forthcoming inspection, not that he had any illusions about its effect. On Saturday the designer-kitchen tycoon appeared on his doorstep half an hour before the appointed time. A man of his own age, a living enigma, he seemed to belong to an unknown human species. Either Eduard had overlooked that species during his Berlin years, or it had settled in the city thereafter: a cross between a pimp and an advocate of the alternative lifestyle. Niessling wore pointed snakeskin bootees, a suit of some iridescent silk-and-linen mixture, and, under the jacket, a collarless black shirt. His long, straggly hair, which sprouted from the periphery of an otherwise bald cranium, was gathered into a ponytail. His Bermuda tan seemed to have been applied with a thick brush, and the large, slightly projecting teeth in his prognathous lower jaw were bared in a permanent grin. No sooner had he entered Eduard's living room than he deposited his leather briefcase on the table, snapped open the catches with a click which, to judge by his tongue movement, he considered erotic, and displayed the contents: nothing but red-banded wads of thousand-mark bills. "This is for starters, no receipt required. A straightforward, one-to-one transaction! Start every deal with a bang, that's my motto. The feel-good factor helps you cope with any problems that crop up later on."

Eduard had never seen so much hard cash before, but he didn't show it.

"Thirty-five thousand, tax-free," Niessling pursued. "Count it."

"What am I supposed to do with it?" Eduard asked, but he couldn't banish a mental picture of his latest bank statement. He had to ask several questions—superfluous ones, the kitchen supremo intimated—before he grasped what was meant by a "one-to-one transaction." Niessling was trying to play him off against Klott, his friend and attorney. He aimed to cheat Klott out of his legitimate commission by paying Eduard an estimated half of it in cash, the proviso being that the buyer and seller dealt direct, without resort to a middleman.

Eduard concealed his distaste. He shut the briefcase with a careless gesture, as if to convey that it ought to contain many more wads of money. "Very nice," he said, "but where are this admiral and ex-squatter of yours?"

"Waiting downstairs in the car."

"All right, let's start by taking a look at the building. I wouldn't buy a kitchen from you without seeing it first."

"That's just where you're wrong!" Niessling retorted with a grin. "Still, suit yourself. What about the cash?"

"Better take it with us," said Eduard.

Later on, when the inspection had set off a chain reaction that threatened to destroy him, Eduard wondered why he hadn't yielded to his initial impulse and kicked the man out right away. Had he suppressed his repugnance so as not to betray his inexperience of the world of real estate transactions? If everyone in a particular line of business disgusts you, you may as well deal with anyone—had that been his crass guiding principle, or had his instincts been blunted by the prospect of easy money?

There were plenty of warning signs even during the drive. The two men at the rear of the armor-plated BMW were quite unlike Niessling's descriptions of them. They sported dark blue bomber jackets and Basque berets. The elder of the two, who sat there with his chest stuck out and greeted Eduard with a curt nod, might in a pinch have passed for a former naval officer. The younger, with his shaved head and butcher's paws, looked like one of those TV wrestlers whose appearance made Eduard reach instinctively for the zapper. If the man had ever strayed into a squat, his only function there could have been to shift furniture or run training courses in unarmed combat.

On the way to Rigaer Strasse Niessling bombarded Eduard with an account of his East–West adventures. How had he built up his empire from scratch in the few years since unification? Used cars? Everyone thought of that idea. No, designer kitchens! Kitchenwise, the former GDR was third-world territory. Niessling didn't stop to ask if Eduard wanted to hear his recipe for success, he gave it to him anyway. "What did the GDR kitchen look like after forty years of socialism? What did it contain? A potentially explosive manually ignited gas stove without an extractor hood, a refrigerator just big enough to chill a couple of bottles of beer, a rusty sink with a dripping faucet. Thermostatic controls, integral working surfaces, deep-freeze compartments, ceramic chopping boards, revolving cupboards, built-in dishwashers? Unknown quantities! But those were just the long-denied luxuries people wanted. Free elections—okay, fair enough, but do you know what reunification meant to the average consumer? A designer kitchen! The electronic ticking of the automatic ignition when the gas is turned on, the hum of the dishwasher, the green glow of the digital clock that looks after the chicken in the oven! And plenty of people, especially the old folk, had a few thousand marks in the bank. They'd saved all their lives because they didn't know what to do with their money—there was nothing to buy but junk in any case. Then came monetary union and the one-for-one exchange, and suddenly their savings were worth something. They weren't enough for an apartment, still less a house, but just enough for a designer kitchen. And now comes the psychological part. Nobody really needs a designer kitchen. The salesman knows that, the customers know that too. But the salesman also knows that the customers don't want to know what they know; they want to be convinced of their need for a designer kitchen. That's where the salesman starts showing off his paces, his talent, his skill, because a kitchen fitter doesn't just sell kitchens. He knows he must first sell the customer something else: a new world, a new approach to life. Unless he does that, he won't even unload a mixer. How does he do it? You won't believe me, but I swear to you, as true as I'm sitting here in my BMW and driving through a red light, I was a lifelong stutterer. I only got rid of that disability after reunification, as a kitchen salesman in the new provinces. I've become a star salesman, a customer seducer, a guru. I give lectures, run training courses— even competitors seek my advice. A kitchen salesman, I tell my people, can't choose his customers for their beauty. Most of the women he has to deal with are old and lonely. They're smart but still open to seduction. They won't be bluffed by charm, only by authority. By firmness. I go into an apartment and cast an eye at the kitchen—an expert eye. I get the lady to show me her gas stove, I inspect the refrigerator and listen to the motor. I make no comment. Instead, I run my finger along a shelf—without thinking, as it were—and look surprised at the dust on my fingertip. I hold it up to the light in disbelief. Even if there isn't a speck of dust on it I convey that only my customer's aging eyes would miss it. That's where the deal begins. The lady's rattled. She apologizes and I forgive her. I turn the gas on and off, slam the cupboard doors, look up at the dim overhead light and shake my head pityingly. You mean you've had no accidents here for thirty years? You've been very lucky! The successful salesman doesn't sell, he promises salvation. I now detail the overdue steps to be taken to renovate the entire kitchen. A kitchen is an apartment's visiting card; it must not only function but satisfy the aesthetic sense. Now comes the most ticklish part: finance. I can't accept credit cards, of course. Who knows if they're covered? Besides, addresses are in chaos in the East, streets are being renamed every day and the customers are often pensioners or unemployed. Only cash will do, 50 percent down and the balance on delivery. There's often a hitch with the second installment. That's when you have to bring on the heavies. The sight of them usually does the trick."

Niessling gestured vaguely over his shoulder. Eduard wondered later why he hadn't asked the man to stop and let him out. Instead, he merely eyed him askance with mute revulsion and allowed him to conclude his lecture with an aphorism: "Nine out of ten people are born to be fleeced."

The building on Rigaer Strasse had acquired some new graffiti since Eduard's last visit. Most of the frontage had been painted and oversprayed in a variety of colors. The shutters were down not only on the second floor but on the third as well, as if the squatters feared an assault with scaling ladders.

When Niessling and his men got out of the BMW, Eduard felt in his bones that some disaster was imminent. They didn't waste time surveying the place, they marched straight up to the metal door and hammered on it with their fists. Nothing stirred, so they proceeded to kick it.

"What do you think you're doing?" Eduard shouted. "This place doesn't belong to you. I never said you could—"

"You don't understand these things," Niessling retorted calmly. "They don't teach them in your trade. Stand clear!"

The admiral shouldered Eduard aside; the younger man took a run and hurled his bulk at the door. It opened at the fourth or fifth attempt, only to close at once behind a figure with an unmistakably rounded belly and a cell phone in its hand. The woman from the bar! Eduard was torn between shame and admiration. Alone and unarmed with anything save the insignia of burgeoning life, she was confronting the intruders' brute force while her militia remained, for the moment at least, in reserve behind the door. Niessling and his assistants, too, were not immune to the effect of this apparition.

"You're trespassing," she said in a businesslike, clearly audible voice. "I'm calling the police—they'll be here in two minutes flat."

The admiral wavered, the thug awaited instructions. Niessling's derisive laughter sounded unconvincing. "You're the one who's trespassing!" he bellowed. "You've no right to be living here!" But that was the extent of his ingenuity. He looked and listened in disbelief as the young woman dialed an obviously familiar number, gave her name as Vera Rheinland, reported "a breach of the peace" on Rigaer Strasse, and accurately described the four guilty parties.

Silence ensued. No one knew what to do. Frau Rheinland, who continued to stand there calmly, was already engrossed in another phone call. Niessling swore to himself. "Squatters accusing the owners of creating a disturbance? That takes the cake!" The admiral stood straight as a ramrod, like a man in a trance; the bully boy seemed to be awaiting orders. Eduard, whose dearest wish was simply to disappear, felt compelled to await the arrival of the police with the others. The windows were now thronged with squatters. "Hey, Schwarzenegger, show us your pecs!" someone yelled. "Come on in, we'll give you a workout!" Niessling commanded his men not to be provoked. Someone else tipped a pail of water, or something worse, out of a window. Vera Rheinland made a gesture indicating that such frivolities must cease. Everyone waited for the patrol car to arrive.

By the time the Wartburg with the flashing blue carbuncle on its roof turned onto Rigaer Strasse, the situation seemed to Eduard to have been defused merely by the delay. The patrol car disgorged the unforgettable duo familiar to Eduard from his visits to the police station, the dream team from a German cops-and-robbers series still to be made. Out of the driver's door sprang the athletic superior from victorious West Germany; out of the passenger door scrambled the elderly East German of junior rank. The younger man left it to the elder to make inquiries. The latter addressed himself to Frau Rheinland in a fatherly tone. She explained in legally proficient language that the self-styled landlord, who had already drawn attention to himself more than once, had attempted with the help of a gang of toughs to break down the door and force an entry. Niessling stepped in. The so-called gang of toughs consisted, he said, of the owner of the building, Eduard Hoffmann, plus himself, Rolf Niessling, a businessman, and two of his employees. Abruptly, he struck a comradely note and lapsed into broad Berlinerish.

"Look, what's the problem, my friend? It's an internationally accepted custom to inspect a building before you buy it. Friedrichshain or Charlottenburg, exactly the same goes for both."

But his Berlin dialect proved a definite misjudgment. The investigating officer responded in standard German, loud and clear.

"Did you give advance notice of your visit?"

"Herr Hoffmann and I wrote three times," lied Niessling. "I can show you copies."

"That's a lie, of course," Frau Rheinland declared, just as stoutly. "We never received one communication, let alone—"

"But this isn't a regular address," Niessling cut in. "There isn't even a mailbox here!"

At a loss, the investigating officer conferred with his superior. The latter, with an air of detachment, had been standing beside the driver's door throughout, seemingly engaged in deciphering the slogans and symbols on the front of the building. His manner was more that of a philologist or field researcher than a policeman. "Permit me to suggest a compromise," he ventured, looking at Frau Rheinland. "This building will be inspected a week from today at 1700 hours precisely. And now push off, the lot of you."

Niessling nodded, Eduard nodded. Coolly ignoring them, Vera Rheinland turned on her heel. One or two squatters applauded. The senior police officer got back behind the wheel of the Wartburg, waited for his fat subordinate to join him, and roared off, blue light flashing. It was all over now, no winners, no losers. The howl of derision and triumph from the upper windows was predictable and tolerable.

Eduard swiftly crossed to the other side of the street. The last thing he wanted was to wait for his frightful companions or bid them goodbye, still less be driven home by them; his one desire was to walk away without looking back. Except that there were these noises behind him. Superimposed on the hum of the moderately busy street, they grew louder and louder: thuds, groans, yells—the din of battle. He halted, keeping his back toward the developments he still perceived only as a soundtrack, as if that would dissociate him from them. Turning, he saw that Vera Rheinland had disappeared. The metal door was wide open, and in front of it, barely distinguishable by their clothing, several men were belaboring each other with a variety of weapons: cudgels, iron bars, blackjacks. Clearly, some of the squatters had been just as reluctant to accept the policeman's ruling as Niessling's men. Three or four of them must have sallied out the door and fallen on the kitchen tycoon's bodyguards. Nothing to do with me, thought Eduard, let them beat each other's brains out, just walk on and don't look back. But, even as he did so, he caught a glimpse of a frail, undersized figure wielding a stick—a mere scrap of humanity. What on earth was *he* doing there? Eduard felt a sort of knife thrust in the chest on recognizing the boy with the shock of fair hair. What are you doing in the midst of those savages, those dogs of war? This isn't a fairy tale or a video, boy, get out of there! Drop that stick and go inside, the door's open. You don't have to prove anything, find yourself another initiation rite!

But the boy was the most courageous, most adventurous, of all the squatters. In an incomprehensible moment of concentration, almost of deliberation, he raised the broken billiard cue and brought it down hard on the muscle-bound thug's head. Quick as a flash the man seized his arm, spun him around, and drove an adult knee into his childish back. Stop that, stop it at once, that's enough, more than enough, there must be a way of stopping the clock between that blow and the next, it's impossible that so much irreparable harm can be done in so short a time! Stop it, can't you see he's a mere child, a twelve-year-old? Help him, someone! Help, murder, police! Eduard was shouting in a voice he didn't recognize. But the absurd, still stoppable process refused to stop. Unimpeded by his shouts, it simply took its course, insisted on unfolding from one second to the next. The street still lay between Eduard and the madman on the other side. How long would it take to cross? Far too long, five seconds are an eternity to a raging thug. With terrible clarity, with the avid magnification of a telephoto lens, Eduard saw the boy's head fly back, saw his body fold up as if it lacked a spinal column, saw the man's boots thud into his head as he lay on the ground, once, twice, many times, saw the handsome young face, now smeared with blood, jerk back and forth under the blows like a doll's head coming loose from its neck.

All this had happened before Eduard hurled himself at the hulking brute and wrapped his arms around him, before his face was clawed by fleshy fingers, before they both crashed to the ground, before his opponent broke free with a head butt, regained his feet, and fended off the squatters with a series of wild roundhouse punches. Eduard saw the dancing, trampling boots close to his head. Then he saw them disappear into the back of the BMW, which had pulled up beside the curb and promptly roared off again. He scrambled to his feet and ran for his life from the squatters' flailing fists and cudgels, conscious as he ran that all that happened from now on would belong to another time.

Somehow he got to the police station and made a statement there describing his own actions and those of the perpetrator. The trembling in his hands and knees persisted until he was on the S-Bahn and several stations down the line. Heedless of his orders, an internal projector kept replaying the sequence in slow motion, freeze-framing some shots, zooming in on others. It falsified the essential element, the speed of the original incident. In reality, everything had happened so fast, it almost seemed that nothing had happened at all.

11 EDUARD AVOIDED LOOKING at the other passengers, whose curiosity or suspicion clearly dated from the moment when he'd gripped his trembling knees with hands like steel cramps. Outside at eye level, looking absurdly incongruous, he saw a motorcycle mounted on the roof of a used-car showroom. A few hundred yards down the track they passed the site of the city's open-heart surgery with the skeleton of the Reichstag building some distance away. Close at hand, the huge, yellowish-white expanses of sand in the center of the city were interspersed with mounds of gravel, yellow dump trucks, stacks of steel girders, and the powerful floodlights that illuminated everything. A passing train briefly dissolved those images into a vortex of whirling specks of light. Then, when his eyes had reaccustomed themselves to the construction sites gliding past, he saw the city's body laid open like that of a patient on a gigantic, brightly lit operating table. Dark, stagnant fluids had oozed out everywhere to form lakes on which bulky construction plants floated amid ice floes. Seemingly airborne surgeons bent over the lifeless body with eyes and instruments, probing the wound with remote-controlled arms, curetting it, making room for new organs, new sinews and arteries. Seated high above the open body or before their monitors in distant, darkened rooms, these unseen surgeons searched for the hidden tumors that had to be removed before the new heart could be implanted. For the doomed body was riddled with encapsulated or dormant tumors. Diagnostic instruments daily came across new deposits and obstructions that made headlines people scarcely troubled to read anymore. Hitler's bunker had been demolished after the war, but its concrete foundations and outer walls still existed. So, nearby, did the Führer's garage bunker with its "folkish" murals and half the big Reich Chancellery bunker, likewise the air-raid shelters of the Foreign Office, the Ministry of Food and Agriculture, the Hotel Adlon, and Propaganda Minister Goebbels, the latter soon to have a Holocaust memorial superimposed on it. Lastly, there was the monitoring shaft the CIA had driven a hundred yards into GDR territory during the Cold War. There were permanently employed as well as unofficial speleologists who explored these extensive tunnels beneath the center of the city. What heart would be inserted in this chest and start beating within it, and what life-form would it awaken?

From behind Eduard's back there came, softly to begin with but steadily increasing in volume until it filled the whole car, a startling sound: someone was singing. Standing at the far end was a gaunt, white-bearded man in the threadbare military greatcoat of the army that had once entered Berlin victorious and left it defeated. He sounded at first like an opera singer practicing his morning scales, but the notes gradually combined to form a sustained melody. A lover's song or a true believer's prayer? A derelict's lament, perhaps.

Although Eduard couldn't understand the words, the beggar's bari-tone was so fine and so powerful it brought tears to his eyes. Under the aegis of the song he had a renewed vision of the boy falling back-ward as if poleaxed, and now knew for sure that the incident had really occurred.

He had to wait in Klott's outer office for half an hour before being admitted. Having described what had happened as briefly as pos-sible, he informed Klott of his decision: he was going to renounce his inheritance, no matter what the expense, and go home to San Francisco.

"You really must watch your step," said Klott. "Giving way to panic like this could land you in real trouble." The deadline for renunciation had expired long ago, Eduard knew that perfectly well. Legally, he and his brother were the owners. "Going home" would be construed as absconding.

Even more important, said Klott, was the moral aspect of the mat-ter. If he knew him, Eduard would be unable to live with the image of a greedy reunification profiteer who had indirectly caused the death of a child and then disappeared. Eduard must face the music and prevail. He hadn't done anything very wrong to date. He had at least done his best—any judge would respect that—to stop the fra-cas. Nobody could reproach him for not being the possessor of a black belt.

Eduard said nothing. It suddenly seemed to him that the most obvious result of Klott's gluttony was a hide like an elephant's. He detested this cold, legalistic approach. Didn't Klott realize that as far as he, Eduard was concerned, the whole rotten inheritance affair was over and done with?

"We go way back," said Klott. "I don't have to explain my atti-tude, but I warn you against premature self-accusations. If some-thing serious really has happened to the boy—and there's no news as yet—he's as much a victim of the squatters as of Niessling's pair of thugs. From what you say, the youngster started the rough stuff. What is one to make of parents who incite their own children to defend an illegally occupied building by paramilitary means? You must drop this readiness to shoulder the blame at once. If the worst happens, your opponents in court will trot out all the accusations you're leveling at yourself, coupled with a demand for punitive damages. This isn't a psychotherapy group where your tears would do you credit. You must prepare yourself for a public hearing. An accused person who accuses himself is bound to lose."

Two hours later Klott called him at home: the boy had emerged from his coma and was out of danger. Eduard's sudden thrill of relief was quelled by Klott's addendum: the doctors couldn't tell how serious his internal injuries were or whether they would leave him permanently disabled.

Eduard said little for a long time when Jenny called him two days later. Where to begin? He couldn't inform her of two life-altering developments in the same breath. In fact, the outrage in Friedrichshain had long since overshadowed the adultery that had started in Neu-Karow. Jenny detected the dismay in his voice when he told her about the boy wielding the billiard cue. With a series of rapid-fire questions she forced him to recount the sequence of events and turn his mind to what had to be done next. One head on the block was enough, she said. First he must find the hospital and visit the boy— his parents as well, perhaps. The thugs were to blame, not him. Then he must get Klott to issue a public clarification of the incident, possibly call a newspaper, organize a press conference, publicly demonstrate his, Eduard's, anger and revulsion at the thugs' barbarity. He mustn't simply sit back and let things take their course. Once in circulation, a false version of events would prevail. No one would take any notice of a correction printed on page twenty in two weeks' time.

Eduard marveled at her presence of mind and the hardheaded ingenuity with which she analyzed his position. She had viewed his bequest with instinctive misgivings from the first—"I advise you, quite simply, not to touch it with a barge pole!"—but now that the affair had taken a disastrous turn she didn't waste a moment on I-told-you-so recriminations. Her incorrigible husband had ignored her warnings and fallen overboard, and here she was, unhesitatingly throwing him a life belt. Why on earth was he tinkering with her love? Why did he persist in focusing a microscope on the tiny little splinter that probably hurt no one but himself? If he needed any proof of her love and devotion, this was it. Why do you always need evidence, Herr Professor? What about showing a little courage, or better still a lot of courage? Not everything in this world is capable of proof, you have to take the plunge sometimes!

"I kiss your hand, madame," he said. "No, first your feet and then the rest of your lovely self."

"A pity that only occurs to you when you're thousands of miles away. All right, now have a word with Loris. He's been sitting beside me the whole time, waiting for me to hand him the phone."

"She talks and talks. She never lets me have a turn!" Loris's voice sounded as if he'd just woken up. It was evening over there, possibly dark already.

"You've got a cold," said Eduard.

"No I don't, I'm chewing a candy."

She's so erratic, Eduard thought, forbidding things in the morning and allowing them at bedtime. Her prohibitions are merely passing whims, the children learned that even before they knew the alphabet. Aloud, he said, "Do you think of me sometimes?" Stupid question! What was the boy supposed to say?

"We all miss you, but sometimes I think I miss you most of all. It seems like you've been away four and a half years."

There it was again, the boy lying on the sidewalk with his head jerking to and fro, and there too, as if he'd seen her long ago, was the boy's mother wearing a green visitor's smock in the intensive-care wing, only her eyes visible above the mask that obscured her face.

"We'll soon be seeing each other again."

"I can play the guitar, did you know? But I think I could do that before you left."

"I love you."

"But I only got a D in math."

"Why? I always thought math was your strong point. I love you just the same."

"Me too. Can you water-ski in Berlin?"

"I think so. You have to rent a boat, that's all."

"Could you rent a boat?"

"Sure."

"I've got to stop now, Mom says it's getting too expensive."

Eduard remembered the night, not long ago, when Jenny had gone to stay with some friends of theirs. He'd been roused in the small hours by a whimpering sound that rose to a scream. Loris was in the bathroom, writhing on the tiled floor, fighting for breath. Eduard embraced the boy, pressing him close, squeezing his small rib cage as he carried him back and forth across the room. Loris, his forehead bathed in sweat, arched his body, little hands clutching his heart, then crumpled. "Give me something, something that'll help! I'm choking, I'm dying!" he wailed. "Easy, easy, take deep breaths, I'm here, nothing can happen to you." Panic-stricken, Eduard called the doctor. Until he arrived Eduard paced the apartment with the boy's back pressed against his chest. He'd discovered that this pressure temporarily postponed the next attack of breathlessness.

It was an age before the doctor came and another age before he opened his bag, got out his instruments, and finally examined the patient. He took Loris's blood pressure, shook his head, took his pulse, shook his head, and looked in his ears. It's nothing, he said with a smile. A slight inflammation of the middle ear—too soon for antibiotics. Eduard was amazed to note the soothing effect on Loris of the doctor's slow ritual movements, the calm voice, the pat on the head, the shutting of the bag, the filling out of forms. The boy had tried to offset what was actually a mild and quite tolerable pain by hyperventilating, said the doctor; that was why he'd found it hard to get his breath. So it was all imagination? Imagination, replied the doctor, wasn't the right word for it. Did some situation exist inside the family that compelled the boy to compensate—possibly a lack of attention occasioned by stress and nervousness on the part of one or both of his parents? Half a Valium would calm him down.

Lying sleepless in the darkness of his penthouse apartment, Eduard knew that half a Valium wouldn't help the boy from Rigaer Strasse.

The next morning Eduard found his access to the laboratory barred by strips of red plastic tape. The workmen merely shrugged when he asked where the entrance was. They understood neither German nor English.

For a moment he was assailed by a fear that the laboratory had been barricaded against him personally. It was only when he discovered the new provisional entrance, this time at the rear of the building, that he noticed that the recently renovated section was shrouded in plastic sheets and enclosed by scaffolding. Later it occurred to him that Rürup had forewarned him of this mysterious phenomenon a few days ago. The preliminary renovation, Rürup explained with a wink, had been only a transitional stage; work was now in progress on the next phase of modernization, which itself was doubtless only temporary. He advised Eduard to read Alfred Döblin, Joseph Roth, Theodor Fontane, and Heinrich Heine. All of them had testified that Berlin was being rebuilt in their day. The city had been undergoing reconstruction for centuries, but it would evidently never be finished.

It was days since Eduard had emptied his pigeonhole. The sheaf of green, yellow, and red memos in which the management commended all kinds of trivia to his urgent attention contained a blue slip bearing an invitation printed in boldface type. A glance at the clock told him that the lecture had already started. Although he wasn't duty-bound to attend the weekly evaluation session, that didn't entitle him to skip it. The main privilege enjoyed by professors as opposed to junior staffers consisted in voluntarily making it their duty to fulfill the Institute's expectations.

So he hurriedly retraced his steps. He traversed the expanse of loose earth that separated the White House from the main building, avoiding the puddles and mudholes, ascended the stairs flanked by blue plaster busts of the Heroes of Science—at Stanford the total absence of a woman among them would long ago have provoked an inquiry into sexual discrimination—and entered the lecture hall.

The decor reminded him of the control room in the starship *Enterprise*. (The choice was as follows: the Institute's still-unrenovated rooms continued to radiate the charm of an East German Army officers' mess; the ones that had already been done over adhered strictly to the styling customary in American sci-fi movies.) The white plastic chairs with the absurdly high backs made his colleagues look like children playing grownups. He tiptoed over to the nearest one available. Although he'd reckoned with the inevitable head-turning that greets any belated arrival, Dr. Santner's searching gaze puzzled him. Did Santner know something he shouldn't, by rights, know at all? The morning papers had carried no report of the incident in Rigaer Strasse, but no doubt he followed the news on the radio and the Internet and might even have visited the "Schizo-Temple" Web site Eduard had searched for in vain. Santner was always well informed and probably browsed the Internet incessantly, so the squatters might be in direct touch with him. Eduard shuffled far enough forward on his chair to be completely hidden from view by the high backs of those in front of him. It was only when he'd adopted this crouching position that he managed to concentrate on the lecture. The longer he listened the stronger his suspicion became that the guest speaker from Göttingen University had been specially invited to undermine him, Eduard, and his research project. With barely suppressed emotion, this expert, a man of his own age, was delivering a pseudoscientific tirade against the whole thrust of his research. Any attempt to explore the genetic origins of human behavior would open a Pandora's box, he declared. In particular, to posit a biological basis for an alleged predisposition to conspicuously violent behavior and account for it by a genetic mutation based on the X chromosome, namely the monoamino-oxydase A, was tantamount in itself to a crime of violence. It was but a short step from such research to the eugenic concepts of National Socialist genetics. To proclaim violence a natural attribute and divest human beings of responsibility for their actions was ultimately destructive of morality, justice, and religion. Any such science was merely a substitute for the latter, and would inevitably have evil repercussions.

When the guest speaker finished Eduard wished he really was aboard the starship *Enterprise* and could get Mr. Spock to beam him into a world without a past. Every eye, he felt, was focused on the back of his chair in expectation of a response. He forced himself to raise his arm.

He congratulated the previous speaker on his impressive lecture. Unfortunately, he said, his esteemed colleague had not always been careful enough to divorce scientific from political objections. He himself knew of no reputable scientist who talked in terms of a "criminal-behavior gene." Furthermore, should anyone go looking for such a thing, the Germans would be the first to be suspected of carrying and passing it on. No one seriously contended that any behavioral characteristic was 100 percent genetically determined. The probability was that we would never discover what proportion was determined by environmental influences. Fifty-fifty—that rule of thumb would probably continue to hold true. The new science did not, therefore, negate morality, religion, and tradition or restrict the scope for freedom of choice. That scope was substantially diminishing, however. Only a few years ago it had been thought politically incorrect even to surmise a genetic predisposition to cancer or obesity. Nowadays people spoke, often as a matter of course, of genetically preprogrammed tendencies toward love of adventure, homosexuality, depression, alcoholism, speech defects, drug addiction, and world-class athleticism. It was surely only a matter of time before genetic components in the individual's ability to control aggression were discovered. But even this genetically preordained ability, if it existed, would naturally be subject to environmental influences. Eduard's colleague from Göttingen clearly failed to realize how far to the left a molecular biology based strictly on chemical processes could end up. The most recent American research had demonstrated beyond a doubt that a readiness to resort to violence was influenced by the level of the transmitter gene serotonin. The lower the level of serotonin in the brain, the greater the tendency toward violence. It had emerged, at the same time, that this level was itself affected by environmental influences. A low serotonin level often reflected humiliating social experiences injurious to the individual's self-esteem. Thus the cat was biting its own tail—or, to put it another way, human genetics was biting Marxism.

Although Eduard inferred from the volume of his colleagues' applause that they thought him almost on a par with his opponent from Göttingen, he took advantage of the next coffee break to make his excuses to Rürup and disappear.

12 "TURN ON the local television. And don't hang up, I'll stay on the line!" Klott sounded agitated. He seemed to take it for granted that Eduard had a television set in his laboratory. Eduard dashed into a small room full of still uninstalled computers, monitors, and fax machines and turned on the set there. He shut the door behind him and picked up an extension.

He saw shots of demonstrators making for the Palace of the Republic from Karl Liebknecht Strasse. The camera angle made it impossible to tell how many of them there were, but some of their banners could be deciphered in closeup: BACK TO YOUR LAIRS, NAZI HEIRS!—ARYANIZERS, TERRORIZERS! From time to time chanting could be heard: "Forty years they lived in clover, now they want to take us over!" One placard, which bore a photo of the boy playing billiards, was captioned "A victim of restitution!" Eduard tried to read the rest of the writing on it but failed. Then, for some seconds, he was distracted by a discovery. Or was it a case of mistaken identity? That figure in shades and a bomber jacket, arm in arm with some squatters beneath a banner reading HANDS OFF MARWITZ & CO.!—could it be Dr. Santner?

The procession halted in front of the Palace of the Republic. The camera panned over the bleak, interminable façade with the tinted windowpanes, once the pride of the socialist republic, which had always reminded Eduard of a gigantic gym. The immense, white-edged slab that shut off the Schlossplatz like a domino on its side, a horizontal version of the Trade Center, looked deserted. But something was moving on the roof. When the camera went in closer Eduard made out a few figures from Rigaer Strasse dressed in their well-known black outfits. They were holding aloft a red banner with the following legend clearly inscribed on it in black: PRUSSIA AGAIN? NEVER!

Klott signaled his presence at the other end of the line. "Did you see that slogan just now? Marwitz & Co., was it? What's that?"

"No idea."

"Marwitz, Marwitz, it rings a bell . . . They've got a flair for the symbolic, those friends of yours. Really smart of them to present their case against that backdrop. You realize what they're aiming at? An analogy between the fight for your property and the fight for the Palace of the Republic. These pictures will get worldwide coverage!"

Eduard didn't understand a word. While Klott was giving vent to his forebodings the procession had moved on and abruptly assumed a different character. The demonstrators seemed to have strayed into another era. They halted in front of an imposing edifice which Eduard found vaguely familiar. Their rather sparse ranks looked suddenly impressive, almost frightening. It was as if these television pictures of the present protest march were being underlaid by earlier, black-and-white newsreel shots of revolutionary workers on the march in the 1920s, by the oil paintings of 1848 familiar from illustrated histories of Berlin. The procession had moved from the Palace of the Republic across Marx-Engels Platz, but—did his eyes deceive him?—the screen was now displaying a long shot, and the southeast side of the square was empty no longer. There, as if conjured by magic from the asphalt, stood the massive, freshly stuccoed baroque façade of the Hohenzollerns' castle. He rubbed his eyes. He'd cycled down Unter den Linden only a few weeks ago, but there hadn't been any castle there then, just a huge parking lot and the Council of State Building with Eosander von Göthe's celebrated portal embedded in it like a thorn in flesh. And now that portal had crossed the parking lot on ghostly feet and reinstalled itself where it had always been: in its original wall.

"Hands off the Palace of the Republic!" yelled the demonstrators. They had now reached Eosander's portal. All at once, high above their heads, Eduard spotted the unmistakable profile of Vera Rheinland. Her leather-clad militiamen were carrying her shoulder-high for the benefit of the television cameras. Head shorn and banner in fist, she was reminiscent of some revolutionary figure. Joan of Arc? But Joan carried a sword, not a flag. No, the celebrated lady in the legendary Delacroix poster! Yes, that was who she was, a reincarnation of Eugénie at the head of her intrepid freedom fighters, forging a path to the Bastille through powder smoke and over dead bodies— Eugénie holding the flag on high. Only the bare bosom was missing.

Was it all just a historical allusion? Were they only playing at revolution, or were they in earnest? Some of the demonstrators started to hurl stones at the castle's lofty windows. But the glass didn't shatter, the missiles failed to penetrate it. The dark panes inexplicably bowed inward at the point of impact to form elastic craters from which the stones rebounded like foam-rubber balls. One demonstrator stabbed the massive doors of the portal with the pole on which his placard was mounted—and transfixed them. The camera zoomed in on the ragged holes and proved what Eduard had found hard to believe: the entire castle was itself just a picture—a painted backdrop.

At the other end of the line Klott curtly explained what everyone apart from Eduard apparently knew.

For the past two years, controversy had raged over how the city center should be rebuilt. At first purely academic, the debate had developed into a war over Berlin's history and identity, an accumulation of all the touchiness, resentment, and hatred that existed between the inhabitants of East and West Berlin. It had all begun when the municipal government—the first since reunification, be it noted—proposed to demolish East Berlin's Palace of the Republic on the ground that the health and safety inspectors had pronounced its asbestos content dangerously high. The East Berliners had scant affection for "Honecker's lamp store," as they derisively nicknamed it, but they'd grown used to it over the years as a place where weddings, birthdays, and comings-of-age could be celebrated at affordable prices. When plans for its demolition were published, many East Berliners saw them as another attempt by the "colonialists" from the West to rob them of a piece of their history. Suspicion turned to fury when West Berlin lobbyists advocated reconstructing the historic castle of the kings of Prussia on the square. To kindle the Berliners's enthusiasm for this project, its champions organized an unusual advertising campaign: they got some Paris art students to produce a painting of the whole of the building's west front, true to scale, and secured it to a steel framework. Almost overnight, this created an illusion that the castle had been resurrected. Anyone looking eastward at the bend in Unter den Linden saw, fluttering slightly as if about to take wing, the phantasmal shape of the baroque palace dynamited fifty years earlier.

The campaign had been a spectacular success, Klott declared. All at once, hundreds of thousands of West Berliners discovered a hitherto unavowed love for the vanished Hohenzollern castle and noted that the Palace of the Republic was all that really stood in the way of its reconstruction. The East Berliners just as promptly developed a love for the Palace of the Republic and ascertained by means of opinion polls that they couldn't live without it.

The ghostly duel between palace and castle unexpectedly assumed symbolic dimensions. In East Berlin signatures were collected and vigils held, Klott recounted. There were even fears of a self-immolation. The socialist palace suddenly stood for the derided and disregarded identity of former GDR citizens, its planned demolition for a Western attempt to destroy that identity once and for all. The reconstruction of the castle, in its turn, was considered a symptom of the return of every German iniquity: Prussianism, the monarchy, and fascism. "Yet both buildings are almost unconnected with the passions that are raging in their name," Klott remarked spitefully. "The kings of Prussia disliked the castle and shunned it, Hitler never set foot in it. As for Honecker's Palazzo del Prozzo, it wasn't cut out to be a symbol of socialist political authority. It was probably the only parliament building in the world to house a dozen restaurants, a dance hall, and a first-class tenpin bowling alley. But who cares about the truth when their identity's at stake?"

The broadcast ended on a surprising note. There appeared on the screen a face Eduard knew perfectly well but couldn't put a name to. The soft-featured man was around his own age, but for some reason Eduard felt there should be a scar near the corner of his mouth. Where had he seen that face? He seemed to recall that once upon a time, when dress was indicative of political persuasion, the man used to part his hair and wear a jacket and tie. He'd stuck to his principles, sartorially speaking, but what about his voice? Had he been taking elocution lessons? In the old days he couldn't speak to save his life. Whenever he took the floor at a campus meeting he used to trip over his tongue and be laughed or shouted down.

Since then he'd acquired a remarkable facility for public speaking. In the quiet but audible voice of an experienced consensus creator he reeled off printable sentences from the "true, but . . ." repertory. He referred to property rights, "which we all uphold." ("He'd have to say that," growled Klott. "His constituents are sticklers for those.") Like all rights, however, even property rights had their limits, and that was when "sensitive areas of German history" were affected. "Some people trample on such sensibilities," continued the face Eduard knew so well, seeming to look straight at him. "We Berliners find it disconcerting to see how people who turned their backs on our city years ago are suddenly smitten with nostalgia as soon as they inherit something here."

Where's your scar? That was what they'd all chanted at him in the old days. Eduard remembered now: this fellow student, now a senator, had belonged to a dueling fraternity but never acquired a scar throughout his time at the university. Someone had discovered in the end that he owed his unblemished cheeks not to superior skill with the saber but to the sissification of his fraternity's honor code. Certain members were permitted to dispense with the duty to fight a duel.

But their roles were now reversed. What had happened? The unscarred mouth opened and, in a discreet tremolo, drew attention to the lessons of history. "Property unjustly acquired during the Nazi era cannot, of course, be returned, least of all to putative land-lords who break into their premises with the help of hired thugs and endanger the health and safety of the occupants." Questioned by a journalist on how the Senate proposed to deal with the squat on Rigaer Strasse, the senator came out with a surprising response: "The occupants aren't squatters, they're temporary residents. Until the claims at issue have been resolved before a court, I see no need to intervene."

"Damned cheek!" commented Klott. "He'd be careful not to take that tone if some squatters occupied a branch of the Dresdner Bank, but he's ready to sacrifice your hovel to the palace lobby for the sake of peace on the streets. Don't worry, though, we'll give him the scar he never got!"

Klott insisted that Eduard drop everything else for the next few days. They simply must discover how his grandfather acquired the Rigaer Strasse building and how much he paid for it.

Eduard hung up. The eighth of his brain responsible for self-preservation, which was still functioning, told him that something was very wrong. How could it have come to this? Could it really be that the bogus duelist turned city father was defending the squatters and posing as the guardian angel of a population overtaken by events, by unemployment, industrial closures, and cultural alienation, whereas he, Eduard, the erstwhile hope of the biology students' Red cell, was being made to look like a rabid landlord, the evil jinni of expropriation and colonialism, and a representative of the castle lobby?

He was furious with them all: with the city, the senator, the squatters, and Klott, who had failed to warn him and carry out sufficient research—furious, too, with himself and his precipitate sense of guilt. It was true: he felt somehow guilty even before learning anything definite about his grandfather, paralyzed by the very suspicion that he might have profited from "a forced sale arising from persecution." What did the others really know? No more than he did, probably. Suspicion sufficed, inquiries were superfluous, *sauve qui peut*. But he wasn't going to knuckle under, certainly not now. He would investigate matters thoroughly and then decide whether, quite irrespective of the legal position, he was or was not entitled to the Rigaer Strasse bequest.

A news bulletin had mentioned the name of the hospital. Having studied the route on the map of that medical metropolis, Eduard followed the arrows to the trauma unit. He had witnessed the atrocity in Rigaer Strasse, he told the intensive-care nurse, and wanted to leave something for the boy. Knowing him, he thought the gift might remind him of a game he was fond of.

"We'll pass it on," said the nurse. "What is it?"

"Some billiard balls. Could I give them to him in person?"

"He's not in a fit state," the nurse replied, taking the bag from him. "He wouldn't recognize you in any case."

Eduard was tempted to walk straight past her, but he didn't even know the boy's name.

He recognized him by the splendid shock of fair hair above the plaster collar. In the hospital grounds he'd noticed a young woman pushing an adolescent in a wheelchair. He couldn't bring himself to approach the pair and accost them, but he followed them along par allel paths, screened by hedges. Once he saw the boy at quite close range, his white face shadowless under a cold sun. He was immensely relieved when he heard him talking. Or had he only imagined the sound? He was too far away to permit himself a definite decision as to whether the mouth above the plaster collar was uttering coherent sentences. Perhaps the boy was merely moving his lips, or genuinely talking but in an inarticulate, unintelligible way. Speech did not betoken consciousness; perhaps he was in that linguistic limbo that shies away from the trauma and blurs every recent recollection. Loris had taught Eduard how quickly and defenselessly children come to terms with almost any fate. They're as ready to believe the person who predicts they'll win an Olympic title as the one who tells them they're going to be wheelchair-bound for the rest of their days.

BOOK 3

1 EVEN BEFORE he opened the *Berliner Tagblatt* the next morning, Eduard knew it would contain something that demanded a rebuttal. He didn't have to look for long. "Riot in Friedrichshain . . ." He skimmed through an account of the origins of the dispute. "Landlord moved in with gang of heavies . . ." Nothing about the boy that would genuinely have eased his mind: ". . . out of danger . . . severe internal injuries." Then came the "background," imbued with all the authority of a printed and quotable press report: "The rights of ownership are in dispute. The squatters claim that until 1933 the building belonged to Marwitz & Co., a Jewish family firm compelled to dispose of all its assets and quit Germany within a year of the Nazis' coming to power. The present claimants, E. and L.H., are said to be descendants of a former Nazi entrepreneur who acquired the Jewish owner's firm for a derisory sum thanks to his good relations with Julius Streicher's 'Central Committee against the Jewish Boycott and Incitement Campaign.' The legal heir, one of Kasimir Marwitz's daughters, is reported to be living in Florida. The squatters have established contact with her."

Klott insisted that they drive at once to the Real Estate Registry Office in central Berlin and clear up a simple matter of fact. The photocopy of the restitution certificate had stated that the vendor was a Frau Schlandt; it did not mention any Kasimir Marwitz. Eduard must go back a page and check the preceding entry.

A neo-baroque building with a protuberant balcony surmounting granite columns, their destination looked like a foundling beside the anonymous architectural cubes that flanked it. Eduard followed his attorney into the interior and paused to marvel. They were in an imposing lobby with a vaulted ceiling supported by ornate columns. Two curving stairways led to upper galleries whose bulging, loge-like excrescences made the lobby look even more like the court theater of some eighteenth-century principality. It was apparent from the elaborate restoration work that, unlike Eduard, the government had nothing to fear from any unresolved claims to title. Immediately after the takeover, hordes of painters and restorers must have been mobilized to create a working environment worthy of senior civil servants from West Germany.

Having followed the arrows that led to the Real Estate Registry Office along the ocher-colored, vaulted passages of a lateral wing, they knocked at a newly stripped pine door. Once inside, they found themselves in a time warp. Outside, in the lobby and the passages, they had been in the decade of reconstruction; here in the office itself, the GDR lived on. The walls preserved that unmistakable "GDR-specific" smell which incredulous Western visitors had noticed without ever managing to identify its source. But the linoleum-covered floor, the two regulation desks equipped with clumsy-looking desk lights, the massive black typewriter, and the stiff-backed female official who didn't deign to look up—all these reminded Eduard of the time when anyone entering such premises reached instinctively for his passport and entry visa. Klott, who was evidently known here, introduced Eduard as his client and left him alone. He himself was scheduled to appear in court.

The woman at the desk handed Eduard a slip of paper bearing a reference number and gestured vaguely to some shelves on the left. Her look of dismissal conveyed that any further questions would be superfluous.

Eduard had pictured the Real Estate Registry Office quite differently: a bewildering labyrinth of passages on four or five floors, shelves on which huge ledgers had been moldering unopened for decades, the history of a city's real estate recorded first in Sütterlin script, then in roman copperplate, then in typescript churned out by one of those mechanical monsters of which an example stood on the desk, and finally, only a few years ago at most, by computer. There might be a few arrows to direct him from one urban district to another until, on the second or third day, possibly after he'd dozed off among the shelves, he found the one book he was looking for.

But this place contained no passages, no other rooms. The book he sought must be here on the left, before his very eyes. It probably wasn't a book, either, but one of those thin, shabby folders on the Ikea shelves. Seated at the tables he saw readers whom he assumed to be engaged in the same quest as himself. But they weren't reading or turning over pages with other books piled high beside them. For each reader there was only one "book," his book, the book of books. And in that book, which was merely a folder, there was one page, and on that page one entry that would determine whether he became rich or continued to vegetate in his former financial state. Other readers in other real estate registry offices were probably seated in the same attitude at this same moment, poring over their "books" in reverent silence. Some had magnifying glasses in their hands and were transcribing the register's oracular pronouncements with fountain pen or ballpoint, others feeding the fateful pages into handy battery-powered photocopiers, others still had brought digital cameras along.

Why on earth had the young revolutionary government preserved all these documents? Why hadn't it simply burned the real estate registers—those most sacred pillars of the old bourgeois establishment—just as the youthful Soviet Union had done? Had the German revolutionaries secretly counted from the first on the recoverability of their new property regulations? Or did they simply find it inconceivable that their state was mortal, and that the owners' descendants might surface in the future? Klott had told Eduard of Schloss Barby, the country mansion in which all the real estate registers had been corralled, as it were. Immediately after the East German state was founded the authorities had dispatched nine million files to Barby and stored them in its two hundred rooms. There the title deeds had lain moldering, long guarded by pigeons and rats alone, awaiting the return of those who bore the relevant names. After reunification some belated revolutionary had tried to burn the house down. Part of the roof went up in flames, but not the files. Files don't burn as readily as roofs, and even if they had caught fire, whether during that belated act of arson or during a more timely one forty years earlier, they would have been rescued. Files were always rescued in Germany. Files had not only outlasted the Third Reich and the GDR but would probably outlast any other German regime.

Eduard didn't take long to find his folder and the original entry, which was familiar to him from the photocopy enclosed with the restitution notice. He turned back a page and winced: Frau Edita Schlandt, who had sold the Rigaer Strasse building to Dr. Egon Hoffmann in November 1933, was referred to in an entry two years earlier as Edita Marwitz and registered as the property's co-owner. It seemed that when Hitler came to power, and for reasons on which Eduard needed no enlightening, Kasimir Marwitz must have transferred the property to a relative, possibly a daughter who had married in the interim and acquired the surname Schlandt. However Eugène, alias Vera Rheinland, had obtained her information, she hadn't made it up.

This discovery rewrote his recollection of what had happened in the last few days. The demonstrators, the senator, the author of the article in the *Berliner Tagblatt*—weren't all the people who'd been gunning for him in the right, and hadn't the only one who'd blindly disputed the truth been himself? He couldn't have known that his and Lothar's claims might not hold water. No one, probably, guessed how little he would miss his bequest. What he found embarrassing, almost unbearable, was all that had already been done in further-ance of those claims.

Not so fast, just a minute! The fact that his grandfather had acquired the building from a Jewish owner didn't automatically imply that he'd taken advantage of her predicament. Legally speak-ing, Klott had said, a sale that predated the Nuremberg race laws was considered valid if the purchase price corresponded to the prop-erty's current value and had demonstrably been paid.

The bookstore at the Savigny Platz S-Bahn station! It surprised Eduard that, after so long away, he'd been struck by the sign he'd only vaguely noticed in passing.

The sales assistant, a tall, resolute-looking person, seemed to real-ize she was dealing with a customer who'd mistaken the bookstore for a first-aid post. Did she have a history of Berlin apartment houses, asked Eduard, specifically of the Friedrichshain district? She led him unerringly through the vaulted rooms to one of the huge bookcases. From the lowest shelf, tome by tome, she extracted a three-volume lifework so heavy she found it hard to rise from a crouch.

He quickly discovered that the second and third volumes dealt with the period that interested him. Rigaer Strasse was represented by a single illustration, but several streets in the immediate neigh-borhood were fully documented. The fate of individual buildings, the eviction of their Jewish owners by the Nazis, the changes under-gone by buildings and streets in the last sixty years—all were recorded in detail. The streets of the now familiar district seemed to pass before Eduard's eyes like a time-lapse sequence as he turned the pages, constantly changing shape. The industrial upsurge after 1871, the 1920s, the Nazi era, the postwar period, the GDR years. The curved 1930s balcony railings had been replaced with simple uprights, the re-entrants and concave curves of the frolicsome gabled roofs simplified after the war and reconstructed flat, the late-nineteenth-century façade ornaments replaced with smooth stucco and the four-pane sash windows with casements, the Venetian blinds abolished, the basements walled up, the street-corner taverns converted into dark apartments, the 1920s advertisement pillars superseded by trees. The author's lifework was incomplete, having been printed before the squatters got busy with their aerosol cans.

Now that he was more or less in practice, Eduard let the pages run through his fingers the other way around and saw a century's changes parade in reverse order. The building on Rigaer Strasse, which was not illustrated anywhere, passed through all the stages of decay and renovation common to the surrounding streets. May Day in the Workers' and Peasants' State . . . As Eduard leafed backward the little hammer-and-sickle flags in the window boxes on the crumbling balconies transformed themselves into the homemade lengths of bunting adorned with swastikas that had fluttered from the still intact balconies on the same date a decade earlier. What of his grandfather Egon, the testator? What had his balconies looked like then?

He came across the name in a series of photographs depicting the Prenzlauer Berg district: above a shop flanked by a cigar store and a pharmacy, in very legible white lettering on a black background, were the words "Schuhhaus Marwitz."

Klott, by now on the way to Leipzig, rather curtly made it clear by mobile that the Rigaer Strasse building wasn't the only restitution case on his books. He was, however, able to tell Eduard that his likeliest source of information about the fate of the Schuhhaus Marwitz during the Nazi period would be the Berlin Document Center.

The walk-in memory bank of recent German history had a picturesque address. Surrounded by tall fir trees and retirement homes, it lay at the end of a blind alley named "Wasserkäfersteig," or Water Beetle Lane, in which cyclists and dog walkers abounded. From outside the place looked like a farmhouse with adjoining stables where families hungry for a taste of country life spent the weekends with their children. Only the fence topped with rolls of barbed wire and the iron grilles over the windows betrayed that the buildings housed hundreds of thousands of crime stories from the Nazi era.

After producing his ID and Klott's letter of authorization, Eduard was made to fill out various questionnaires. Under the headword "Marwitz" in his computer the American official found a registration number, which he handed to Eduard together with a diagram of the building's layout. In the designated room Eduard exchanged the numbered slip for a microfiche. The archivist showed him how to insert this microfiche in the viewer and print out individual pages. Eduard was startled to discover how simple it all was, and how quickly he could sift the countless documents for the one that was relevant to him. He hadn't done more than run a preliminary check on the microfilmed documents when he came across his grandfather's name and signature and an abbreviation that temporarily deprived him of all hope. Instead of writing his name, Grandfather Egon had repeatedly identified himself as "Pg"—Party Member—Hoffmann.

Eduard had to roam the microfiche for hours and print out dozens of pages, arranging them in the correct order, before he formed a mental picture of the events that had led him to Rigaer Strasse sixty years later.

American troops had discovered the documents in 1945 at the home of Julius Streicher, the Jew-baiter. Made up of correspondence between various Party offices, letters of denunciation, boycott proclamations, and court reports, they chronicled the campaign of expropriation and persecution that had driven a wealthy Jewish industrialist named Kasimir Marwitz out of Germany and, ultimately, into his grave. The retail outlet in Prenzlauer Berg was not Marwitz & Co.'s only business in Berlin. It maintained a long-established and successful footwear factory that had greatly expanded during the 1920s, thanks to a novel sewing technique invented by Kasimir himself, and it owned over two dozen shoe shops in Berlin alone. In May

1933 Marwitz & Co. had been the first major concern in Nazi Germany to be "Aryanized." The firm's correspondence made repeated references to two of its employees: Pg Dahnke and Pg Hoffmann.

But the more Eduard immersed himself in these documents, the more of a mystery his grandfather seemed. Where Pg Dahnke was concerned, there was only one member of the firm whom he detested more fiercely than its Jewish owner, Kasimir Marwitz, and that was its legal advisor, Pg Hoffmann.

Dahnke was quite well off. However, although he managed Marwitz's branch on Uhland Strasse with his wife, Hertha, and received a fixed salary plus a commission on sales, he clearly felt victimized. His denunciatory letters to Streicher's Central Committee against the Jewish Boycott and Incitement Campaign were full of allusions to his own services to the Fatherland and Party: ". . . sent to the Western Front in 1914 at age seventeen, five times wounded, certified war disablement 40 percent, later reduced to 30 percent . . ." He was motivated not by poverty but by the fact that other people, who in his opinion had no business being in Germany at all, were faring substantially better. Pg Dahnke felt sure that Kasimir Marwitz would not survive the new era and his tireless denunciations, but the person that riled him even more was the Party member senior to him, "who helps the Jew Marwitz to rob the German people and carries out his orders to the letter."

Eduard's grandfather, it transpired from a well-meaning memo from the Nazis' Economic Section in Berlin defending Pg Hoffmann against a hostile inquiry from Streicher's office, was anything but a shining light. "Formerly active in a students' organization" (like his grandson, thought Eduard) "he joined the movement back in 1931 and, at the time of the national revolution, expressly advocated that the firm be streamlined in accordance with its principles." Pg Hoffmann had been employed as the firm's attorney since 1929 on a salary, as Dahnke noted bitterly, of five hundred marks a month. But he evidently used his contacts with Nazi functionaries whom he'd known since their student days together to block or water down Pg Dahnke's attempts to Nazify Marwitz & Co. Dahnke's detailed lists of the Jews it still employed were meat and drink to Streicher's office. The humble manager of the Uhland Strasse branch contrived to get the firm boycotted on April 1, 1933. The smaller storekeepers and footwear manufacturers who could not compete with Marwitz's prices at last had a pretext for driving their successful rival out of business: being "in Jewish hands," the firm must be made to close down. A so-called Association of Middle-Class Businessmen organized demonstrations outside Marwitz branches. The boycott worked, the firm's sales plummeted. Marwitz was anxious to sell his business and offered it to Wollgraf, a leather-goods manufacturer from Weinheim. The latter bided his time and banked on acquiring the firm for a half or even a tenth of the price in a few months' time.

Dahnke not only noted but promptly reported that Pg Hoffmann had endeavored to sabotage the Party's instructions in one crucial respect: he persuaded his boss, Marwitz, to appoint him, the firm's attorney, managing director and chairman of the board while Marwitz himself continued to hold a majority of the stock. Pg Hoffmann thereupon compelled the whole of the board to resign and dismissed thirty Jewish employees on the spot, but he retained thirty others on the ground that "the National Socialist authorities had failed to demonstrate that he had the requisite amount of skilled labor." In the trade journal *Schuh und Leder*—Eduard read the paragraph word for word—Egon Hoffmann professed his belief in the "Führer principle" and "the national community concept." In the next paragraph, however, he demanded—under the protection of that preamble?— that the boycott be lifted forthwith because the firm had now been "streamlined." Pg Hoffmann's article may have deceived some of his Party pals at the Economic Section in Berlin, and even his emotionally torn grandson Eduard, but not Pg Dahnke, who continued to complain to the firm's "strong Jewish taint." Pg Hoffmann, he said, had not "fired a single Jew" from Marwitz & Co.'s businesses in Berlin. "At the head office he is not only surrounded by Jews but advised and, of course, egged on by them. Herr Dr. Egon Hoffmann keeps Party members down as best he can so that no one disrupts his relations with the Jewish community around him." Dahnke dissolved the "Marxist" staff committee and placed himself at the head of a "German Christian" successor organization founded by himself. The new managing director took prompt action. He reinstated the original staff committee and fired Dahnke—"for no good reason," as Eduard, suddenly proud of his unknown forebear, read in Dahnke's letter of protest to Streicher's office—"stating only that he was compelled to dismiss me on purely emotional grounds." Eduard gave his grandfather special credit for having been clearly unimpressed by Dahnke's perpetual moans about his war wound. "I had that day been released from the hospital after a major operation on the wound in my upper thigh," lamented Dahnke. "Since it was still very painful, I asked to see Herr Hoffmann at the head office. He declined, ostensibly for lack of time, so I had to limp downstairs again . . . At nine the same night a messenger brought me my notice of dismissal." Dahnke took instant revenge. "Egon Hoffmann is just a figurehead. The Jew Marwitz continues to run the business as before. He issues his directives to Hoffmann, who carries them out to the letter . . ."

Eduard was becoming fascinated by the Dahnke–Hoffmann duel of sixty years ago. The handwritten letters to Streicher's office lent the informer's vengeful voice a strange immediacy. But his unknown grandfather, whose own voice never appeared in the records, communicated itself to him in an unmistakable manner. He couldn't yet decide whether his professions of faith in the Führer and the National Socialist ideal were genuine or just lip service. In close combat with his adversary Dahnke, however, Pg Hoffmann had shown himself a daring player, almost a gambler.

Thanks to his connections with the brownshirt leadership, Dahnke had succeeded in engineering the arrest of Managing Director Hoffmann and two senior Jewish employees "for political offenses." Brought before the labor tribunal the next morning, the accused man lost his temper. Dahnke's accusations, he declared, were a pack of stinking lies. He challenged District Cell Leader Dahnke, who was present in court, to a duel. Instead of sending his second, Dahnke called the police. Hoffmann was jailed for "insulting a public official."

There followed a tragic farce. Kasimir Marwitz clearly found his Aryan managing director's treatment of the devious Dahnke an embarrassment. Dahnke triumphantly reported that Marwitz himself had withdrawn his notice of dismissal, assured him that he'd never approved it, and said that "on the contrary, he thought my wife and me were the nicest Berlin managers he knew." Not content with this success, Dahnke sent two brownshirt relatives to Marwitz's house in Dahlem to demand that Managing Director Hoffmann be dismissed forthwith. Unless Marwitz himself resumed that post, the brownshirts warned, his factory would be "badly damaged." It never came to that. The very next day Marwitz sold his firm, for far less than it was worth, to Wollgraf, the time-biding leather-goods manufacturer. The new owner, himself a longtime Party member, promptly dismissed all the firm's remaining Jewish staff.

He did not, however, reengage Pg Dahnke, who had "de-Jewed" the company on his own initiative and handed it to him on a plate. Egon Hoffmann, the former managing director, was not reengaged either. Pg Dahnke now had even more grounds for complaint. In one of his last letters to the Streicher office, "sent on behalf of my wife Hertha as well," he wrote: "And now we're out on the street, not because of incompetence, but because we held the political beliefs that now guide the German nation." A good year later, the eternal victim could chalk up a moral victory: submitted on December 20, 1934, his request that Pg Hoffmann be expelled from the Party had at last been granted. But even this belated triumph over his direst foe was vitiated. "How can we be expected to endure the fact," he wrote to his father confessor, Streicher, who doubtless simply filed his letters from now on, "that we're confronted in our own home—I refer to the apartment house built for his deserving branch managers by the firm's original founder, Jonas Marwitz—by that convicted enemy of the Party Egon Hoffmann, who is now our landlord and puts our rents up?"

Eduard stared incredulously at the sender's address on the letterhead, which he had hitherto overlooked on each of Dahnke's epistles: Rigaer Strasse.

2 | THAT NIGHT, after his session at the Document Center, Eduard called Klott and asked him to obtain an injunction preventing the *Berliner Tagblatt* from repeating its assertion that Eduard's claim to the Rigaer Strasse apartment house was based on a "forced sale arising from persecution." Egon Hoffmann, whose ownership was proven by the real estate register, had in fact defended the original owners, Marwitz & Co., from "Aryanization" by the Nazis.

Eduard found Klott's disclaimer in the newspaper two days later, accompanied by the usual rider: although obliged by law to print it, the editor could not vouch for its accuracy.

Füllgraf, the journalist who had recently offered to escort Eduard through Berlin's intellectual zoo, devoted an article to him in the

local news section. Its tone was defamatory. The moral value of the
restitution concept was based, among other things, on the plan to
return the Aryanized assets of German Jews who had been expelled
or murdered. That this concept had been nightmarishly abused with
tragic results was the responsibility of a clumsy oaf of a German, not
long back from the United States, who was laying claim to an apartment house on Rigaer Strasse. The legitimacy of his claim could not
be debated here, wrote Füllgraf, but there were times when a decent
person should be governed by historical sensitivity, not by the letter
of the law. Historical remorse was sometimes a better guide than a
greedy lawyer. What was particularly embarrassing was the claimant's
attempt, clearly motivated by cupidity, to prettify his grandfather's
career. E.H. himself admitted that he had never known the testator,
nor did anyone, E.H. included, know how this unknown forebear
had gained possession of the building on Rigaer Strasse. The only
certainty was that, as managing director of Marwitz & Co., he had
been responsible for firing thirty Jewish employees. That fact alone
should suffice to bring a blush to his grandson's cheeks. Historical
revisionism motivated by rapacity? Surely *that* couldn't be the aim
of the restitution concept. The grandson's efforts to beautify his
grandfather into a friend and helper of the persecuted owner of Marwitz & Co. were suspiciously reminiscent of the abominable routine
formula to which many postwar Germans had resorted: "My best
friend was a Jew."

It was all Eduard could do to finish the article. He felt himself
blush as Füllgraf so urgently recommended, but that was as much
the effect of rage as of shame. How could such a friendly and intelligent man, who had not only made his acquaintance but asked him
for an interview, suddenly portray him as a rapacious Nazi heir?
Why hadn't Füllgraf called him and requested information? Berlin's
winter sky and the cult of guilt by suspicion—life in California had
made him forget them both. After two decades of silence and denial
on the subject of Nazi crimes, the younger generation had begun to
put their elders on trial. But there had been something panicky about
this process from the outset. It was as if the perpetrators' children

were striving to appease the Moloch of German guilt with a continuous supply of sacrificial victims from their own ranks. The accusers
had become infected with the climate of accusation and exposure,
which often served to generate mutual suspicion rather than call
genuine perpetrators to account. Those who denounced an idea as
"fascistoid" or an acquaintance as an apologist for Nazi crimes
seemed to be proving that they themselves were free from all sin and
had gained a temporary lead in the race for innocence.

In the first flush of his anger Eduard felt tempted to remonstrate
with Füllgraf, but he abandoned the idea after debating it briefly. On
the phone and in private Füllgraf might possibly agree to issue a correction on this point or that, but the article had already appeared
and taken effect. In any case, the insinuation game sold more papers
than honest journalism.

The ground beneath Eduard's feet was treacherous. You thought
you were walking on asphalt, only to go through it and find yourself
wading around in subterranean vaults and tunnels whose roofs you
mistook for the sky. To Eduard the ubiquitous excavations and man-
made lakes in the soil of Berlin now seemed like recklessly exposed
entrances to another city beneath it. Disembodied spirits crept forth
and clung to the ankles of the living, hampered their progress, be-
fogged their brains. It seemed that the inhabitants, usually so sensitive
to environmental hazards, had no inkling of all these subterranean
forces which, like an odorless gas, were productive of suspicion, malice, cynicism, and *sauve qui peut* reflexes.

In conversation with Rürup at the Institute the next day, Eduard
asked what accounted for the fact that, in Germany, children and
grandchildren felt so little curiosity about their relatively decent
forebears, who had been neither criminals nor docile fellow travelers. Why did they feel vaguely threatened by the discovery that
there had been one or two courageous people among the preponder-
ance of cheering conformists? He wasn't talking about great heroes or
death-defying resistance fighters who had banded together against

Hitler—after all, people in this part of the world agreed on nothing so readily as sentiments like "I'm no hero myself" or "I don't know how I'd have behaved." He was talking about little, flawed heroes, intermediate quantities like his grandfather—people who, though unwilling to lay down their lives, nonetheless ran certain risks for their persecuted neighbors, friends, or fellow citizens. Why, for instance, was a man like Rürup almost as thoroughly ostracized today as he had been under the communist dictatorship?

Eduard hadn't found it easy to ask Rürup for an appointment. They'd had no opportunity for an informal chat since his welcome to the Institute. When he saw Rürup sitting at his desk in his bleak office, he regretted that the professor wasn't better at projecting himself and his authority. Rürup's whole appearance seemed governed by the ideal of unobtrusiveness. He was never to be seen in anything but his brown-checked tweed jacket and a dark gray shirt whose collar turned up slightly at the ends. His shoes and the slacks with the permanent creases still seemed influenced by the taste of the regime he had morally rejected. Eduard looked upon Rürup as something akin to the father he wished he'd had, but he was surprised that such a quaint genius of a character should be so modest and so heedless of externals. He himself had another conception of the scientist's role in society. Although the media generally showed representatives of his craft attired in their smocks in a cold and somehow abstract working environment, even the public were slowly coming to realize that these faceless figures in laboratories were the revolutionaries of the future. They, who were deciphering the alphabet of life with their unimpressive-looking diagrams and diffraction patterns, would change society more lastingly than any social revolution or political genius. The only way to develop remedies for the fatal diseases of industrial society was to discover how they had arisen. The defense of the planet against the ozone layer and the greenhouse effect, the elimination of human ailments, the discovery of new sources of energy and foodstuffs—these things were to be expected not from any future Lenins, Maos, or Che Guevaras, but from the unremarkable people in lab smocks.

Rürup's expression conveyed that Eduard was only feigning naïveté. "Ostracized?" he said, almost aggressively. "Nothing odd about that. The fellow travelers feel they had no choice, and they want to preserve that sensation. It wasn't seriously impaired by the heroes who deliberately put their lives at risk—heroism is too much to ask of anyone, as we all know. The petty dissidents who didn't actually risk their lives but opposed the regime spontaneously, without any set plan or organized backing—*they're* the spoilsports, *they're* the ones who injure the conformists' self-esteem most of all. They disprove the myth that 'you couldn't do anything' because anyone who failed to conform was doomed to imprisonment or the hangman's noose. In the Nazi period, no one who refused to shoot a civilian was ever put up against a wall for disobeying orders. Likewise, no one who refused an invitation to collaborate with the Stasi—and many did just that—had to fear for his life or liberty. Like successful resistance to a dictatorship, a successful dictatorship is dependent not on its leaders but on the morale of the little people, so called. 'Woe to the nation that needs heroes . . .' Brecht's hackneyed dictum should be amplified. A handful of heroes will never save a nation of cowards."

Eduard thought he read something more into Rürup's answer. For some time now, the professor had struck him as withdrawn and almost unapproachable. Criticism of his leadership qualities was growing at the Institute, where a strange coalition had formed. The younger scientists from the West, whose courage had never been put to the test, got on far better with the flexible Dr. Santner, who had traveled widely even in the days of the GDR. It was whispered that Santner had received a summons from Washington, and that he'd been offered the directorship of the Institute to keep him here. Eduard had often wanted to ask Rürup about this gossip, but the professor's aloof manner discouraged such questions. Suddenly sensing that his unapproachability was just a defensive stance, Eduard asked if there was any truth in the rumor, and if he could do anything to help.

Rürup looked at him with a faintly mocking air, as if the question related to Eduard's own future. It was a real shame, he replied, that Eduard's talents were currently being applied to social rather than scientific experiments. He would gladly have deployed him against Santner's ambitions, but word at the Institute was that "the American" was setting a work rate that would once have been termed "socialist." He, Rürup, would be unable to protect Eduard for much longer because he was being urged, in a friendly but unmistakable manner, to take early retirement. He wasn't averse to the idea. The dictatorship had tested his moral integrity and punished his attitude with scientific isolation. The agents of the new era, who were now testing his ability to withstand competition, found that he had only learned how to be obstructive, not to win.

"They may even be right," said Rürup. "We shall see." And he bade Eduard *au revoir.*

3 THE FOLLOWING NIGHT Eduard was roused from his bed by the doorbell. He almost failed to recognize Klott, who was wearing a track suit, a beanie, and a pair of heavily tinted shades. Klott the former urban guerrilla, decks cleared for action!

"It's on fire," he said breathlessly. "Quick, get dressed, grab your raincoat, and stick this on your head." He removed the beanie and thrust it into Eduard's hand.

Klott drove his Rover like a fire engine, deaf to all remonstrances. Every traffic light was the same color to him. Buildings flashed toward Eduard and past him as if propelled by a seismic wave; street-lights, trees, and kiosks simply bent aside.

"Don't ask questions," Klott mumbled around the dead cigarillo in the corner of his mouth. "I've told you all I know: it's on fire!"

He pulled up not far from Rigaer Strasse. The housefronts were illuminated by warning lights flashing in heartbeat rhythm. Although the fire engines and police cars parked nearby could not be seen, countless curious spectators were thronging the balconies and open windows. Some were pointing across the roofs, but most were staring into the darkness and fending off the little black specks that flared up like glowworms when caught by a stray light. There was a smell of burning plastic bags and car tires, mattresses and refrigerators, charred wood and scorched plaster.

"Why did you bring me here?" Eduard yelled. "I can already see the headlines: 'Furious landlord stoops to last resort: eviction by arson!'"

"Don't worry," Klott retorted curtly. "A landlord who's months behind with his fire-insurance premiums will hardly be suspected of torching his own property."

"Who was it, then, the squatters?"

"They're bound to be suspected, but for no good reason," said Klott, lighting his cigarillo. "Who's going to torch a building they're living in rent-free, without having to pay for water, power, or trash collection—a building they feel quite at home in after so many years? Maybe a gas pipe exploded."

"You don't believe that crap yourself!"

"There is another possibility," Klott said thoughtfully. "Perhaps there'll be an anonymous confession before long. You know: 'Jews and squatters out! Germany for the Germans!' It was a bit easier to feel in solidarity with you twenty years ago, my friend!"

They made their way to Rigaer Strasse in the crowd of rubbernecks streaming out of the buildings nearby. The fire department had cordoned off such a large area that Eduard could form no idea of the extent of the damage. The fire itself had obviously been extinguished; the site of the fire was identifiable by the dense cloud of smoke rising from the roof at the rear of the building as if blasted into the sky by a bellows.

Klott proposed that Eduard accompany him to his office and spend the night on one of the comfortable leather sofas there. They must visit the police station promptly in the morning and inspect the results of the investigation. Eduard agreed, but he was far too agitated to think of sleeping. Having driven back in silence, they spent a long time sitting on the window seat in Klott's office, drinking scotch and looking out at the deserted, festively illuminated Kurfürstendamm.

Would he now, on top of everything else, have to pay for the debris of the fire to be removed? Klott laughed and, when Eduard didn't join in, firmly shook his head. It wasn't clear what he found so hilarious, Eduard's question or his predicament. Eduard accused the attorney of fobbing him off with vague information. He would never, he said, have accepted the bequest if warned of even one of the traps he'd fallen into since. In a furious attempt to find the initial link in his chain of misfortunes, he went so far as to impugn Klott's entire profession. He failed to understand how a man like Klott could bring himself to earn a living from these flimsy restitution claims. The whole principle was absurd and immoral.

Klott had let Eduard's outburst flow over him quite unmoved. Eduard could hear nothing but the crunch of the pretzels he kept stuffing into his mouth by the handful. Suddenly, however, the attorney lost patience.

"You don't know what you're talking about," he said sharply. "Look out the window. Nearly opposite you can see the Hotel Kempinski. Further along the Ku'damm there's Karstadt, Wertheim's, KDW, and Hertie's—formerly the Tietz department store. Don't you realize that they and thousands of other Berlin businesses were built up by German Jews and stolen from their rightful owners by Aryan informers and competitors just like Marwitz & Co.? Take the Hotel Kempinski, opened by Berthold and Helene Kempinski just after Bismarck founded the Reich. The Kempinskis' businesses, which also included the Haus Vaterland on Alexanderplatz, were squeezed by the boycott against Jewish owners. The Dresdner Bank cut off their credit and they were jointly acquired at dumping prices by Werner Steinke, an 'Aryan' employee of the Kempinskis', and the financial director of Aschinger's, one of their competitors. The Kempinskis emigrated to England, Steinke moved into their luxurious home, and Walter Unger, their last remaining German Jewish co-owner and associate, was deported in 1943 and murdered. Or take the story of Ignatz Nacher, the Berlin brewery owner. He was the first to hit on the idea of selling beer in bottles, and it made him one of the wealthiest men in Germany. Less than a year after the Nazis came to power he was compelled, once again with the complicity of the Dresdner Bank, to sell the Engelhardt Building on Alexanderplatz and resign as managing director of the Engelhardt Brewery. All he got for his business was less than 10 percent of its value, roughly the sum he had to pay for permission to emigrate six years later. When he died in September 1939 he left nothing. His brother had fifty-five reichsmarks in his bank account when he was deported. Precisely the same fate overtook other Jewish businesses, large and small. Dozens of Aryan applicants stood in line for each of them when it was put up for auction. Anything left over was sold off at street markets, labeled 'Jewish property.' Thousands of people, all of whom knew full well where the stuff came from, fought to buy their deported fellow citizens' china and furniture, drapes and bed linen. During the war auctions were held in the deportees' homes themselves, and it was often their next-door neighbors who snapped up their household effects. Restitution would be justified even if its sole purpose were to give back exiled German Jews their land and buildings. Large tracts of central Berlin used to be owned by them. Some twelve thousand cases with a market value of several dozen billion marks remain to be settled here alone, because the GDR—the 'better' or 'antifascist' Germany—simply perpetuated this Nazi injustice. What the Nazis had stolen from German Jews was expropriated once more by the Sozis and became—to use communist officialdom's magnificently mendacious term—'national property.' That property included the desirable residences taken over by the self-styled guardians of the nation."

While they were on the subject, Klott went on, he didn't see, either, why the status quo should be accepted by millions of refugees from the GDR who had been dispossessed of their homes by the state or had had to sell them for derisory prices. True, there were unpardonable gaps in the law that left room for innumerable dirty tricks, and in many cases it would be fairer to pay compensaiton than return the properties in question. Some of the prospective clients who entered his office referred with profound emotion to the sentimental value of a house or piece of land they'd never seen, but he wasn't obliged to take them on.

Eduard said nothing. It was absurd, he felt, that Klott should have to tell him all these things. At length he asked why he'd taken him on at all. Was there some good reason, aside from their long-standing friendship, why Klott should be grappling with his claim to the building on Rigaer Strasse? The attorney seemed gratified by this question. If Eduard's claim were based on Aryanization, he replied, he would be the first to warn him off or, if necessary, leave him out in the cold. However, he was pretty sure the squatters' allegations were false. He had renewed an old acquaintance from the contemporary scene and would probably be in a position to give him the address of Frau Schlandt, née Marwitz, in the next few days.

Eduard knew the way to Friedrichshain police station better than Klott. He didn't have to introduce himself to the brace of sheriffs from the still-unwritten evening TV series, but they seemed put out by Klott, now back in his double-breasted suit, who looked authoritative and clearly took exception to the fact that the police officers were engaged on a second breakfast two hours after the start of office hours. Eduard was tempted to dig him in the ribs when he loudly introduced himself as Eduard's attorney and demanded to look at the investigation records. Klott behaved as if he had landed in Normandy four years ago, fought his way to Friedrichshain with his division, and must now submit the two policemen to a process of reeducation.

He leafed through the file with a bilious air. Why, he asked, was there no record of his admonitions about the exposed electric cables dangling down the front of the building and in the stairwell? "I repeatedly drew attention to the danger of fire. Either the commissioner of police doesn't pass my letters on to the relevant precinct, or you neglect to file them!" The cause of the fire was being investigated by experts, the younger policeman retorted brusquely. In any case, he had eyes in his head and didn't need any lectures on the subject from a Kurfürstendamm attorney. They were investigating the possibility of arson by a person or persons unknown.

For the record's sake Eduard was asked his whereabouts on the night of the fire. The information that he'd been asleep at home when roused from his bed by his attorney was duly noted.

To his surprise the newspapers attached little importance to the incident. All it rated was a three-line report in the local news section.

4 EDUARD RELISHED the silence that followed the fire, although he cherished no illusions about its cause. The Rigaer Strasse building had for some reason attained the status of an alpine hotel in which peace is suddenly restored after a bombardment by every thunderbolt in the area. It was as if the interested parties had temporarily agreed to avoid making any new moves. The dispute had placed all of them—squatters, municipal authorities, Klott, and Eduard—in positions they had never previously dreamed of occupying. Eduard was represented as a picture-book, street-theater capitalist whose conscience terminates where the profit motive begins. The senator had seized the opportunity, in a case that was costing the city nothing, to demonstrate a historical sensitivity he would never have shown toward insurance companies and banks, the major beneficiaries both of Aryanization and restitution. As for the squatters, surprised to find themselves taken under their arch-enemy's wing, it was probable that they were secretly wondering where they had gone wrong.

While becalmed in this way, Eduard received a phone call from Marina. She promptly rejected his instinctive attempt to apologize for his silence. "If I'd wanted to see you any sooner, I'd have called you," she said, and suggested a weekend trip to Weimar. "Weimar?" he repeated in disbelief. It sounded like the destination of a dream journey that had never figured in any of his dreams. To him, "Weimar" had been a parental word. Something unreal and vaguely, objectionable clung to the name, an aura of injured dignity and greatness. Weimar was the home of the new German Parsifals, the Camelot of those who invoked a better, more wholesome Germany. He couldn't get into his head that this, of all places, might become the destination of a "pleasure trip" with Marina, a health resort for his wounded manhood.

Whatever she had gleaned about his inheritance problems from the newspapers or from Institute scuttlebutt, she asked no questions. They had tacitly agreed to keep their assignations quite separate from the rest of their lives. Each time they met they would sample a different newly opened restaurant, a new theater, a neighborhood they'd never been to before. The forever self-redesigning city, which devised new playgrounds every week, presented an ideal background for the illusion of a second, quasi-extraterrestrial existence untouched by the first.

The events of the last few weeks had upset this equilibrium. Even at their most recent dinner together Eduard's interest in a new rendezvous had been only feigned. His head was too full of voices, too preoccupied with explanations, justifications, accusations. Divorcing their first and second existences suddenly struck him as childish, and he had also become alive to the pressure this was exerting on Marina. He inferred from various allusions that she herself was contending with problems he hadn't wanted to know about. She was about to move, and her ailing son required so much attention that it was jeopardizing her position at the laboratory. She was obliged to report sick more and more often on his account. The boy's father came to see them but would never make a firm arrangement in advance. He'd been known to stay away for a whole year without disclosing his whereabouts, with the result that their son had to think up a succession of desperate excuses when questioned by his classmates. On one occasion he'd claimed that his father managed a ranch in Brazil, on another that he'd hijacked a plane and been sent to prison. Most recently he'd informed his friends that his father was dead.

Eduard had once met the boy and Marina at a café. He surmised from the offhand way she introduced him that she didn't want them to become better acquainted. But the youngster had gazed at him with big, intent eyes—Marina's eyes—as if wondering whether Eduard would make a worthy substitute for his inaccessible father. It was impossible to evade the mute question, and Eduard could not help trying to find the answer. Nowhere near as good-looking as his mother, the boy had obviously inherited his broad nose and reddish hair from his father. Eduard thought himself capable of gaining his trust. What perplexed him, however, was the strange mixture of intimacy and irritability that prevailed between mother and son. The twelve-year-old behaved with Marina like a temperamental lover who decided when and whether he would grant a request or obey a prohibition. Any man who wanted to join that alliance would have to gain access to it with a crowbar.

Once Eduard and Marina were in her Golf GTI convertible and heading south down the autobahn, he felt as if the weight of the city were lifting from his shoulders with every mile. He hadn't left Berlin since returning from America. The different light, the open country-side, the color of the asphalt, the speed and mode of travel—all were unwonted experiences. The sky's dimensions seemed to differ from those on the other side of the Atlantic. High above in the firmament floated pale, almost motionless wreaths of vapor that robbed the sun of power; lower down, differing in density and velocity, clouds like huge sable beasts came flying toward them.

He was having to reaccustom himself to the beauties of restraint. White and yellow flowers whose names he'd almost forgotten were hiding, barely visible, in the youthful green of the fields. Broad swaths of heather stretched away to the dark, clear-cut edges of the forests whose somber expanse was relieved only by the reddish branches of the pines and the cones that seemed to have sprouted from them at the last moment. Seen against an orderly background of beech, linden, and maple, the silvery trunks of birch trees resembled unauthorized intruders, dummies cursorily dusted with chalk. Visible on the hills, like strange grazing animals, were the bright red gabled roofs of new housing developments. In the dips stood gigantic, angular monoliths of glass, steel, and plastic that might have fallen from the sky like the excremental droppings of some alien civilization.

Eduard tried to explain his wonderment to Marina. He was constantly tempted to remove his sunglasses, he said, just to satisfy himself that he wasn't wearing any. In California he'd experienced the spring as an explosion of blossom and color, a luminous symphony orchestra in which the instruments were brought in by an unseen conductor: crescendo, please, the oleanders; now, cantando, the bougainvilleas; and now, fortissimo, the ornamental cherries. Even the verdant backdrop to the whole performance had vibrated in a thousand gradations. The green of German field and forest was more restrained and monochrome than its counterpart across the Atlantic, Eduard declared; it lacked radiance. He was struck for the first time by the singularly matte appearance of grass and foliage in Germany, which might, he said, be attributable to a combination of weaker sunlight and greater chromatic uniformity. There was too little yellow and red in it. Everything seemed to have been painted by an artist who used too few tubes of paint and shrank from mixing them. Germany's matte coloration, like its passions, its eternal alternation between diffidence and arrogance, might somehow be connected with the sun, which slanted down at an angle even during the summer and was always threatening to go in.

Marina tapped her forehead. His meteorological and chromatic comparisons meant absolutely nothing to her. Personally, she said, she liked the slanting German sun and the matte green beneath it; in any case, she much preferred "matte" to "glossy." She found a good word to say about all that irritated him, even the speed demon who'd been sitting on her bumper for a couple of miles and was angrily swerving out to overtake her. She'd let Eduard drive her Golf only once and never again. His driving habits had been tamed in the States. After initially complimenting him on his patience, she condemned them as dangerously lax and lethargic. Sorry, she said, but she felt safer when she herself was behind the wheel. The mode of driving she favored, locally known as "sporty," was clearly indicative of her determination not only to hold her own in the duel on four wheels with largely masculine tailgaters and know-it-alls, but to emerge victorious.

She seemed in general to get a kick out of disputing Eduard's impressions of the native land to which he had become a stranger. When they spoke about the Institute she sided against their Wessi colleagues. She inveighed against the conceit of second-rate careerists who missed no opportunity to parade their superior knowledge in front of downgraded Ossi colleagues by embellishing German scientific terms with English ones delivered in a ludicrous accent. As a woman, she said, she felt far more at ease among her East German colleagues, who reacted far more humorously to her occasional habit of dressing up like a bird of paradise. Then again, she would astonish Eduard with her harsh strictures on GDR males. With their bushy beards and deficient clothes sense, she said, they were Stone Age representatives of the species. GDR women she extolled all the louder, albeit with a hint of irony. Wouldn't they make ideal partners for West German men who'd been rattled by the women's libbers? "Self-confident professionals but—wonder of wonders—feminine notwithstanding!" To judge by her acquaintances, the male Wessi–female Ossi combination worked excellently, whereas its inversion had always been a recipe for amatory disaster.

And Marina herself? Eduard still didn't know for sure whether she was a Wessi or an Ossi, and she made him pay for having asked

the question at all. Scarcely had she "betrayed" herself by express-
ing a predilection for a little-known perfume obtainable only in the
West than she teased him by singing a communist "Young Pioneer"
song she claimed to like.

"How much more would you really know about me if you knew
it?" she asked, looking at him belligerently.

"Nothing. Still, don't you think it's a bit ridiculous to make such
a secret out of it?"

"It's no secret. GDR women have more orgasms than women from
the West, hadn't you heard? Well, what does that tell you? Guess."

Perhaps it was more than a guessing game—perhaps it merely
symbolized the indeterminate nature of their affair.

"Before and afterward are out, so please don't ask me for my passport or special peculiarities. For all that, my dear, even our relationship has its rules. There's something you should know: I can never
love or sleep with more than one man at the same time, and if that
man—regardless of whether I've known him three weeks or three
years—breaks the rules and I find out—"

"How would you find out?"

"I always do, then it's over."

"You break it off?"

"Yes, I do, and with one exception the decision has always been
mine."

"That sounds ominous."

"Really? I don't regard it as a moral question, it has to do with
myself. Men are incapable of making swift, irrevocable decisions in
matters of the heart. They're born to maneuver, to lie, to hover three
feet above the ground. That's not in my nature. If I thought it necessary, I've never postponed or shirked a goodbye just to wait for 'the
right moment.' I always take a while to make up my mind. It's an
awful struggle—relapses and self-abasement, weeping and gnashing
of teeth—but once I reach the crucial point there's no turning back.
My decision is final."

Was that a warning? He studied her in profile, chin jutting and

curly head tilted for a glimpse of the rearview mirror as she prepared
to overtake. She glanced at him for a moment before looking straight
ahead again. Her eyes were alight with belligerence.

The façade of the Hotel Elephant was an almost exact copy, to the
nearest door and window, of the engraving on the old postcard
Marina had shown him; the lobby, on the other hand, was ruled by
art deco and international hotel standards. The man at the reception
desk keyed their names into a computer. To Eduard it seemed a kind
of statement that the who's who of European celebrities from Grill-
parzer to Thomas Mann and Adolf Hitler, who had given his occupa-
tion as "Writer," had checked in on this very spot in the course of
two centuries. Was anything here really older than the computer
behind the reception desk? The whole hotel might have been a successful replica that happened to be standing on the same spot as the
world-famous original. He stared in sudden panic at the room key
the receptionist handed him. Someone had told him a long time ago,
with an equivocal smile, that the rooms on the Elephant's top floor
afforded a view of the watchtower of Buchenwald concentration
camp. The number on the key indicated that they were staying on
the third floor.

The windows of their room looked out on Marktplatz. The
Renaissance buildings around the cobbled square looked as if they'd
celebrated their topping-out ceremony only a few months earlier.
Eduard experimentally flopped down on the big bed and watched
Marina standing at the open window. The line of her slightly
inclined body lent enchantment to the room and the square outside
it. When he came up beside her and put his arm around her shoulders he felt an almost imperceptible tremor run through them. He
was going to ask if she felt cold but stopped himself just in time. It
dismayed him that he had momentarily misinterpreted such a reaction. The gentle answering pressure of her body reconciled him to
the scenery outside, which looked, even in daylight, as if it were
illuminated by candlelight. All at once he found it forgivable, the

look of innocence and security that had so often infuriated him
about the spruced-up, half-timbered aspect of German country
towns. The housefronts, the church, and the town hall seemed to be
outlined with a light pen. His gaze even glamorized the Berolina
double-decker buses in front of the hotel and the calves of the sweating tourists, many of them in shorts and sandals, who were tumbling
out of their open doors and onto the square like kids on a waterslide.
He listened without rancor to the new arrivals calling to Hans,
Heinz, or Karin, the yells of "Wait a minute!" and "Stop!" that had
made him quickly cross the street whenever he heard them in San
Francisco.

Marina shut the window. To Eduard her hand on the handle was
like the conductor's raised baton when the lights go down and the
audience stops coughing. Others might shut the window because
the noise outside was too loud; Marina did so to muffle the imminent
explosion of sound *inside* the room for the benefit of those outside.
He was touched by the absentminded but dependable way in which
she performed this prescient task. She shut the window just as a
solicitous lady's maid, knowing her mistress's uninhibited and
incorrigible behavior, might prepare the bedroom for a tryst. Then
the lady's maid vanished, leaving Marina behind.

In front of the drawn curtains she slipped her dress over her head
but retained her black body stocking. She liked to display herself in
this transitional state, which could always be revoked, and arouse
him by the mere sight of her. He sometimes felt she deliberately surprised him with her multifarious lingerie. It was as if, with a research
scientist's detached sense of humor, she meant to run the gamut of
his erotic notions. But her curiosity wasn't unlimited. She had once
taken the precaution of listing the male practices he should avoid if
he didn't want to risk putting her off him for evermore.

It would have seemed like vandalizing a work of art, as she stood
there before him with the champagne glass in her hand, to undress
her completely. She was doing it for herself, she said, not for him;
she enjoyed pleasing herself. He marveled yet again at the absence of
false moves in his sexual relations with Marina. She would signal her

displeasure if he hesitated or asked what she wanted him to do. Did he suffer from an urge to prove himself? The only instruction she issued seemed to be to follow his own inclinations. He almost felt cheated that it was all so simple, that there was nothing to learn, discover, or divine. If he stopped short, alarmed by his own violence, she said she was capable of defending herself and urged him to continue. All that irked him was the notion that he might only be a surrogate—that Marina's explosions owed nothing at all to himself and his skill as a lover. Those disturbing thoughts were probably part of the psychological damage he'd brought with him from his life outside this room. It was as if he had to persuade himself, again and again, to accept the gift of Marina's devotion.

Slanting rays of afternoon sunlight sent their will-o'-the-wisp messages through the curtains. The objects in the room moved to and fro like puppets on luminous strings, becoming transformed into creatures of light and shade that seemed to halt the instant you looked at them. The strips of light on the windowsill established contact with the glowing green champagne bottle on the table, roamed across the glistening beads of sweat on Marina's belly, and touched her lips, which seemed to be illuminated from within. Then, from one moment to the next, a passing bank of cloud extinguished all the lights except the little red and green glowworms of the hotel room's electronic gadgets. Marina's open mouth, the armpits lit till just now by the shimmering skin of her upper arms, the dark furrow between her legs—all that had earlier been in shadow sank back into the gloom. Eduard subsided with it and let himself fall. As he did so, like a distant memory, he had a vision of Marktplatz. He felt he'd seen the square before at another time, in another place, in quite a different light. Then, too, it had been thronged with people, but they'd hailed him with false enthusiasm. The whole scene of jubilation had been counterfeit and insidious, staged by a personal enemy. His descent was suddenly checked. Beneath their window, one or two of those within earshot of Marina's cries would involuntarily pause and look up, wondering if they'd heard aright, and then walk on, shaking their heads in amiable amazement.

The guidebook hadn't exaggerated: you really didn't need to take more than a thousand paces to explore thousand-year-old Weimar. With a hint of derision, Marina assumed the role of a guide who was showing a "belated homecomer from the USA" the workshops of classical German literature. She patiently helped him to decipher the commemorative plaques and inscriptions that traced the careers of the famous. Eduard was unimpressed by closer acquaintance with their dates of birth and death, their relocations and ailments, their feuds with each other and the court—by all the gossip that had been worked up into a staple part of the school syllabus. What really surprised him was the evidence of his legs, which told him how small the place was. He failed to understand how so many of the great and good had lived within a thousand paces of each other. An art-loving princess having engaged first one, then another as a tutor, she was emulated by her friends, and within a few years there came into being a small, radical, incredibly prolific minority made up of painters, architects, composers, poets, educational theorists, scientists, and the personal physician to them all, Christoph Hufeland, who was almost daily obliged to trudge across town to minister to his difficult, often hypochondriacal patients. Perceptibly inspired by easygoing Italian masters of the art of living, there arose in the midst of their German forest a provincial metropolis in which, subject to fits of genius, envy, folly, and morbidity, the finest minds of their generation had mingled, clashed with, and tolerated each other. What accounted for this combination of spatial constraint and superabundant talent? Had one been conditional on the other? Hadn't Lorenzo's Florence also produced five or six outstanding men of genius within a small compass and a short space of time?

The winding streets of Weimar, too, had now been conquered by the victorious army of bulldozers and cranes, masonry saws and pneumatic drills. Scaffolding draped in fluttering plastic enclosed buildings familiar from countless photographs, construction sites were piled high with cobblestones, historic roof tiles and rose windows salvaged by hand. Berlin and Weimar seemed to be catapulting themselves out of the present at the same speed but in opposite directions. Berlin was fleeing into the future, Weimar into the past. Even the most famous modern building in the world, the experimental Versuchshaus, widely regarded as the mother cell of all modern architecture and the original blueprint for cities of the industrial age from Los Angeles to Novosibirsk, was undergoing renovation. Incredulously, Eduard strolled through the inconspicuous bungalow and examined the unfinished sketches on the walls, which might have been dashed off just for fun. No poem, no stage play, no classical novel had so radically changed the visible, man-made world as the sketches of the little priesthood that constituted itself here in April 1919 and proclaimed the formula for the architecture of the future: simplicity, openness, functionalism.

Goethe's "garden house" evoked memories of Eduard's German literature teacher—of his quivering lip and the knuckle of his forefinger as he beat out the rhythm of the hexameters on his desk.

> Pleasure we take in true, naked Amor and his gratifications,
> And the agreeable, creaking sound of the teetering bedstead . . .

The German teacher had probably tapped out the same rhythm on his desk at the college for sons of the Nazi elite in Karlsruhe, his former place of employment. That a poet's love nest should have become a national shrine to be deployed against Buchenwald concentration camp as proof that the Germans were a civilized race had blighted the place forever in Eduard's mind.

He felt relieved, almost disappointed, when he saw the house with the delicate ornamental half-timbering and steep slate roof among the beech trees, looking as if it had somehow outgrown its strength. Like the town, the garden house made an infinitely smaller and frailer impression than his mental picture of it. He was dumbfounded by the apparent impermanence and decrepitude of the place. It was as if the rooms were still illumined by the *coup de foudre* that had smitten the poet prince when he first saw poor Christiane Vulpius on the grounds. The whole house seemed to be on rollers, as collapsible and transportable as the great man's legendary traveling bed.

Marina and Eduard differed in the speed at which they looked, perused, and walked on. Being the quicker she often left him behind, only to rediscover him through the doorway to some other room. For him, the sight of her figure appearing and disappearing, the momentary glimpses of her profile, her bare arms and back, brought the sketches and silhouettes on the walls to life. Nonsense, he told himself. Stop it, you're being as absurd as he was, only in another way!

But he couldn't help it: the relics of passion displayed here like museum exhibits were kindling his desire. With a dismissive shake of the head, as if preserving the decencies, he obeyed the call of the place. Marina's intuition and presence of mind amazed him, that was all. Without prior intimation or intention, she was offering him a homecoming long renounced and somehow forbidden. Was he not, with Marina and Goethe's aid, bridging the chasm he'd chosen to insert between himself and "the Germans" by marrying Jenny and making a second home in California? Wasn't this straying off to Weimar, this cultural adultery with Marina, far more serious than any sexual transgression? And wasn't the damage to his marriage a consequence of Jenny's unallayed mistrust of the Germans and, in particular, of a self-mistrustful German named Eduard? Help! Never had there been a more convenient explanation of a personal mishap!

Inadvertently, as it were, Marina had put her finger on a hiatus. Wasn't it remarkable how easily, indeed, almost triumphantly, he and an entire generation had accepted being deprived of this part of German history without even realizing that they were missing something? Remembering how allergic schoolchildren were to the saints of German classical literature, he suddenly thought how splendidly compatible that allergy had been with acceptance of the country's division. It wasn't just separation from a piece of land they'd penitently accepted. They'd also been generous enough to renounce an engaging mode of thought and existence and let it go hang.

Eduard hesitantly noted that he was on the road to reconciliation. How long would it be before he discovered a penchant for loden coats and lederhosen, for pork knuckle with sauerkraut, for sweet Baden wines, for soccer chants and the painful German slap on the back, for linking arms and swaying to brass-band marches at Carnival time?

Later they lay beneath the trees in front of Goethe's garden house, he with his shirt off and his head on Marina's lap. His skin prickled, unaccustomed to the feel of the ground and the unseen creatures crawling around beneath his back. His eyes strayed up the beech tree's trunk, which was green with mold, to where specks of sunlight flickered between its branches, which seemed to be rocking to and fro on a choppy sea. The hot, almost Mediterranean afternoon sun was firing volleys of luminous arrows through the leaves. When Marina sat up he saw her chin just above him and followed the movements of her lips. She was reading a small volume she'd bought, almost at random, at the book counter. Dedicated to Christiane, it told of the ups and downs of their well-nigh hopeless relationship. Of her struggle for acceptance by Goethe's clique, who derided her as a "plump zero," a "blood sausage" and "maidservant;" of G. the drunkard, whose bloated body was mocked by Frau von Stein; of G. the glutton and voluptuary, who wrote innumerable plaintive letters about his provision with wine, cold cuts, and the long-denied pleasures of love; of G. the "media victim," the object of hatred and envy, whose unseemly "sensual proclivities" reviewers loved to censure. Surprising and never mentioned was the famous man's courageous stand on behalf of his socially inferior mistress, which almost led to his ostracism at court. Finally, G. the traitor, who had once, "with fumbling hand, counted out the hexameter's rhythm on her back" but could not, at the last, bring himself to enter the room where she lay screaming and dying in agony for days on end.

Far overhead between the leaves Eduard saw the sky like a diver looking up at the surface from a great depth, and, just above him, the line of Marina's neck and translucent chin. Once, when she stopped reading, he caught her eye and uttered the hackneyed phrase for which no substitute exists, adding that he wished things could go on like this for ever and ever. "Like what, exactly?" she asked. Her parted lips conveyed a hint of strain. They closed again in the next breath, and she turned her head away.

When they headed back to the hotel in a stream of tourists it was as if time were running out. Marina now had only impatient, weary glances to spare for the remaining stops on their cultural itinerary, for the home of Frau von Stein, which still seemed to be glaring up at the frivolous garden house, for the Anna Amalia Library and the Pushkin Monument. She almost snapped at Eduard when he paused to ask a question and hustled him along when he lingered over the plaque bearing greetings to Goethe from Pushkin, whom the Czar had forbidden to leave Russia.

They hurried into the hotel like two hunted beasts. In the gloom of their room Marina threw herself on the bed, curled up, and pulled the pillow over her head. Eduard suddenly grasped the cause of her anger. He had violated their tacit agreement. Carelessly, on an emotional impulse, he had opened a door he'd avoided until now and would never leave permanently ajar. In reality, though, they had long ago broken the rule that was supposed to shield their hours or days together from any claims to a future. He was looking at a proud woman castigating herself for allowing a hope she'd hitherto kept under control to escape her and become the master of her emotions. She proceeded to reproach him for worming his illicit way into her heart without any encouragement on her part.

"I hate the way you've been letting our affair drift along. I've never had much time for feminists' fanfares or the marshaling of the sexes into battle order. No, my dear, this isn't about 'role definition.' It's about the simplest thing of all: human rights, lovers' rights. Never a day goes by without my thinking of you. Every day I feel I could spend my whole life with you, not just an hour or two, and I can never really understand why you leave me. I can't fathom the process, and I'd betray myself if I did. I can't save up my desires for the few hours or days you dole out to me with a teaspoon. Let's call it a day—*I'm* calling it a day. Please spare me any belated explanations. I know you'll make all kinds of promises tomorrow, but tomorrow'll be too late. It was too late from the start. You'll never leave your family, and I can't even hate you for it. I'm more inclined to hate myself for letting it drag on so long."

He looked at her lying on the twilit bed, her naked, motionless form contorted with chagrin and rejection. Her face was in shadow, expressionless, speechless. She wept, fought back her tears, and wept because she was weeping.

The next morning she drove him to the station. She was going to visit a woman friend in Nuremberg, she said. "In a couple of months or so, maybe we could have dinner at the Palmetto or take in a movie. But please don't call me. I'll tell you if I feel like it." She didn't wave when the train pulled out. Unlike all the other leave-takers, she turned on her heel and walked back along the platform without even turning her head.

He vainly scanned the landscape speeding past for the images he'd perceived on the outward trip. His senses seemed incapable of recognition, as if he were traversing an unfamiliar continent. There was nothing around him but a great black void. In sudden, momentary flashes of memory, reason sought to challenge sorrow by replacing snatches of Marina's indictment. She'd given him his marching orders not because she'd had enough of him, but because she wanted more of him than he was prepared to give. So why did he keep staring at the automatic door as if she might appear at any moment? Why did he hope for a loudspeaker announcement summoning a passenger named Eduard Hoffmann to the telephone aboard the intercity train? Was it just the male ape's well-known, atavistic, prehensile reflex, the instinctive urge to cling to a receding object? Or was he afraid that the last chance of a lifetime had eluded him on that platform in Weimar?

The red light on the answering machine in his Berlin apartment was winking. There were two messages. For a moment, when he heard Jenny's voice, he feared a flash of jealous intuition, a probing question. But mistrust and jealousy were not in her repertoire—she had an aesthetic distaste for such emotions. "They make women mean and ugly," she had told him once.

Jenny informed him that the Debis Corporation, after making endless additional and wholly unnecessary inquiries, had indeed offered her the post of press officer, starting in September. This had really thrown her. "To be honest, I don't know whether to cheer or get goose bumps. I can't say moving to Berlin appeals to me, but I admit that the prospect of regular trips to that renovated turret in the Weinhaus Huth makes me view the city more favorably. At all events, we'll soon have to decide which roof to continue our experiments under—or on."

After Jenny and the beep came a voice he'd never heard before. An insistent voice that vaguely reminded him of Niessling's, it sounded younger and less experienced. Norbert Kühlmann introduced himself as a member of an "association of friends." "We've been closely following your valiant fight for home and hearth, and we'd like to express our admiration for the action you took in Rigaer Strasse. We're prepared to continue to help you secure your rights, and we offer you our association's firm support. Never again must German property, German soil . . ." At that point the message broke off as if the caller had been interrupted or disconcerted by the possibility that his words were being monitored.

Should he wipe the tape or turn it over to the police? In Germany the reaction to such twitches of the Nazi muscle was either insufficient or excessive, though agitation over the excessive almost always ended in shoulder-shrugging acceptance of the insufficient. What made Eduard go weak in the knees on second hearing was the little word "continue." Was it a form of admission? Precisely what sort of help had allegedly been extended, and what more such help could he expect? The suspicion brought a cry of disgust to his lips. It had become unendurably loathsome, the whole business. Not even Windsor Castle would have been worth so much aggravation.

In the middle of the night, when he'd almost given up hope, he was roused by a phone call. But it wasn't Marina. "I congratulate you on your sangfroid," Klott said plaintively. "Fancy fleeing the eye of the storm just like that! Strength of character or a split personality—it must be one of the two." For the sake of their long-standing friendship, which had survived the growing discrepancy between their ways of life, physical girth, and political views, he'd managed to get in touch with the Rigaer Strasse squatters and was at last in possession of a phone number for Edita Schlandt, née Marwitz, whom Vera Rheinland held to be the legitimate heir. Frau Marwitz—she'd reverted to her maiden name—lived in West Palm Beach. Klott advised Eduard, both as his attorney and as a former comrade in arms, to go and see the lady at once. "Besides," he concluded rather cryptically, "it's time you realized something: even squatters belong to a generation that'll inherit some four billion marks in the next few years."

Eduard looked at his watch. The sun hadn't set in West Palm Beach. He dialed the number.

"Yes? Who? Eduard Hoffmann? You must have the wrong number . . . Sorry? The wrong number, I said."

The voice at the other end of the line sounded too young to belong to a woman whom Eduard estimated to be well over eighty, but her accent, which still betrayed her mother tongue after so many years, prompted him to ask her not to hang up.

"You don't know me, but you knew my grandfather, Egon Hoffmann."

"Egon? Sure I know him—knew him, I mean. Are you certain, though? He never mentioned having a grandson named Eduard. How come you're calling me?"

"There's something I have to find out about him."

She chuckled briefly. "After all these years? Why? You're probably a grandfather yourself by now."

"I'll explain when I see you."

"Where are you?"

"In Berlin."

"And you're proposing to come all the way to West Palm Beach? When?"

"Tomorrow."

"But that's absurd. What for?" She hesitated. Then a softer note came into her voice. "You're his grandson? If you're half as nice a person as Egon was, you're welcome."

The next morning he asked Rürup for four days' leave of absence on urgent family business, booked a round trip to West Palm Beach and San Francisco, and sent Jenny and the children a brief fax warning them of his arrival.

5 | THE PLANE, which was crowded with American and German vacationers, had been overbooked. Eduard took it as a good omen when the flight attendant apologized to him, a latecomer traveling on his own, and conducted him to a seat in business class. He enjoyed the surge of acceleration before takeoff, the ever-increasing vibration of the huge fuselage that silenced conversations and tightened the passengers' grip on the arms of their seats. It gave him a feeling of lightness and freedom when he saw the runway and, within seconds, half the city career away beneath him. It was like a big, deep sigh of relief, being yanked so suddenly up and away. Relaxed and unreproachful, he saw Berlin spread out below him in a setting of luxuriant—but matte!—greenery between the arms of the Spree and its many lakes. The city's location favored it in spite of everything. It wasn't beautiful and could never become so, but it did possess a flawed kind of beauty.

"To revert to my losing battle," he wrote to Klott, "if I owed the bequest to 'Aryanization,' I wouldn't waste a moment fighting for it. Even if it is mine by right, any pleasure I might have derived from it has been marred long ago. I'd dearly like to kiss the whole cramped, dilapidated, squatter-infested place goodbye, and I only regret not doing so in good time. But there's more at stake now than a title deed. Let's call it the truth of an affair that doesn't concern me alone but was wished on me by circumstances. Which book of the Bible contains that bit about the Almighty sparing the city if there are fifty righteous men within its walls? I think it's Genesis—you might look it up for me sometime—but I'm afraid the Almighty wasn't thinking of the special case that's been worrying me, as Egon Hoffmann's grandson, for quite a while. How would the Almighty treat a city that won't have anything to do with the righteous men who lived within its walls—that actually disavows them in the hope of convincing the Almighty they never existed? The inhabitants' defense is that the unrighteous imposed such a complete and utter reign of terror that even the most righteous gave up and became unrighteous."

Having finally reached cruising height, he was glad to be unable to mail the letter. Perhaps the worst aspect of the city far below and behind him was its lack of sufficient breathing room for chance. Nothing remained as small as it had been, everything was somehow interconnected, every triviality thirsted for importance and fled into a wider context, aspired to higher rank, developed into megalomania, yearned to become a symptom, a myth. A stupid row about a ruin in Friedrichshain had inflated itself into a dispute between the Palace of the Republic and the Hohenzollern Castle. A wholly banal falling-out between two lovers was indirectly prompting him to follow a genocidal trail, sucking the strength and emotionalism from the wounds of the past and parading itself as an antifascist reflex. And he, Eduard, was well on the way to becoming a fisher in these troubled waters.

When he awoke he wasn't sure whether the sun, which was wreathed in a reddish haze, had just risen or was just setting. Through rents in the clouds he made out vast expanses of water gleaming like beaten metal, bounded here and there by the darker outlines of countries or islands that swiftly disappeared from view, while far beyond, on the extreme periphery of the window-framed sky, a band of pale pink seemed to separate the vault above from the horizontal plane below.

The screen of the cabin monitor was displaying a map of the world across which an airplane that might have been drawn by a child was jerkily advancing. The computer simulation was as little verifiable from a glance out the window as the stated speed. All that proved they were even moving was the drone of the engines and the leisurely, gliding progress of successive armies of extravagantly accoutered clouds. Eduard was irritated by the red umbilical cord on the computerized image, which hung from the belly of the phantom airplane above the Atlantic and led back to Berlin. Jerk forward as it might, the ridiculous winged object never succeeded in breaking free from its point of departure.

Humid heat smote him in the face as he came down the steps at West Palm Beach. His skin was instantly coated with a varnish of hot moisture by the air rising from the asphalt in visible, almost palpable eddies. He couldn't recognize the passengers disembarking ahead of and behind him, having so far perceived them only as seated figures. He now saw that nearly all of them had boarded the plane in the standard dress affected in Florida all year around, irrespective of the wearer's sex or age group: sneakers, shorts, T-shirt. Weimar was probably the only place in Europe where so many old legs could be seen in shorts. Eduard was conscious of the glare dive-bombing him from the sky, of the different weight of the air.

The taxi drove past orderly groups of palm, banana, and grapefruit trees, past trees whose crowns were often exceeded in diameter by their krakenlike aerial roots. Not for the first time, he delighted in the playful, unscrupulous way in which the country stage-managed itself. Shimmering between the palm fronds were white hotels with gilded battlements and turrets reminiscent of a Disney film. On the lawns could be seen white-clad, panama-hatted men and women.

Huge limousines braked in panic whenever a white trouser leg emerged from the shrubs beside the road and planted an immaculate golf shoe on a pedestrian crossing. Eduard had been told by a friend in San Francisco that many a pedestrian dreamed of being gently nudged in the knee by a bumper. With the aid of a good lawyer, the victim of such a mishap could easily become a millionaire.

They headed toward a gigantic triumphal arch that spanned a gleaming vista of sky and ocean. Only when they got closer did Eduard realize that the edifice was painted on the lateral wing of a hotel resembling a castle. Jenny had always been more amused by such frivolities than he. The art of illusion, she said, was probably older than any other. Why should he object if theme parks and the skyline of private residences or major shopping centers—not to mention the interior decoration of department stores, hotel lobbies, and movie theaters—were governed by a theatrical stage designer's aesthetic? Didn't it worry her, rejoined Eduard, that the whole decor turned out on closer inspection to be a sham, the balustrades pure stucco, the stucco moldings plastic, the crystal chandeliers acrylic resin, the mirror frames papier-mâché, the marble tables chipboard, the antique carpets factory-made? The illusion worked only at a distance. That, Jenny had replied, quite unmoved, was just why America sold itself so well on film. On the screen a dummy worked better than any original. The ideal distance between customer and product was that between the tenth row in a multiplex and the screen. It occurred to Eduard later that she might also have been hinting that it was the ideal distance between herself and him.

The cabbie slowed to ask a passerby for the address Eduard had given him. The oceanfront neighborhood where Frau Marwitz lived seemed to have been designed by someone obsessed with love of contrast and bold aberrations of taste. Eduard had never seen such a juxtaposition of opulent homes in so many different architectural styles. Each vied with the other for the honor of being noticed first. A private residence in the style of a Turkish mosque drew the eye away from its neighbor, a retirement home resembling a Gothic church; a Tuscan villa with a copper-sheathed roof strove to hold its own beside a Greek temple. Further prizes were awarded for the art of topiary. All these residential castles and libraries, monasteries and churches, were enclosed by dense, neatly sculpted hedges. Only one architectural element was universal: in addition to the steps leading up to them, all the houses were provided with switchback paths for the wheelchair-bound.

Edita Marwitz lived in the only apartment house in this exclusive residential district. Eduard could tell from the surviving wild palms and remnants of scrub that it had once, not so long ago, been surrounded by tropical forest. The black doorman announced him on the house phone in the lobby and showed him the elevator. The door of the seventh-floor apartment didn't open until several locks had been turned. Eduard felt boundlessly relieved when he finally set eyes on Frau Marwitz. She was a tall woman, and rather on the plump side. The broad face under the thinning hair, which had a few blond strands in it and was scraped back into a bun, looked shrewd, almost defiant. Her brightly painted lips and the countless wrinkles around them seemed to form an autonomous system, a face within a face. She eyed him closely, with a hint of mockery, as if comparing him with some picture in her head. "No," she said at length, paused as though about to elaborate on that verdict, then gently shook her head. Eduard couldn't decide whether the shake of the head was negative or a symptom of age.

"I know," he said quickly, "this is by way of being a surprise attack. I apologize."

Off to a bad start, he thought. The corners of her mouth turned down—disapprovingly, it seemed—when she heard his voice. She said nothing more for a while, as if replaying his words in her head. "No," she repeated, "you don't look like him. Don't sound like him either. No resemblance at all. Do you ever sing?"

"Should I? I used to as a boy. Just one of those things . . ."

Abruptly, she broke into a laugh that took years off her age.

"Oh, let's speak German," she said irritably. "It's silly for two people whose mother tongue is German to show off their English. Incidentally, he used to stick his tongue between his teeth when he said 'th,' just like you. Come in."

Eduard, in turn, was puzzled by the sound of her German. The vowels and harsh gutturals reminded him a little of the German favored by Hollywood movies set in World War II. It was only when he followed her into the apartment down a long, whitewashed passage that he noticed she leaned on the cane in her left hand. The two interconnecting living rooms were bounded on the street side by a glassed-in walkway. At the far end were some sliding glass doors that opened onto a terrace. Light flooded in on innumerable plants, lending the apartment the look of a greenhouse in which tropical flowers, shrubs, and small trees flourished amid choice pieces of antique furniture. Embroidered slipcovers reposed on the arms of the chaise longues, sofas, and armchairs, and a crocheted cloth was draped over the marble chess table. The hand-carved frame of the art nouveau mirror hanging on one wall was overloaded with flowers and vine tendrils in relief. The silver tea service on the mahogany table, with its finely enchased sugar bowl and cream pitcher, looked more like a museum piece than something in daily use. The table and floor lights, all of which were on, illuminated the group and portrait photographs set out on the desk and the piano.

Frau Marwitz offered Eduard a wicker chair on the terrace and excused herself. It was a long time before she returned with a pot of tea and some cognac.

"How come this sudden interest in Egon? What made a grandson of his fly halfway around the world?" she asked. "Did he leave you something in his will?"

Although she might only have meant to test his quick-wittedness, Eduard promptly started justifying himself. He recounted, far too hastily, how he and his brother had first learned from a friend of their father's of "a" bequest—he avoided the possessive "our"—on Rigaer Strasse about which they had known as little as they did about the testator, their grandfather Egon. He went on to tell her of the dispute over the occupied building that had almost cost the life of a twelve-year-old boy; of the squatters' allegation that he was a Nazi's grandson attempting for a second time, fifty years after the Nazis, to dispossess the rightful heir, Frau Marwitz herself; and of the strange prominence the whole affair had attained.

He couldn't tell if she was listening. She continued to look at him as if searching his face and voice for evidence of his claim to be Egon Hoffmann's grandson. Her mental picture of Eduard's forebear was evidently much clearer and more detailed than his own. He was also flustered by the way she kept gently shaking her head all the time. Then came another brief, mocking laugh.

"I don't envy you the country you come from," she said. "Divided or united, as soon as you start digging there, Nazi filth comes spurting out again. You get splashed even if you're standing on the sidelines." She clearly enjoyed talking in riddles, keeping him guessing.

"They didn't do their homework properly. Slipshod research!" she went on, looking at Eduard as if that verdict applied to him. "Frau Rheinland and her friends have gotten a few things mixed up. They must have heard or read somewhere how two elderly ladies from Florida lost their temper in the lobby of a Berlin courthouse and became violent. You didn't know? Where have you been? It was in all the newspapers. The two old things—you're looking at one of them right now—had the nerve to slap the face of a criminally stupid young man, the grandson of a former Nazi industrialist. For a derisory sum, his astute grandfather acquired and Aryanized my father's firm within a year of Hitler's coming to power. After the war he was allowed to keep his ill-gotten gains provided he paid an indemnity of 20 percent. He died a very wealthy man; my father committed suicide in Berlin in 1935. You'd think an affair like that would end sooner or later, at least legally, but nothing of the kind— it goes on and on and on. Now to that slap in the face. Hardly had the two Germanys miraculously united when the Nazi industrialist's grandson came forward. Not with an apology, not with a gesture of contrition—no, with legal claims! That twenty-year-old innocent wanted to reacquire the land and buildings his noble grandfather lost possession of after the war because they'd been expropriated by the East German government. Young Wollgraf brazenly alleged that my father had disposed of all his assets 'voluntarily,' and that the indemnity payment agreed upon in 1950 naturally included assets situated in the GDR, among them the Rigaer Strasse apartment house. Do you get it now? Frau Rheinland has simply confused you with the grandson of a Nazi industrialist!" Her laugh betrayed a hint of a malicious glee. "I can't really blame her. You can't help the fact that your grandfather was different, that you can be proud of him— you didn't even know the man. It's always surprised me that none of the Hoffmanns ever tried to find out more about him."

She rose, led Eduard over to the piano, and indicated one of the framed photographs. It depicted a string quartet: four young men of university age. Edita Marwitz watched Eduard as he searched the faces in the photograph for some distinguishing feature. With sudden decision he pointed to the figure at the music stand in the foreground, a mustachioed violinist in a wing collar. "That's my father Kasimir," Edita Marwitz said with an implacable smile. "Your grandfather was responsible for the notes in the bass clef."

Going closer, Eduard scrutinized the young man with the cello. He was holding the instrument unusually far from his body and depressing a string with the fourth finger of his left hand, right up near the bridge. The eyes behind the rimless glasses seemed to be looking impatiently, almost angrily, at Kasimir, the first violin.

"Of course, you don't even know what he looked like! Your grandmother's pride was so badly hurt, she must have obliterated him from the family's collective memory. Well, yes, Egon probably made a disastrous husband and father. He was a show-off, a gambler, an incorrigible ladies' man. But isn't it rather odd that a man incapable of fidelity should be punished for it with repudiation by his children's children? Plenty of faithful German husbands of his generation were guilty of quite different offenses—they became informers, racists, murderers. Were *they* reproached by their families, let alone disowned? No, having done their dirty work they were welcomed back with open arms by their faithful spouses and beloved children. Egon, naughty Egon, had a quality that's rare in Germany."

Little by little, Edita Marwitz's reminiscences built up a picture of a difficult friendship. Kasimir and Egon had studied law together at Leipzig. On taking over his father's footgear firm, Kasimir recruited his former fellow student as legal director with a seat on the board. When the Nazis followed up their victory at the polls by organizing boycotts against companies owned by German-Jewish industrialists, Egon advised his friend to save the firm from Nazi "streamlining" by initiating the process himself and appointing him, Egon, managing director in his place. After some hesitation, Kasimir agreed. The two men developed a strange rivalry, a relationship that alternated between trust and suspicion. Egon, who always liked to play a prominent part, not only in the string quartet but businesswise as well, made no secret of the fact that he relished his new position of authority. No sooner had he moved into the managing director's office, with its three windows overlooking the Kurfürstendamm, than he implemented the directives of the Reich Ministry of Economic Affairs with such vigor that Kasimir became uneasy. He and his friends sometimes debated in an undertone how much of Egon's behavior was genuine and how much playacting: his public persona as a Party member and devout Nazi, or his privately expressed abhorrence of "those brownshirted philistines." But the chief bone of contention between them was their differing assessment of the gravity of the Nazi threat to Germans of Jewish extraction. Kasimir forbade himself and everyone else from even entertaining the idea that a monstrous campaign of theft and murder had been launched against him and his kind in a country where his family had lived for centuries. He was convinced that the Nazi nightmare would soon be over, and that they must simply grin and bear it for a year or two. When Egon urged him to sell and quit the country as soon as possible, taking his family with him, he blew a fuse. He could well imagine, he said, why Egon was painting such a gloomy picture of his, Kasimir's, future. It seemed that Eduard's grandfather left the Marwitz house in Dahlem without a word, and that he received Kasimir's subsequent apologies with no outward sign of reconciliation.

When Kasimir was threatened with arrest, however, Egon hid him at his home and used his Party connections to get the warrant rescinded. In the fall of 1933, when Marwitz & Co.'s turnover had steadily dwindled because of the boycott and the threat of closure, Kasimir decided to sell his majority stockholding to his main supplier, Wollgraf, the leather-goods manufacturer. The latter was in no hurry. Such were the circumstances under which Egon advised his friend to hive off the Rigaer Strasse apartment house and sell it to him.

When negotiating a price, said Edita Marwitz, Egon showed, once and for all, "where his affections lay." He insisted on paying Kasimir a sum 25 percent above the asking price and remitted it at once to an account in Paris. The money enabled Kasimir to arrange for his dependents to emigrate and get some of their furniture out of the country. From Amsterdam the family managed to sail for New York complete with their household effects.

It was dark by now. Frau Marwitz stopped answering Eduard's questions and fell silent.

Through the picture windows he could see the white and yellow dots of streetlights, the harsh, pulsating glare of neon signs, and, further away, luminous ribbons of cars passing each other in opposite directions like two endless railroad trains. In the black sky far above, with only their central or upper sections illuminated, floated the gargantuan cubes of the high-rises, man-made mountains in which the troglodytes of the twentieth century had taken up residence. In a few years' time, thought Eduard, Berlin would inscribe the same outlines on the sky. Modern cities didn't grow, they enlarged themselves in sudden, furious bursts, repeating on a vast scale the pattern programmed into a computer.

The semidarkness had painted out the wrinkles on Edita Marwitz's face, leaving only the deeper lines visible. "However," she said suddenly, "Egon's magnanimous gesture wasn't quite as altruistic as my father thought. He'd failed to notice that Egon's motive in attending our chamber music soirees wasn't confined to his love of Brahms and Schubert."

When he played solos and transformed his cello into an orchestra, she went on, he used to throw her glances like declarations of love. In the end, despite his notorious reputation, she accepted him as her lover. It was a clandestine passion; both of them had differing but equally cogent grounds for discretion. Edita's marriage to the bank clerk Martin Schlandt had failed within a year, notwithstanding all her parents' admonitions and attempts to mediate. For his part, Egon attached great importance to secrecy because even a whiff of the affair would have given his greatest enemy inside the firm, a resentful branch manager and staff representative named Dahnke, a rope to hang him with. But above all, though courageous by nature, Egon couldn't bring himself to tell Kasimir that he was his daughter's lover. "The curse of secrecy pursued us halfway across the world to Florida, where we saw each other again two years later," said Frau Marwitz. "It was here in this apartment that he came to see me and my family after my father's death. We resumed our affair, but secretly as in Germany, always in different places, always afraid of being seen together."

Once the Rigaer Strasse property was sold and the purchase price credited to his account in Paris, her father had done something incomprehensible: far from following his family to the States on the next available ship, he changed all but a small proportion of the money back into reichsmarks and returned to Berlin. He left the family in the dark about his plans, having apparently taken it into his head to try to buy back parts of the business or found a new one with the help of his old friends in banking and the Chamber of Industry and Commerce. But his old friends didn't want to know him anymore, Frau Marwitz learned later, nor did his son-in-law Martin Schlandt of the Dresdner Bank, who couldn't divorce her fast enough once the firm was sold. Two years after returning to Berlin, Kasimir took his own life.

"After that it seemed even more impossible to burden my mother with a confession," Frau Marwitz went on. That probably suited Egon quite well, she added. He kept reproaching himself for having abused Kasimir's trust by worming his way into his daughter's affections. But perhaps it was all just a smoke screen. What the Nazis' racial mania, Edita's fear of her mother's wrath, and her American acquaintances' mistrust of this family friend from Naziland had failed to do, namely, drive them apart, Egon himself achieved by indulging in the vice he could never give up in good times or bad: his philandering. At some stage the signs became too obvious, the excuses too threadbare. "One day I did as your grandmother had done: I put his bags on the doorstep." There it was again, that mocking, pugnacious laugh.

"And now? Now the sad story has turned out well after all, at least for Egon's grandsons. What are you going to do with your unexpected windfall?"

Eduard felt weary all of a sudden. He'd lost the desire to correct any misapprehensions, to defend himself, to mind his tongue.

"No idea," he said. "Till now I wasn't even sure the building really belonged to us."

"What? No idea at all? Maybe you'd like to make me a present of it? Or give it to the nice young people who are living there rent-free? Or, better still, sell it and send the proceeds to a charitable organization? What about the Jewish Claims Commission?"

"I'll have to give it some thought."

"Don't give it even a moment's thought!" she snapped. "That's just goyish nonsense, the idea that profiting from something is morally contaminating. True, you can't claim credit for the courage and decency your grandfather displayed. It's like winning the lottery, having a grandfather like Egon and inheriting a property from him as well. But now that you've hit the jackpot it's your duty to make the best of it. Why is it always us, the rescued, who plant trees for the few Germans who helped us and pin medals on their chests? Why don't you do that? Any German third-grader can spell the names of Hitler, Goebbels, and Eichmann, but he's never heard of the Egons. You're doing a regular PR job on those murderers! What sort of examples do you want to imprint on your children's hearts and minds?"

She struggled out of her wicker chair, took her cane, and turned on the lights. It was time to go.

"That altercation with Wollgraf's grandson," Eduard said as he rose, "how did it end?"

"In farce," she said. "The judge dismissed his charge of physical assault with consequent nosebleed. He did, however, allow young Wollgraf's claim to all the Marwitz properties in the former GDR. Perhaps he knew it was a backhanded decision. When informed of all the mortgages he'd have to take over and all the jobs he'd have to preserve, the beaming victor promptly renounced all claims to title. Oh, by the way, if that's why you came: somewhere among my papers I have the bank statement detailing your grandfather's payment to my father. Want me to dig it out for you?"

"No need," Eduard said quickly. "It exists, that's the main thing."

He detected an ironic glint in her eyes as she shook his hand.

6 | THE BLACK DESK CLERK greeted Eduard as if he knew him and had been looking forward to his arrival for days. Although this exuberant welcome was all part of the service, it was gratifying nonetheless. Together with his room key he was handed a note from Jenny: "Get today's *New York Times* and look at Section D. Call me."

The *New York Times* was about as popular in West Palm Beach as the *Frankfurter Rundschau* in Oberammergau. The salesgirl at the hotel kiosk drew him a complicated obstacle course of a sketch map that led to a newsdealer's specializing in what she called "those foreign papers." He passed the time on the way there by fantasizing that some ingenious correspondent assigned to the story had unearthed links between the neo-Nazi scene in Friedrichshain and the grandson of a deceased Nazi named Eduard Hoffmann.

It took him a long time, once he finally had the newspaper in his hands, to find the item Jenny must have meant. A four-line report headed "Mysterious death of German poet," it stated that Theo Warenberg, often characterized as "the poet of reunification," had been found dead in his apartment. There was a possibility that he had committed suicide.

Eduard's first impulse was to dismiss the report as a mistake. Then he told himself that he was only trying to anesthetize himself against the consternation that afflicts someone confronted by the actuality of a dire development he has long foreseen but failed to prevent. As if seeking to test or refute the news, images flashed through his head in quick succession. Theo handing him some pages from his brother's Stasi reports and watching him read them . . . Theo barefoot with the remote control in his hand, filling his lofty apartment with the strains of his latest pet CD . . . Theo's face close beside him in the gloomy room overlooking the Spree Canal as they sat at the open window in the depths of winter, listening to the faint sound of ice floes breaking up and grinding together as they drifted past on the inky water . . . Theo drunk, flawlessly reciting a page-long sentence by Kleist and winding up intoxicated with words alone . . . Theo in a bar, head cocked like a trustful child as he engaged the two women beside him in a conversation about his latest spat with his latest girlfriend and enlisted their advice . . . Theo in a wine store, flirting with the attractive salesgirl and unerringly asking for the only bottle of grappa, inaccessibly located just below the ceiling on the topmost shelf. (Theo the awkward customer who invariably and successfully insisted on putting restaurants to as much trouble as possible. "Waiter, those people at the next table are boring me. Get rid of them!") Theo holding the ladder for the salesgirl to reach the bottle of grappa and—half with her approval because he did it so blatantly and unashamedly—looking up her skirt . . . Theo wearing an overcoat in his apartment, bare feet on the parquet floor, eyes huge in his emaciated face . . . And now, as he clung to that recollection, Eduard suddenly felt that Theo had meant to say something more when seeing him off in the lobby—something important which he, Eduard, had missed by opening the door too soon.

All at once he knew why, irrespective of his shock and grief, he couldn't believe the *New York Times* report. That Theo had finally forestalled his relentless creditors and taken the decision himself was conceivable—self-determination in death as in life! But that he should have admitted the Grim Reaper to his home for a final bargaining session—that was unlike him. His aesthetic sense alone—the thought of what he would look like after a few days' decomposition—would have ruled out an unobtrusive demise. Theo was a star. He would have staged his own final appearance, for example in a luxury hotel and doubtless with some female companion, after consuming a choice dinner and the most expensive scotch on the bar list (at the hotel's expense), and he would also have taken care, after the last long swallow, to be discovered in a memorably photogenic condition.

Eduard called Jenny from the hotel. He'd already said a word or two of greeting when he realized that the person at the other end of the line was Ilaria, not Jenny. Ilaria had perfectly mastered the rather curt "Hello?" that was Jenny's greeting on picking up the phone, but she reverted to her old, girlish tone as soon as she recognized his voice. "You have to go back to Berlin right away? Shit! We've got a chemistry exam coming up next week." He told her his best friend had died. "Sure," she said, "I'd go back too. Friends are more important than family, really." Jenny was out, but Ilaria had some consolation to offer on the subject of their delayed reunion. A few days here or there didn't matter, she said, not now. Mom had promised to take them all out of school two weeks before the summer vacation and fly with them to Berlin.

Having armed himself against the return flight with two sleeping tablets, Eduard survived the fifteen hours by dozing for extended periods. He didn't wake up until he was ensconced in a Berlin cab.

Back home he dumped his bag, briefly satisfied himself that those rooftop-view invariables, the television tower and the Mercedes star on the Europa Center, were still in the same place, and set off for the Volksbühne.

The city's state of flux seemed almost homey to him when he surfaced after negotiating the temporary stairways and detours of the Alexanderplatz S-Bahn station. Even on the way to Rosa Luxemburg Platz he came across ubiquitous signs of the sense of loss that had clearly smitten the whole neighborhood. Posters bearing Theo's verses were pasted to doorways, walls sprayed with (suddenly legible) graffiti: titles of plays by Theo and excerpts from his poems or interviews such as "Civilization of the Undead" or "Dogs must turn back into wolves." Now that Theo was dead, it seemed that the graffiti writers were espousing the translation of their hieroglyphs he'd always offered in his writings. Flying from the bulky, boxlike roof of the Volksbühne, which still bore the direction OST in big neon letters, was a black flag whose present significance was presumably twofold: rebellion and mourning. The theater's two side wings were draped in strips of bunting sixty feet long. The left-hand one read FOR SOMETHING TO BEGIN, the right-hand one SOMETHING MUST END. The projecting portico with the massive columns resembled the entrance to a hero's tomb. The hermaphroditic building, midway between a power station and an ancient Germanic council chamber in appearance, had now professed itself a mausoleum.

A screen mounted on the kiosk outside the theater entrance was showing video clips: Theo reciting Beckett amid mounds of trash in Berlin's garbage-collection depot . . . Theo on the roof of the Weinhaus Huth, taking a run and pretending to jump off . . . Theo on the john, tearing pages out of a book—his first volume of poetry?—and, after reading them aloud, wiping his ass with them . . . Theo at a prize-giving ceremony, attired in a suit and ten years younger, leaving the academy president's outstretched hand unshaken in midair . . . Then came a short sequence that took Eduard's breath away: Theo just as he'd left him in the lobby of his apartment. As though awaking from sleep or a drunken stupor, Theo came toward the camera, waved it away—dismissively or only in jest?—and then gave the requisite information. The camera panned down and captured the bare feet under the summer overcoat.

The fliers being handed around told Eduard what he already knew. The theater was presenting a dramatized reading from Theo Warenberg's last and still unpublished play. But what were *they* doing here, all these dark blue Mercedes and BMW limousines with dummylike chauffeurs visible behind their tinted windows? The foyer was crowded with individuals most of whom had nothing in common with the audience Eduard had seen there in the winter. Whenever people paused to whisper at the sight of a clutch of dark-suited figures passing them in some live situation—at an airport, for instance—he always found it hard to associate the celebrity in their midst with the person he'd just seen in awe-inspiring closeup on the evening news. But now, as they all surged toward the auditorium, he was able to identify one or two faces—the faces of party chairmen, senators, publishers, authors, literary critics. He stared at one face with such undisguised amazement that its owner abruptly turned his back. It was thirty years since he'd seen, at such close quarters, the former fellow student from the dueling fraternity who'd never fought a duel. What Eduard had forgotten, and the television cameras concealed, was the senator's diminutive stature. He was pleased to note, among the faces prepared for photogenic action at any moment, the unkempt white locks of the old man who had delivered the tirade against West German colonialism at Santner's party. Most of the other guests at that dichotomous function had also turned up, though they couldn't keep their distance here, in the shoving, jostling throng. Also present were the regular attenders with the colorful hairdos and the rings and studs in their noses, lips, and ears. Unobtrusively rubbing shoulders with the linen, cotton, and black silk of property owners and city fathers, the squatters' habitual black leather involuntarily assumed the character of mourning attire.

But why wasn't everyone proceeding into the auditorium—why were they congesting the cramped foyer? It wasn't until Eduard stood on tiptoe that he discovered the focal point on which everyone was converging: a group of five women in black. Eduard recognized two who had been Theo's partners in the days before his womanless period. The others could only be their predecessors or successors. All five looked remarkably similar and surprisingly youthful. Eduard was reminded of something Theo had once told him in his customary, confessional mode: he recognized only thirteen years in a woman's life, those bounded by the twenty-second and thirty-fifth inclusive.

The senator, having elbowed his way to the fore with the aid of his minders, was clearly in a quandary. No one had whispered a helpful hint in his ear, so he didn't know which of the five widows to console first. To be on the safe side he imposed a handshake on all five and murmured some words that evoked the same mouth movements five times over. Next came the mayor of Berlin, and after him a woman with a diamond stud in her black-lipsticked lower lip. She not only joined the gaggle of widows but stood there like a sixth. It was Vera Rheinland, belly now flat, breasts beneath the partially unzipped leather vest swollen with mother's milk! Good God, Theo, thought Eduard, if only you could see this! In death you've achieved what not even your worst enemy, i.e. you yourself, could have predicted in your lifetime. Everyone loves you and is reaching out to you! People who never speak to each other as a rule are leaning, in the grip of a shared emotion, over the gulf you celebrated in words. They're acclaiming you, the canal rat, the implacable satirist and schismatic, as a bridge builder, a savior from the gutter. The poet of reunification—that's you all right!

Hailed by a voice coming from somewhere above and to one side of them, the theatergoers gradually fell silent. All heads turned to the actor on the foyer steps. He was standing like a sentinel in front of one of the five sets of double doors that led to the inner sanctum, the only one now open. Accompanied by rhythmical synthesized music, he was chanting some verses by Theo in a low, deliberately hoarse voice. Under the impact of that voice, sometimes low and seemingly hesitant, sometimes abruptly incisive, an atmosphere of concentration arose. An old but never quite forgotten ritual took its course. Some of the younger theatergoers led off, followed by the widows, until all present—the dignitaries and their bodyguards and the wearers of the nose, lip, and ear insignia of the alternative society—were seated on the floor. Eduard was witnessing a sit-in by all the factions, possibly all the political parties, that had fought and abused each other ever since the establishment of the two German states but were now bowing their heads and lowering their weapons in reverent silence. The only ones unable to sit down were the late arrivals near the exit doors, who were being crushed and almost lifted off their feet in the pressure zone between those crowding in from outside and those seated in the foyer. Among them was someone Eduard had seen somewhere not long ago. Someone whose sideburns, bow tie, and white, turned-up shirt collar seemed to stamp him as a member of the new human species now invading Berlin—a fashion designer, an accountant specializing in liquidations, a stock-exchange yuppie? Someone Eduard thought he knew—someone the sight of whom transfixed his cortex like a laser beam. Surely Theo's Stasi brother couldn't have had the gall to turn up!

What was it murmuring, groaning, bellowing, that voice overhead? Songs of rage about the life of the zombies, the undead, the McDonald's civilization, hymns devoted to the predator called history and the blood rituals of the oppressed from whom the New Man would arise, prophecies of disaster and swan songs utterly devoid of any promise of cessation or redemption. "Horror, the primary aspect of the New . . ." Eduard had a fleeting recollection of his urge to laugh during Theo's premiere. Where did it come from, the audience's almost addictive desire for castigation?

Another voice took over from the first, an elderly woman's voice, but the hoarseness and hesitation had ceased to be an artistic device and become symptoms of barely suppressed emotion. "Many of you sitting here knew him, each in your own way. And each of you will miss him in your own way. We have long been aware that he was and will remain a luminary in the poets' republic, which neither celebrates nor needs any national day. I should now like to speak of his modesty. For he, a master and renovator of language whose faltering but inexorable voice induced the whole world to listen to him, was himself a listener of genius. Meeting him before or after a rehearsal, whether in the theater cafeteria or in one of his three hundred regular drinking haunts, one was astonished, almost shocked. The spokesman of a whole outlawed epoch, he not only spoke but knew how to listen. More courageously and artistically than any other, he cried aloud the scandals of a century. He was too modest, one might almost say too heedless of himself, to define his own life. We're told by the doctors that his exact cause of death is unknown. But we who saw and spoke with him in the last few weeks and months—we know the disease that afflicted, consumed, and ultimately killed him. The name of that disease? The Federal Republic of Germany! It's good that this poet should now have been heard and acknowledged by those he indicted in his lifetime. But that doesn't mean he belongs to everyone. We cannot allow people who are depriving us of our land, our businesses, and our homes to appropriate our spiritual property as well and claim it as their heritage—to supervise our obsequies, to determine our list of speakers, to arrange a state funeral in their own honor. They are welcome as mourners, but as mourners listening in silence, not as usurpers."

A low murmur ran through the foyer. The nature of the occasion precluded any public display of approval or disapproval. But even those who might at first have sympathized with the old lady's emotional outburst seemed upset by the shrill note on which it had ended. Grief at the loss of Theo had clearly prompted her to complain of other, wider-ranging losses. Her lament had developed into an accusation impossible to dismiss with a dignified lowering of the eyes. The tension and suspense became excruciating, for the target of her accusation, the man politically responsible for all the shortcomings named and unnamed, was not, after all, visiting some abandoned East German coal mine. Disguised as a mourner, the guilty party was seated in the lotus position only a few feet from the widows' circle, surrounded by his victims. Not content with a hostile takeover of the other half of the city, he had insinuated himself into the last remaining bastion of the dispossessed, their emotional interior, their utopian refuge. Everyone, Eduard included, tried not to look at the usurper.

The senator rose, straightened his necktie, and began to speak. There it was again, that wondrously transmuted voice so versed in the art of compromise and conciliation. No one could deny his courage. This wasn't home ground, nor was it exactly routine practice for a politician to address a hostile crowd of bereaved mourners off the cuff and unscripted.

"I wouldn't wish to intrude on anyone's grief," said the senator, "and I've got a tough hide, but I refuse to let anyone deprive me of the right to pay my respects to Theo Warenberg. I knew him long before the Wall came down. I knew him in the early years as an awkward but always humorous provocateur, later as a skeptical advisor, eventually as both at once: opponent and friend. I don't mean to boast, but I believe I was the last person to see him alive and walk him to a cab—after a long conversation at my home. And I think the best tribute we can pay this great German is to refrain from erecting new walls above his grave—walls which Theo Warenberg nimbly vaulted long ago in the verses he wrote during his lifetime. The previous speaker was quite entitled to intimate that he never entirely abandoned utopian socialism—though I myself am not so sure!—and that he mocked and pilloried the shortcomings of the Western system—within which, incidentally, he made his home for many years—in verses that merit admiration for their poetic power and audacity alone. But it is equally true to say that he defined the incurable diseases of practical socialism, not only in good time but, to borrow the previous speaker's phrase, more courageously and artistically than any other. I don't say it was the socialist dictatorship that killed him. That, with respect, would be going too far. But it was of course the other Germany, which he considered the better in his storm-and-stress period, and on which he bestowed his talent and his intelligence, that proved his life's greatest disappointment. Capitalism he credited with every kind of iniquity, so he was never disillusioned by it. That is why we should eschew any foolish mutual attributions of responsibility for his death. No, Theo Warenberg belongs neither to one side nor to the other, neither to East nor to West; he belongs to literature. For him as for all true poets, realpolitik was ultimately no more than copy, the backdrop against which he presented his despair at the foundering of an ideal on the reefs of human nature. That is why I earnestly entreat you not to monopolize the right to mourn. This is a public place. Not only you but his many friends from the West of the city are entitled to lend expression to their feelings and take leave of him in a dignified manner."

Not a sound. The senator had gauged his riposte so artfully that the only course open to any subsequent speaker would have been a resort to personal abuse. His mode of self-ingratiation was harder to resist than that of his predecessor because it was directed against any attempt to ingratiate himself. But that could hardly be the reason for the ensuing, horrified silence. Everyone including Eduard was chewing over one of the senator's seemingly incidental remarks. To think that it was he, of all people, who had walked Theo to his last cab! It was impossible but conceivable. Maybe Theo really did belong to everyone.

7 | KLOTT HAD CALLED Eduard in West Palm Beach the night before he flew back and asked for a report. He interposed several flippant remarks about Eduard's grandfather, then grasped that Eduard wasn't in the mood and limited himself to saying that, as soon as he got back, he would introduce him to a wholly unexpected but—this time—perfectly respectable prospective buyer for the Rigaer Strasse property.

Once in Klott's office, Eduard was deluged with reproaches. Why in the world hadn't he insisted on bringing back proof of the purchase price paid by his grandfather? Documentary evidence of that kind would settle the whole affair in short order.

He couldn't find it in his heart to trouble the old lady with such a request at the end of their long conversation, Eduard replied.

However, if Klott drafted a declaration renouncing all claim on the building in Rigaer Strasse, he was sure Frau Marwitz would be happy to sign it. She genuinely wanted him, Eduard, to assert his right to the bequest.

Klott used three fingers to fish an extended family of jelly beans from the jar on his desk, crammed them into his mouth, and gave Eduard a look that questioned his sanity.

"I don't know what's the matter with you," he said, "jet lag, mind lag, Alzheimer's, Schmalzheimer's. Come down to earth. You take a Lufthansa flight to Florida, hear a few nice things about your suddenly beloved grandfather from a Jewish ex-girlfriend of his, and come back a little innocent—a Band-Aid for the lacerated German psyche. What do you plan to do, put up a plaque on Rigaer Strasse? 'Here lived'—no: 'This building was purchased for humanitarian reasons by Egon Hoffmann from his best friend Kasimir Marwitz . . .' Are we all expected to lay wreaths for noble Egon on the date of the sale? And please, spare me and your future congregation any more talk of that love affair!"

All he wanted, Eduard said coldly, was to gain possession of a building that rightfully belonged to himself and his brother and sell it as soon as possible. What was eating Klott? Why was he getting so worked up?

"Don't you realize how many Dahnkes there are to one Egon—how many incorrigibles will seize on your story and make a meal out of it? 'My grandpa saved a Jew too!' Doesn't that have a horribly familiar ring?"

"I think you're wrong," said Eduard. "My grandfather's story wouldn't make a suitable apologia for the Germans, far from it. On the contrary, if it's a question of volume, the story of *one* relatively decent individual magnifies the guilt of innumerable conformists and accomplices rather than minimizing it. It shows that it was possible to sabotage the machinery of persecution and destruction. If there had been more such saboteurs, they might have slowed or even stopped it."

Klott brushed this aside and glanced at his watch. If he might be permitted to summarize Eduard's instructions to his attorney, he said, was their gist that he didn't care who bought the property as long as it was soon?

Eduard nodded.

"Then I can introduce you to someone right away," said Klott. With that, he picked up his jacket and hustled Eduard out the door.

Eduard recalled—too late—his last drive with Klott. It was daylight this time, but the dense curtain of rattling raindrops that obscured the windshield made him feel like someone imprisoned in a car wash. The windshield wipers revealed only momentary glimpses of the neighborhood they were traversing at high speed. From the nonchalant way he drove, Klott might have been behind the wheel of a video-game race car. He could only give his best on a rain-soaked surface, he declared, and added that he disliked talking while he drove.

They took the route they'd taken on the night of the fire. Eduard found it hard to recognize the environs of Rigaer Strasse. A steadily growing army of building contractors was advancing from both ends of the street, but also from the side streets around it, and had encircled the apartment house. All the street signs were new. Roofs had been replaced, one or two buildings faced with marble up to the second floor, many front doors stripped and fitted with brass knobs. In these surroundings, Grandfather Hoffmann's bequest resembled a black-and-white still from the silent movie era. The front of the building was unchanged aside from a few new slogans, and that was precisely where Klott parked his lime-green Rover, right beneath the open windows, as if he'd never heard of butyric acid and paint bombs.

From under Klott's umbrella Eduard peered up at the dangling cables and loose-fitting window frames as if he were seeing the place for the first time. Why bother about this ruin, why all the financial and emotional expenditure? Half a country had quietly changed hands in parcels of varying size. West German banks and insurance companies had, without fuss, taken over their former branches or head offices together with any liabilities incurred under the GDR; West German political parties had quietly renovated their old head-quarters, or what they declared to be such; "homeless" Prussian aristocrats, barons and counts who had settled in West Germany, were moving back into their villages and country mansions east of the Elbe; West German concerns had inherited their former mother companies in the "new provinces," looted them, and discarded the residue—in fact, 95 percent of the productive capacity of the former GDR had somehow found its way into West German hands. And he, Eduard, hadn't even managed to rid his ruin of a few fantasists who, far from paying any rent, were saddling him with their bills for power, water, gas, and trash collection!

The metal door was only propped against the frame. Eduard followed Klott inside. It clearly wasn't the first time his attorney had come this way. Having without difficulty found the hallway light switch behind a dismantled door, he trudged up the stairs, panting and cursing. Eduard was astonished to note how the character of the stairway changed from one flight to the next. The bottom two floors were clearly occupied by genuine squatters, fundamentalists who regarded any lick of paint as a symptom of ideological degeneracy. The upper floors, from the fourth onward, had been taken over by the squatters' clandestine bourgeoisie. Eduard identified preliminary signs of domestic refinement in the bare electric light bulbs dangling from the ceiling and the doormats outside the doors. Missing banisters had been replaced with new ones, either hand-turned or filched from intact staircases. From the fifth floor onward, unabashed corruption reigned. Passing stripped pine doors with stylistically correct brass locks, they came to the final flight, which boasted a red stair carpet held in place by brass rods.

Klott opened a door without knocking. The big room beyond it was obviously an erstwhile apartment whose interior walls had been demolished—without Eduard's permission. Several squatters were seated at a long dining table covered with white bedsheets. To Eduard's amazement, Vera Rheinland waved to them, rose, and greeted Klott with a kiss. He recognized no one apart from her and Jeff. The fair-haired boy was nowhere to be seen.

Vera Rheinland bade Eduard welcome with no perceptible emotion, her manner that of a politico who had resolved to negotiate with the opposition. The political wind had changed, she explained. The new senator for internal affairs had abandoned the squatter-friendly "Berlin line." The municipal authorities were grooming Berlin for its future role as the German capital. Measures to that end included not only the establishment of a demo-free zone, the introduction of a dog tax, and the removal of prostitutes and sidewalk dwellers from the city center, but the eviction of squatters from occupied buildings.

All that surprised Eduard afterward was how quickly everything had gone. The squatters undertook to defray all his expenditures on the running costs of the building. The fire damage they were already repairing themselves. "We reject the concept of private property on principle," said Vera Rheinland, "but the only course open to us, for a longish transitional period, is to become property owners ourselves."

Next, a squatter with a sea horse tattoo on his arm—a slender youth barely out of his teens—proceeded to negotiate a selling price with Klott. Eduard was perturbed to note how calmly and professionally he justified his impudent offer, which was just over half Klott's asking price. It seemed that transactions of this nature obeyed a universal grammar. When it came to haggling, Eduard reflected, the differences between political camps and creeds evaporated. But jet lag was steadily prevailing over his duty to remain more than usually vigilant. He came to once more with an indignant start when he heard the sum Klott described as his "rock-bottom figure." Nine hundred and fifty thousand for the entire building? The gaunt youngster countered with six hundred and fifty thousand. Ridiculous! Come on, Klott, we're going!

Eduard drifted off again. As he did so he suddenly heard his brother's voice. Instead of inveighing against Klott for conniving at a sellout, however, Lothar adopted a superior tone and told him about a deal he had witnessed in New Zealand. When Christchurch University had finally, after a protracted dispute over a plot of land, agreed terms with the original Maori inhabitants, the entire clan had accompanied their chief to the signing ceremony in tribal dress. Lothar became incensed. What entitled this youth with the sea horse on his arm to speak for the whole gang of squatters? Merely his father's bank balance? Fair enough. But what did Lothar think of the offer, Eduard insisted. Procedural criticisms apart, Lothar replied angrily, he had no comment to make on the whole affair. So saying, he vanished.

A kick on the shin. Eduard awoke with another start. Klott's bulky torso was visible with crystalline clarity as far as his neck, which was constricted by the collar of his white shirt, but further up something had changed. That head with the plate in the lower lip and the idiotic-looking crest of hair on the otherwise bald pate, could that be Klott's? Despite his attorney's guise, was he really the chieftain of the enemy clan?

"Eight hundred and fifty thousand, okay?"

Eduard saw Klott's face draw menacingly nearer.

"Pretty damn good for a half-gutted building with squatters still in situ!"

"But I'll have to call my brother," said Eduard after a pause which, to judge by Klott's eyebrows, lasted far too long. And he affixed his signature to the binder at the spot indicated by Klott's forefinger.

8 KATHARINA'S BLOND PONYTAIL was the first thing Eduard spotted beyond the arrival gate's glass partition. She called something inaudible. All he saw was her hand, which she wagged in front of her face, American fashion, like a little windshield wiper. Next he saw the uninhibitedly laughing, grimacing face of Loris, who pushed past Katharina and flattened his nose against the glass. Behind them, studiously preserving her distance, stood Ilaria, who had grown half a head. The children's pleasure at seeing their father again after nearly six months seemed proportionate to their physical size. Ilaria didn't wave, presumably because she thought it proper to dissociate herself from the younger ones' crude display of delight. Instead she removed her baseball cap, ostentatiously lowered her head, and, as if in forewarning, ran a hand back and forth over her cropped hair. All that lovely hair, not only shorn off—with a scythe, from the look of it—but dyed pink! She might have a pierced lip or nostril as well for all he knew—he couldn't tell at this range. Jenny must surely have been just as appalled, but what would she have said when her daughter first appeared looking like that? "Great, I love it!" Where was Jenny, anyway?

He suppressed a pang of disappointment when he saw the children emerge from the gate pushing the baggage cart. Two canvas grips and a couple of suitcases looked more like a vacation trip, a fleeting visit, than a permanent move.

"Hi, here you are at last!"

"How do you like my hair?" asked Ilaria.

"Great," he said. "That color's just spectacular."

The expectant smile on Ilaria's face died. His acquiescence had obviously disappointed her. When giving Katharina a hug he sensed, rather belatedly, that her adolescent body recoiled a little. For a moment he thought his second daughter was already afflicted with the "don't touch me" disease. Then he realized that the catlike arching of her upper body was merely an attempt to avoid any physical contact, however inadvertent, with the tiny breasts she'd just sprouted. Jenny, shivering slightly, her face still infused with California's more munificent sunlight, stood in the background as if devoid of any further connection with the children she'd brought into the world. She waited patiently for Eduard to welcome her last of all. A hug, a dry kiss—parental ritual.

A moment of euphoria came when they were all standing on the terrace of the apartment in Charlottenburg. Jenny was pleased with it. She drew a deep breath. It seemed to her that up here at roof level another, second city had arisen, an airy, translucent, supernal world. She felt that another human species must live here, rendered freer and more lighthearted by its proximity to the birds.

In defiance of Eduard's advice they all went to bed in broad daylight. By one o'clock in the morning Loris was wide awake and keen to go waterskiing.

Eduard helped him dress as quietly as possible. He'd forgotten the boy's sleep smell. For a second or two he buried his nose in the tousled hair on the hot skull, which seemed to throb. They tiptoed out of the apartment and drove to the Wannsee. Loris's eyes sparkled when Eduard lifted him over the barrier that separated the landing stage from the lakeside promenade. They walked along the wooden planks to the far end. Black water lapped unseen against the piles, emitting an occasional gleam when it reflected some light or other.

Although the night was warm and clear, only a sprinkling of stars could be seen. For a while they sat on the landing stage, dangling their legs and gazing across the dark, almost motionless surface at the bushes on the far shore. From time to time their faces were fanned by a puff of wind. The lights of the buildings opposite swayed in the breeze as if suspended on strings. Loris looked for the "big truck" in the sky and said the stars looked much farther away than they did in San Francisco.

When they got cold, they stood up and inspected the moored craft. Loris was fascinated by a twin-engined speedboat whose long, pointed bow protruded from the water like a fighter's cockpit. Eduard towed the floating projectile toward him by the painter and held it steady while Loris jumped onto the stern. He sensed the boy's private exultation at this forbidden act of trespass. For a while they sat in the bucket seats and let the water rock them. Loris turned the big steering wheel this way and that and worked the throttle lever back and forth with his plump little hand. The dashboard and the curved windshield probably reminded him of the starfighter he flew in his computer games. Instinctively, his left hand felt for the control button that would ignite the inboard rockets.

They embarked on their next dream voyage aboard a yacht, which they reached by using the intervening craft as a pontoon bridge. For a long time they lay on the deck on their backs. They might have been the only people on earth. Not a sound could be heard save the gentle bumping and chafing of hulls, the creaking of masts, and the reverberant echoes of Loris's exultant voice.

When Eduard saw his son poised on the bow of the yacht, he had a sudden vision of the Rigaer Strasse boy collapsing, smitten by the keen and painful certainty that a moment's lapse in the sequence of events could be enough to transform an entire young life into a mush of blood, spittle, and excrement.

To Eduard, Jenny's observations were like a replay of changes in the city he no longer noticed. He sometimes wondered whether the things that surprised her had ever been different at all. That the double-decker buses displayed three-digit numbers and terminated in places they used not to stop at; that the Berlin telephone directory comprised a stack of five volumes; that Russian could be heard everywhere on the sidewalks of Charlottenburg . . . Hadn't it always been so? Jenny claimed that even the East Berlin traffic lights had changed. The flashing pedestrian lights had been slimmer, she said, not as plump and prosperous-looking as they were now. Another symbol aroused her disfavor: the suddenly ubiquitous German eagle. "I've nothing against heraldic beasts in general or eagles in particular, but take a wholly impartial look at that example in the parliament building. Rounded wings, feet far too big and talony, head so tiny as to be almost invisible. Your eagle looks as if it can only waddle and scratch like a capon, not fly anymore. Compare the Polish eagle, the heraldic eagles of Washington or Pisa—trim, elegant birds you can credit with an ability to leave the ground occasionally. Couldn't you slim your eagle down a bit in honor of the new republic—couldn't you make it look a bit more elegant and airworthy?"

She was pleased to be recognized and greeted at the Tent as if she'd never been away. Pleased, too, by the Berliners' habit of asking no questions about people's temporary desertion of their city and treating them as if they'd walked out the door only yesterday. One danger signal, on the other hand, was that the Tent's outside tables and chairs had now to be removed from the sidewalk by ten o'clock at night. "The introduction of Bonn conventions," said Pinka, the proprietress. "The rapid degeneration of an international metropolis into the German capital," Jenny amended.

She was infuriated by another change that struck her while walking down the Kurfürstendamm one night. "Haven't you noticed?" she demanded as they passed the heavily made-up women who stood at mathematically regular intervals in the lee of the buildings. "They used to stand here on their own and run the business themselves. Now they do it under the watchful gaze of thugs with Rolex watches and pointy shoes, who loiter in doorways with their slave girls' passports in their pockets."

Not for the first time, it was a cabdriver who redeemed the entire city from Jenny's wrath. During a discussion of the disadvantages the fall of the Wall had brought in its train, she told him, "Please don't get me wrong. I was always an anticommunist." The cabby's response enchanted her: "It's none of my business what kind of communist you were."

Eduard had quickly dismissed any thought of burdening Jenny with a confession of his adultery. She would have intimated at the first hint of it that she wasn't prepared to be his confidante.

Sometimes she looked at him as if she expected him to take the initiative. What are you waiting for? There isn't a best time! Not a best time, certainly, but there were favorable or unfavorable attendant circumstances. Among the latter were children who might burst in at any minute because they were bored or unputoffably hungry for an omelette. Or rain and an outside temperature of fifty degrees. Eduard had ceased to believe in the possibility of a lucky fluke in bed. He pictured a well-prepared love feast, a festive showdown in which at least the outward scenario met all Jenny's requirements. At the same time, an abusive voice laughed him to scorn. The one thing you must not leave to chance, it said, is chance itself.

Meantime, there were two nuisances rampaging immediately below their bedroom. All Eduard had at first noticed about the occupants of the apartment downstairs was the surprisingly large kidney-shaped swimming pool on their balcony. He kept meaning to ask them where they'd bought it; Loris complained daily that he'd been promised one just like that. Now, as if to provoke or annoy Eduard and Jenny, their neighbors had chosen the balcony room, which was obviously unoccupied, as the venue for their nocturnal delights. Punctually at half past midnight, sometimes via the open balcony door, sometimes via one of the water pipes or drainpipes that functioned in old Berlin buildings as sound conductors, the woman's moans of pleasure traveled upward with such volume that Eduard and Jenny were tempted to expel the couple from their own bathroom. Jenny had made the woman's acquaintance—"She's a singer"— and instantly classified her as a sham.

"She sounds pretty convincing to me," Eduard protested.

"I ask you, those absurd, high-pitched squeals! It's opera, you can tell that yourself. She does it to train her voice."

"Noises like that can be genuine sometimes."

"I don't deny it, but listen closely now . . . There! Sounds like a band saw, doesn't it? She's probably got a tape recorder hidden under the bed. Be honest, do you find it titillating?"

"Not titillating. It sounds enthusiastic, that's all."

"Really incredible, how easily a man can be fooled."

"Not this man."

Jenny looked at him with a blend of amusement and pity. "Where that's concerned, no man in the world can ever be sure. Not unless he's an idiot."

He didn't tell her about the dream he'd had the night before. He was standing on the terrace watching a strange figure clambering up and down the roof opposite. The briefcase, the turned-up collar and bow tie, the sunglasses—none of those suited a chimney sweep. The man sat down on the ridge tiles and gazed intently at Eduard through his dark glasses. Go away, Eduard shouted at him. Who or what are you looking for? At that the figure vaulted off the ridge like a clown, slithered down the tiles in Eduard's direction, and ended up sitting cross-legged in front of him. The mannequin cocked his head, looked up at Eduard, and removed his sunglasses. Eduard recognized him. He'd spotted him at the Volksbühne commemorative, that yuppie disguised as a sales representative, Theo's Stasi brother. But then he heard the voice, the familiar, three-packs-a-day voice. Jesus, that was great! said Theo, ripping off his sideburns. I've never been treated so well in my life, he prattled on. All those wonderful speeches! The money's rolling in too, for once. Reprints, special programs, special issues, special performances. Only a pity I can't give interviews. You won't tell anyone you've seen me, will you, not even Jenny? The thing is, I plan to stay dead for a while. Where have you left Jenny, anyway? In San Francisco, Eduard told him. What? Theo blurted out between frightful paroxysms of coughing and laughter. You mean you still haven't done it? He smacked his lips lecherously. I can just picture her, the poor thing, waiting in bed behind those huge windows of yours. What a woman! But now—not scared of me, are you?—give me your hand! He hauled himself up by Eduard's outstretched arm, light-bodied as a boy of fifteen, but once on his feet he clasped Eduard tightly, as if trying to prove that he was still capable of choking the life out of him. I owe you something, he said. He rummaged in his briefcase, produced two objects, and thrust them into Eduard's hand. One felt round and hard, the other soft and pointed. Jenny's place isn't where you've been looking, he whispered in his ear, it's between the second and eighteenth vertebrae . . . Suddenly Eduard was beside Jenny holding the flask and the feather, conscious that Theo was watching him through the French doors. Playfully, Jenny tried to knock Theo's two aids out of his hand. You've absolutely no need for that sort of thing! she laughed, flailing around with her legs and turning over on her tummy. Hurriedly, Eduard anointed her back with a drop of liquid from the flask. At once he saw a shudder run through her. When he drew the feather across the same spot it was as if warm rain were falling on her back. She reared up, froze, and subsided again. Simultaneously, lightning and laughter filled the air. No sooner had she recovered her breath, however, than she sat up, elbowed him out of bed, and swore at him. Dirty beast! Scrounger! What's the big idea? Who said you could do that? Sneaking up on me from behind and taking what you've no right to! Nobody asked you to. Get lost! Get out and never show your face here again! With tears of rage spurting from her eyes, she snatched up the irreplaceable feather and the precious, almost unde-pleted flask. Having snapped the former and smashed the latter, she hurled the remains at Eduard and chased him out of the bedroom.

Theo grabbed Eduard and drew him close. They were now stand-ing perilously near the edge of the flat roof. You still haven't grasped the crucial point, Theo yelled in his ear. You must risk your neck! You must jump, jump . . . Incidentally, did you know I had a six-year-old daughter? He giggled. Where? asked Eduard. In San Fran-cisco, but never fear, you don't know the mother. I'm going there now. Pay me a visit sometime! Theo jumped, but instead of falling he dematerialized into a dark, fluttering creature and soared off. Briefly visible was the little briefcase beside his billowing coattails; then all that could still be seen was his gleaming bald patch, a pale dot speeding westward.

The evening Jenny sent the children off to see a three-hour Holly-wood monster movie had defied the forecasters: it was warm and cloudless. The predicted depression, nicknamed Bea, had strayed off to Scandinavia, thereby refuting Jenny's contention that Berlin marked the precise spot on the weather map that every bad-weather front storming in from the Atlantic strove to reach without stopping along the way.

At the back of the flat roof separating the front of the building from the rear, their apartment's unknown previous tenant had erected a wooden platform, a kind of raised blind that afforded a view of areas of the city normally obscured by the roof of the build-ing opposite. Just big enough to accommodate a table, a bench, and a couple of chairs, this structure was the venue for Eduard and Jenny's first evening alone together. He had prepared her favorite fish dish, an *imperiale*, or reddish variety of sea bream. They were on a level with the tops of the backyard linden and chestnut trees whose luxuriant foliage surrounded the festively bedecked table like oversized houseplants. The discordant look of the roofscape, with its planes of carmine, purple-brown, and grayish black and its often abrupt indentations and protrusions, conveyed that life on and under the roofs of Berlin was an afterthought. A tower crane loomed over one building in every four or five. In the twilight, however, the integuments of scaffolding looked like pupae from which brighter and friendlier creatures would emerge in due course. Still visible beyond the gold and violet streaks of cloud at the farthest extremity of the horizon was the sun that had already set for the denizens of the floors below. Now and then an airplane threaded its way toward the airport or out of the city between the flashing red beacons mounted on cranes, church towers, and factory smokestacks. Eduard wondered whether he and Jenny could be seen by a passenger with a good pair of binoculars. Jenny's attention was monopolized by a cat that suddenly darted along the knife edge of a nearby roof, leapt onto a chimney, and hunkered down with its head on its outstretched paws. One could almost see its outlines dissolve into the swiftly gathering dusk until it was absorbed by the two different darknesses of the chimney and the sky, and only its phosphorescent green eyes were left.

Jenny had bribed the cat from day one by putting out tidbits and saucers of milk. She had also gotten to know its name, Hera, and its owner, who was none other than the Singer. For the sake of the solidarity prevailing between mothers of all species, said Jenny, the Singer had refrained from spaying Hera so as to enable her to sample motherhood at least once. But Hera always returned from her walkabouts frustrated, their only result being the half-dead birds she generously deposited in her mistress's kitchen. It was the Singer's Polish cleaning woman who had explained the reason for Hera's lack of success: all German tomcats were sterilized. A she-cat in heat would have to trek to Poland if she wanted to find an able-bodied mate.

Seated on the shadowy platform with her swan-necked head erect, Jenny looked first at the cat's eyes, then at Eduard. She opened the second bottle of wine and clinked glasses with him. An almost inaudible breath of wind fanned one of the treetops that hovered in front of them like a dark captive balloon. She seemed in that instant to be leafing through myriad memories in quest of that initial flash of recognition when their eyes had first met and held each other's gaze. Things had been so promising at first. They'd envisioned an around-the-world trip, camel rides across the desert, days and weeks with nothing to do but lounge on the deck of a yacht and make love to the point of exhaustion, either on the swaying planks or on a rock high above the breakers. When she rose and came over to Eduard she seemed to have turned back into the woman in whose eyes he had drowned in the days when everything seemed possible—the days before they'd had to prepare school lunches, sign report cards, whisk the children to the emergency room, become their domestic staff.

"You're not going to make me walk all the way to Poland, are you?" Jenny giggled and kissed him. "Will you do me a favor? Take me just as I am—carry me over the threshold."

"Which threshold?"

"Which do you think? Carry me inside, I mean."

He couldn't conceal his astonishment. She looked at him inquiringly.

"Where did you get it from, this obsession with making love al fresco, high above the treetops?"

"From you, who else?"

"From me? There must be some mistake. The best place for what we're going to do is bed. And this time, sweetheart, we'll play by my rules, not yours."

She laughed as he carried her down the wooden steps and onto the flat roof. "Sure you're still up to it? Your poor back!" She rewarded every labored breath with a kiss. "Too smashed to know what you're doing anymore, is that it?"

"I'm as smashed as you are, neither more nor less."

"Great," she said. Then, when they were inside, "Hey, was that your idea?"

They stared out the window in disbelief. Thunderous detonations could be heard. Some unwitting accomplice, presumably a building contractor, had mounted a fireworks display—one of the countless topping-out celebrations that broke over the city every few days. The only pity of it was that the luminous edifices the builders erected in the sky were so much more ephemeral than the shows they staged on the ground.

"Pretend it's the first time," said Jenny's voice. "I've told you nothing, just that you've got to have plenty of stamina and refrain from asking questions. You must obey my signals and not come before I let you."

They soared away, or rather, Jenny did. Below him Eduard saw the huge ocean liner of the city with its twinkling portholes, above him the man-made fandango of lights in the black sky, in front of him Jenny rising and falling. "Don't give up on me," she said. "All right still? Think of the never-ending roar of the surf below the cliffs, the yacht that never stops rocking, the Bach cantata and the wonderful voice that keeps repeating two syllables: Pa-tience, pa-tience . . . And if that doesn't do the trick, think of something sobering like a miles-long traffic jam or traffic lights that refuse to turn green."

He was suddenly aware that Jenny had stiffened and stopped short. Then, after a long pause and with no perceptible intake of breath, she said crisply, "The children are back."

Eduard listened to the noises of the night. He heard the hum of the fridge in the kitchen, further away the muffled roar of traffic on the main street, elsewhere the bawling of some infant silenced a moment later, doubtless by the insertion of a handy bottle. The key whose sound had startled Jenny had only turned inside her head. No one had come, neither the children nor Jenny herself. Cold air from the open terrace door caressed Eduard's sweating body like an icy hand. He felt nothing but a disyllabic certainty that slowly rose from his loins and engulfed his brain: E-nough, e-nough . . .

"That's it," he said, "I give up, I resign. I've disappointed myself, disappointed you, been disappointed by you. Whatever I give you, it's never enough. I must be an even bigger fool than I thought if I failed to grasp the simplest of truths: you just don't love me and you never have. You must have known that from the start, though.

There's something about me that puts you off, that repels you, something immutable and incurable, insurmountable, irremediable. Why
did you never tell me? Why did you stall us both for so long—why
did you set me a problem I could never solve? It must be something
quite simple and straightforward: the wrong smell, the wrong-
colored eyes, the wrong skin texture, the wrong way of moving—at
all events, something far more banal than all those noble, overriding
reasons why you felt inhibited, which I strove so hard to overcome.
Your problems with the Germans and their chilly city, your funda-
mental mistrust of a husband belonging to that murderous race, the
price of a multicultural marriage—all crap, pretense, a waste of time.
There's no marital contretemps that lends itself better to smoke
screens of that kind, of course, and none that has so many potential
causes. You kept on dishing up new riddles, and I, like that idiot in
the fairy tale, did my docile best to solve them all in turn. I pored
over sex manuals you should have read, dreamed up scenarios you
should have staged. I climbed every rung of the ladder although it
had long been obvious that the ladder was endless. Why? Because I
refused to acknowledge the simplest fact: there's something about
me you just don't like, something as unalterable and repulsive as the
hands of the Hunchback of Notre Dame."

"You're forgetting something," Jenny said almost inaudibly,
"Gina loves him in the end in spite of his shaggy hands."

"She loves him because she's sorry for him, but she wouldn't
dream of going to bed with him."

"Why are you messing around? What are you doing?"

"What do you think I'm doing? I'm getting dressed—I'm
leaving."

"But I love you, you idiot, when are you going to get that into
your head? Where are you off to?"

"No idea. All I know is, I want to get away from a woman who
doesn't want *me*."

"Do as you please, but don't go out that door."

That she was preserving her self-control and wouldn't let go,
even on the brink of his final departure, only strengthened his

resolve. He had no specific goal in mind, only an overpowering urge to get out, to do at last what he should have done the first time he became aware of the problem. To go, just go, unmoved by any belated protestations of love or childish tears.

"All right, go! Leave, but not by *that* door! It's the wrong one, you hear?"

He wouldn't have dreamed of heeding her. There was more than one door and window up here in the terrace room, and all would have suited him equally well. He turned the handle with a jerk and— Q.E.D.—there he was: outside. A long way outside, though . . . He head Jenny cry out, not in pleasure but at least in fear, he thought, and simultaneously noticed that, from the practical standpoint, she'd been right. There was something fundamentally wrong with the door. Instead of opening onto the wall-to-wall carpet of the landing, it revealed a precipitous expanse of roof. Instantly, he slithered down the tiles for a couple of feet, still retaining his grip on the handle of the door, which swung far, far out over the void. He hung there for a moment; then the lever handle turned under his weight and slipped through his fingers. What followed was pure dynamics, Isaac Newton, gravitational pull. He landed with a crash on the sloping roof, slid helplessly down it to the gutter, which projected him forward and upward like a miniature ski jump—and found himself traveling at a different speed. From now on he perceived everything in slow motion, like a beneficent and intoxicating rallentando. He saw the flashing red beacons above the roofs, the yellow windows across the way, the cars gliding past on the street below. The whole city came up to meet him, bade him welcome to its pallid lights and unyielding surfaces. What took you so long, dear Eduard? We've been expecting you from the first . . . Then he felt as if it wasn't happening to him, to that crude, alien mass of flesh that had once belonged to him and would be unpleasantly distorted by the force of the impact while he himself, detached from it long ago, was soaring off into an orbit of his own. All that seemed incongruous was that he heard his body land, felt moisture on his face, and could marvel at the fact that he was lying in water. Some woman offered him her hand and asked an incomprehensible question: "Are you all right, Herr Hoffmann?"

Suddenly Jenny's voice was there too. "Does that hurt?" she asked, kneading his feet and ankles, knees and thighs in turn.

"No," he said indignantly each time. After all, why should a dead man feel pain?

"In that case, get up," she said.

Getting up was easy, standing far less so. He was dripping wet and had a nasty pain in his ankle.

"No real harm done," said Jenny, as if it were her duty to console the Singer, not Eduard, and apologize for his unseemly behavior. "I guess he'll get away with a bruise or two."

"How did it happen?"

"He took the wrong door," said Jenny. "Lucky you've got such a nice big balcony!"

They spoke little. Jenny applied cold compresses to his ankle and avoided his eye. By degrees he forgot the pain. He was an idiot, she whispered. How could he have scared her like that? What had come over him? Had he known his dramatic exit would end in a swimming pool?

It might have been hours or days later when she draped the wet cloth over his eyes instead of his feet. She excited him with her icy hand, then settled herself on top of him. At some stage—he'd done nothing a man himself would recall—he heard a sound like the whistle of an arrow leaving a bowstring, saw Jenny arch her body as if in pain, heard a celestially beautiful sigh like the expulsion of a breath pent up for a lifetime, and felt the sort of convulsion in her limbs that might have been caused by a cold shower on hot flesh. He couldn't see her eyes.

"Yes . . ." she said.

He lay beside her for a long time, nestling against her armpit, and listened to the dying echoes of the tumult in her bosom as if he were hearing the reverberations of the big bang held by scientific legend to be the beginning of all Creation.

"How and why?" he asked eventually. "In bed, with no effort, almost in my absence? What about the fear of heights, the danger?"

"You misunderstood me from the first. I kept telling you: it's not a question of scenarios or techniques or specific positions. That's all man talk."

"So tell me!"

"You're dealing with a difficult case," she replied, not looking at him. "I've no idea where I got my crazy notion from. You half guessed it and then misinterpreted it completely. It was absurd, the way you bent me over the parapet in that turret and nearly pushed me off. It was never a question of whether *I* would fall and land in the mud—the very idea! What was required, of course, was the opposite of that: a man who would risk his life for the woman of a lifetime—risk his neck to conquer me. When you disappeared into space like that, something snapped inside me."

"Where do we go from here?"

He saw a single tear shining in her eye.

"I don't know," she said. "You can't jump out the window every time."

ACKNOWLEDGMENTS

All the characters in this novel are fictitious. Any resemblances to persons alive or dead are fortuitous and unintentional.

My account of the so-called Aryanization of Marwitz & Co. was inspired by an article by Catarina Kennedy-Bannier in *Der Tagesspiegel* (Berlin, December 14, 1992) and by the fourth chapter of Johannes Ludwig's *Boycott, Enteignung, Mord* [*Boycott, Expropriation, Murder*] (Munich, 1992). It was reading those works that also prompted me to carry out research of my own at the National Archives, Washington, D.C., and at the headquarters of Schuhhaus Tack in Burg, near Magdeburg.

My grateful thanks are due to the Woodrow Wilson Center, Washington, D.C., for its generous grant.

I should also like to express my gratitude to the Stiftung Preussische Seehandlung for its assistance.

P. S.